GENRENAUTS

THE COMPLETE SEASON ONE COLLECTION

MICHAEL R. UNDERWOOD

*To the 321 Kickstarter backers that made this omnibus possible. This book exists because of **you**.*

Episode One:
The Shootout Solution

Prologue
Inciting Incident

Mallery York pressed her back against the outer wall of the saloon while bullets flew on Main Street. Her breath came fast as her hand fumbled, ripping the hem of her skirt and tying another bargain-basement tourniquet around her right arm. It'd keep the bleeding down, but she'd taken three hits, and addressing them all would transform her outfit from "Western" to "Jane of the Jungle."

The report of gunshots came around the corner, impacts sending splinters of wood flying in the dusty street. Mallery flinched at each one, every hit refreshing the sharp pain from only moments ago. She'd gotten lucky, in that "not all bullet wounds are created equal" kind of way. But no matter what, the mission had gone down the latrine and it was time to bug out.

Mallery dug into her petticoats for the polished chrome and Gonzo Glass phone. Doubling over to make herself a smaller target, she pressed the big red button, shielding the phone from view. Even with bullets flying, she kept to the concealment protocol, just as regs demanded.

The call picked up on the second ring.

"This is King. What's your status?"

"Floundering in a sea of gunfire and dust."

"Just hold on," King said. The voice of her boss and mentor was a life preserver. She grabbed it and held on for dear life.

"The showdown was a bloodbath. Our White Hats are down to the last man, and I saw him turn tail and run a minute ago. The bandits are going to finish off the wounded in a minute, and I need immediate evac."

Someone moved on the other end of the line, set to speakerphone.

Probably Preeti rolling over to another station. "What happened?" King asked. "You said you had the posse assembled, they had their bonding scene around the card table and everything."

"Tell that to the three dead deputies in the street, boss. What's my ETA on an extraction?"

Low chatter between Preeti and King. Then, "Roman will be there in ten minutes. Can the story be salvaged?"

Mallery risked a look out into the street, concealing the phone beneath her sweat-and-dust-stained hair. The bandits were tying bags from the bank to their saddlebags, but the gunfire had calmed down.

"Not today. We'll need to assemble another posse."

"Understood. Stay out of harm's way, and Roman will be at your location in fifteen."

Mallery winced. "I thought it was ten?"

"Dimensional disturbance. Preeti has plotted a new course, but it's going to delay the crossing."

"Well, I'll just hang out here and bleed some more, then. No big problem."

"Try to keep that to a minimum," King said.

"Aye aye, captain."

"Preeti will stay on the line with you until Roman arrives. Be careful, Mallery. King out."

"Careful isn't going to stop the bleeding," Mallery said, watching her skirt go red. Next time she came to Western-land, she was wearing the chaps. They were at least something resembling armor. Though they couldn't be turned into bandages nearly as easy. You give a little, you get a little.

"Roman is on his way. We've got your location locked, so just sit tight," Preeti said.

"You know, this is why I prefer Romance world. At least there I'd be having mortal-danger makeouts while under fire."

"I'll put in the request on your duty roster. More mortal-danger makeouts."

"I don't know about more, but I'll take it."

Preeti stayed on the line, trying to engage Mallery with small talk, keeping her bleeding friend focused when the world started to go black. Mallery leaned into the conversation, shutting her eyes and focusing on Preeti's story about spending all Saturday digging through the source text archives to find her favorite childhood storybook.

Mallery ducked her head out to check on the bandits. The Williamson gang had finished loading up and was riding for the hills with half of the town's silver. "When I get back, I am so kicking someone's ass."

Another impact hit mere feet from her head. She ducked and said through clenched teeth, "This is *not* how the story was supposed to end."

Chapter One:
Everyone's a Critic. Even Drunks.
Especially Drunks.

Leah Tang was dying on stage.

She knew she shouldn't expect too much from a college bar crowd, but this was beyond the pale.

Her *The Last Action Hero* bit? Interrupted every ten seconds by the table full of bros up front yelling for her to show some flesh.

Her breakdown of why the Star Wars prequels failed, from the lack of a scruffy-looking-Nerf-herder rogue figure to the bungling misuse of the Jedi Order? Nothing but heckling.

Even her story about the Epic Ice Fortress Snowball Wars from when she was in middle school fell flat, and that bit had killed before.

It sure didn't help that the drunk first-timer before her had gotten a hooting-and-hollering standing ovation with nothing more than five minutes of boob jokes.

He'd primed the audience so much that when she took the stage, one of the bros up front asked her to flash him. It was a testament to her professionalism that she didn't just dump her water on his head to start off her set.

In fact, so far the only person in the room who seemed at all interested in her routine was the intense black guy sitting on his own in the second row by the entrance. He hadn't taken his coat off even though the bros up front were sweating in the lights. This guy, this one appreciative audience member—he liked her genre commentary, so she'd be happy to oblige.

This guy had been at her last open night too, if she remembered right. So he was either digging her work, a creeper, or maybe both. Hopefully not both. That wouldn't bode well for her future fan base. "I'm huge with the 'overly intense and creepy' crowd!" Not so good.

Not that she had a fan base to begin with. The rest of the crowd—the townies at their regular tables and the drunk-ass students up front—the best they managed was polite disinterest.

Leah heard her father's voice in her head. "Oh, Leah, don't go to the coast and become a comedian. Make a responsible choice; stay here with your family and go to optometry school like your brother."

The bros up front catcalled again, asking for her number for the third time.

"Come down here, baby!" one said. "I'll make your fantasies come true."

Cal, the owner, had a very high bar for throwing out belligerent hecklers, so she was on her own. It was three strikes and you're out here at the Attic, and she was in the middle of Strike Three. So she might as well enjoy herself.

"Fantasy, eh?" Leah asked.

Perform for the audience you have, not the audience you want, she thought. She grabbed the available segue and ran with it, squaring off to the audience and zeroing in on the bros in the front row.

She affected a coquettish bedroom voice. "Let me tell you about my fantasy."

That got the bros' attention.

"My fantasy"—hooting and howling nearly drowned her out. She resumed, trying to shut them out. "Discovery. New races, new kingdoms, new magics. I loved that when I opened a fantasy book or found a new author, I knew I was in for a tour through someone's imagination."

The bros were crestfallen, their interest shorted out. But the guy in the coat leaned forward, elbows on the table, his drink sitting forgotten beside him.

"But as I grew up, I realized something that was incredibly rare in fantasy: people that looked like me.

"In most fantasies, an Asian girl like me only shows up as a topless witch in need of rescue or killing, with snakes crawling over her boobs. And that is just not my scene.

"My fantasy is less about the whips and the PVC, more about self-actualization and hope. And you know what? That's just as sexy to me."

That got a chuckle out of one of the college guys up front. From the look of him, thickly muscled, wearing a tank top that read "No Fat Chicks," he was probably not laughing at the joke the way she meant him to be.

"In my fantasy, Asian girls like me can do anything we want. We can be fighters, wizards, and rogues. We can save the day and fall in love with the person we want, not be de-powered or married off as a prize for the square-jawed hero.

"When I was a kid, I read so much fantasy that I was convinced I was The Chosen One. My parents yelled at me for introducing my friends as my Sidekick or my Nemesis. Because heroes in fantasy can do it all—they learn magic, pick up languages in a montage, and become master swordsmen in a month on the road headed from their village to the Dark Lord's tower, winning the heart of the elven princess and besting the champion swordsman from the pointy-hat-wearing Pseudo-French kingdom along the way."

She saw a dim flicker of light coming from the back of the room, right next to the million candle power spotlight that would have her seeing dots through the weekend. It was Alex, the host, giving her the one-minute warning.

At least she'd caught the signal this time. Last month, she hadn't even seen the timer and they'd cut her mic when she went over.

Even low on time, she plowed ahead.

"So when I was eight, confident that I was The Chosen One, I decided to begin my heroic skills acquisition. I spent six months awaiting my parents' tragic death with Wednesday Addams–level fascination.

"Thankfully, they lived, and I forged on un-orphaned. First, I tried to become a master alchemist. My parents bought me a My Little Scientist kit, but even after eight weeks, all I could do was almost blow up our garage. My older brother's bike is still stained mad-scientist red, more than fifteen years later. Whatever, it's not like he was using those eyebrows.

"So I gave up on alchemy and focused on riding—every good fantasy hero can ride, right? Except it wasn't fourteenth-century England, and I wasn't royalty, and my parents unsurprisingly did not accept my argument, in a bad British accent, that if they didn't max out their credit cards on horse-related expenses, that an evil wizard would rule the world." Leah made the sad trombone noise into the mic. That was good for a couple of chuckles.

"And that's when I knew. Sword fighting. Every good Chosen One knows their way around a sword. So I guilted my parents into enrolling me in a fencing class, and I tell you what. You have never seen someone happier than ten-year-old me running around with a kid-sized épée pretending to be Aragorn or Inigo Montoya." Leah mimed some slashes and thrusts.

"I practiced and practiced—stayed with it way longer than anything else. Even got into some tournaments. I got all the way to the finals in my division.

"And you know what happened?"

She waited a second, let the suspense build.

Another flicker of light from the back. Her time was up. Just as she was getting some momentum.

Leah stopped, turning to the audience. She'd keep practicing her blocking and timing, even if she was performing to an effective audience of one.

"What happened is I got my ass handed to me six ways from Sunday by a kid from Iowa that had been fencing since he was four.

"I was fuming after the bout. But my parents made me go congratulate him. He introduced me to his parents, and guess what? They were farmers. And the kid? Adopted.

"You never *choose* to be the Chosen One. You just *are*."

The guy in the coat nodded, his arms crossed.

"And you know what? That kid sent me a friend request two weeks ago. He's headed to the Olympics.

"But even though I never won a tournament, I found something I loved even though it was hard, even though I would never be the best. Those stories made me believe in myself. That's what fantasy means to me."

Alex approached the stage, not remotely happy with her for going over time. His little light was flashing like a raver strobe.

"But I tell you what—if you come across a farm boy and an old wizard, shiv them, take their horses, and go make your own destiny.

"Thank you, and good night!" She bowed (shallow, so as to not give the bros anything to look at), then clomped off-stage, still grumpy about acquiescing to Cal's creepy demand that all women wear heels to perform. Flats were wonderful, she loved flats. Even heels couldn't make her tall on stage, so why even pretend?

Alex gave her a falsely enthusiastic high-five, resuming his thankless job as host.

"How about that Leah Tang. Quite a kid! Keep it going now for our next comic, Kyle Jones!"

One person's solid applause and another half-dozen golf-claps were her reward for the night.

Well, that and the free booze. Cal's one bit of generosity. Even if you washed out, open mic performers always got a drink on the house.

Leah made a beeline to the bar and ordered her customary post-gig Jack & cola. She preferred Laphroaig on the rocks, but her comps didn't go anywhere near that far. And she was expecting a whole lotta nothing in tips.

Though surprisingly, No Fat Chicks tossed a ten-dollar bill in the can Alex walked around for her. That'd pay for her cab home, at least.

"Not the best night," Inez the bartender said, mixing the drink. Inez could be counted on to enjoy the show, but she couldn't play favorites. Not since her very noticeable dislike of a misogynistic-as-hell show a few months back got her in hot water with Cal.

The bartender kept her black hair short, since she "hated ponytails worse than she hated well tequila"—an exact quote that Leah had logged away for use in a future set. Leah had a thousand little lines like that jotted across a half-dozen notebooks that she used to stitch together ideas on the whiteboard in her room.

"I think the guy in the coat was paying attention to something other than my ass."

"It's a fine ass, kid. You should be proud of it. But if it's ass they're looking for, they should be at Whistlin' Dixie's, not here." Inez topped off Leah's drink with an extra pour of Jack.

Leah raised the drink to salute the bartender, then took a long swig.

Someone appeared to her right, and Leah turned to see No Fat Chicks, drink in hand. Up close, she saw how sloshed he was.

"That was fantastic, dude," he said, slurring. "Hot and funny. Plus," he whispered, "I'm really into reptiles and I think you'd look amazing covered in snakes."

So not only had he completely missed her point, now he was going to sloppily hit on her. Sigh.

"An impressive performance, Ms. Tang," said another voice, stepping from around No Fat Chicks's broad shoulders. It was the dude in the coat.

Perfect timing.

"Thanks, man," she said to the bro, then turned to face the guy in the coat, hoping her other admirer would get bored and wander off.

Leah saluted with her drink. "I wish a few more people here shared your perspective." She took another sip.

The drunk bro stood there like a loading cursor, trying to figure out what to say.

"Perhaps your insights might be better used elsewhere," the guy in the coat said. He reached into his pocket and pulled out a business card with a Johns Hopkins logo.

"I'm Dr. Angstrom King, Department of Comparative Literature. I run a narrative immersion laboratory, and I'm looking for new staff. I think you might be an excellent fit." King had the upper-class Yankee accent that she associated with the Ivies, but he wore it well. Some folks used that accent like a weapon, a constant reminder of their superiority.

He wasn't coming off as scary, thank goodness. And Leah knew from scary, thanks to her share of sketchy dudes trying to pick her up after sets.

Speaking of which, No Fat Chicks had lost interest and wandered off. Thank goodness.

"Immersive Narrative Laboratory?" Leah asked, looking at the business card, which announced King as a Visiting Professor of English. "Mind de-academia-ing that a bit for me?"

"My team are narrative specialists working with stories in very much the same way that your routine did. We have a big project running right now, and I could use someone with your perspective."

"I've got a job, thanks," Leah said, turning her back to King and reacquainting herself with her drink. She'd put college in her rear view several years back and was glad of it. This "Immersive Narrative Laboratory" was a load of crap if she'd ever heard of one. And while working the reception desk at the accountants' office was far from glamorous, it kept her afloat financially and didn't expect her to work overtime.

"I understand your reluctance, Ms. Tang. The Refusal of the Call is especially strong for persons of your generation. But we pay very well, and the benefits are quite hard to beat."

"Going Campbell on me isn't going to change my mind," Leah said, taking another drink, "but I could stand to hear more about the pay."

Leah looked to Inez for confirmation one way or another. "Is this guy legit?"

Inez nodded. "Word is he helped Tommy Suarez land that HBO special."

Leah froze. Oh, he was *that* kind of weirdo. The "eccentric as all get-out but really well-connected and potentially very useful" weirdo. She perked up.

Tommy hadn't made it big yet, but he'd gone straight from working the regional circuit to an HBO special, which did not happen in the normal world. And if this was the guy who helped Tommy make that jump, she could take the time to check out this "lab."

Plus, this place was tapped out, so she'd need a new lead. She'd made the rounds in the Baltimore circuit, and she was getting nowhere. She needed a break.

"You should have had Inez vouch for you in the beginning," Leah said.

"It means more if you do the asking for yourself. If you've changed your mind, I'd like to introduce you to the team tonight. And if you come along, hear me out as I explain what our team does. I'll ensure that you have a weekly gig here or at any other club in the Baltimore-DC area you want for as long as you like."

A steady gig, indefinitely. She hadn't gotten close to graduating out of the open mics. If this guy could guarantee her a steady gig, give her time to sort out her material, find an aesthetic that could connect with audiences … Leah tried to avoid salivating at the idea.

Leah checked her phone. "But it's eleven o'clock. Your team works that late every Thursday night?"

"Tonight we do. Shall I bring my car around?"

Leah shifted her weight from one hip to the other. She took a long swig and asked, "You have to tell me if you're going to axe murder me, right? Some kind of professorial code of conduct?"

King's expression brightened. He mimed a posh British accent. "Indeed. It's a condition of my tenure. Along with the requirement that I be absentminded and wear tweed jackets with patches."

"Well, if that's the case, sure." Leah finished off her drink and left a tip for Inez, who made the glass and bills vanish with her magic.

King lead the way and Leah followed, reassuring herself that her mace was in fact where it was supposed to be in her jacket.

The two made their way out into the ever-humid Baltimore night. King worked a key fob and a too-nice-for-a-visiting-professor Audi came alive three spots up the street.

"Where's this lab of yours?"

King opened the door for Leah. "South of the city. Shouldn't take but twenty minutes to get there."

Leah held the door as King went to the driver's side, not quite ready to climb in and commit to doing something quite this dangerous. "And a reminder. No axe murdering."

King climbed into the car. "Ms. Tang, if I wanted to find someone to kidnap and axe murder, I'd be looking for victims that are far more trusting than you. And I wouldn't be hunting in Baltimore. Things tend to go poorly for men who look like me when we're suspected of crimes in this city."

"Point."

King started the engine, which purred to life, running quiet. "As a university professor, I specialize in the disquieting reassurance. It means that my office hours are blissfully uneventful."

The sound system turned on, leaping into an Eddie Izzard CD. One more layer of resistance peeled off, and she took her seat.

Chapter Two:
The Story Lab

True to King's word, about twenty minutes later, they arrived at a two-story-tall office building off I-97.

The car had already passed several turnoffs to nowhere in particular, so if he was going to axe murder her, he was taking the long way there. That was comforting. Sort of.

The building had a dome on one side that arched up another story's worth. IMAX, maybe? Maybe that's what he meant by narrative immersion. She could think of worse jobs than getting paid to watch IMAX documentaries about penguins and hummingbirds.

King rolled the car into a spot that read "Team Leads."

"What I'm going to show you may seem incredible, but know that it can all be explained by science. Our mission is one of exploration."

"That's not ominous at all," Leah said, stepping out of the car. On the drive over, she'd texted two different friends to check on her in an hour to make sure she was okay. Mr. and Mrs. Tang didn't raise no dumbass. Smartass, yes, but not dumb.

King opened the door with a quick scan of a passcard, revealing a stark corridor with an institutional look. The rooms were labeled innocuous things like "Archives, 1970–1979" and "Personnel Files" and odder things like "Probe Reports," "Skill-acquisition Lounge," and "Dimensional Barometric Chamber."

Her nerves had resumed assembly of a worry-henge when King threw open a set of double doors at the end of the hallway, leading into a room that looked half like the NASA command center and half like a newsroom.

The room was nearly empty, only a half-dozen of the stations filled by men and women in polo shirts, each watching several screens of TV shows, none of them immediately recognizable.

"My team is through here," King said, leading her along one side of the room. At the far wall, wide windows showed a room that looked for all the world like a hangar. If her spatial sense was working, that would be where the IMAX dome was.

King led her into another long hallway that spanned the length of the building. Part of the way down the hall, voices prompted Leah to turn and see a crash cart round the corner behind front of them. Lab-coat-and-scrubs-clad figures pushed the cart, checking the IV drip, taking pulse, and more. The patient was a white woman, blond, very banged up, and wearing an outfit that belonged at a kitschy Wild West party. The cart raced by, and King peeled off to join them, pointing to a nearby room.

"Wait in there," he said.

Leah stood befuddled for a moment as the cart and its entourage rounded a corner.

What *was* this place? A shiver ran down Leah's spine, fear tackling curiosity into a confusing melee.

The doors King had pointed to revealed a break room, and a nice one at that. It had several flat-panel TVs on the walls, treadmills with built-in screens, a full kitchen, several fridges, couches, tables, and a library in one corner.

An older Middle Eastern woman with silvery hair sat in the rocking chair amid the library. She held a massive hardcover in her lap.

Noticing Leah, the woman set her book down and stood.

"Hi," Leah said.

"You must be Leah. I'm Shirin Tehrani." Her voice was a smooth alto, welcoming and kind.

Shirin crossed, heels clicking on the floor, and extended a hand along with a warm smile. "Pleased to meet you."

"So King told you I was coming, did he?"

"Of course. He keeps us apprised of candidates and solicits our input. Your evaluations in improvisational thinking and threat responses were very impressive. You have to be quick on your toes in this job."

"Threat responses?" Leah asked. "I thought this was a lab. What is it, really? There was a crash cart or something, and King went off and said I should wait here."

Worry crossed Shirin's face, but didn't stick. Why was she so calm?

Leah's danger senses were going off. She had a few minutes left to send the all-clear text. It didn't seem like anyone was hiding axes for murdering, but they might all be delusional.

Or maybe it was a cult. A story cult? Granddaughters of Grimm or something?

"It's as he said—a narrative laboratory. This will go more smoothly if you wait for him to explain. Please help yourself to coffee or a snack or anything while you wait. But try not to worry about the woman you saw. Our medical facilities are top of the line."

Shirin's smile was gracious. The woman's whole demeanor said "classy aunt." Leah could use some classy aunts in her life. All of her aunts were back in Minnesota.

Leah looked around for some normalcy to latch on to. *Hey look, coffeemaker. Yes.* Java was needed to face the fear. "Is the coffee any good?" she asked.

"It's good for office coffee. And the granola bars are passable, if you're hungry. They're in the second drawer to the left of the fridge."

When Leah looked back, Shirin had plopped back down and was once again consumed with her book. She was acting like this wasn't weird, but it clearly was.

Leah's pulse quickened, and she tuned in to her peripheral vision, wary.

Think about the gigs, Leah, she thought, trying to find her calm.

The coffee was, in fact, passable. More importantly, it was hot. She passed on the granola bar, and walked the room, not comfortable enough to sit down when she had a hundred questions and the only other person in the building she'd met so far didn't seem interested in talking.

A few minutes later, Leah's coffee buzz was in full effect as Professor King returned. He wiped off his hands and tossed the bloodied rag in a bucket beside a waste bag.

Leah asked, "Are you going to tell me what this is all about, now? And who was that on the gurney?"

"The woman on the gurney is Mallery, a member of my team. She's being treated now. As for what this is about, why don't I just show you?" King said, his voice level. King escorted Leah to the command-room thing. Shirin put her book down and joined them.

As they entered the command room, King made straight for a woman Leah's age with thick glasses and an incredibly bright wardrobe, patterns on patterns set against a traffic cone orange shawl. She sat in a wheelchair, a complex set of monitors and two keyboards within arm's reach.

"This part is really cool," King said. "Preeti, can you bring up the orientation video on Big One, please?"

"Sure thing, boss."

The woman's hands blurred, typing at court transcriptionist speed. A moment later, one of the large screens went dark. Preeti held her over-the-ear earphones out to Leah.

She took the wireless headset, which played the opening riffs of an orchestral score like an epic movie trailer.

Earth popped up on the screen, clouds and storms and oceans and all that jazz. The screen zoomed out, showing Earth surrounded by a rough circle of red light, a dozen other worlds in fragments around it. The orbiting was replaced by circular logos—crossed revolvers, a heart, a magnifying glass, a rocket ship.

I am surrounded by crazy people right now, Leah thought, already prepping her escape strategy.

A familiar voice started to narrate. It was King.

"Stories are the DNA of the universe."

Wait, what?

"We think of life in three dimensions. With time, that makes four. Some scientists posit that we live in eleven dimensions.

"But for our purposes, there are only five that matter.

"The fifth dimension is narrative. In the fifth dimension, Earth is surrounded on all sides by worlds that are simultaneously familiar and irreducibly distinct."

The camera panned to the side, zooming in on one of the adjacent worlds. Getting closer, every bit of land area on one continent was covered by city, towers and factories, and the circuit-board of lights that reminded Leah of flying into Southern California by night.

"Each world hosts the inspiration for a narrative genre. This world inspires our stories of Science Fiction."

The world spun, resolving into shots of iconic science fiction scenes—a launching rocket, a massive laboratory filled with androids, a cityscape with flying cars, a bustling space station.

"There are dozens of others." The screen showed a Western boom town, a mine shaft entrance in the distance.

Next came a contemporary American city filled with people going about their lives. The camera moved inside a café, where every table was filled with couples. Some were awkward, stealing glances and then looking away. Others were twitterpated. One woman was on her knee, proposing to her girlfriend. Another was having a knock-down drag-out fight.

"Romance."

The screen flipped through other worlds more quickly.

First, a fantasy kingdom, with gnomes, dwarves, and elves walking around a market town, castle towers in the background. A flourish of colorful magic erupted from the gnome's hands as a crowd looked on. It was her bit come to life.

"Fantasy."

Then the screen jumped through several more, offering views of worlds Leah pegged as noir, horror, and one world populated by pirates with shirts open to the waist, oiled chests, and tight breeches, and women in gigantic Elizabethan dresses corseted within an inch of their lives.

Finally, the screen returned to the picture of the earth, surrounded by the other worlds.

"Because of your specific skills, you've been selected to join this elite team and protect not only Earth, but dozens of other worlds, from destruction."

This was too much. Leah pulled one ear of the headset off and sniped back at King. "Are you serious? This is some Rylan Star League ridiculousness."

She started walking for the door. The playback continued. "In any system, there is entropy. When something breaks down in one of these worlds, when a story goes wrong, it ripples back on Earth.

"When a story breaches in the Western world, violence runs rampant on Earth Prime."

She looked back as she passed Preeti, starting to take off the headset. On the screen, a newspaper showed the headline "Shooting Spree in Omaha. Seventeen wounded, two dead."

Leah took the headset off entirely. "Hold up. You're telling me that broken stories affect our world? Some kind of feedback?"

"Keep watching," King said, his patience clearly wavering.

The video continued.

Leah's curiosity grabbed her, and she donned the headset again.

"Every world has a different influence on Earth."

The worlds again.

"The mission of the Genrenauts Foundation is to minimize these dangerous ripples between the worlds. When a story world goes off-track, it's our job to set it right. Using inter-dimensional vessels launched from this and other facilities around the world, teams travel to the impacted world, investigate the story breach, and put it back on-track."

The screen resolved to a logo—Earth surrounded by a dozen worlds, with "GENRENAUTS—MID-ATLANTIC ASTRODOME."

Leah took the headset off and turned to the group. Her disbelief, her desire to not be caught by some weird gotcha, took center stage.

"This is some kind of History Channel documentary, right? On after *Ancient Aliens?*"

King was nonplussed.

"Some kind of lab hazing prank or something? I thought this was going to be a touchy-feely writing job, like High Culture TwitFeed or something."

Preeti paused the playback.

"It is exactly what the pretentious video says it is," King said. "Maintaining balance between the worlds is of incalculable importance. We stand in one of several bases that monitor and respond to dimensional disturbances. There is one such disturbance right now, in the world that inspires our Western genre. One of our team has been severely injured in a failed attempt to patch the story breach, and I would like to bring you along with my team to observe as we resolve the situation."

"Tell me more about these ripples."

King had to be a professor, he had the sigh of the put-upon down pat. "When a story breaks, that breach creates a thematic-semiotic ripple effect, which crosses over from that world to our own Earth. Each of those story worlds has its own distinct signature derived from the genre it represents, and each signature has a different effect on Earth when it ripples over. Identifying and patching story breaches as quickly as possible minimizes these ripple effects and keeps the earth roughly as we know it."

Heady stuff. No wonder they hired a lit professor to run the team.

Leah made the "go on" hand gesture. "And now, unpack that one more time like I'm stupid. Because this still sounds crazypants."

Another sigh, this one more exasperated. "Right now, a story is broken in the Western story world. Western world's signature is about violence, order vs. lawlessness, and taking the law into your own hands. Do you remember the shooting in Vegas yesterday?" King asked.

"Yeah."

"That was only the first of several identified ripple events over the last forty-eight hours since the breach began."

King turned to Preeti. "Bring up the news feeds."

Preeti tabbed through to another program, and pulled up a news site.

The headlines read:

VIGILANTE SHOOTER KILLS FIVE BURGLARS IN EVANSVILLE, IN

UNIDENTIFIED GUNMAN SHOOTS SEVEN IN WASHINGTON PUBLIC PARK. ALL IN CRITICAL CONDITION. GUNMAN STILL AT LARGE.

SWAT RAID GONE SOUTH: FIVE OFFICERS IN CRITICAL CONDITION.

"And if we don't fix this story breach," King said, "the shootings will continue. The whole world will shift. More people will take the law into their own hands, will take what they think they deserve by force."

King jabbed a finger at the screens. "That's what I mean by thematic-semiotic resonance. A story breaks, and then people die, lives are ruined. I need to send a team to Western world and fix the story now. I brought you in because I thought you could help. Do you want to critique stories your whole life, or would you rather fix them?"

"Hold up. I have friends in Vegas, and you're telling me they might have gotten killed because of some broken story in a whole other world?"

"Those are the stakes, Leah. Now it's time to make a decision. You have ten minutes."

King turned and made his way out of the room, apparently done with the conversation.

Shirin watched him go, saying, "He gets what we'd call 'passionate' about the job."

Leah turned to watch the news feeds. She'd heard about the shootings, but had blamed it on the social media age, where a small story can become a huge story within an hour.

"So you're script doctors, but for real worlds? And somehow also dimensional cops?" Leah said, trying to parse the unbelievable.

Shirin smiled. "That depends on what you mean by real. The people on these worlds have their own lives, their own desires, but they are bound by the rules of their world. We help keep their worlds running as they're meant to. It's the best job you could ask for. Adventure, excitement, a new challenge every mission."

Preeti had turned back to her workstation, watching three screens, each showing a view of what had to be the Western world—Old West buildings, saloons, cowboys on horseback, and a trio of Native American men from a Great Plains tribe trading with a merchant on a street corner.

"So how finely sliced do the genre worlds get? Is there a Slasher world, a sports movie world?" Leah asked.

Shirin gestured to the wall of screens. Looking closer, she started to pick out different worlds. Each pack of 3x3 screens seemed to show one world, but with different styles. "Each world has one umbrella genre which sets the tone for that world. Fantasy world has dark fantasy, epic fantasy, and sword and sorcery, all on different continents far removed from one another. Slasher would be a region in Horror world. Sports stories happen all over, but something like *A League of Their Own* would go to Women's Fiction world.

"I hate that label, by the way," Shirin added, "but unless we convince the High Council to rename it, that's what it is." That sounded like an argument that had gone around the block more than a few times. "I guarantee you that this will be more exciting than answering phone calls, scheduling meetings, and processing expense reports."

"Don't knock expense reports. There's a kind of magic in paying bills with other people's money," Leah said.

Shirin said, "I could see the appeal in that. But what we do is storytelling at the highest possible stakes, determining the fate of individuals, nations, and entire worlds all at once."

Gulp. "No pressure, right?"

Shirin nodded. The woman seemed to be shooting straight, not sugarcoating it to get her to sign her soul away.

But curiosity wouldn't let her just walk away. She might as well see how deep the rabbit hole went before deciding whether to take the leap.

Leah waved at the screens. "So, what does it take to cross the dimensional barriers or whatever you do?"

"For that, we go to the Hangar."

* * *

Bakhtin Hangar contained several berths with snub-nosed rocket ships under repair and reconstruction, as well as launching stations.

One of the ships stood on end, scaffolding and a set of stairs attached—for maintenance, most likely. The ship was twenty feet tall, with a glass port on the top, and a larger hatch near the back. Techs in red jumpsuits surrounded the nearest ships, running diagnostics, moving hoses, and generally making with the busy.

King watched the scurrying preparations, tapping through menus on a tablet.

"So you cross dimensions in that?" Leah asked.

"Exactly," King said.

"So why haven't I heard about the weird rocket launches by BWI?"

"Because they never cross above that hoop. These ships travel in the fifth dimension, they're designed to traverse the boundaries between Earth Prime and the narrative dimensions. And this one is about to launch. What do you say?"

"I say this is still totally bonkers."

"That's fair. But the offer stands—come with us, and you'll have a steady comedy gig for as long as you want it."

"So what are the chances that I get killed in your little excursion?" Leah asked.

"Not at all likely. I'd give it a seven percent chance. Only three percent if you follow all of my directions."

"The fact that you know those percentages without thinking makes me think that the actual odds are way worse." Leah looked at the ship, at the dome above, and thought about the drudgery awaiting her at the office tomorrow.

It was totally ridiculous that this place was even here, right under everyone's noses. A whole multiverse of possibility and semio-thematic thingamawhatsits and professional dimensional story doctors jumping between worlds as regularly as corporate troubleshooters.

The smart thing to do would be to get them to call her a cab, text her friends that she was coming home, and forget this whole thing. She could try the Attic again, promise to use different material, and keep trying, keep grinding until she got a break. That's what made sense.

Watching the techs cluster around the ship, King barking orders, rushing the team to move faster, Leah imagined what that normal life would be like.

Banality by day, frustration by night. Weekends in coffeeshops writing material, late nights dying on the stage again and again.

Or ... this. This bizarre, dangerous job with infinite possibility. And, even if she didn't like it—wasn't suited or whatever—she could take the gig. King had delivered for Tommy Suarez, and Inez vouched for him. And wasn't a steady gig worth an evening of bizarreness?

She thought about the woman on the gurney, the mention of "casualties," weighed it against the chance to fly in a rocket ship, to see impossible vistas, to take her passion for stories and use it to make a real difference. That is, if all of this was real. But she'd never know unless she gave it a shot.

And there was her answer.

Leah popped off a quick "all clear" text to her friends as she walked toward the rocket.

"Hey, King," she shouted. "Do I get to wear a cool bubble helmet?"

"Not this time," King said, turning with the hint of a smile. "First, there is some very exciting paperwork for you to fill out."

Much less cool.

But still, spaceship.

Chapter Three:
Blast Off

Leah held on for dear life, sitting with her back to the floor, gravity pulling like a tilt-a-whirl, minus the spinning.

King was at the helm. Shirin had the copilot seat, calling out sensor data. Leah sat in the second row, alone, with boxes of supplies secured behind her.

The ship rocked and rattled at a dull roar. Colors kaleidoscoped across the windshield like an acid trip mixed with a music visualizer. Leah tried to keep her regretfully greasy dinner down as the ship lurched and shook.

"What's with the rattling?" she yelled, distracting herself from her fear by complaining—a tactic she borrowed from pre-K kids everywhere.

"It's dimensional turbulence," King said, his voice lacking its usual level calm. "The dimensions rub up against one another more sometimes than others, and that friction disturbs our passing in the fifth dimension."

"That sounds crappy." She stopped for a moment to consider. "And yet kinda cool. Has it ever killed anyone?" she asked, not really wanting to know the answer, but fear was in the driver's seat, and the question was out before she could swallow it.

"Not often," Shirin said, her knuckles white on the sides of her seat.

A strap broke behind her, and Leah saw gear tumbling to the ground. A bag spilled old-timey Western clothes—ponchos, starched shirts, dusters, and chaps. Another bundle went clang with the sound of metal on metal as a rolled-up tube of guns toppled to the floor.

"The universe is coming undone back here," Leah said. She caught Shirin looking on, the older woman's eyes evaluating the damage, worry showing through a hastily applied mask of calm.

"If you get me killed before I even get to see *Westworld,* I'm going to be ridiculously pissed-off."

King worked the controls, hauling back on a lever and slamming a button. The ship lurched to the left, and a few bumpy moments later, the turbulence faded. The windshield view-screen resolved to a flat white, which then receded into a horizon, a sun-drenched desert at high noon.

"Can we skip that part on the way back?" Leah asked, taking deep breaths and locking her vision on the horizon to try to reassemble her shattered equilibrium. They were pointed up, gravity tugging on her back.

"Seconded," said Shirin.

King's smile was meant to be encouraging. Her stomach was still too sloshy for it to help. "That's one hurdle you've already made it past. Fascinating, no?"

"The light show was impressive, but I could have done without the rock tumbler ride."

"Tumblers take off the rough edges, don't they?" King gave a wry smile. Shirin rolled her eyes as she unbuckled.

"Why do we have to travel with our backs to the ground? Or is dangling from one's seat considered a perk?"

"Now she's getting it." King unbuckled, then adeptly climbed out of the chair, dropped to the chair beside Leah, and reached over to help her out of her seat.

"I got it, I got it." Leah swatted at his hand, working the X-cross straps that had kept her mostly stable in the seat during the crossing.

"Shirin, see to the gear."

The woman descended a column of rails at the side of the ship. Leah tested the strength of the rails, then followed.

King said, "Now that we've arrived, here's what you need to know: to do our jobs and keep the worlds stable, we need to make as little an impact here as possible. We're surgeons, not sawbones. We nudge the story back on track, and do it from the shadows whenever possible. If the people of this world realize that they're being messed with by outsiders, then even more stories will go off-track, and the whole problem will only compound until we're all quite screwed."

Leah climbed onto the stairs and made her way down to the pile of rucksacks. "Tread softly, got it. But won't we stand out regardless? Westerns aren't exactly known for their diversity. Black guy, Asian woman, and a

Middle Eastern woman wander into a saloon, people are going to notice. And then make a joke. And then shoot us."

King nodded. "Sad truth is, you're right. That's why we have these." He gestured to the Marshal's pin on his jacket. "This is a Personal Phase Manipulator, or PPM. They let us project an illusion and fit in to the story worlds. We'll look like any other three lily-white red-blooded cowfolks. We try to only use them on worlds where our operatives wouldn't otherwise be able to move unnoticed. Here, the various historical regions on Romance world, and so on."

"Anywhere that the three of us would get run out of town if we showed up looking like ourselves," Leah said.

"Exactly. That's why Mallery and Roman went first in this world," King said. "The Phase Manipulators are incredibly expensive and sometimes unreliable, so we try to minimize the need for them."

"That and Western world is usually one of the most dormant, the most stable," Shirin said. "There hasn't been a genre-redefining Western for years. The breaches here tend to be small."

Leah said, "So all the racist storytelling tropes happen in these worlds: black guys *do* always die first in Horror world, beautiful white people are ninety-five percent of the leads in Romance world while the 'ethnic' friends get paired off with one another in the credits—that kind of thing?"

"Pretty much, yes." King helped Shirin sort out their gear while Leah looked on. "Thematic-semiotic resonance is a two-way street. The way we tell stories manifests in the story worlds. The dominant narrative here is reflected on the genre world. Any given world has some room for minority narratives and counternarratives, but those are just as marginalized."

"Counternarratives. Like parodies?"

"Parodies, deconstructions, feminist or antiracist interventions into the genre, and so on."

Shirin walked by, a bag over each shoulder. "We should probably save the literary theory lecture for after the mission, Professor." She put a hand on Leah's arm. "Go ahead and get changed. The less work the Phase Manipulators have to do to make you fit in, the more reliable they are."

Leah gestured to the ship. "What about this thing? It's a bit more conspicuous than the Minority Musketeers riding into town."

"The ship has its own Phase Manipulator," King said. "It projects the image of something that makes sense in the world—like a boarded-up ranch house or a rock outcropping. Due to the size difference and the fact that it's inorganic, the phase shift is more stable."

"Because technobabble, got it," Leah said. "Glad to hear the chameleon circuit's not broken."

Shirin draped a heavy leather coat over Leah's arms, ignoring the reference. "This will make you look bigger than you are. We need to look dangerous. The best way to blend in on this world here is to come off as big and bad. Normal folks don't get in the way of people they consider to be threatening."

King opened the hatch, heading outside to give Shirin and Leah their privacy.

* * *

Leah adjusted her ten-gallon hat, looking in the mirror bracketed to the inside of the ship's hatch.

With her Phase Manipulator on, Leah saw a stranger before her. Leah moved, and in the mirror, a white man with Norse coloration echoed her. The illusion had sandy-blond hair, an angular face, and hair shorter than she'd had since she cut her own hair as a six-year-old.

The illusory man had Leah's build, so she wouldn't have to worry about people looking her "in the eye" at her forehead or her chest. The whole thing had the feel of LARPing an episode of *Quantum Leap* by wearing a virtual reality rig.

She turned away and looked back, catching her "self" out of the corner of her eye. If she was going to keep up this act, she would need to not be startled by seeing this illusion casually in washrooms or watering holes or whatever reflective surfaces were at hand.

Having to travel in whitewashed drag in order to not get harassed wasn't exactly what she'd call comforting, but the fascinating bizarreness of having a full-body illusion was fairly distracting from the unfairness of it all.

"Adjusted yet?" came Shirin's voice from behind her.

Shirin's cover illusion was that of a grizzled white woman of about sixty. She had a time-worn face and bone-white hair.

"This is weird, right?" Leah said, watching her hands as she talked. "I mean, we're wearing illusory white people. This is straight-up science-fictional future shock weird."

Leah put on her hat, which was two sizes too big. It dropped right down

27

onto her nose, blocking her vision. She flicked the brim and the hat eased back so she could see, weighing heavy on her ears.

"It's weird, but things were worse when we tried to go without the PPMs."

"So, how do I look?"

Shirin doled out another one of her classy aunt smiles. "Not quite dangerous, but it'll do." Shirin bent down and reached into another bag. She came out with a leather belt holding two holstered revolvers. "This will help with the dangerous part."

"I'm not a big gun fan," Leah said, her hand drooping as she took the weight of the belt.

"You don't have to like them, but for now, you definitely have to wear them." Shirin strapped on her own gun belt. She drew each of the guns in turn, checking the wheel and action.

"I checked yours before we went. Leave them be for now if you're not comfortable."

"I'll do that. I'm a whole lot of uncomfortable, and kind of wishing I'd taken a nap today before my set.

"Also, why isn't your illusion a dude?" Leah asked.

Shirin flinched, hurt crossing her face. Leah was about to open her mouth to apologize, but Shirin cut her off.

"I spent more than twenty years pretending to be a boy. That's enough for several lifetimes."

"Sorry, what?" Leah asked.

Shirin dropped her shoulders, taking a breath. "I'm trans. I left Iran after the revolution in '79, when it became very clear that women like me were especially unwelcome."

Ah. Leah shut her mouth. "Sorry. I didn't know. Didn't mean to …"

Shirin raised a hand. Her forgiving smile wiped away some of the awkwardness. "No worries. I'm old enough that folks here won't police me quite as much as they would a spring chicken like you. Just remember to speak at the bottom of your register so you can pass for a boy without the PPM having to do it for you. Lean into the drawl and you'll be fine. And remember, here you're Lee, and I'm Atlas Jane. Now let's disembark and put this bit of awkwardness behind us, why don't we?"

"Yes, please."

* * *

The hatch opened as Shirin aka Atlas Jane let the harsh desert sun back in. King stood on watch adorned in a brown leather vest and slacks, a bandolier across one shoulder, a shotgun resting on the other.

"We're about a mile outside the town," King said, gesturing off into the distance, beyond some dunes. His illusion was of a black-haired Germanic white guy, grizzled enough to wear the mantle of a Marshal.

They'd arrived in scrublands, setting down at the base of one of a set of rolling hills. There were mountains off in the other direction. Cacti spattered the landscape, along with the light scrub vegetation. The view could have come from one of a hundred soundstages at MGM or any of the Studio's other golden-age Western sets.

Leah climbed down out of the ship, the boots pinching her feet. Such were the joys of being a five-wide. Shirin said she'd had to guess on the fly when they were packing, and next time she'd get tailored gear.

The earth dusted as she touched down, and she could feel the heat sucking all the moisture out of her skin.

She took a breath, the air dry, sun beating down like it was being paid. All that was missing was a tumbleweed.

And there we go, she thought, seeing one roll and bounce by on a gust of wind.

"Lead on, pardner." Leah tipped her hat, her voice as low as she could take it. King furrowed his brow and started walking.

Shirin leaned into Leah. "You're his new best friend."

Leah responded, sotto voce, "Hey, he hired me from a comedy club. Don't know what he was expecting."

"I was expecting that you would be a natural at this," King said over his shoulder. "Let's see if I'm right."

* * *

Walking into the town, Leah could almost see the cardboard behind the storefronts. It was every Western town from every movie brought to life, with washerwomen, mud-stained miners, vest-wearing gentlemen, prim and proper schoolmarms, and more.

She had to contain her sense of wonder, the mix of excitement and worry at seeing the tropes of a genre brought to life and plopped right in front of her. She held her hat in place as she craned her head up, scanning the buildings, squinting her eyes to make out what looked like an office for a mine in the distance, beside the ridge of rocks that stood at the town's back.

But this wasn't a happy-bouncy Western town, townfolk and ranchers greeting one another with tipped hats and the frontier hospitality of people who were all on the edge of something new together.

This town was scared.

Mothers hurried their children along from storefront to storefront, watching the horizon over their shoulder. Ranch hands stayed close by their livestock. Leah's eyes found the bank (inventively labeled "Bank and Trust"), and suddenly understood. The windows had been busted in, the door swung on one hinge, and the wooden walls had bullet-holes, as did the storefronts opposite and beside the bank.

There'd been a shootout here, or her name wasn't Montana Lee. If she was going to be Lee, and Shirin was Atlas Jane, she should get to be Montana Lee. Leah hadn't played Montana Lee since she was seven and living in the Twin Cities, but the genre-tastic sensory overflow brought back those memories, games of cops-and-robbers fueled by classic films and their glorious parodies.

Her friend Cenisa had been the sheriff, because Mel Brooks had proven that black sheriffs were cooler than the grizzled old white ones. But Montana Lee did not do karate. Or kung fu. She was a gunslinger. The best gun in the West from the Far East.

The memory left her in the right mind-set for the world, remembering the diction and drawl, the swagger that came from being bowlegged from riding and wearing boots for too long.

"The shootout was here, but the bandits are gone," Leah said, taking in the street with Shirin and King from their vantage point at the end of Main Street. "So where do we pick up the story?"

"First, we find Roman. He'll be there," King said, nodding toward the saloon, which was indicated by a gaudily painted sign showing a petticoats-laden blonde sipping from a frothy mug in a not-at-all-suggestive manner.

"This place is really on-the-nose," Leah said as an aside to Shirin.

"There's no genre awareness here. All of the tropes, the archetypes, they're just a way of life. You've got to roll with it, use it. We come to these places and we can see two steps ahead—it gives us the edge."

"I'm so paralyzed by low-hanging comedy fruit that I cannot even."

"Then I'll even, and you stay odd," King said, walking across the street to the saloon.

At least King was holding to the rule that all bosses were required to pun.

The head Genrenaut pushed open the swinging doors and stood astride the threshold for a moment, cutting an impressive silhouette with his shotgun over his shoulder and his hat seeming to take up the whole doorway.

Now *that* was an entrance. *Guess that's why he's the boss.*

Leah found herself taking mental notes, partially as a distancing technique to avoid cracking up, part because the world was so perfectly a thing unto itself. Foucault and Plato would go gonzo with this place.

King walked straight over to a booth, and Shirin followed, Leah close behind.

Entering the saloon, Leah felt a dozen sets of eyes on her, narrowed eyes below brimmed hats sizing "him" up, not in the piece of meat way she got walking by a construction site or frat or many other places.

They were getting his measure, deciding whether "he" was a threat. In the heavy coat, with her hair pulled up, and the PPM doing its job, her disguise seemed to hold up.

The attention was still intrusive, but it felt a whole hell of a lot less creepy than being ogled on the street by a bunch of construction workers. Also, this time she was armed. The guns she ignored, but the knife in her boot was reassuring.

But the size-up wasn't all only for macho reasons. There was a hint of fear at the edge of people's movements. This town had been shaken, and bad.

A tall man with sun-beaten skin sat in the corner booth, a rifle propped up beside him. He played the "don't stab yourself" game with a bowie knife, moving just fast enough to be scary. He left the knife stuck in the table and tipped his hat back as King approached the table.

This would be Roman, then.

He slid to the side and made room. There was an all-but-empty bottle of beer on the table, and a fresh one waiting beside a worn and smeared newspaper that looked like it'd been read thirty times.

Roman was probably over six feet tall, though it was always hard to tell when someone was seated. He had a heroic square jaw and corded muscle that showed through Western garb that had seen long and hard use. Of the four of them on Western world, he looked the most like a gunslinger.

He fit into the scene, but it was almost like his gravity was greater than the men around him. *Could the people here tell if someone was from a story world versus Earth? What did it mean to be of a story world?* She kept it together, thinking of

31

the steady stand-up gig. Stay out of trouble, and one day's worth of sightseeing would pay off for years to come.

And it wasn't like she'd ever been on a job interview this bizarre or fascinating. Though once she'd been asked to sit in a room and work on logic puzzles with three other candidates while they were being observed through a one-way mirror for "leadership skills." That had been one weird summer camp.

"This must be the new recruit," Roman said with an Afrikaans accent. That'd explain the name. She didn't know many American born-and-bred Roman De Jagers. On the other hand, she'd never lived in Dutch Pennsylvania, so who knew?

"Around here, folks call me Lee," she said, offering a hand. They shook, but Roman didn't make eye contact. He sat back down as King, Shirin, and Leah filled the booth.

"Any sight of the Williamson gang?" King asked.

Roman shook his head. "They said they'd be back in two days for the rest of the bank's money. Word in town says their horses could barely trot, they were so laden down. Folks are scurrying, trying to settle their affairs and leave on tomorrow's train. Some of the bank staff rode off with as much as they could carry an hour ago. Unless we can give these folks hope, this place will be a ghost town by the time the Williamsons get back."

"Miners and ranchers both?"

"The ranchers are threatening to take their stock to the next town over, sixty miles north." Roman talked only to King, and even so, never made eye contact. The gunslinger's gaze stayed locked on the street, watching through the windows. "The miners can just head one stop down the rails to another operation. There's only silver here, no gold. The place is, in reality, perfectly vulnerable, but this isn't how the story's supposed to go. You can feel it in the air. It's not just fear. The whole world's ten degrees off-course."

King waved to the room, his voice low as they slid out of character and into story analysis or whatever it was they did in the field. "The best way to tell when a part of the story is off-track is to look at the edges of things. If someone—or some*thing*—has gone off-track, their story momentum diverted or disrupted—there's an effect at the edges, like their borders have been chewed on, or shredded. Sometimes it manifests as a fading or another form of discoloration. The effect varies by world and by story. Here, you often see colors filtered through sepia tones."

"What? That's … weird. So it's like Pleasantville in reverse. People lose their color or something?" Leah asked.

"Sometimes, yes. No one here can see it. It's only visible to Genrenauts, not folks from the story world itself. It takes certain detached concentration, like learning to see Magic Eye pictures. Be on the lookout, but don't go scaring anyone by staring at them like they're on fire."

"Got it. Stare, but don't stare. This probably isn't a good time to admit that I was never any good at Magic Eyes."

"No, I'd suggest you keep that to yourself," King said.

"So, where's our survivor?" Shirin asked, moving the conversation along.

Roman pulled the knife out of the table and sheathed it at his hip. "Frank Mendoza. He's here somewhere. I've been asking around, but most everyone's clammed up tight. Maybe you can get more out of people."

Shirin stole Roman's beer and drained it. "I'm already there. Come along, this will be fun," Shirin said to Leah as she stood. The older woman made her way to the bar, an exaggerated sway in her hips, her whole body language opening up like a sunflower. Where Leah had to move to mask her femininity, Shirin embraced it. She wove through the saloon, doling out compliments, leaning over poker games, and breaking the ice like an arctic steamliner.

So, that's why she's here, Leah observed. Roman's B.A., King's Hannibal, and Shirin's the Face.

But those weren't Western archetypes. *How did they fit in here?* Mapping the team members to the genre, King would be the Marshal, Roman the Gunslinger, and Shirin was what? The Woman Who Can Actually Fight? The Kindly but Tough Matron, more like. Already they were straining the confines of the genre, though her knowledge of Westerns had never moved much beyond the playground scenarios. And where did that leave her, archetype-wise? *I don't want to be the Kid. I'm always the Kid.*

And if they were supposed to stay in the shadows while also fixing a story, what roles could they really play? Maybe it wasn't about what archetype you fit so much as what impact you had. Make a difference wearing the hat of a Gunslinger, but not so much that people call you the hero. That made sense. Mostly.

"Come on, Kid," Shirin said, waving Leah over to join her at the bar.

Leah cut a straighter path through the crowd, avoiding contact as actively as Shirin had embraced it. But it was easy to move in the woman's wake once she'd swayed the mood of the room.

The saloon was almost all men—no schoolmarms, washerwomen, or other acceptable women archetypes present. Nothing but the working girls on the stairs. But Shirin made her way through the crowd on sheer determination and craftiness.

Leah took a stool beside Shirin at the bar. "I can't imagine what you're like at dinner parties." Behind the bar stood a thick-set man in black clothes and a white apron. He had the wispy echo of hair clinging to his polished head, and his hands were busy pouring whiskey in Shirin's bartenderly conjured glass.

"This fella with you, ma'am?" the bartender asked. Shirin nodded, all bright smiles and steady ease.

"One for me, thanks," Leah said, not wanting to look soft on her first day on this bizarre adventure that purported to be a job.

So far, Leah would have paid for the experience. Her mind galloped off into imagining the other story worlds, the narrative sightseeing she could do in a Diana Wynne Jones–esque Fantasyland or Hard Boiled-opolis.

Shirin brought Leah back to the present by raising a toast.

"To new friends."

Leah raised her own glass to match. Shirin downed her drink like a pro. Never one to be outdone when it came to shots (though often one to be carried home after them), she drank as well.

The rotgut burned like napalm going down. The booze made her wistful for the generic paint-thinner-grade stuff she and friends had drunk in high school before any of them knew better.

Leah set her glass down and gave Shirin a questioning stink-eye, interrupted by coughing.

"When in Rome."

"He's the Roman," Leah said, gesturing back to the corner.

"Exactly. He fits in perfectly." Shirin spun on the stool and leaned back on the bar, taking in the room.

"Now where would you begin if you were looking for information?" she said at a whisper. "Remember, think genre tropes."

"Shouldn't I be looking for the sepia thing?"

"That comes with time. And if you rely on the micro, you can lose the macro. Let's start with what you already know—story. We can develop the rest later."

Leah scanned the room, trying to read it like a crowd before a set.

There were ten tables and five booths. A small elevated stage filled the wall opposite the bar, with a player piano and dingy red curtains and trim. A trio of dancers in red and black finery perched at the far side of the bar, turned in toward one another to ward off drunken advances.

Another set of women draped themselves around the railing heading upstairs, all painted to the nines—those would be the working girls, though for all Leah knew the women might do both. The saloon patrons were divided between miners, ranchers, and folks Leah supposed were the town drunks or vagabonds. Most draped over tables in a stupor, their tables cluttered by half-empty bottles of the same rotgut that would be plaguing her, later on.

"First things first, I'd ask the bartender. If he's like the ones I know, they keep a close eye on who comes and goes. After that, I'd look around for any friends or family the guy had in town—if anyone's left."

Shirin said, "Good. Now you watch the room while I talk to the bartender. See if anyone listens in. Chances are, anyone close to Frank is going to have their ear to the ground to see if anyone is after him."

With that, the older woman spun on the stool and raised her glass to the bartender. "Another round, please, Ollie."

His attention ensnared, Shirin continued. "You seen Frank Mendoza since the shootout?"

A shadow passed over Ollie's face. He looked down, settling his gaze onto the bottles and glasses.

Leah turned from Ollie to look across the room to the team, focusing on the edges of her peripheral vision. Thankfully, she had years of experience, thanks to keeping an eye on hecklers and skeevy people on the street, dating all the way back to being an early blossomer as a kid.

The working girls continued their chatter, mugging for the room, half-paying attention to everyone and no one at the same time. The gamblers were getting almost raucous, the pall of the Williamson gang deferred temporarily by drink and the promise of a big win.

Nothing yet.

The bartender said, "Ain't seen Frank since the fight, no. Who's asking?"

Shirin answered, "Someone who isn't about to let the Williamson gang stampede right through this town. But if I'm going to do that, I need to know how the Williamsons fight. And for that, I need Frank. If you haven't seen him, who has?"

"You with that big fella in the corner?"

Shirin raised her voice, talking to the bartender but clearly meaning to be heard by more. "That I am. He's the fastest draw you or I will ever see, and I've been all over this county, from the Mississippi to the Big Easy and up through the plains. And he don't cotton to bullies. If someone here knows Frank, it'd be for the good of the town for us to meet him."

The bartender continued. "Don't suppose I know anyone who ran with Frank, aside from his poor brother. They came to town 'bout a month ago, hadn't made many friends."

While the bartender dissembled, one of the working girls descended the stairs by a step. She was younger, no more than twenty, with amber-brown skin and night-black hair done up at the top, ringlets at the back. She leaned against the railing nearest to the bar, disengaged from her companions. She was attempting (poorly) trying to mask her intent by pointing her face toward the stage. But her eyes were fixed on the bar.

Leah figured the girl gave herself away because she wasn't comfortable in the clothes, fidgeting and adjusting every few seconds. New to the job, most like. Leah adjusted her archetypal assessment of the girl and made a judgment call.

Leah nudged Shirin with her elbow and whispered, "Nine o'clock, on the stairs."

Shirin leaned back from the bar and said, "Well, if no one else in town knew him, I guess we're on our own. Thank you kindly." Shirin set her drink down, her sigh matching the sound of glass on wood. "And in that case, I'm going to need some help getting my friend to relax. Who do I talk to about the working girls?"

Leah spun on the stool to watch Shirin work, her target already pegged.

"You'll want to talk to Miss Sarah, there. She takes care of folks what need relaxing." On the stairs, a woman about Shirin's age nodded to Shirin. Her dress was fine, if worn. That'd be the madam, then.

After buying another whiskey and a beer to go with it, Shirin slid off of her stool and led Leah back to the corner. Leah followed, and the group re-formed at the booth.

"The Kid here pegged our lead," Shirin said. "The youngest working girl on the stairs was a bit too curious when I was asking around about Frank."

Roman joined in. "Mallery suspected that Frank and Juan were hiding a sister."

King said, "What's your play?"

Shirin slid the beer over to Roman, replacing the one she'd taken. "I mentioned that Roman here was in need of some comfort. The Kid takes Roman to ask for the girl, and then Roman goes up to pump her for information."

"But thankfully, nothing else," Roman said.

Leah said, "If I knew you better, this is where I would make a joke, but I don't want to offend."

King pointed a finger at Leah. "And once he's up there, I need you to keep an eye on him. Establish and maintain direct visual or aural contact. We don't like to send agents into unknown situations without backup nearby. Roman can handle himself, so this is a test for you. I want to see how you think on your feet."

Roman took a long swig from the drink, then slid out of the booth. "Come on, Kid. Let's go get me a woman," Roman said in a low voice, hamming it up for her.

"Me, too? Kinky," Leah joked.

"I'm too embarrassed to ask for myself, so you get to go with me and make sure the girl is nice. I haven't been with anyone since my wife died, so you're being careful on my behalf."

"That's a cover, right?"

"Got it," Roman said, tipsily swaggering across the room, though he'd been stone-cold sober in the booth. Were the whole team actors, then? "King says you did improv. Just roll with it."

Leah made a show of steadying Roman, accompanying him to the stairs. Leah looked up to Miss Sarah, a regal woman who held herself like the dust and grit of the town was simply not allowed to wear her down.

"You'd be Miss Sarah?" Leah asked, pitching her voice low.

The woman nodded. "I am. How can my girls help you?"

"Why don't you sit down, Roman?" Leah said, making a gesture of lowering the big man to a seat. Leah took a step up and leaned in to whisper the story that Roman had made up on the fly while the woman fanned herself, masking her lips.

"I see," Sarah said. "Does he have a preference? Girls?" She leaned in. "Boys?"

"If he's going to get over his wife, I think he'd need a woman's attentions, Miss Sarah. I caught him stealing glances at the young lady at the top of the stairs...."

37

Miss Sarah turned and beckoned the woman down.

The younger woman questioned her every move, not confident about taking up the space she occupied. Seeing her closer, she was maybe eighteen. Not out of adolescence, with all of the self-consciousness that came with it.

Improv had been what helped Leah get past that. Presumably, sex work could do it, too, but if the girl had come into town with her brothers, she wouldn't have been at the business long. But how did it work in the genre world? Was it the sanitized version of sex work from the movies and books, or was it actual early modern sex work, warts and all?

"This is Maribel. She'll take care of your friend."

Leah repeated Roman's made-up backstory to Maribel, who nodded.

"I'll do my best, Miss Sarah."

Maribel descended to Roman, who had stuck to character, tipsily sulking at his empty table.

"Come on, Roman. Miss Maribel would like to speak with you upstairs." Leah mimed helping him to his feet. Thankfully, Roman did all the lifting himself, because Leah was pretty sure she wouldn't have been able to get him to his feet on her own.

Roman got one hand on the railing, and Maribel looped her lace-gloved hand through his other arm, guiding him up the stairs.

They stopped at the landing and Leah turned to Sarah, who watched the pair move while smiling for the crowd. Her respect for the madam kept ratcheting up. She was the best version of the archetype brought to life.

"Uh, Miss Sarah. There's one more thing. I wanted to ask if I might wait by the door, make sure he goes through with it and stops moping all over our campfires."

Miss Sarah crossed her arms. "My girls are plenty encouraging on their own."

Leah tried to improv a reason why the madam should let her go up anyway, and the only good ones involved paying for her own company, which she decided against.

"Fair enough." Leah stepped back, starting to turn.

Think. Think. Think.

Ah.

"You got an outhouse? That whiskey goes straight through me."

"Out back, up against the rocks," Miss Sarah said.

Leah tipped her hat to the madam. She "helped" Roman up the stairs, and then made herself heard as she came right back down and left by the front door.

The street was almost totally empty, save for some people packing wagons and loading saddlebags.

Rounding the corner to head for the outhouse back, Leah put a hand to her ear to activate the comm. "Roman's upstairs with Maribel, but I couldn't get permission to go up and watch his back. Finding another spot now."

King's voice answered her. "Just act casual. The PPM will help you blend into the background if you let it."

"Got it."

Through the comm, Leah overheard Roman and Maribel exchanging niceties. The Afrikaaner was playing coy, inviting Maribel to be more active to draw him out. Problem was, it wasn't working. So they were mostly not talking. Leah imagined the awkwardness of two fully clothed strangers looking at each other in a bedroom, saying mostly nothing. She'd had dates like that.

The saloon's backyard rolled right into a rock outcropping twelve feet high, a natural wind block. Leah found the outhouse no problem, but what she was looking for was another way in or upstairs. There was a back door to the saloon, which she bet had a stairwell for staff to supplement the grand stairway in the main room.

A quick peek in the window showed a kitchen where off-duty girls sat eating and chatting. No way she'd be getting in there. As she began to pull her head back, something caught her eye.

The cook, a younger man, looked familiar. Really familiar. As in, family resemblance familiar.

Bingo.

Leah scooted away from the back door and took a long arc to the tree, plotting a path up to the first-floor awning that stretched along the back wall of the saloon. More than enough for her to crawl along, if she were industrious. Since she'd been climbing trees and jungle gyms since she was three, the answer to that question was a confident yes. Sitting up in the tree would get her close enough for visual contact, if the angle was right and if Roman was on this side of the building. And she bet she could get to the window in about thirty seconds if she had to.

Leah angled her path to the outhouse to make sure she wasn't being watched as she moved to the back side of the tree. Then, using skills earned with many skinned knees and sprained ankles, she scurried up, perching herself among the leaves and finding a stable position with a view of the rooms. The shades were drawn, but they were all light-colored, and still yielded silhouettes.

She had eyes on three rooms from her angle. One was clearly not Roman and Maribel, as the silhouetted figures were already very much in the middle of things. But two other pairs were in the "just talking" phase.

"In position. Roman, if you can stand up now, I'll confirm your location."

A figure in one of the rooms stood, taking a step forward.

"Confirmed. I have eyes on," Leah said.

"Well done," King said. "Now stay put, and don't get caught."

"One more thing," Leah added, happy that King couldn't see her self-satisfied smile. "I'm pretty sure our sole survivor is working in the kitchen."

A moment went by, and Roman said, "Is that so?" presumably waiting for a chance to say the same line for both conversations.

With no one around, there was no reason to hide her proud grin. "Thought you might want to know."

Leah settled in, getting comfortable in the tree. The flaky bark made that hard, but she'd spent many an afternoon reading in trees. *Okay, big guy, it's all you,* she thought, locking in on Roman as the pair continued to talk.

* * *

Roman stood two paces from the bed. The room was practically hotel-bare, without even the faux-homey gestures that chain hotels indulged in to show that they cared. Maribel hadn't been here for long, the place hadn't taken on her style, her character.

The room held a bed, a chair, a small dresser, and a closet. Maribel had a bag leaning against the closet door, propping it closed. Good chance she had a knife under the pillow, for protection, maybe a revolver in the bag if things went really poorly.

Maribel lounged on the bed, splayed out in an awkward imitation of a come-hither look. The room hadn't fit her, and she didn't fit it. She patted the simple yellow cotton sheets of the bed, saying, "Why don't you take a seat, let me get those boots off of you."

Roman kept an eye on the closet as he joined her. Maribel slipped off of the bed and kneeled to pull off his boots, which had been worn to as close a comfortable fit as they would ever be, still pinching at the heel.

"How long you been in town, Ms. Maribel?"

"Not too long. A month or so." Maribel set one boot aside. Roman stretched his foot, feeling the grains of sand roll against his toes. Oh, the shower he would take after the mission.

"Why here? Why not head all the way to the coast, San Francisco or the like?" he asked, trying to lure her out to get more information. Mallery figured something was up with the Mendoza brothers, but she hadn't been certain, at least that's what her notes said. Comparing Maribel to the feeds Mallery had sent back to HQ, the girl was almost definitely Juan's kin.

He'd bet good money Maribel was connected to the story, but he didn't know how aggressive to play the scene. But he was certain that he wasn't about to jump in bed with a teenager.

The girl struggled with the other boot, slipping it back and forth to shimmy it off of his heel.

"Oh, you know. Big city dreams turn out to be more expensive than you think. One delay and suddenly the money you had to get to the coast only gets you as far as Nowhere, Colorado, and you have to learn to make do."

"You came out West all on your own?"

Maribel finally got the other boot off, and set it beside the first.

"Yes, sir," she said. Maribel paused, no more boots to fixate on. The next logical piece of undressing would be his shirt or pants, a substantial step up in intimacy.

She wavered in place and steadied herself on the bed frame.

"Miss?" he asked.

The girl raised a hand to bid him wait. She took several long breaths. But her breathing wasn't strained.

If he was a gambling man, and on worlds like this he was, she was faking it. But to what end?

"I'm not feeling so well, Mister Roman. If'n you don't mind, I think it'd be best if I ask Miss Sarah to send up someone else to look after you while I take a sit-down."

"I didn't ask for the other girls, Maribel. I asked for you."

Maribel stopped, body freezing. But not out of fear. More like she was weighing her options.

Roman scooted back on the bed, giving her space. "I'm going to make a guess, and if I'm wrong, I'll leave and you'll get your money, no fuss. But if I'm right, hear me out."

Maribel's hand slid across the bed, probably toward a knife or a holdout pistol.

Roman moved slow, raising his hands. "I'm not here to hurt you. But I'm guessing that your last name is Mendoza, and you had two brothers, Frank and Juan, until Matt Williamson and his gang killed one and scared the other one off."

He watched Maribel's eyes, already knowing the answer. "So am I right?"

"What do you want with me, then?" her words came out half-question, half-accusation.

"I'm mighty sorry about your brother. My friends and I, we're here to stop the Williamsons, but we need Frank's help. So can you tell us where he is?"

"Oh, I wish I knew. He ran off from that fight, and I ain't seen him since. Miss Sarah said she'd shut me up tight when the Williamsons come 'round again, make sure they didn't know he still had kin in town."

Still dissembling, then. Roman sighed. "It's a shame. Would have been awful handy to meet the only man to survive a showdown with the Williamsons."

Roman let the words hang in the air, tuning his ears. He heard the creaking of wood in the hall.

Story worlds had a way of bending to your plans, as long as you set your intentions to match the tale types. What he needed right now was for Frank Mendoza to come and check on his sister.

And that was it. "But how could he have abandoned his little sister, with those bloodthirsty men sworn to come back for another try at the town? I mean, your brother's no coward, is he?"

Wood creaked again. Maribel stole a look to the door.

"I couldn't say, mister. Now why don't you lay back, and I'll get someone up here to help you forget all about those Williamsons."

Instead, Roman shot to his feet and pulled the door open, revealing Frank Mendoza, wearing a stain-worn apron.

Frank reached to his belt and came away with a revolver, flour-covered hand shaking. Roman stood perfectly still, not wanting to give Frank any more reason to shoot, having already startled the man.

"Frank Mendoza, I presume."

Frank shook in place. "We don't want no trouble, mister. So you best go on mosey yourself downstairs and forget about both of us." It was far harder to take Frank's threat seriously when his hand was shaking like he was in an earthquake. The gun was plenty dangerous, assuming it was loaded. But without control, that pistol was more hazard than weapon.

"How about you put that gun down, Frank," Roman said, trying to make his voice as calming as possible. "Shaking like that, you're more likely to hurt Maribel than me."

"This fella and his friends are going after the Williamsons." Maribel turned to Roman. "You gonna give us all the bounty on the Williamsons if he helps you get rid of them?"

Much better. "Of course. My friends and I, we heard about the Williamsons, and we mean to help you drive them off. Get justice for poor Juan and your other friends. But if we're gonna win this fight, we need you, Frank. You're the only one who has faced the Williamsons and survived."

Roman smiled, trying to warm up the situation. He didn't have the charm of Mallery or Shirin, but he'd been in scrapes like this before, sweet-talking at the business end of a barrel. He could just snatch the gun from the young man, but with Frank's finger already on the trigger, it was a risky play. "We drive them off, then my friends and I will get you and Maribel the next train to San Francisco, with some extra money besides. Plus whatever we recover from the bandits."

Frank was still shaking, but less so. Terror had given way to confusion, and Roman saw a flicker of hope in the young man's eyes.

And a flicker was all they needed to plant the seed of heroism.

Maribel crossed to her brother and pushed his hand down, lowering the gun. They talked in whispers, too low for Roman to hear anything other than that it was in Spanish.

The gun away, Maribel turned. "Why don't you bring your friends up here to talk, Roman?"

* * *

Leah came in to fetch Miss Sarah, and once they'd explained, the madam gave the nod. The three of them went up discreetly over the next ten minutes to avoid suspicion. Well, any more than they already got as outsiders.

The group sat and stood in the room, Maribel sitting with her brother on the bed. Frank was jittery. Leah imagined if she'd walked away from a gunfight only twenty-four hours ago, she'd be jittery, too.

King introduced the team. "I'm King. You've met Roman. This is Lee, and Atlas Jane." Even King saying her cover reminded Leah of how strange it was to look down and see a stranger's body. She remembered to adjust her stance, switching from a cocked hip to leaning back against the wall, arms crossed.

Think dudely thoughts.

King continued. "I'm a State Marshal, and these are my deputies. Governor sent us over in a hurry after he heard what the Williamson gang did. And I don't cotton to bullies."

King pointed at Frank. "We'd like to help you with the Williamsons. And we've got a plan that will see them run off or bleeding on the street. But we need you for this fight."

"Your sheriff died in the shootout, and the deputy, too?" Shirin asked like she didn't know the answer. A fine interviewing skill. It was also a stand-up skill.

"Yep. Both of 'em," Frank said.

King steepled his hands, a chess master with words for his playing pieces. Dude was scary in action. "That means the town needs a new sheriff. Who could do the job?"

Frank looked to Maribel. "There ain't many gunslingers around. Miss Sarah says the town hasn't had trouble for a few years. Most folks ride right on by to the bigger towns, or hit the train coming out of Sandborne."

"That the truth, then?" King said. "In that case, I think we've got our new sheriff right here. The only man to face the Williamsons and live."

Frank froze like a deer in the headlights back home, refusing to move even as Leah's father yelled at it and waved it off the road.

King read the room, then turned back to Frank and Maribel. "Here's the offer. You help us take out the bandits, we get you set up as the new sheriff, or we get you train tickets to the coast. Either way, you get a purse to look after your sister and get your brother a proper burial."

Frank looked to his sister then down to his shaking hands.

"I ... I'll try. But I can't promise nothing, Mr. King. I ain't no hero."

"You became a hero the moment you stepped up to face the Williamson gang the first time," King said. "What we're going to do now is make you a gunslinger. With training and my team at your back, we'll put Matt Williamson in the ground, restore peace in this town, and get you and your sister on your way to the coast."

King offered a hand. "Do we have a deal?"

Frank met King's hand, twitching from head to toe. "Deal."

"Excellent. We've got a few hours of sunlight. Meet me behind the saloon in five minutes." King nodded to Roman, then walked out of the room.

Chapter Four:
Y'all are pullin', not squeezing

Squinting, Leah looked down the sight of the heavy revolver at the tin cans and bottles that King and Roman had set up along the fence at the edge of the saloon property. A small hill in the background served as the backdrop, keeping their misses from endangering the neighbors.

"Both eyes open. Squinting kills your depth perception," said Roman from behind.

Leah opened her eyes, refocused, and pulled the trigger.

The gun kicked in her hands like a cat in 2 a.m. freakout mode, roared like a cannon shot, and yet her bullet smacked into the hill, at least a yard off-target.

Beside her, poor Frank was doing even worse. He held the revolver in both hands, his body recoiling from the gun, head turned away. Almost everything Leah knew about guns before that day came from watching TV, and even she knew Frank was holding it wrong.

"Grip, Frank. Let's start again." Roman stepped up beside the timid gunslinger, keeping a wary eye on the muzzle of the revolver. He put a steady hand on Frank's wrist, then took the gun and wrapped the scared young man's right hand around the grip, setting his finger along the stock.

If she didn't know better, Leah would have guessed that Frank was playing up the awkward to make "Lee" feel more comfortable. But that wasn't the way of it, and his twitchiness mostly made her more nervous. Nothing like your neighbor on the shooting range being as shaky as a jackhammer to tank any semblance of calm and focus.

Leah squeezed off a few more shots, going wide to the left, then to the right. She aimed again and put a bullet straight into the post … six inches below the can.

She adjusted again and fired, winging the can, which wobbled and then dropped off of the post.

Leah whooped.

Frank despaired. "He's already got it. I got shooting lessons from my pop and I ain't never hit nothing 'cept nothing. Are you sure I have to shoot to take the Williamsons out? Couldn't I just convince them to leave the town alone or something?"

"Silver-tonguing ain't going to get justice for your brother, Frank," King said. "You're the hero this town needs. You stand up to the Williamsons again, people here will notice. And you stare a man down, a man who tried to kill you and failed, you've got something."

"I know what I'll have. Shame. Shame I couldn't save my brother."

"The dead don't hold nothing over you, Frank. There will be time to bury Juan, but if you don't learn how to shoot, you'll be running your whole life. Someone has to protect your family."

Frank looked to Maribel, who leaned against the back of the saloon, pointedly not watching the scene. It looked like Maribel was even less interested in guns than her brother, but wanted to show her support.

"Okay, now try again," Roman said.

* * *

A half hour and another fifty bullets later, Leah had hit ten targets, Frank had hit one. Accidentally. Ten feet from the target he was aiming at.

"Okay, that'll have to do for today," King said. "Frank, why don't you and I have a talk about breathing and focus. My years as Marshal taught me more than a few things about how men's minds work, and I reckon your problem is that you're your own worst enemy. Let's see if we can't get your mind and your body on the same side, okay?"

Frank nodded, eager to hand the gun back to Roman.

"Roman, you keep working with Lee," King said.

Leah shook out her wrist as the two men headed back inside, Maribel joining them after one parting look at Leah.

Either something in her grip was off, or guns really hurt to hold and fire.

"Can you show me that grip again? I think I'm doing something wrong," Leah said.

"No problem. Let's start from the beginning, with your stance."

Leah adjusted her footing, going for the square stance she'd been taught all of an hour ago. "So, how did you get into this crazy business?"

"Try this." Roman pushed her right leg out, widening her stance. "I did a little bit of this, little bit of that, traveled in Africa and the Middle East, and decided I wanted to get out of the corporate violence business. I was looking for a way out, and King found me."

"Seems like he's got a neat little talent for that. Finding people."

"That what happened with you, then? Getting tired of comedy?" Roman took the gun and placed it back in her hands, wrapping her right around the grip, her left on her right. "Finger off the trigger until you're ready to fire. Make a strong frame with your hands, arms, and shoulders. Connect everything through the torso to the feet, or the recoil will spoil your aim."

Leah adjusted, trying to figure out what it felt like to connect the hands, arms, torso, and feet with this weapon. She'd learned just enough about guns to know she didn't like them. "Tired of comedy, no. Tired of receptionisting, yes. You were what? Security? Private military contractor?"

"Something like that. It was the best way out of a bad situation. Until King came along and showed me a better way." Roman pointed to the fence. "When you're ready to fire, sight down the barrel, center your target, place your finger on the trigger, and squeeze."

"And when was that?" Leah fired, hitting the fence beneath the can. Better than missing the target zone entirely.

"Almost ten years ago," Roman said. "You're flinching before you fire, anticipating the recoil. Stay steady, exhale as you squeeze the trigger."

"And you like it?" Leah took a long breath, recentered on the target, checked her stance and grip, and exhaled, squeezing the trigger.

And the can went flying. Mostly sideways, a glancing blow, but she'd hit. "Yes!" she said, throwing both hands up in the air.

"Careful," Roman said in a level voice, hands out and calming.

"Ah, yeah," Leah said, remembering the lethal weapon she was cheering with, bringing the gun back down to a ready position.

"Better. And yes, I love it. Best job I've ever had. The cause is good, the pay is better, and life is better when I'm not on-mission. Out in the field, kicking around in a F.O.B., there's a lot of down time, but unless you're back home, there's always that niggling sliver of fear, that need to be always ready, the idea that even when you're shirtless and gambling while the guy next to you is dreaming up some stupid prank to pull on his buddy, some a-hole could be about to drop a bomb on you."

"Yeah, not a lot of bombing going on in southern Maryland." Leah stopped herself. "Right? The genre worlds can't, like, send bombs over from War Movie world to take us out?"

"Line up another shot," Roman said. Leah detected a chuckle under his instructor seriousness, and marked herself a point in the comedy success column.

Leah did her best to repeat the ritual Roman had given her, taking aim at the next can. This shot went wide, but barely.

"Close. Go ahead and move over so you've got the straight shot headed uphill," Roman said. "And no, the other worlds don't know that we even exist. Science division says things would get really bad if they did."

"Yeah," Leah said. "Imagine a whole world suddenly realizing they're in the Matrix all at once."

"No one likes to realize they're not in on the joke. These worlds make sense internally, and even when stories break down, they carry on without any outside interference. If we did more than small fixes, or if the worlds knew what else was out there …" Roman stopped, as if trying to remember. "I think the phrase Preeti used was 'Absolute ontological deterioration,' which sounds like a bad time."

"No one gets to see behind the curtain. Got it." Leah squared off and fired, hitting the can and sending it flying back.

"Dead on. Nicely done. When you get out of your way, look what happens?" he said, walking over to retrieve the can. Leah lowered the gun, remembering the muzzle discipline that had started the lecture, along with trigger discipline and ten minutes of other safety discussions. Roman plucked the can up and turned it to show Leah a hole straight through the middle.

"Story of my life."

"Getting out of your own way, or a bullet through the heart?" Roman asked, his instructor's demeanor cracking.

"That's an affirmative to both, good sir," Leah said.

"Fair enough. Now, let's try without moving to recenter."

* * *

King sat Frank down on the bed in the room he shared with his sister. King remained standing.

"You and your brother stood up to the Williamson gang in the first place. That means you've got some courage already. The fact that you ran means that you have fear. Courage and fear go hand in hand, like a horse and rider. Courage is knowing a bronco is bucking and deciding to jump on its back anyway, knowing you may get thrown. So what we need now is to figure out how to get you back on the horse, calm your nerves, until you can prove to yourself that you can ride, that you can conquer your fear. That clear?"

Frank nodded. "Yes, sir."

"Why did you and your brother step up? What were you thinking when you said yes, when you strapped on that gun belt and went out into the noonday sun to face those bandits?"

"My brother, he volunteered first. And I ... I couldn't let him go alone."

"Loyalty, then. You wanted to protect your brother."

"Yes, sir."

"Just like you want to protect your sister."

Frank flexed his hands, looking at the floor. "Yes, sir."

"You won't have to do this alone, Frank. My team, we've solved problems like this before. But if some outsider solves a town's problem for them, what happens? Solving people's problems for them never made them more capable of anything."

King knelt down to speak to Frank, eye to eye, ignoring the popping in his knees and the accompanying pain. "What I want is to help you save this town. For folks to be able to remember Frank Mendoza as the man who avenged his brother's death, who ran the Williamson gang out of town with the help of some Marshals. You haven't lived here long, but this town claims you as their own, that much is clear."

"Well, we've tried to make friends, since our money ran out. Miss Sarah's been mighty generous, putting us up here in the saloon."

"And you can repay that generosity by believing in yourself."

King stood slowly, not interested in spending his aging knees on a pep talk when there was a gunfight on the horizon. Frank was a tricky case. Most heroes-in-waiting just took the smallest push out of the door to get started on the path.

But this was a breach, and if his brother was meant to be the hero, that'd explain some of the hesitation. But they had the time they had, he just needed to solve the puzzle of Frank. "Think back to a time when you were perfectly calm, when you stood up and licked whatever the problem was."

Again, Frank looked at his hands and the floor below.

"There has to be something. Some time in your life—"

Frank cut in. "It's stupid."

"I'm sure it's not. Everyone's life is their own, Frank. Your triumphs are still triumphs."

"I was cooking. It was a dinner party for my cousin's engagement. The milk went sour, so I had to go and get more, and I forgot about my tortillas, so they burnt and I had to start over. But instead of getting frustrated and giving up, I started over. And it got done, and it was delicious, and the dinner was perfect. After that …"

King cut Frank off, sensing the dip in Frank's mood. He had to keep the boy focused on the positive.

"That. That right there. Why did you start over without wallowing?"

"I knew it had to get done, and worrying weren't going to help no one."

King stopped, pointing a finger. He tapped Frank on the shoulder. "That's how you need to think. The Williamson gang needs to be stopped. Worrying and panicking won't help nobody. We can teach you how to shoot, how to move in a fight, find and use cover. You just have to get back on that horse, see?"

"I was never good at riding, Mr. King. Might be better for you to find another way of talking 'bout this."

It'd been a while since King'd had a hero quite this reluctant. But this wasn't the first time a story breach had gone weird. HQ was getting troubling reports from the other bases, on top of the missions he and the Mid-Atlantic teams had been working. Something was rippling across the worlds. These breaches were different. Maybe some kind of dimensional El Niño or the like, a system of incongruities in the breaches. Yet another topic for his next report to the High Council.

King went to the door.

"Here's a thought. Why don't we get a head start on dinner, and you show me what you can do. If I see you in your element, maybe I can get an idea of how to make gunfighting make sense, seem less terrifying. And if we don't, then we still have dinner for everyone. Seems reasonable, don't you think?"

Frank stood, more light in his face than he'd seen since he met the boy. "Yes, sir. Everyone needs to eat, and being on the frontier is no excuse for eating poorly."

King stepped aside, leaving room for Frank. "In that case, after you."

* * *

Leah had seen firsthand that Frank Mendoza was a public menace with a revolver, but it turned out he was a saint with a saucepan. Which, for a Western, was pretty odd.

Miss Sarah arranged for the team and the Mendozas to take dinner in the kitchen alone, so Frank could come down without being seen in public. The six of them crowded around a table, making stutter-stop attempts toward conversation that happened with people you'd met, especially in groups.

Frank was as calm and confident in the kitchen as he was clammy and shaky on the shooting range. Put him in an apron and set a stove and some pots in front of him and he was The Man With No Name. No wasted motion, no hesitation. He poured water and worked a spoon with precision and grace, happily explaining every step.

Frank had some core of confidence to work from, so getting him to step up would be a matter of connecting that core confidence he had with cooking to shooting.

Or maybe coming up with some crazy crossover Iron Chef kind of way to make cooking into fighting. Have him go into battle with a meat tenderizer and paring knife.

Still, as funny as that image was, it was odd. In Leah's memory of Westerns, most of the reluctant heroes were farm hands or would-be ranchers. They wanted to be gunslingers, but didn't believe in themselves. Frank definitely didn't believe in himself, but in any other story, he'd be a supporting character. But King and the team seemed pretty confident that this was their hero. Something about the story just didn't fit. Maybe that was because the world had gone so off-kilter.

Everyone was feeling one another out—Maribel and Frank played it close to the chest, King and the Genrenauts were trying to steer conversation away from themselves as best as they could, presumably along their Prime Directive-y agenda to tread lightly. Leah was mostly content to watch King and the Genrenauts work, like having a movie unfold right in front of your eyes, one where half the cast knew they were in a story, and the other half didn't. *Cabin in the Woods* without the blood sacrifice.

Frank chatted up a storm. "You should have seen poor Juan with that dog, they looked like they'd been put through the wash and left out to dry."

Shirin and Roman played the role of the easy audience, and Leah remembered herself enough to smile along. The weirdness of the situation, the onion-tastic meta was hitting hard. The wrongness of the story niggled at her mind, like a chunk of popcorn that she couldn't quite pick out with her tongue. The more she tried to relax and observe, the more the wrongness stood out to her.

Food, however, made sense. Leah held her plate out for another serving of cornbread. Cooking and serving, Frank was almost a whole other person, completely in his element, not a shaking hand to be seen. But did that mean he could stand up to the bandits?

Frank dished out food to the entire Genrenauts team, as well as filling plates for saloon staff and customers. All while keeping up his end of a conversation about the Mendozas' life before they'd come out West.

"Why leave Texas?" Shirin asked.

Frank shared a look with his sister, who had changed out of the frippery and was wearing a simple floral dress.

Maribel picked up the conversational thread. "Well, you see Frank here wants to open a restaurant, but there weren't no way he could do it in Wichita Falls, Texas. He won't settle for anything less than the fanciest of clientele, with the prices to match. So we saved up as much as we could, sold most everything we owned aside from Frank's pots, Juan's guns, and my books, and bought ourselves tickets as far west as we could manage. That got us here. We'd only meant to stay long enough to buy the tickets to San Francisco."

"I know I could get a job in any restaurant out there, if they would only give me a chance," Frank added.

Maribel set her dish in the sink and kissed Frank on the cheek. She said something in Spanish, then walked out the back door.

Leah wiped her mouth with a napkin and stood, following Maribel on a hunch she didn't know she'd had until she was halfway to the door.

But King and company had talked about following your instincts and everything, so she went with it.

Winds drew sand into swirls, catching the red-pink light of the setting sun. The same wind tickled at the hem of Maribel's dress. The woman leaned against a wooden pillar of the back porch, looking west to the sunset.

"Everything alright?" Leah asked, stepping into Maribel's field of vision. The woman bristled for a moment, then relaxed.

"I'm fine. Just like watching the sunset, is all. It's the same sun, no matter where you go, but it seems a little brighter here, the moon a little closer. Or maybe this town's really that much smaller."

"I thought you came from a small town?"

"Small, but not tiny. This here's a stopover town, perfectly fine aside from the bandits, but nowhere for us to put down roots. Especially after ..."

"I bet. I imagine if I were in your shoes, I couldn't put this town in my"—Leah caught herself before using totally out-of-genre language—"dust fast enough."

"Turns out it's not easy to just up and make money when you're away from home. Ms. Sarah's been right kind to us, and she treats Frank better than any fancy San Francisco restaurant would, I reckon."

"And how are you dealing with, I mean, having to ...?" Leah asked.

"I ain't had to take no customers, if'n that's what you're asking about. And I don't intend to start, if you're asking."

Leah wondered if the PPM would hide a blush. She focused on the story, trying to hold the structure in her mind, the moving parts that were Maribel and Frank and the bandits. But how did it all fit together? Her gut told her Maribel would play a bigger role in this story. She stood out too much to be just the doting sister.

"I made a deal with Ms. Sarah," Maribel continued. "She needed to look like she had more girls on her roster, so I dress the part but if someone picks me, I fake like I'm sick. I was faking a fainting spell when your friend started in about the Williamsons."

"Wouldn't people notice eventually?" *There's more to her. But what?* Leah thought, racking her brain for the right angle.

She shrugged. "Eventually. Ms. Sarah looked to be getting a bit nervous, but she didn't want to lose Frank's cooking. And the other girls are plenty nice to me, especially since I ain't taking their money. And on account of me looking out for their little ones while they work."

"That's ... a lot simpler, I guess. So what are you going to do when you get out to the coast?"

Maribel looked out to the sunset, like she was looking all the way to the coast, to her future. "Keep Frank out of trouble, run the parts of the restaurant he can't be bothered with, assuming he can get the money together to give it a shot. Frank talks big, but he's not the one for follow-through."

Ding ding ding. That's it. "But you are?" Leah said.

Maribel closed her eyes, wrapping an arm around the pillar. "'Fraid so."

"How's that?"

Maribel looked up at the darkening sky, clouds stretched thin in staggered lines.

Leah could swear she was right on the edge of something. King was agitated about Frank not stepping up, and something about Maribel couldn't help but stand out—she wasn't your average Western leading lady. She wasn't a schoolmarm, wasn't a prostitute. There had to be some "supportive sister" characters in the genre somewhere, but all of the narrative math added up to tell Leah that there was more going on here.

Leah repeated her question. "What do you mean by that, Maribel?"

It was probably her mind playing tricks on her, but Leah thought she could see frayed edges at the end of Maribel's elbows and at her cheek. Just for a second, like a shadow passing overhead. But the feeling stuck once the visual irregularity faded. Leah already knew Maribel's story was off, so what was this telling her?

"Is there something we should know, Maribel?"

"Shit." Maribel looked Leah straight on, her eyes moist. Her instincts said to lean on the woman, to push a bit harder. Something would come of it. "If Frank goes out with your boss, the Marshal, he's going to get himself killed, isn't he?"

"I don't know," Leah said. "The others in my posse, they've been doing this for a while. But they need Frank for their plan to work. If he steps up and then freezes again, he's going to die, and maybe the rest of us with him."

Maribel wiped the almost-tears from her eyes and stood up straight, taller than Leah had thought she really was.

"I love him like the sunset, but Frank's no gunslinger. Never was, never will be. Juan wanted to be, but he never had the gift."

"But you did?" Leah asked, connecting the dots. *They said trust your instinct. Hope it doesn't blow up in my face.*

Maribel sighed.

Leah knew that sigh. That was the sigh of regret. It was the sigh she'd used when she questioned moving out to Baltimore, questioned her desire to do stand-up. It came up a lot, actually. "I had the skill," Maribel said. "Just not the judgment."

"How's that?"

"Why don't we go back inside. I don't have it in me to tell this story more than once," Maribel said, then without another word, walked back inside.

Leah turned on her heels and followed. *And cue the revelation scene.*

* * *

Leah watched as Maribel walked up to the table and looked King in the eyes.

"Y'all need to know something. My brother's a lot of things. He's kind, he's funny, and he's the best hand in the kitchen I ever met. But he's no hero. You can't take Frank out there to face those men. I ain't going to stand by and watch another brother get gunned down."

"Maribel, we don't have to tell …" Frank said.

"I have to, Frank. We been running for too long."

Maribel squeezed her brother's hand. "He's no fighter, Mr. King. He and Juan joined that posse so I wouldn't have to."

"Explain," King said, fingers steepled, expression flat.

"Back home, I got into a whole passel of trouble. We lived in Wichita Falls, you see, home of Kid Cole. He was always strutting about town like he owned the place. He took a shining to my friend Sue-Anne, shot dead three other men who came calling on her. But Sue-Anne, she didn't want nothing to do with Cole.

"So one morning, when he was standing on Sue-Anne's porch again yellin' at her to get out there and talk to him, I took Juan's gun and went off to pick a fight. Put two in the air before he could shoot once. Shot him dead, I did. But the other bullet went wide."

Maribel closed her eyes, looked down to her hands. "It ricocheted off a pole behind Kid Cole and hit Sue-Anne through the window. Struck her dead before she hit the ground. So there I was with two deaths on my hands and more guilt than justice."

Frank squeezed Maribel's hand as she sniffed back tears.

"Then it got worse. I knew Kid Cole had rich family, but no one told me he was the nephew of a circuit judge."

"We had to get away from the judge," Frank said. "So we packed up and left."

"Figured if I dressed up all feminine-like, we could lie low and make it to the coast, far out of the judge's jurisdiction."

"But you can't," Leah said. "Someone needs to stand up to the Williamsons. It should be you."

"Did you see the Williamsons?" King asked Maribel.

Another nod.

"How bad are they?" Shirin asked.

"One-on-one, I could do for Matt. But there's five of them. And after Sue-Anne, I swore I wouldn't touch another gun 'til the day I die."

"We're talking about your brother's killers," Leah said.

"And I want them dead as surely as you do. But if I pick that gun up, I'm saying that what I did to Sue-Anne didn't matter."

"The way I hear it, you took up the gun to do something she couldn't do for herself," Shirin said. "Your brother can't take up the gun, but you can. Let us help you put your brother's spirit to rest, and you might find that the ghost of Sue-Anne is put to rest, too."

"Here's what we'll do, then," King said. "You get to square off with Matt and the gang when they come back, say your piece, and then we put the lot of them in the dirt. And when it's done, you and Frank get the bounty on the Williamson gang. That should get you to the coast with enough left over to get you started on that restaurant."

King opened his hands, his body language open, approachable. "What happened to Sue-Anne—that was Cole's doin', not yours. Would Sue-Anne want you to just stand by, knowing you could have done something to help this town? A town that can't save itself? You made a terrible mistake and you're living with it. But you're never going to make one like that again, are you? You're going to be better."

And that was why he was the boss.

Frank squeezed his sister's hands. "Don't do it. We can lie low, put the money together somehow, get out of here once things blow over."

Maribel wrapped her shaking brother up in her arms, hands running through his hair. She looked King dead in the eyes. "I ain't going to leave this town until I've put those men what killed my brother in pine boxes."

Leah said, "You got yourself a hero. Now don't make me regret it."

Roman joined in, "You already know how to shoot. And you know what you're fighting for. But if you want to kick the dust off, I reckon we've got about a half-hour of light left between twilight and the torches."

"That's a fine excuse to get out of doing the dishes," Frank added.

King scooted out his chair and stood. "Lee and I will handle those."

The dinner party broke up, each to their next task.

Leah shot King a look, hoping to mean "Look at that! I did something!"

His response was hard to read. Guy was made of poker face. But Leah knew she'd done good. She could boast later.

* * *

After sunset, the group reassembled in the saloon, again claiming the corner booth. Maribel changed and joined them, far more comfortable in spats and a collared shirt than in a working girl's frills and lace. Frank stayed upstairs, wanting no part in Maribel getting herself killed, so he said.

Shirin rolled out a piece of paper and took charcoal to it, drawing out a map of the town.

"Where'd they come in from, last time?" Shirin asked.

Maribel tapped the paper on the east end of the street. "They came in this way. The Douglas ranch saw them first, sent Joey to ride into town and warn folks. Frank, Juan, and the sheriff's posse met them here," she said, pointing to the bank.

"Got it," Shirin said. "In that case, our best spots are here, on the roof of the bank, the church bell tower here, and the roof of the saloon."

"Ain't no way onto the roof of the saloon unless you got a ladder," Maribel said.

"We'll find one," Shirin said. "If not, Roman here's a fair climber." Roman nodded, showing the hint of a grin.

"Or we make it simple. Shirin can set up in the bell tower with the long rifle, the rest of us will be on the ground with you," King said to Maribel.

The woman considered the map. "Five of us, five of them. The sheriff winged at least one of 'em last time, so we've got that on them, too," Maribel said. "You keep the others busy, and I'll do for Matt Williamson just fine."

"We'll have your back," King said.

"Why not set up an ambush?" Leah asked. "Take them out as they're coming in?"

"I want to see the light go out of those bastards what killed Juan," Maribel said.

King didn't challenge her. Leah filed the question away for later.

Chapter Five:
High Eleven-Thirty-Ish

Leah woke to oppressively loud knocking on the door. She fumbled about the room in a haze. Dimensional jet lag had kept her up for hours, and when she did sleep, it was poorly.

"Yeah, yeah," she said, waving at the door, holding her other hand up to her eyes to block out the morning sun that cut through the window.

Ms. Sarah and the saloon had put the team up for the night. Her room was small and sparse, but really all she needed was a place to pass out. Though in creaky retrospect, maybe a nicer bed would have helped.

The washing facilities made her miss camping trips with the family, which was saying something. After her cold sponge bath, she made her way down to the kitchen. Frank manned the stove, grilling and frying and looking far more comfortable wearing an apron than she wagered he would wearing a bandolier.

The rest of the team was already assembled, looking like the Western version of firefighters sitting and waiting for the call. King had shaved, Roman had not.

Shirin pulled up a chair. "Good morning, kiddo. Coffee?"

"Please yes now," Leah said, her brain not done spooling up. She'd taken exactly one 8 a.m. class in college, a chem lab the school didn't offer any other time. If it'd been at eleven, she was sure she'd have gotten an A. Instead, she swallowed her C+ and moved on, glad that the science requirements for a theater degree were minimal.

Shirin handed her a tin cup of coffee. She didn't bother sniffing, and went straight to pouring the java down her gullet. It was thick, and fairly pungent, but it did the job of ripping off a layer of her fatigue like it was a waxing. Painful, but over in a moment.

Maribel walked into the room, holding her own tin of coffee. In pants and without a bustier, she moved like a ranging big cat. Ready to pounce in a moment.

"Today's the day, then," Maribel said. "Ms. Sarah's got the word out that we'll be waiting for the Williamsons. I figure they'll show by noon. Everything set on your end?"

King set down his coffee. "All ready. Atlas Jane's got enough shells to take on an army."

Maribel leaned in, and Leah did her best at concealing her eavesdropping. Luckily, Leah was excellent at being nosy.

"Anything happens to me, you get my brother out of town. Get him somewhere so he can be the fancy chef he was supposed to be."

"It'll be done," King said. "But don't worry. I've been at this for a very long time, as have my posse." King raised his voice back to normal conversational levels. "Aside from Lee here. He's new, and we haven't decided if he's going to run off or if he'll be running circles around me within a year. He's already a champion eavesdropper."

Leah's cheeks went hot. She leaned back in her chair, facing King. "Can you blame me? If I'm going to walk into a firefight, I'd like to know what I'm getting into."

"That's fair," Maribel said. "Walking into a fight blind is a great way to end up with a permanent view of the inside of a pine box."

Roman raised his cup to toast.

"Okay, grub's up!" Frank said, moving with enthusiastic precision, doling out sausage, eggs, and hash from his skillet. "Sorry I can't do anything more— limited materials and all. I picked up a gumbo recipe back home before we left, and I've been dying to try it out." Frank stopped, a chill passing over him. "I mean, I wanted to try it. But the general store here doesn't get none of that sort of thing. I ain't seen a shrimp or saltwater fish in weeks."

"It's wonderful," Shirin said. "Thank you for the breakfast."

"I just wish I could be of more use than frying up eggs. Maribel here's the real deal."

"When we get to the coast," Maribel said, "it's your picky palate and steady hands that'll be making us rich. I figure we can get to owning three restaurants by next winter, we play our cards right."

Leah saluted with her coffee tin. "That's what I like to hear. What will you call your restaurant, Frank?" she asked, hoping to distract the siblings from the coming danger. Hell, herself, too.

The cook moved between the stove and tables without pausing, his face bright.

"Oh, that's been the hardest part. I want to cook so many different styles of food, so it'd need to be something not so specific to one cuisine."

"What about The Globe Café?" Leah suggested.

Frank stopped and cocked his head to the side, then resumed serving. "The Globe Café. Not bad. Better than Maribel's idea."

Leah turned, expecting the answer.

Maribel shrugged. "I think Little Brother's Bistro is a great name."

"But I'm older than you," Frank said.

"You get to be the older brother when you make us our fortune. Until then …"

Frank slid hash and eggs onto Leah's plate. She raised a hand as he approached with the sausage. "I don't eat meat, sorry."

Vegetarianism was a thing then, right? She hoped that cover would play in Western World. Traditional Western heroes were always steak-and-eggs types.

Shirin elbowed Leah. Maybe she should have been "not very hungry" instead.

The older Genrenaut covered for her. "Lee here got the runs last time he had meat on the road."

"Ah, that's a shame," Frank said. "I promise, this meat's plenty fresh, and well-cooked."

Roman offered up his cleared plate. "I'll take the kid's share if he's too lily-livered."

Frank dished out the sausage to Roman and came back with more hash, which Leah accepted with her most gracious smile.

"Get your breakfast down quick," King said. "We need to get ourselves into place. Frank, maybe you could wrap up some of those sausages for us in case the Williamsons make us wait?"

"Sure thing. But they won't be as good when they're cold."

"I'd rather be on time with cold sausages than late and dead with a full stomach."

"Sign me up for death by full stomach," Roman said. "In another forty years or so."

"You keep eating like that, your heart won't give you forty years." Shirin pointed to the plate full of second helping, slathered in grease.

"Yes, Mother," Roman said, making a face.

* * *

Shirin's earpieces had been tested, retested, and were in perfect working order. Leah had never seen a radio that small, not one that wasn't limited to Bluetooth networks. And they would be way outside Bluetooth range, especially with Shirin in the tower.

"Some places, we can get away with tech. Other worlds, we have to be inconspicuous," Shirin said, fitting Leah with the earbud in the washroom before heading out to their positions. "Just don't fiddle with it. The hat should do most of the work covering it up, and the PPM will do the rest."

"Why can't you take them out one by one as they come into town?" she asked Shirin on the comm.

"The more resonant the story, the stronger the patch. We need to play in-genre," Shirin said. "Sneaking around and assassinating bandits doesn't fit."

Shirin raised a finger of exception. "But when we go to Spy world, you and I can sneak around and assassinate to your heart's content."

"Next time we come here, can I skip the giant-sized hat?"

"Oh, honey, there are things you get to complain about, and the wardrobe is not one of them. This is what every new team member has to go through. Even King and me, though that was ages ago."

"You two have been at this for a long time, haven't you?" Leah asked.

"That we have. Best job I've ever had. Not every mission is as scary as this, though. A lot of the worlds aren't violent. Romance world is especially fun. It's all musicals and meet-cutes and schmoopiness."

"Note to self: ask for the rom-com beat," Leah said.

Shirin held Leah gently by the shoulders. "Good luck with that—Mallery has that niche locked down hard. So for now, you watch our back and keep the Williamsons out of the bank."

* * *

Leah stood inside the front room of the Bank and Trust, ten feet wide and twice as deep. One teller and the manager were all that remained of the staff. And no customers had come by in the two hours she'd been standing by as they waited for the Williamsons.

The streets dried up about eleven, everyone rushing to get their errands done or take the last train out before the bandits came back. The train whistled its departure as townsfolk piled in to escape to the next town over or stay with friends. As far as she could tell, only a few dozen folk remained, hiding behind boarded-up doors and watching from second-story windows. Even if they drove the Williamsons off, this town might not recover.

Leah knocked on the window, catching Maribel's attention. Roman and King shot the breeze on the porch beside her, watching the street but playing casual.

"How's it look out there?" she asked.

"Still dead quiet. No one 'cept the horses, and most of them are gone, corralled off the main street. No one wants to be in the crossfire."

She would think about that, wouldn't she? "I imagine the horses appreciate that."

"They would if you could tear them away from their feed. Dumb things."

"Aw, I like horses."

"How much time you spent on 'em, Lee?"

"I like *looking* at horses," Leah said.

"Well, try living—"

Maribel was cut off by Shirin's voice in Leah's ear. "Five riders on the horizon. It's time."

Roman knocked three times on the horse post, the signal that the Williamsons were coming.

"Here they come. Good luck." Leah looked back at the empty room, the terrified staff. There was still money in the vault, if not much. But the Williamson gang didn't know that. All they'd know was that there was a new posse between them and the silver.

Leah wanted to be able to help, but even with an afternoon's worth of training, she wasn't going to stare down a band of killers, gig or no gig. King hadn't asked her to put her life on the line, and she hadn't offered. She just hoped she wasn't going to stand by and watch them gunned down the way Mallery had watched her posse lose.

"Smoke 'em," Leah said as the posse squared off in the street.

* * *

Roman stood at the ready as the Williamsons advanced.

King called the fight. "Roman, you take the woman on the right, I'll take the big guy on the left. Leave the ones in the middle for last. Shirin will cover us.

"Talk to them first," King added, "but if they draw, all bets are off."

Maribel snapped her holster open, ready to draw. "I'm no Marshal, and I don't need no excuse to put down the men what shot Juan."

A short man with a several-times broken nose and an unkempt beard climbed down from his horse. Four others joined him.

The first was a tall woman with a rifle. The short guy's taller brother held a shotgun, but the others had six-shooters on their belts. Roman trusted that Shirin could drop the shotgunner or rifleman as an opener, make things easier for the crew on the ground.

"Well lookey here. What do we have today?" the short man said with a Tennessee accent. That would be Matt Williamson. "A little girl playing dress-up in her brother's clothes. And she's found herself a posse."

King addressed the bandits. "You can lay down your arms and go to jail, or we can let our irons do the talking."

"Who the hell are you? The Governor actually waste another lawman on this piss-hole of a town?" Matt said.

"I'm Maribel Lucia Mendoza." Her hand hovered over her holster. She took a step forward, breaking ranks and not stopping.

"Maribel, wait," Roman said.

"Mendoza?" said Matt. "I killed a Mendoza a couple days ago. The one went down before he could fire, then his kin dropped his gun and ran to hide behind Miss Sarah's skirts. That don't make me inclined to be afraid of their kid sister, dress-up or no." He grinned wide, teeth stained and rotted.

"I ain't my brothers." Maribel drew so fast Roman only saw a blur. She fired, and the big guy to Matt's right dropped on his ass. Western Genre rules applied, with bullets causing knockback impossible outside a story world.

Maribel kept Matt and Tom Williamson in her sights as she spoke to the rest. "You best get back on your horse and keep riding if you don't want to end up being dragged out of the town in a pine box."

In response, the Williamson gang scattered, drawing to fire. Roman drew and the street was swallowed in clouds of dust and the thunder-crack of gunfire.

Tom Williamson fell facedown in the dirt. That'd be Shirin. Roman took a spot behind a watering trough, shooting at the woman with the rifle while Maribel charged Matt Williamson. Maribel winged Matt and put another round in the big guy.

The riflewoman bolted for the alley between the general store and the blacksmith.

"Keep them from getting away!" King shouted, firing after her.

Williamson fired on Maribel, who dashed right, heading across the street, firing suppressing but not dangerous shots back toward the bank.

"Aaah!" came Leah's voice on the comms.

"Stay down, Kid. We've got this," Roman said.

Shirin's voice crackled through the earpiece. "I've lost eyes on the riflewoman."

Roman took another shot, catching a bandit in the off-arm. This was nothing like shooting at the range. The guns were lower-quality, and the rising dust kicked up by the fight was obscuring everything.

"I'll get her," Roman said. "Drop masquerade protocols and end this?"

"Just keep on them!" King shouted over the din. Another shot rang out, clipping his gun arm. The team lead dropped to a knee, then crawled for cover.

With King down, Matt Williamson took the free path for the saloon. Maribel fired after him, but Williamson was a fast bugger. He was inside before she could fire a second time, and once he was off the street, she stopped. She wouldn't risk another bystander, not with the ghost of Sue-Anne haunting her.

Roman launched to his feet, sprinting down the street toward the general store. "I'm on the riflewoman. Someone go help Maribel with Matt."

"King's wounded," Shirin said. "He needs first aid."

"I'll do it! I can go around back," Leah said.

"Negative. Do not engage." King's voice was strained, but resolute.

"Gotta start pulling my weight some time, right? Don't worry, I don't intend on getting myself killed for a lousy stand-up gig."

As he turned into the alley after the riflewoman, Roman saw Leah hightailing it across the street, holding her hat down with one hand, the other shaking by the holster.

"Go get 'em, Kid," Roman said.

Chapter Six:
Improvisation

Leah kept her head low, running with her torso bent over her legs, the dust kicked up by bullets and shuffling proving enough concealment to make it across the street as the gunfire continued. She'd seen Maribel head into the saloon through the front door, following Williamson, so instead, she ran for the back door to cut him off from the kitchen.

"Pulling some daft heroics is not going to impress me, Ms. Tang," King said.

"I got this. I'm not going to try to take him on alone. All I need to do is find a way to help Maribel. She's the hero, right?" Leah grabbed the back corner of the building and caught herself to turn, not as gracefully as she'd like. She slowed as she reached the door, then tried to move as quietly as she could.

The door creaked as she stepped into the kitchen, where one of Ms. Sarah's girls sat drinking lemonade. She yelped when she saw "Lee." Leah put a finger to her mouth in the hopefully inter-dimensional sign for "Shush."

"Where?" she mouthed, pointing toward the main room. The working girl gave an exaggerated shrug.

Leah pressed herself up against the wall, inching toward the swinging door that led between the kitchen and the bar. She looked through the narrow band of glass into the main room. People cowered behind overturned tables, with Ollie the bartender hiding behind the bar, apparently not the type to keep a shotgun next to the rail liquor. More's the pity.

Maribel stood a step inside the swinging front doors, her gun out. Opposite her, Matt Williamson stood at the base of the stairs, holding his gun to Frank's head.

Dammit, Leah thought to herself, wishing Frank had stayed out of the way. But of course he'd have been watching as close as he could, with his sister putting her life on the line.

"Put down that gun, or you'll be fresh out of brothers," Matt said. Mirabel had tipped her hat, owned up to being a Mendoza, so what did Matt do, he went straight for Frank. The situation was as trope-y as they got. Family hostage, hero has to choose between getting the bad guy and saving their loved one.

Maribel spun her gun around, slowly, holding it by the sight and cylinder, no position to fire. "Just hold on, now. Don't nobody else need to get hurt today. My brother ain't even shot none of your crew, unlike me. Why don't we step outside and settle this, like I said."

"Little girl playing cowboy. You had enough yet? Put that gun down and I let your yeller brother leave town. You're fast, but not that fast," he said, pressing the barrel of his gun into Frank's temple. The chef shook from head to toe, wet eyes closed like he was shutting out the world with the hope that it'd go away.

Leah tried to work out a plan.

If she made noise to distract Matt, would Maribel have the time to fire?

Would she be able to hit without hurting Frank? Or would the noise just make Williamson shoot Frank?

Could she hit Williamson through the glass?

If she opened the door for a clear shot, would he notice?

There were too many variables, too many possibilities. They slammed at her from all sides like hail on a corrugated metal roof, her heart pounding in time.

She wasn't a hero, not yet. She was the Kid, the helper. And the helper usually ended up kidnapped and/or killed.

"Think, Leah, think."

But what if I'm not the Kid? she thought. *What if I'm the Rookie Sidekick?* She'd been the one to get Maribel to open up, to step up to join the cause. That could be the Kid or the Sidekick.

And in a finale, the Rookie Sidekick fought with whatever they could get their hands on. Their role was to give the hero the chance they needed to make the shot.

The back stairs. That was it. She turned and pointed to the girl, trying to use completely incorrect sign language to tell her to keep Williamson from coming into the kitchen. The girl shrugged again, apparently nonchalant about the gunfight in the room next door.

Leah grabbed the pitcher of lemonade right off the table and made for the work stairs beyond the kitchen, the set Frank had used to come and go out of sight. She walked the line between speed and stealth, making her way up, over, and then to the top of the L-shaped stairs that led down from the second floor to the main room.

Which put her above and behind Matt Williamson. Upstairs, all the doors were closed, unsurprisingly. Anyone who was getting busy had better things to do, or were at least smart enough to put a closed door between them and people with guns.

Leah stood at the top of the stairs and yelled, in her best Tough Miner voice. "I ain't paying!" She set the lemonade down, soft, at the top of the stairs.

In an exaggerated feminine voice—with a strong thread of Betty Boop—Leah shouted, "You rat! After two hours! Ms. Sarah, Ms. Sarah!"

Leah fired her gun at the thick side wall, no chance of hitting anyone or anything on a ricochet. And at the same time, she kicked the lemonade. The carafe shattered on the stairs, spilling and sloshing and making a marvelously distracting racket. Directly behind Matt Williamson.

Looking down to the first floor, she saw that her trick had done what it needed to. Williamson, confused, looked up and back. Leah waved a taunt, but before he could move, Frank dropped to the floor as a gunshot rang out.

Matt Williamson fell back onto the stairs, his revolver clattering to the ground beside him.

Lemonade spilled down the stairs, soaking the bandit's back as he went limp, red blooming on his chest.

Frank dashed away, and Maribel walked up on Williamson, kicking the gun out of the dying man's hands.

"That's a nice trick, there," Maribel said.

Leah stared at the body, her hand still shaking. He was dead. Because of her. He deserved it, but that was a dead body in front of her and he wasn't coming back. She sat, steadying herself on the railing to the stairs, the world closing in and zooming out at the same time.

"Status!" came King's voice, impatient and strained.

Leah breathed, words not yet coming. She took her eyes off of the body and turned away from Maribel. "Williamson's ... dead," Leah said.

"What about the tall one?"

"She got away," Roman said. "She's got some serious hand-to-hand chops. Caught me by surprise."

Silence for a moment. That woman must have been something serious to give Roman the slip.

"The other bogies all down?" King asked.

"Nothing going outside," said Shirin.

"That's what I like to hear. Meet up in the saloon so we can debrief and denouement."

Leah wobbled to her feet and walked the other way, doing everything she could to put the image of Matt Williamson's body out of her mind. She knew it was coming, but to see death up close, to watch it ... she wouldn't get that image out of her mind, probably ever.

And that's why Western heroes were defined by their grit.

Chapter Seven:
Ritual and Reward

With the bandits dead, tied up, or gone, the Genrenauts returned to the dinner table in the kitchen. Maribel had removed her hat, hair down but braided behind her back. Frank was cooking once again. The smell of beans and rice filled the kitchen, as well as the crackle of tortillas frying.

Leah tried to help tend to King's wounds, help preserve life to cancel out helping to end life just minutes ago, but the team leader waved her off. Roman bandaged the man's arm and put it in a sling, but he looked about as good as you could expect for a guy who had been shot.

Leah poured herself a drink and downed it in one peaty gulp. Her hand stopped shaking after a few minutes.

"So you always lose control of things like that?" Maribel asked with a smile. "I don't recall anything about distracting Williamson by enacting a stage show up on the second floor."

"No, that was all on the fly," King said. "And none too shabby, either. 'Cept for the fact that he was told not to go off and do something stupid like that."

"I'm just glad I came up with the idea between the back stairs and the second-floor landing."

"You made that up on the spot?" Frank asked, aghast.

"I was on the stage back home. I'm used to thinking on my feet."

"Looks like you picked your posse well, Marshal," Maribel said.

"I like to think so," King said. He leaned over, wincing, and pulled a bottle of far nicer liquor out of a bag. "Lee, get me three glasses."

Leah rose and retrieved glasses.

"Not those," Frank said as she pulled down the tin cups. "They have nice glass." The chef opened another cupboard and passed her three fine wine goblets.

Leah set the glasses down in front of the Genrenauts.

"Now get one for yourself," King said.

Frank grinned as he handed Leah another glass.

"Newbie or no, you're in our outfit, now," Roman said.

King poured a finger of amber-colored liquor into each glass. "We have a ritual on this team, whenever we complete a job. Victory without a celebration, well, that's like a story without a proper ending. Every story has its shape, and in this one, we found a hero, set things right, and broke in a new member of the posse." King raised his glass to Maribel, and to Leah, respectively.

"Should you be drinking if you got shot?" Leah asked.

"Hell, that just means he should drink more," Roman said.

King cleared his throat, taking control of the conversation again. "To another happy ending," King said, toasting. Leah raised her glass, and they clinked together in a happy mess of sound. Shirin gave Leah an affectionate squeeze on the shoulder, and Roman winked, leaning back as he drank.

Leah tossed back the drink as a shot before she realized that everyone else was sipping.

But as a testament to the alcoholic rigor of her college days, she did not do a spit-take when the peaty-as-a-barrow-wight's-butt liquor hit her tongue and nose.

She set the glass down hard, only gasping a bit.

"Did I forget to mention this was a sipping scotch?" King said.

"Tarnation!" Leah said, half-coughing, half-chuckling.

King leaned forward and poured another half shot into Leah's glass. "And to Maribel, the hero of the day. May the word of her deeds spread from the Mississippi straight to the coast. And may her brother's restaurant become the toast of the town."

Maribel toasted with her own cup, filled with a heavy portion of what Ollie had declared "the best whiskey in the house."

"What do you think the town will do now for a sheriff?" Frank asked.

King said, "Once we report back to the Governor, he'll send someone along soon enough. We heard a larger response was needed, and we were closer than any of the folks available."

"We'll be long gone by then," Frank said. "There was some … I mean, now that the Williamsons are gone …"

Maribel took over for Frank. "What my brother's trying to say is that I'm asking for the bounty we were promised. Matt, Tom, plus two more. Even those what your team brought down, like you offered."

"And as the Governor's representative, I'll make good on that promise." King reached into his bag again, pulling out a pouch the size of his fist. "You put your life on the line, so you ought to be able to ride out of this place and make a better life for yourselves." King tossed the bag onto the table, landing with a lucrative *thunk*. "We'll go over to the bank to settle up the rest."

"Assuming they have enough left," Frank said.

"If'n they don't, I'll see to it that you get a promissory note from the Governor."

Maribel tested the bag's weight, opened, and poured out a small waterfall of Western-world cousins to gold doubloons.

"We can get a coffin for Juan, a proper burial," Frank said.

"With enough left over to get us ahead on the restaurant," Maribel said. Looking up from the coin, she asked, "So, where you headed next?"

Leah watched King as the team leader formulated their extraction plan. She still had a zillion questions about how everything worked, and couldn't wait until they were on their own so she could break cover and get some answers.

"We'll head on to the next town that needs us. Don't like to stick around and put down roots. Doesn't sit well with me."

"King here gets antsy if he sleeps in the same bed twice," Roman said. "That's why we always trade out bedrolls."

Shirin winked at her teammate. "It's actually because Roman flattens them like an iron."

King excused himself to the facilities, and they sat and drank and talked for a good while longer before he came back and pulled the team upstairs.

* * *

King reported that HQ had given the all-clear on the patch, the breach and ripple effects over. He debriefed the team in a room of their own while Maribel and Frank made funeral arrangements for Juan.

The High Council had called the team back immediately, but King had convinced them the patch would be stronger if they stayed for the funeral.

So that afternoon, the Genrenauts stood in their finest, un-blood-stained clothes with Maribel and Frank as the local priest held a service for Juan Louis Mendoza. The Genrenauts helped lower the casket, then watched as Maribel and Frank let a handful of dirt pass through their hands as they said goodbye to their brother.

Leah stepped outside the moment, thinking about the shape of the story—beginning, middle, and end. Which brought them here, burying the dead alongside Mallery's fallen posse.

Once the caskets had been lowered to their final rest, the townsfolk lined up to thank Maribel.

The whole town.

Maribel had a receiving line four dozen folk long. Merchants, ranchers, the schoolmarm, the blacksmith, the two bankers left, and more.

The team stood by as the town embraced Maribel and Frank as their own. Some folks came over to thank them as well, but King waved them off, saying, "Maribel's the hero. We were just glad to help."

Leah watched the townsfolk with Maribel and her brother. "They're not going anywhere, are they?"

"Doubt it," King said, arm bound in a sling under his duster, one sleeve hanging empty.

When the townsfolk had said their piece, Maribel and Frank came to see the Genrenauts. Maribel's vest sported a shiny new tin star.

"So I reckon you're staying, then," King said.

"When an entire town begs you to stay, you consider."

Frank added, "And they offered to build my restaurant for me. Right there on the rail line. Folks will come from either coast."

Maribel looked back to the graves. "I just wish Juan could have lived to see it."

"We're going to call it Juan's Café," Frank said, squeezing his sister's hand.

"I think that's a fine way to honor him," King said. "It might be a long time before we make it back here. You look after this town now, you hear? I'll make sure the Governor gets a full report so you're not left on your own the next time trouble comes around."

Maribel settled into a wider stance, already embracing her role, like she took up more of the screen. "You got it. And make sure you look after each other too," Maribel said.

Roman and Shirin tipped their hats. Leah followed suit, and the four of them turned to walk off into the sunset, the cherry on top of the genre cake.

Mission Accomplished.

When the town was out of sight, the team turned and headed back to their ship.

Along the way, Leah unloaded her backlog of questions.

"So, what will happen to them now? If their story is done, do they disappear? If the whole world is supposed to be Western stories, what happens when your story is over?"

"They keep going on. The people here have real lives, but everyone is always in the beginning, middle, or end of a story. They get their happily-ever-afters, too," Shirin said.

"We only ever see people in the middle," King added. "When things run smooth, our presence actually disturbs the world more than it helps."

Roman said, "And regs dictate that we can't stay in the field for longer than a week unless absolutely necessary."

Cresting a hill, they returned to the rock outcropping that disguised the ship. The illusory stone was a shade off from the ones around it. Or maybe that was her nascent genre-senses tipping her off. Another one for the question bucket.

"Why a week?"

"Stay on a world too long, and the place gets its hooks in you," Roman said. "You start to get boxed in by the story—"

"That's enough about that," King said, cutting him off. The team leader had a remote-looking device in black plastic and pushed a button. The Phase Manipulator image fizzled out of existence, revealing the dust-coated rocket ship.

And the rest of the team's disguises dropped at the same time. Leah looked down and saw her own skin again, saw Shirin and King back to their real appearances. She felt like she'd exhaled a breath she hadn't known she'd been holding. She flexed her fingers and ran a hand over her arm.

"There'll be time for a proper debrief when we're back in HQ. Shirin, get our preflight going. Roman, the walk-around, and take the newbie with you."

Roman and Leah broke off and took a wide arc around the hill to approach the ship at ninety degrees to everyone else.

The Afrikaaner slipped back into teacher mode. "We go wide in case someone's been camping on the ship. We have proximity alarms, but even those can be disabled. Coming up on the ship, one, preferably two, members of the team do a visual inspection of the ship, looking for any holes in the fuselage, loose bolting, anything that seems out of order."

"Like a commercial flight, then?" Leah said, remembering the safety videos from the last time she'd gone home to visit her family. As far as she could tell, the ship looked fine, for an inter-dimensional snub-nosed rocket-ship. Still, anything that could keep them from having to deal with that amount of turbulence on the way back was worth a thorough check.

Roman ran his hands over the hull of the ship, feeling the seams. He sidestepped his way around the ship, tracking the base of the ship's trunk, where the tripod fin-legs splayed out from the body. "Any flight, really. Unless the pilot's lazy. And of course, when we have to get off-world in a hurry, that walk-around gets pretty cursory."

"And how often do you have to jet out like that?"

Roman opened a panel below the hatch and booted up a green-scale screen. "More often than I'd like, but not as often as you'd think. King's team has the highest completion rate in the organization. He's thorough, and he gets first pick of prospective recruits."

"How old is this ship?" Leah asked, pointing to the aged display.

"This one's fifteen years old. Most ships serve for about twenty years before they're retired. It's a Mark III. The Mark IVs are just now going into service at the Hong Kong and Mumbai bases."

"And where do we get all of this tech?" she asked.

Roman responded with a thin smile. "We, eh?"

"Hey, I risked life and limb, I think I've earned a we."

"So do I." Roman tapped at the console, the screen scrolling through dozens of lines of text. "Most of the tech comes from subsidiaries owned by the High Council. The workers don't know what they're making, everything is subdivided out, double-blind, then assembled at each base."

"Sounds absolutely Soviet."

"It's the best way to keep everyone safe. What we do is bigger than countries, bigger than economics, it's a literal world-saving kind of mission. But it's easiest if almost no one knows about it and they go about their lives happily oblivious. The blowback we'd get if the truth got out …" Roman shook his head.

"I can imagine Badger News going to town with something like this."

"Most people wouldn't even be able to appreciate the stakes, and even if they could, we'd immediately see people trying to travel between worlds for kicks, and others blaming every little social ill on some screw-up by a Genrenaut team."

Leah could just imagine what some politicians might do with the truth, let alone religious zealots. You'd see whole religions pop up or metamorphose into something new and probably even more bizarre. "Got it. Sacred burden, sworn to secrecy, all that jazz."

"Hey, the pay's good," Roman said. "Worth not being able to tell anyone I date what I really do."

"What do you tell them?"

"I work in a lab."

"That King's go-to?"

"It is. Ninety-nine percent of folks don't know enough science to poke a hole in the cover, and those that do, we distract with theoretical quantum physics and doctoral lit crit from King. It's not even really a lie. We're using a different version of the many worlds theory."

"Positing a relationship between parallel dimensions instead of individual emergence and digression, I guess." Her physics class had been at 2 p.m. Much better.

"Right in one. I was never much for science. You'll want to go to Shirin or King for the detailed breakdown. Or buy Preeti a drink and let her go to town. She's got a doctorate in Dimensional Theory."

"I disbelieve that that is a real thing in which one can get a degree."

"Officially, no. But the High Council funds a special shadow department at top universities around the world. It's where they recruit most of their tech and science staff."

"I am officially down the rabbit hole, aren't I?"

"Pretty much. But you've handled yourself pretty well. Last newbie we had lost his lunch two hours into the first mission."

"Was that you?" Leah asked.

Roman shut the panel. "No, but I didn't fare much better. That was Tommy Suarez."

Wash out of the Genrenauts, get an HBO special. Not a bad retirement plan.

Roman looked the ship up and down, then said, "We're good. Let's go home."

Epilogue:
Sign on the Dotted Line

The trip back from Western world was far smoother than the way over. There was some chop as they crossed back through the rainbows-on-black sky of the space between dimensions, but on the shake-o-meter, it registered as Bumpy rather than Vomit-Cannon.

As Leah stepped out of the ship and onto the stairs built into the hatch, a support team of ten techs greeted the team. The techs converged on the ship like flies on a corpse. Science flies.

"How's Mallery?" King asked as soon as he touched down.

One of the techs said, "She's out of surgery and recovering. I'll let the nurses know to expect you. Council will want your report first."

"I imagine they'll understand if I check in with medical first," King said, waving the bandaged arm. "How did Louis's team fare?"

Leah tried to squirrel these details away, loose puzzle pieces to be assembled later, when she knew more about this brilliant and mad place.

"Last report said that they were on level twenty of the tower, under heavy fire."

"Something is definitely going on," Shirin said, the last out of the ship.

"I'll report to the Council once medical has cleared me, you three head over to see Mallery. I want familiar faces greeting her when she wakes up, let her know we finished the job."

"Come on, Kid," Roman said. "It's only fair to show you what happens when things don't go as smoothly as they did for us."

"That was smooth?" Leah asked.

* * *

Roman double-timed it toward the medical wing. Leah had to jog to keep up with Shirin, who was only a couple of inches taller and yet managed to power walk almost as fast as Roman. The doctors had taken King off to another room, away from recovery.

The trio was greeted by a middle-aged nurse—a black woman who looked like she'd been up for twenty or so hours, wearing blue scrubs and bright pink Crocs.

"She's awake, but only one of you should go in at a time. Don't let her move. She lost a lot of blood."

"Thank you, Ms. Rachelle," Roman said, moving immediately to the door.

"I guess he's going first," Leah said.

Rachelle said, "He's usually the one with the gunshot wounds. This is a nice change of pace." She turned on one foot and returned to her station, filled with file folders and a pair of flat-panel screens. How often did the Genrenauts get hurt that they needed their own medical facility? Though with the focus on secrecy Roman had indicated, it made sense to make their HQ its own contained facility, a one-stop world-saving shop.

Shirin put a hand on Leah's shoulder. "While we're here, let me take you on the tour and show you what we're up against. Roman will come get us when he's done."

"I assume they're close, then?" Leah asked, treading right over the matter of propriety.

"She's like a little sister to him."

"This is one of those 'team-is-like-your-family' things, isn't it?"

"Right in one." Shirin walked over to the next room. She double-checked the chart and said, "This is Eve. She caught a poisoned arrow running from an enraged tribe defending its sacred artifact in the Pulp world."

"Will she be okay?"

"We hope so. The poison isn't known on Earth Prime, but we think she's past the worst of it."

"Yikes. How many teams are there, here?"

Shirin continued down the hall "We've got thirteen Genrenauts on staff at this base, enough to form three teams if we all have to mobilize at once. But right now, we're down three agents. The third is Perry here—he lost a duel with the Baron of Farthingmunster, trying to defend the honor of the Lady Whipton."

"Regency world?" Leah hazarded. Shirin nodded.

"This job doesn't usually have this high a casualty rate, right?" Leah asked. "You mentioned that something is off."

"That's why King has to report right away. The disturbances on the story worlds have gotten bigger, like a dimensional monsoon season. And when we try to put things back on track, the worlds fight back, harder. I've never seen anything like it. The Council is taking a measured stance, not officially acknowledging that anything is wrong, but King is worried. That's why he went ahead and brought you in. We're getting short-staffed, having trouble keeping up with all of the disturbances."

"Sounds like an awesome time to start the job."

Shirin crossed her arms. "Come on. You're telling me you'd rather go back to working reception?"

"Hey, the only danger there is dying of boredom."

"Uh-huh. We'll see about that. In the meantime, let's head to the break room. I could use some coffee that doesn't taste like it was brewed with molasses."

* * *

After all the fuss about reporting immediately, King ended up standing at attention for twenty minutes in the broadcasting room, waiting for the High Council to call in.

The bullet had gone straight through the meat of his arm. He'd be shooting lefty for a while, but Dr. Douglas said it wouldn't take too long to heal, especially if they deployed on story-worlds like Action or Science Fiction that had rapid recovery.

King stood at the focal point between the three wide-screen flat-panel monitors that filled one wall of the room. Behind him and on both sides were the servers, processors, and transmission equipment to live-cast at three angles at high-fidelity across the world, while never being able to tell him where exactly his superiors were speaking to him from. He guessed they were based in Europe, but he'd always met the Councilors here, at his base, or at European HQ outside of London. But the London team was as in the dark as he was about where the Councilors really lived.

It'd been like that the whole thirty years he'd been with the organization, one of the first Genrenauts recruited by the Council during their initial expansion.

The screens changed from flat black to the loading screens, showing the array of dozens of worlds in their orbits around Earth, each marked by its official symbol. Pistols, hearts, fans, swords, magnifying lens, prayer beads, and so on. His team's beat was a small selection of the dozens of story worlds the Genrenauts patrolled and protected.

The title screen dropped, revealing five shadowed figures. They always stood in shadow, seeing King but never being seen during meetings. It'd been the same five of them, as near as he could tell, the entire thirty years. He'd only ever met three of the High Council. The other two, the most senior, never made public appearances. King had taken it as the eccentricity of the rich, germophobia, or something. They were a constant—inaccessible, unbending, but just.

The Council's leader, Gisler, spoke from the middle of the screen. "Angstrom King. Report."

"The breach has been patched, Councilor."

King unpacked the mission in exhaustive detail, relating Mallery's initial patch attempt, the complication, and his team's response, down to Leah's impressive first outing and the resolution, solidifying Maribel Mendoza as a hero and securing the town.

Fifteen minutes later, he was done.

"What is your agent's status?" another councilor asked.

"Mallery York is in serious but stable condition. She's the third operative from this base to be critically injured in the last month. I'm concerned about the nature of these recent breaches—"

D'Arienzo, friendliest of the Council, cut King off. "We are aware of your concerns, and the reports from team leaders about these so-called aberrations in the breaches. Our science division is investigating the readings, but thus far, we have no reason to believe that this is anything other than a seasonal high tide of dimensional disturbances—"

"With all due respect, Councilor—"

Gisler cut him off. "Respect means not interrupting your superiors."

Status. Respect. Propriety. His own team called him a stick in the mud, but if they only knew the Council …

D'Arienzo continued. "We thank you for your efforts, and for your report. Debrief your team and stand down to ready status."

"Understood," King said. And with that, the call dropped, the screens going blank.

"Pricks," King said under his breath once he was certain nothing would pick up his back talk.

Which was outside the room and ten paces down the hallway.

But that was the way of things. The Council were mysterious and aloof. But without them, none of this would be possible. They'd discovered dimensional breaches and travel between the worlds, and kept their eyes on the big picture, maintaining the delicate balance between dozens of worlds. They had earned the right to dictate terms.

* * *

Two coffees in, Leah watched King walk into the break room and make himself some tea.

"So, what do you think of this operation?" he asked.

"You're all kind of suicidal. But I love it. There's no way even being a professional comedian could be this cool. Sure, it'd be less dangerous, but … cowboys, and lasers, and spaceships!"

"And that's probably all in your next two pay periods," Shirin said from the couch. Boots off and legs up, she had her nose in a thick tome of a biography.

"With Mallery injured, my team's understaffed for the foreseeable future. So, if you want it, there's a probationary position here for you. Your start would be back-dated to yesterday when you walked in the building."

"Isn't there some security screening I have to do?"

"I did all of that already. So, do you want the job?"

Leah was expecting the offer, since she'd manage to pull off the fight with her slapdash plan, but seeing the Genrenauts in traction had given her some pause. She could walk away right then and if King delivered, she'd have the solid gig, she could build her career and put this all behind her.

She thought back to the team at the table, to the look in Maribel's eyes as Matt Williamson dropped to the floor. She thought about Frank's cooking, Shirin's laugh, and the feeling of jet thrusters beneath her.

Red-pill, blue-pill time. She could go home, keep filing other people's paperwork while daydreaming material for her shows, or go down the rabbit hole into a totally bizarre and dangerous but exciting line of work hacking dimensions and saving the world with stories.

Mom and Dad would say to stay with the familiar, to dig deep and commit to her comedy that she had chosen over her family. But she'd gotten into comedy because it was the best way she knew to make a difference, to tell the stories she wanted to hear. In the Genrenauts, she could do all of that and never have to take minutes during a Strategic Revenue Best Practices presentation again.

"Can I Sandberg for a moment and ask about the pay and benefits?" She'd never argued a salary before, but she'd gone into a firefight for this job. A little negotiation wasn't going to cost her the gig.

King pulled a slip of yellow legal paper out of his jacket and passed it to Leah.

She unfolded the paper and was disgusted at the lowball figure until she realized there was an extra zero at the end.

"That first number is salary. In dollars. U.S. dollars?"

King said, "That it is. And below that is the health package."

Leah scanned the bottom half of the paper. The plan was positively *European*. Including a *lot* of life insurance. Unsurprising, but not super-reassuring.

"This job will call for long hours more often than any of us like, but I think you'll agree that the compensation is worth the overtime."

So, to review, she could stick with her mind-numbing but safe job and bang her head against the stand-up circuit with one gig a week until she refined her act enough to earn more work, or take a ridiculous-percent pay increase to do six impossible things before breakfast.

"You've got yourself a deal," Leah said, extending a hand. King's grip was unsurprisingly strong.

"Welcome to the team, then, Probie."

Really? "Why Probie? This isn't *NCIS*."

"The show didn't make that up. Fire departments and other agencies use it. And so do we."

"But this place isn't government, right?"

"No," King said. "We're technically nonstate actors, and if most governments found out about us, we'd probably be locked away forever. So read the NDA very, very closely."

"How's Mallery?" Leah asked, eager to change the subject from how much of a newbie she was and the hazing she should expect.

"She'll be fine," Roman said. "No major arteries hit, and she's already restless. Ms. Rachelle had to come in and up her sedative so she won't tear her stitches."

Roman offered a hand to Leah. "Welcome to the Genrenauts."

They shook. "Hope you survive the experience," he added.

His cribbing of the famous X-Men line put Leah even more at ease. She already felt at home with the troupe, this band of storytellers and hustlers. And she couldn't wait to tell off Suzanne at the office and move her army of office animals out of the cubicle and into the Genrenauts break room.

"Sounds good. But for now, I'm going to go and crash."

"Not so fast," King said. "Just because you've been cleared, doesn't mean you get to skip the rest of the paperwork."

The team lead handed her a pen and a manila folder that was at least three inches thick. "I'll need these on my desk within the hour. Then you can head home. And be back tomorrow by eight for orientation."

"I take it back. I'll die of boredom. Anything to avoid paperwork." Leah hung her head as she exaggeratedly padded to a table, dropping the manila folder to as much despondent effect as she could muster.

A minute later, Roman sat down across from her, a tablet and earphones in one hand, a pair of bottled beers in the other. He twisted off the caps with his palm (nice trick), and passed one to Leah.

They toasted, and Roman put in his earbuds. He opened a digital comics reader on his tablet, leaving Leah to the stack. Leah repeated the ridiculous salary to herself as she scanned the stack of papers.

Camaraderie, adventures in storytelling, a fat paycheck, and health insurance. What more could a girl ask for?

END EPISODE ONE

Episode Two:
The Absconded Ambassador

Chapter One:
Saving the World with PowerPoint

Working as a Genrenaut was like being a member of a theater troupe run by a burnt-out hippie who melded Devising with MBA management: the ideas were outlandish and random, but the execution was 100% corporate. There were reports, meetings, and lots of emails—but while the format was familiar, the content was delightfully bizarre.

Emails had subject lines like "Cultural Trend Forecasting Report," "Best Practices in Alien Relations," and more. The required reading and viewing made Leah Tang feel like a double-booked media critic for the City Post, and the meetings, overseen by the alternatingly imperious and playful Angstrom King, were half weekly process and half crash course in graduate-level dimensional narrative theory, a subject that Leah hadn't even known existed a week ago.

King advanced another slide as the team sat in a conference room. King stood at one end of the table, opposite the screen. Shirin Tehrani sat upright, taking notes longhand on a legal pad, never looking down, but somehow still writing impeccably. Leah would have to ask for lessons on that, too. To Leah's right, Roman De Jager had his boots up on the table, tablet in his lap, chair leaned back five degrees short of toppling. Roman tapped through a pattern-recognition game while King continued his breakdown.

King had never once chewed Roman out for his lack of focus, but Leah had realized over the week since she started the job that Roman was focusing—he just needed something to distract his hands and part of his brain. She'd had classmates like that—too much going on to only ever be doing one thing.

A poster on the wall opposite Leah showed the Genrenauts seal, a constellation of worlds, a regular blue-and-green Earth in the center, all of the others bearing a logo for their genre—crossed revolvers for Western world, a heart for Romance, rocket ship for Science Fiction, and so on.

Memorizing the logos had been a day-one job, right after her genre fluency evaluations.

The organization's motto curled around the worlds:

Every World a Story, Every Story a Proper Ending

The latest slide was so corporate it hurt, showing a set of wire diagrams. But what they represented was anything but normal. "Our Forecasters have reported increased dimensional activity," King said.

"All five bases corroborate, showing narrative breaches up fifteen percent year over year."

"So we can expect overtime to continue, then?" Shirin Tehrani asked. "My son has a recital this weekend, and if I'm off-world, I'll be in the doghouse for months." Shirin sported a pashmina scarf and wore her hair braided, a steaming mug of coffee sitting at her place-setting, making this her third cup of the day.

"I'm afraid not," King said. "Twenty-four-hour on-call status will continue until disturbances taper off or until we're back up to full strength."

Another Genrenaut had come back with serious injuries two days ago, putting their in-house medical wing up to capacity. Rachelle, their head nurse, was threatening to walk if she didn't get the payroll to bring in temporary help.

King continued. "Forecasting expects the Romance world to be the next to show a breach, given the drop in use of and satisfaction with dating apps and a reduction in applications for marriage licenses. However, Wright's reconnaissance run yesterday didn't show anything amiss, and the readouts aren't indicating a breach, so …"

"We wait." Roman slid his feet off the table and leaned forward, setting his tablet in front of him.

"Indeed. You'll find new genre briefing priorities in the team's Cloud Box. Leah, this is your priority for today. Your entrance interview ranked you Yellow on Rom-Com, but Red on category romance."

Leah shrugged. "My mom was the Harlequin fan. I never took to them."

"Your personal tastes will inform your perspective, but any field agent, probationary or no, is expected to be conversant in all of the genres for which we're responsible, which means that you've got a date with your eReader."

"Yes, oh captain my captain," Leah said, saluting with a fist over her heart.

King clicked through one more time, and the presentation ended with the Genrenauts logo.

"You have your assignments," King said, shutting off the projector and walking out of the room. To Leah's eyes, King had been harried over the week, way more stressed back home than he'd been in the field. She was still getting to know everyone, though, so maybe stressed was just his default. She'd noticed that this week he ate ham hocks, collard greens, and skillet cornbread, where all he ever ate the week she started was steamed chicken and broccoli.

Leah snatched up her tablet and turned to Roman. "Any favorites you think I should start with?" Roman gestured to the tablet. Leah handed it over.

He swiped through to a text file and started tapping. "I'm partial to the romantic suspense. But the MacKennas are really witty historicals. Probably more accessible than other stuff the tastemakers put on the reading list. I'll forward you some of Mallery's favorites. She's our specialist for that genre. "

Active agents were evaluated on their genre knowledge: the ability to identify and explain genrespecific archetypes, plot arcs, and aesthetics—the same skills that would let them operate effectively in that genre's world to find and address story breaches.

Leah's first mission had been a whirlwind. She'd only seen a tiny portion of the support staff required for the Genrenauts' operation to function. Besides the field agents, there were medical, admin, the tech division that kept their ships in order, as well as the quartermasters that worked on the various dimensional properties from different story worlds, from cybernetic enhancements to artifacts and spell books.

Leah was amused but not surprised to hear that the tech division recruited heavily from the Imagineers, in addition to the R&D departments of leading tech firms. There was the forecasting team, which brought Big Data analytics to the multiverse, studying stocks, cultural trends, sales patterns, and media coverage to try to forecast and identify ripple effects from story worlds.

Finally, there were the curators, who worked with the forecasting team to determine which films, music, TV, and books were making waves in Earth Prime—the manifestations of flows from story worlds. They studied viewer metrics, distribution deals, award lists, and more. Seeing everything from the outside, it looked and felt like a Rube Goldberg machine at times.

But it was still more fun and more profitable than answering phones and processing expense reports.

Leah plopped her tablet down on a beanbag chair and went to the kitchenette to pour herself more coffee.

Just as she was raising the mug, the divine smell of the local blond roast tantalizing her nose, a harsh klaxon went off.

The Breach Alarm.

Leah took a long swig of coffee, then set it down with the reluctance of leaving a new lover in bed to leave for work. She turned to Roman for commiseration. "Craaap."

Shirin hadn't even gotten to sit, instead turning in place as she walked into the break room to head right back out.

"What? This is the fun part. To Ops we go."

Ops was the nerve center of Genrenauts HQ, where Preeti Jandran and a half-dozen other staffers monitored the weird science end of the business, using sensors and systems no one had bothered explaining to Leah and which she was happy to leave as a mystery, as long as they pointed her in the right direction.

Walking into Ops, Leah once again felt like she had stepped into NASA, or maybe an IMAX room. Or a NASA IMAX room. Twenty screens filled the far wall, the floor packed thick with consoles and sensors and workstations.

King stood by one such station, looking over the shoulder of Preeti, the team's designated handler. Preeti's fingers whirred across a keyboard, one screen showing what looked like seismic activity, the other tuned to a CNN news feed.

"What's up?" Shirin asked.

"We're picking up several red flags. Space X just lost a shuttle in mid-launch, and the ISS is reporting cascading software failures."

"Which means a breach in Science Fiction world," Shirin said by way of explanation. Since each world had a thematic tie to Earth Prime, when there was a breach on a story world, the ripples on Earth would come along specific lines, manifesting on Earth in mostly predictable ways.

On her first mission, a breach in Western world had rippled over to create a rush of gun violence. And when Fantasy world broke, its breaches would ripple over as sectarian violence and destructive tribalism.

Preeti nodded at Shirin's evaluation. "Our latest recon to Ahura-3 showed everything in order, with an upcoming diplomatic summit. But sensors show the station as the epicenter of the ripples." "That's enough to get started," King said. "Suit up, team. Probie, you're with me." Leah followed King as he set off again at flank speed.

* * *

King chewed up the floor as they made their way to Bakhtin Hangar. "This is not the ideal world to have for your second at-bat, I must admit."

"I was raised on Trek and Battlestar, man. I'm good."

"Genre awareness by itself is not sufficient for this world. This breach has been tracked to Ahura-3, in the space opera region. Ahura-3 is a hub to dozens of species, accommodating thousands of languages, biological and cultural variances. Only Roman, Shirin, and one other field agent on this entire base are rated to head an operation in that world."

"But won't it just be bumpy forehead aliens and pseudo-European political intrigue?" Leah asked, going off the first (and shortest) of the matryoshka-like cultural briefings of the story worlds in the base's jurisdiction. The Science Fiction world was dominated by the Space Opera and Military SF regions, alongside contemporary action-adventure stories and Cyberpunk. But the region hadn't seen a landmark formal or narrative innovation since the reimagined Battlestar Galactica. At least, so said the Genrenauts analysts.

King let her question sit as he swung open the doors to the hangar, showing two of the three ships in their berths. The ship they'd taken to Western world was being rolled out to the launch pad, dozens of techs running diagnostics, checking gauges, and so on. The ship was one of three active in this hangar, and so carried the super-specific name of US-3.

Quite a production. And all buzzing away in a corporate campus that looked more like an insurance office from the outside than a base for dimensional adventurers.

"By that logic," King said in the tone of a disappointed professor, "you'd tell me that the blues is simple because it only uses four chords. Try telling that to Nina Simone and B.B. King."

Leah nodded. "But we've got universal translators, right?"

"Thankfully. We couldn't do anything there without them. But linguistic translation and cultural translation are very different. You'll stay with Roman, Shirin, or myself at all times. No running off, even if you have the best idea possible. Your initiative with the Williamsons is admirable, but there are too many pitfalls in this region for a green agent, and we've finally gotten you through orientation.

It'd be terribly inefficient to replace you now."

Leah caught the joking tone he was laying down, and replied in kind. "Gee, thanks. Y'all know how to make a girl feel welcome." Leah looked over her shoulder as Roman strode in, already changed into sexy-grubby space-traveler garb—a ratty sweater over mesh shirt, loose cargo pants, and a shoulder bag which she'd bet dollars to donuts contained guns. Or blasters, or whatever the term-du-jour for the SF weapons of the world.

"Do you have a bag of guns for every world?" Leah asked.

"Of course not. No guns in Fantasyland," he said, not missing a beat.

"But you should see his collection of wands and staves," King said. "I want takeoff in ten.

Roman, you and the newbie on walk-around."

This part, at least, she knew. Roman went to stow his bag of guns and supplies, so Leah started her checks for hull damage or anything else that might cause minor to catastrophic failures during their cross-dimensional flight between Earth Prime and the story world.

She'd done the walk-around as they left Western world, so she knew ostensibly what to look for, but it didn't stop her from starting over and doing another complete circuit when Roman thundered down the hatch stairs to do his own inspection.

"How do I tell the difference between a scuff and a mark that could become a tear or gash or another we're-all-going-to-die kind of thing?"

"Scuffs will buff off. Plus, we don't usually scuff. Dimensional turbulence dents and bends more than scuffs. We keep the ships clean, so you should be able to spot any we're-all-going-to-die things pretty easily."

Leah scanned the ship's hull. "This looks good. Anything I missed?"

"Nope. I'll check the circuitry here, and we'll be good for pre-flight. Ninety-nine times out of a hundred, this walk-around is just for show."

"But nobody wants to be time number one hundred."

Roman tapped his nose. "Especially if King's around. We've got time, so you can change into your off-world gear now. We'll arrive within sight of Ahura-3, and they use visual comms. Protocol says we all have to be in field gear when we launch."

Leah turned to start dashing, ten minutes being nowhere near enough time to walk to the wardrobe room, find clothes that fit, change, and get back to the launch.

But once again, Shirin proved to be a little bit psychic. Crossing the hangar floor in an anklelength maroon-and-yellow robe-dress-thing, she held up a black-and-silver duffel bag for Leah. "Dressing corner there," she said, thumbing at a corner that had a tri-folding screen and a stool.

"High tech."

"Quick changes don't have to be fancy, but they do have to be done. Two minutes."

Leah hustled over, pulling the curtain across the floor behind her as she shrugged her sweater off. While in HQ, all field agents were required to wear VDUs, Versatile Dress Units—aka underwear that could pass in any number of worlds. VDUs didn't apply to all worlds, but eight out of ten wasn't bad, and SF world was one of the eight.

Leah zipped open the bag and pulled out the first item, a black underskirt. She swapped out her jeans for the skirt, and then drew out the expected big damn Science Fiction dress-robe hybrid, similar to Shirin's, but emerald green and less fancy. The bag also had a variety of jewelry—anklets and bracelets and earrings—which would have to wait until they got on-world. No way was she going to try to put on earrings during dimensional chop. Four holes per ear were enough.

That was another thing she missed. Regs meant that she was only allowed the "normal" stud earrings, which meant her other earrings and bar had to stay at home.

Unless SF world turned out to involve Bajoran levels of ear-bling.

She stuffed her Earth Prime clothes in the duffel and then jogged across the hangar floor to climb into the ship. She stowed her bag in one of the airline-esque locked-and-secured box cubbies, and then climbed up the rungs along the side of the ship and slid into her seat to buckle the X-straps that would keep her roughly in place even if they ran into more dimensional chop.

"Not bad, Probie. But next time, finish the job," Shirin said, pointing to her own resplendently adorned ears. "And when we get there, there will be makeup."

"It's the future! Haven't they outlawed makeup already?"

Shirin shook her head. "It's the only way Xenei can tell human women apart, unfortunately." "Well, that sounds horrible and rife for abuse," Leah mused.

King climbed into the ship. "Hasn't even touched down, and Probie already plotting to abuse Xenei? I knew you were a quick study, but this is above the call of duty. Keep this up and you'll make the rest of the team look bad." King closed the hatch and spun the wheel tight. "Pre-flight?"

"Finalizing now," Shrin said. "Preeti says we are clear for crossover, forecast indicates minimal friction between here and our destination."

Roman gave Leah a smile. "Looks like you lucked out this time."

Leah crossed her fingers as King climbed into the copilot seat and strapped in. The team lead opened up the comms, joining Shirin in the switch-flipping game. "Mid-Atlantic Actual, this is US-3, initiating launch sequence." Leah had never been much for flight simulators, so from where she sat, they might as well have been making it all up. As long as it worked.

Leah dug her fingers into the seat as the ship began to rumble.

"Here we go," she said under her breath as the ship lurched ahead, punching through the dimensional barrier between Earth Prime and the story world. Through the view-screen, the inside roof of the hangar disappeared, replaced with a coruscating rainbow and VFX that looked for all the world like the Kirby Krackle from silver age comics.

The ship rattled, shaking her in her seat, but in just a few moments, the shaking receded, replaced by comparatively gentle gravitational force pushing her back against her seat. And the Kirby Krackle out in the void was replaced by ... actual void. As in space. Stars and distant nebulae and a gray-ish dot in the distance.

"So, we're in space now. Like, actual astronaut space." Shirin said, "You got it."

Leah's hair floated up and around, wrapping around her head, bouncing back and forth. The edges of her dress rippled free, held back at the waist by the straps.

Not only were they in space, but their ship didn't come with artificial gravity, which meant zerog. Honest-to-goodness, Sally Ride is my homegirl zero-g.

"I'm in space right now," she said, her brain processing the reality of the situation through the excitement of a five-year-old who had watched shuttle launches like they were the World Series, who had made cardboard spaceships several years beyond the time frame when child psychologists said was "normal." Fantasy had been her first love, but her heart had made space for, well, space. "Quite something, isn't it?" King asked. "Permission to squee, sir?"

"Just don't get it on the seats, Probie." Leah could hear the man's smile, an old theater trick for reading tone when you were upstage of your castmates.

"Aye, captain. Sanitary squeeing only."

"Carry on." Her grin went ear to ear, watching the interplay of light and darkness play out for infinity. What she wouldn't give for a 360-degree viewscreen right about then.

"One hundred thousand klicks to broadcast range of Ahura-3," Shirin said. "No anomalies or other ships within sensor range."

"That is what a dimensional crossing should feel like. Well done, team."

Leah took a few minutes to stare out into the nothing. Internally, she was doing a class-A booty dance.

King turned in his seat. "Leah, see if you can squee and finish getting dressed at the same time.

We'll be hailing Ahura-3 in about ten minutes."

Leah unbuckled and floated out of her seat, hands out to brace herself against colliding with the seat in front of her or the hull above.

"How's it feel?" Roman asked.

"This is so cool!" Leah said, failing to keep her voice professional.

"Get it out of your system—we won't be able to mess around once we port," Shirin added.

Fly in zero-g. That's another one off the bucket list, she thought to herself, grabbing her chair and pulling herself toward the bulkhead, applying Ender's lesson and interpreting the base of the ship as "down."

I need to be able to talk about this with someone outside the team. They've got to have allowances for best buddies or something, right? she thought. But the orientation package had specifically said that no one, not even loved ones, were allowed to know the reality of Genrenauts operations. So she'd have to contain her excitement with friends.

For a moment, she was content to tool around the ship and tackle the challenge of applying jewelry and makeup in zero-g. Necklaces would be … interesting.

Chapter Two:
Not Remotely in Kansas Anymore

Leah could not believe her eyes, even as Ahura-3 filled the windshield, then grew too wide to see all at once. It followed the ring-and-spokes design model, three massive tubes with a dozen corridors, each connecting the tube to the central axle. Shuttles and maintenance drones swarmed around the station, and ships moved in and out of the axle, which seemed to be the main port.

She'd wrestled her jewelry into submission and applied a base layer, ready for whatever weird science fictional makeup job would be required for the station.

"That. Is. Awesome," Leah said, gobsmacked.

Roman chuckled. "It's not even the biggest thing around. Ra'Gar battle-moons are more than five times this size. Around a third of the size of Mercury." On-base, Roman was always doing two or things at once. Here, in the field, he was steady, both calm and more animate. Focused.

"Mercury?" Leah asked, her brain stuck in "WOW" since Ahura-3 had gotten large enough to make out as its own thing.

"Okay, opening coms. Everyone shush and act like you belong." Shirin flipped a switch, and then held a button. "Ahura-3, this is Free Trader Grendel, come in, Ahura-3." Leah restrained from laughing at the name.

A woman's voice crackled through the radio, speaking with a Russian accent. "This is Ahura-3 Command, we copy you, Grendel. Welcome back. We don't have a flight plan from you, but what else is new?"

"Hey, Commander. No plan? Again?" Shirin asked, slipping seamlessly into character. "That's what I get for hiring a new assistant. She must have

94

flubbed the form before sending the Ansible. My apologies. We're about twenty minutes out, what are my chances of getting into the docking queue this side of moonrise?"

"You do like to play right on the edges, don't you, Grendel?" came the commander's response.

"What can I say? Keeps things interesting."

The station-side audio stayed on, chatter and beeping audible through the staticky connection.

"Come on over to bay five. You're behind the freighter Salex Crown."

"You're a peach. Catch you in the Bazaar?"

"You know it," the commander responded. "Mallery with you this time?"

Shirin winced. "Sorry, Oksana. She couldn't make this circuit."

"So be it. I will be happy to claim those apologies in vodka. Twenty-one hundred." "Got it. See you then." Shirin released the comms button.

"Over and out."

"Okay, we're good." Shirin turned to speak to Leah, one eye still on the dash. "Oksana's the executive officer on the station. She's tapped into anything that happens officially and most of the stuff under the table. If we haven't gotten the problem sniffed out by then, she'll be able to point us in the right direction."

Leah asked, "Last trip was you and Mallery, then?" She didn't need to finish, just judging by the shift in Shirin's demeanor.

Maybe ask a few less obvious questions, there, self, she thought.

Shirin flipped some switches and then unstrapped and swung herself down toward the gear.

"Okay, newbie, let's get our faces on."

"So, what did you mean by lots of makeup?"

* * *

Walking across the gangplank into the customs and clearance area, Leah felt like an utter fool. And not just because she was still wobbling after having been in zero-g for less than a half hour.

Mostly it was because she had on more makeup than she'd ever worn in her life, maybe even more than she'd worn for a makeup final in college, which was impressive, since her assignment had been "zombie."

But apparently, the custom for human women traveling in space was to wear red carpet levels of makeup. Red carpet followed by a David Bowie birthday rave.

Though that would be pretty awesome, to be honest.

The embarrassment was made somewhat better by Shirin being as dolled up as she was, but the older woman wore the cosmetic face with enviable nonchalance.

May I give so few fucks when I'm her age, Leah thought.

King went ahead, wearing an outfit that was a combination of shabby chic and Han Solo. He wore a sweet forearm tablet-computer-wearable thing on his left arm, and code-switched into a patois of English, French, and something else with the customs agent, a black woman of maybe twenty-five, wearing a prim-and-proper black-and-silver uniform.

The rest of them stood by at the gate, a glass wall that ran twenty feet up toward the hundredfoot-high ceiling. Light projectors of some sort formed a red laser crosshatching across the only open way through the glass. Beyond, a similarly uniformed man with dark tan skin, in a silver beret, stood by a console.

King bade the guard farewell, and her companion pushed a button, which changed the color of the laser netting to green. King went first, then Roman.

"Go ahead," Shirin said, and so Leah stepped through the netting. The light filled her vision for a second, but it didn't feel like anything else, no pressure, no tactile sensation, nothing. The guard nodded, and she stepped forward.

They passed from the customs area into a long hallway.

"I have to clear our cargo, so you three go ahead and start asking around, discreetly, to figure out what the source of the breach is. Roman has your covers for this mission."

They approached a T-juncture. A sign overhead said CUSTOMS with an arrow pointing left, the other way labeled STATION ENTRANCE. King broke off to head toward CUSTOMS.

"And Probie, don't go wandering off alone. This place is big enough, we might not be able to find you."

Leah watched King stride down the opposite corridor. "Well, that's not terrifying or anything."

Shirin tapped her neck. "Don't worry. We're all chipped, so the wrist-comps can find us anywhere on the station."

Leah rubbed her own neck, though the injection site wasn't sore anymore. "Yeah, I remember that from orientation. But he couldn't resist the chance to be alarming, could he?"

"Nope," Roman said, picking up the pace. "Come on, this place is amazing."

* * *

Roman was not lying.

As they stepped out into the station proper, Leah was greeted by complete sensory overload.

Lights, speech, music, and the sensation of standing on something that was moving. There was no way she could feel the specifics of the rotation on a station this big, but it was distinct from standing in a car or a plane or bus. It was ... its own thing.

The main building looked half like an airport terminal and half like an open-air version of the Star Wars cantina. She spotted a dozen different non-human races, and guessed at another dozen human-ish races, with different head shapes, skin colors, or some combination of the two, from walrus-looking people with large whiskers to tree people to a race that looked like big versions of fantasy dwarves—proportionally short limbs, but instead of being around four feet tall, they were six feet tall, nearly all in the torso, with massive, golden beards in elaborate braids that swung down to their belts like strands of Viking jewelry.

One race walked on all fours, legs as thick as a telephone pole, torsos built like rhinos, but redscaled with the heads a mixture between a rabbit and a Gila monster. Another seemed to be nothing more than brains in jars, floating along on personal hover-disks.

"I should be trying not to stare, right?" Leah asked.

Shirin passed Leah. "Your cover's as a tourist from Mars who has never been off-planet, so you're good. This gives you a bit more leeway, but you're still responsible for knowing the whole setting dossier." The older woman wove her way through the crowds, working the room like she'd done on Leah's first mission. Judging by how many people seemed to recognize her, Leah wondered about the boots-on-the-ground reality of the "don't make waves" commandment that King had hammered home right away, and the orientation material repeated.

Another thing she'd like to ask about, but probably shouldn't. Instead, Leah took the opportunity to rubberneck, taking in the brains in jars, the lizard-rhino-people, and everything else.

A short walk and a longer elevator ride later, they reached a trade district, with more market stalls, airport-esque kiosks, and a two-floor bar called How Bazaar.

Shirin chatted up the hostess, a green woman wearing a dress that was half rave-wear, half space-opera gown, bands of cloth crosshatching an otherwise bare back as the alien woman led them to a black leather booth in the corner of the first floor.

"So how many people here do you know?" Leah asked as they filled the booth.

"I know a lot of people. And they think they know me. But it only takes one or two odd details for people to fill in a whole painting about someone they barely know. It's just another mask, like the others we pick up and put down on the job. Which reminds me, covers."

Shirin slid the sleeve of her dress back to show the wrist-screen. "Works like a tablet. The first file that pops up should be your cover, and then the details for the rest of the team. Read up, there will be a quiz. There's a ton of material to get through, and you've got a couple of hours at most before we'll be working the room trying to sniff out the source of the breach."

Leah poked at her wrist-screen, which pulled up a text file establishing her as Leah Summers, assistant to Freelance Attache Narissa Shirin. Summers was a country girl from Mars, graduated summa cum laude from Olympus Mons University and aced the Stellar Service Exams, now two months into her apprenticeship with Shirin.

Many of the other details were drawn from Leah's real life—parents' names, Han Chinese heritage, and so on.

Roman and King were the Head of Security and Pilot, respectively. Other files showed the team's last three visits over two years, the stories they'd stitched together, breaches they'd resolved. The reports were hyperlinked, with names and races and events linking over to other files. It was a whole story universe wiki, but for a story that was real, was all around her in its three-eyed, antennaed, spinning space-station glory.

"Turn it up," someone across the bar said, piercing her rabbit-holing fugue state.

Leah looked up to see a view-screen above the bar turned to a news feed. A Chinese woman in a sequined suit addressed the camera.

"Gentlepersons of Ahura-3, good evening. This week is expected to see a historic event as

Ambassador Kaylin Reed finalizes negotiations for an Interstellar Alliance, binding Earth with the Ethkar, Gaan, Enber, Xenei, Jenr, Nai, and Yai civilizations. This alliance is expected to create a huge surge in interstellar trade, as well as serving as a mutual defense pact in case of another Ra'Gar invasion.

"For the changes to traffic during the negotiations, we go now to Security Chief Gary Michael ..."

As the anchor continued her report, Roman emerged from the crowd, metal-toed boots clanking on the floor as the crowd parted for him, his presence making its own wake. Roman jumped right in, saying "Smart money says our breach has something to do with this. Shirin, you and Probie work the room here until the commander shows up. I'm going to get King and start working the fringes, see if we can't scare up some gossip."

And then, as quickly as he'd appeared, Roman was off, power-walking in a way that looked entirely badass and not at all like the dorky white people exercise regimen that it was.

"Do we usually get this much of a road sign?" Leah asked.

Shirin wobbled her hand. "Depends. We've gotten to the point where we trust our instincts in the field. When you think you've got the lead isolated, you work it until it's done." Shirin tapped her own sternum. "That instinct that told you you'd spotted Frank in the kitchen, that led you to dig with Maribel, that's what you trust here."

She continued. "Our team in particular has an incredibly high accuracy on breach identification. I'd like to think it's intuition, but King insists it's because of the frankly ridiculous amount of primarysource research he makes us do. It helps that everyone he recruits is already an expert in codeswitching from life experience. Easier to see something out of sorts when you're used to being on the outside looking in."

"Does it often go like this, boys' team, girls' team?" Leah asked as a blue woman with four arms set glasses of white liquid with ice cubes in front of them.

"What'll you have tonight, Ms. Shirin?"

"A Venusian Sunrise for me, and a Manhattan for my apprentice. Commander Bugayeva will be joining us presently, if you can make sure the hostess sends her our way."

"Of course, Ms. Shirin. Good to see you back."

Leah checked her wrist-screen. It showed 20:40, just twenty minutes from their appointment with the commander.

Shirin looped around to Leah's question. "We divide and conquer according to our skills."

"Anything I should know about this commander before she shows up?"

"She's proud, she's aggressively competent, and she would be much happier if Mallery were here in your place. She carries a bit of a torch. Chances are, it won't make things pleasant for you, unless you want to charm her yourself. Best bet is to sit back and listen. You'll get more to do when we learn where the breach is. This place is so big, I'll probably have to assign you to tasks on your own. Click through to the Interstellar Alliance briefing. I need you up to speed as soon as possible."

No job, not even stand-up, had put Leah's improv comedy training of "always say yes" to the test nearly as much as this one, and this was only her second mission.

Leah speed-read her way through the briefings about the Interstellar Alliance while Shirin tapped away on her own wrist-screen.

There were six principal civilizations involved in the proposed Alliance: The Terrans; the Ethkar, a race of warrior-priests with bumpy heads and pointy ears; the Gila-monster-elephant people, who were called the Gaan; as well as the Enber, the tall bearded race she'd seen earlier; the Jenr, the four-armed blue people; and a pair of races that had purple and pink skin, but otherwise looked like humans, called the Nai and Yai, who shared common origins.

The Nai (purple) were ruthlessly capitalistic, and the Yai (pink) had embraced communalism. The Nai lived on a planet, the Yai its moon, and only stopped fighting with one another when the Ra'Gar started nibbling at the edges of their overlapping territories.

"Wait, so no one actually knows what the Ra'Gar look like?" Leah asked as she swiped through the briefings.

"There are various reports. But they differ for every race. There's a "speculation and lore" tab on the Ra'Gar page you should be checking out. They're the Big Bad right now, the reason for the Interstellar Alliance. Ambassador's been banging this drum for years, but now people are scared enough to listen."

"What do you think the breach is? Someone sabotaging the Alliance?"

"That seems the most likely. Assassination attempt, kidnapping, blackmail, maybe even a staged attack on one allied civilization faked to look like it came from another. Or the threat could come from one of the would-be allies, a minority faction trying to throw a spanner into the works."

"Lots of options. How will we run them all down?"

"We won't. We're going to find out what's going on from Commander Bugayeva, or Roman and

King will squeeze it out of some low-grav lowlifes."

The server came by and delivered their drinks. Shirin's looked for all the world like a Tequila Sunrise, while her own was a blissfully familiar Manhattan, complete with maraschino cherry.

"Is this how missions usually go?" Leah asked.

"Often enough. I'd rather schmooze my way through the station than spend days crammed in a prop ship or gathering intel at the end of my fist."

"Schmoozing sounds like more my game." Leah raised her Manhattan for a toast.

Lots of toasting and drinking in this job. Mom would approve.

Leah took a sip of her brilliantly mixed drink and went back to the briefing. She devoured the material, happy for the years of improv practice and LARP experience. It was like diving into an ongoing game half a world away. The rough sketches were familiar, thanks to a lifetime of SF reading and viewing, it was just the particulars that were different. Names to learn, specific cultural biases to apply. Faction A hates Faction B because Reason 1, Faction B distrusts Faction C because Backstory.

And so on, and so on. Until Shirin said, "Eyes front, Probie."

Leah looked up to see a muscled bombshell in a black-and-silver uniform walk into the bar, a waterfall of hair thrown over one shoulder, wearing makeup that was both more excessive and more dynamic than hers or Shirin's put together.

"Game face," the older woman whispered.

Leah gulped.

* * *

Shirin slid out of the booth to stand and greet the commander. Bugayeva was one of her favorite onworld contacts—smart, sharp, if unforgiving of slights. She was a real intelligence operator, though her official position was Executive Officer.

"Oksana, it's been too long," Shirin said, throwing her arms open. The two hugged collegially, then Shirin turned and offered the woman a space in the booth. Leah slid out and extended a hand.

"My new apprentice, Leah Summers. Leah, I give you Commander Oksana Markovna Bugayeva,

Executive Officer of the Ahura-3."

"A pleasure, ma'am," Leah said. "I can honestly say I've never seen anything like the Ahura-3." Good, Shirin thought. Polite and concise.

The woman met Leah's handshake with firm strength. "Thank you, Ms. Summers. We're very proud of the old girl." The women resumed their spots in the booth, Commander Bugayeva sitting opposite the Genrenauts. "Nothing like her in the system. Some of the Plutocracy stations are larger, but nothing beats the Ahura for productivity and diplomacy."

"I've been bringing my assistant up to speed. How is everything going with the Alliance talks?"

"Speaking of which"—the commander raised a hand, and the Jenr server appeared as if conjured. "Dirty martini, two olives. And a Red Stripe back."

The server nodded and vanished as quickly as she'd come. Impressive. As a rule, the Jenr were light on their feet, but this woman was a step above.

Oksana spread out, her presence unfolding until she filled half of the booth. Shirin had seen Oksana stop a turf war between Gaan and Nbere, browbeating each of the leaders until they all put their weapons away and then spent a half hour cleaning up after themselves. She was The Impressive Woman to a T—cast in the mold of characters like Honor Harrington, Commander Janeway, and so on. Not as hands-on as an SF version of Strong Female Character™, but all the more formidable for her choice to command socially rather than physically.

"It'll get sorted out," Oksana said. "The Alliance will move forward or they won't. Get that group together and there's so much waffling you might as well call it a brunch party."

Commander Bugayeva waved the topic away. "I didn't come here to talk shop, no matter what you might have thought. Tell me what you've been doing with yourself. And how is Mallery?"

Shirin leaned back in her seat, gesturing with her drink like a practiced socialite. "She's a lunar moth, here and there and back again." Had to keep up appearances. If she let slip that Mallery was still in traction after her last mission, they'd never get anything out of the commander, the conversational thread would go too far out of her control.

The commander's face darkened, betraying more than Shirin imagined she meant to let on. "Well, please give her my best, and tell her to not be a stranger. I'm just an Ansible away, after all." Then the commander held her drink out in a pose for the question, "So what brings you to our humble little station?"

"The same old same old. I wanted to show my new apprentice the sights, and no diplomatic tour is complete without a visit to Ahura-3. Plus I figured I could pick up some work and top off the gossip tanks while I was here, what with the treaty signing and all."

"I don't think you'll have any difficulty getting nibbles. Everyone's scrambling to be in the right position when the Alliance is solidified or blows up in Reed and Laran Do-Ethar's faces. Do-Ethar is wound so tight on this she's likely to go off like a grenade of mysticism and metaphors." The commander leaned forward, her voice dropping. "And I'm pretty sure the Ethkar can actually do that with their battle-songs. You want work, show up on her doorstep and tell her I sent you and you'll be set."

"I've already beamed her a message. Just waiting to hear back."

* * *

Leah watched the poised women talk like it was a tennis match. But instead of a ball, they played innuendo and subtleties between them, body language and tone their forehand and backhand forms, questions and intimations their rackets. Back home, she'd be paying master class prices to study these women and their verbal fencing, friendly banter over deeper agendas, power plays back and forth from rough equals still jockeying for position. Bugayeva was a straight shooter, responded well to Shirin's polite but direct questioning.

"We'll want to talk with the Enber first. They're dealing with a miner's revolt on Greyen-7, and a trade deal with the Yai and Nai would help them settle things down. They'll be Reed's staunchest allies outside the Ethkar," the commander said, clearly offering an olive branch or trading a favor.

"And if the Enber can get the Nai on, the Yai won't be left out," Shirin said.

"And once both of them are on board, the writing's on the wall. You'll need to run rumor control about the Ra'Gar. Linnan's the gossipmonger there. Calm her down and the proceedings will be much more steady."

Shirin set her glass down and asked, "How is the ambassador holding up through all of this?"

Bugayeva flinched a bit, eyes looking slightly up as she responded. "Tired, but determined. The

Alliance will be the capstone of her career, and she will see it through."

Nope. Don't like it. Years of improv and reading the crowd at stand-up shows told her that something was fishy, and it sure as hell wasn't the food. Shirin and King had told her to trust her instincts.

Leah glanced sideways to Shirin, who shifted, eyes locked on the commander. Leah wished for telepathy, or another few months of working together to be able to read her senior colleague better.

Well, Bugayeva liked it straight, so Leah'd give it to her straight. Breaking silence, Leah said, "Sorry, but you're hiding something. Is this just about stability, trade traffic through Ahura-3, or is there something else? Who's driving the Alliance? Reed, Terran brass, what?"

Bugayeva smiled a predator's smile. "That's a bit direct. But I appreciate the ovaries." The commander took a long sip of her drink, then set it down on the table, making a too-loud clink. "But next time, do me the favor of getting to that answer without breaking your boss's flow. We were having a conversation between adults, and I don't need a knobby-nosed adolescent bumbling through to ask the question that might as well be spelled out in the constellations." Leah flinched as if hit. Daaamn. Harsh. Too harsh.

Commander Bugayeva gestured to the station. "This place is a complex system of interlocking parts. Millions of them. If I can get a few thousand of those parts to start using the same time signature, start working in direct relation to one another, it makes everything else smoother. Smoother operation means freeing up resources for other tasks, means a chance to take this station to the next level, start to think about things outside our system. And that, that will get back to Terran High Command. The Alliance is Reed's baby, but I'm happy to be its godmother. You read me?" "I read you," Leah said.

The commander downed the rest of her drink, then slid out of the booth. "I should get to bed. Duty rotations are accelerated with the Code Orange during the negotiations. Look me up before you go, preferably without Junior here."

She set her drink down, along with a circuit-chip the size of a quarter, then strode out of the bar.

"What just happened?" Leah asked once the woman was out of earshot.

"You made the right guess, but in the wrong way." Shirin took a long sip from her drink. "Next time, hold your questions for the end. But for now, get Roman on the line. We need to download this to them ASAP. I was hoping Oksana would tip us off to what's gone south, but it looks like she's passed that hot potato to the ambassador. Might be a plausible deniability thing." Not two hours on-station, and she'd already screwed up. Fantastic.

Chapter Three:
On the Job

After a half hour of trolling the bar for tidbits about the ambassador, Shirin's wrist-screen got a ping.

She called Leah back to their booth.

"Finally got a beam back from Laran Do-Ethar. We're off to meet her in the diplomatic wing."

Leah set down her drink, number two for the evening and thankfully not more. There'd been no side-eyes from Shirin or the commander when she didn't keep up with their cocktail-pounding, so she was still on this side of tipsy, probably good for meeting alien dignitaries.

"What do I need to know about Laran, then?"

"First, it's Lah-ran, not La-ran," Shirin said, the difference subtle enough that Leah uselessly narrowed her eyes trying to process it. "And second, expect bluntness and evasion in equal quantities. The Ethkar are one of the most culturally alien species in this story world, as far as humanity's concerned."

Shirin swiped a credit stick for the server, and then tossed the bags to Leah, who struggled to rearrange the world while Shirin made for the lift.

"Their value system works deeply off of personal conviction and mystic communion. It'll be like talking to a zealous recent convert," Shirin said, a wake forming ahead of her as she strode, one of those tricks of presence that some people (not Leah) could just make happen.

Leah watched the scenery and little moments playing out in the bazaar as best as she could while also keeping up with Shirin, both physically and verbally.

"The Ethkar don't take slights well. This time, we will want me to do all the talking, but I want you to study her as best as you can without staring too much. Laran is an easier read than some of her colleagues, she's a good Etkhar to meet first. And ultimately, she's on our side. Let's keep it that way."

Beeping told Leah that she had another message. Unfortunately, her wrist-screen was buried under twenty pounds of awkwardly bulky bags.

"Why don't we have roller bags?"

"They're considered gauche now. Thank god. If I never see another roller bag in my life it will be too soon." Shirin pressed a key in the elevator and the doors closed, leaving them on their own.

* * *

The diplomatic wing was anything but peaceful. Robed humans and aliens buzzed around like locusts, moths, or whatever other annoying, buzzing, flying things this science fictional world used to represent chaotic clouds of activity.

All of the races from the Bazaar were present, and more, though they had some things in common —the cost of their clothes. More robes here, but also sashes, coronets, and fancy hats and helmets, some more Upper Kingdom Egypt, some more Project Runway, and others that could have been straight out of the Thor movies.

Shirin wove through the crowds, coming and going with polite hellos and brief chats, translator earpieces feeding her the English equivalent to the clicks, warbles, and other alien tongues. One race —shorter gray-skinned aliens with smooth faces—communicated only in sign language, but it sure as hell wasn't American Sign Language, judging by the translations.

"Here's where my years of ground work pay off," Shirin whispered in the gap between two groups. "The Ethkar are none too trusting of humans, but Bugayeva has a lot of sway here. Let me take the lead and we'll worm our way into the story and start driving."

Leah spotted the Ethkar in a larger crowd in front of a door guarded by security in station blackand-silver. Her translator changed over everything at once, so she had two sets of cacophonous voices coming in. The ambassador was around five-six, but filled the space around her, her movements precise, powerful. And where aural confusion had Leah twitchy, Laran was all smiles. But none of that warmth touched her eyes. Was that an Ethkar thing, or was she just playing good diplomat? Another thing to watch.

"Great light, we bid thee welcome," Shirin said, hands straight out in some kind of special gesture.

"Bright visitor, you are welcome!" Laran answered, throwing her arms open. With this, warmth did reach her eyes. So that's a genuine reaction. Noted.

"Quickly, in here," the ambassador said, waving at the door, which irised open. "This is your apprentice, I assume?"

Shirin nodded, waving Leah into the suite.

And sweet it was. The front room was the size of a penthouse, but clearly lived in. One whole side of the suite was filled with books, but a ten-foot-long dining table dominated the other half, with hallways in back, presumably leading to personal chambers.

Another guard stood astride the hallway, her arms crossed.

"And for a moment, the mob will have to wait," Laran said. She extended a hand and squeezed Shirin's opposite shoulder. Shirin returned what Leah took to be an affectionate greeting. Or a secret handshake. Leah's mental RAM was working overtime, trying to contextualize everything going on. Just as long as she didn't have to actually speak the alien languages. She'd never gotten past "mellon" in Sindarin.

"Can I put these down somewhere?" Leah asked.

"Let's not waste thought on such banality," Laran said.

And that came out of nowhere, Leah thought. Got it. Culturally alien.

"Anywhere is fine," Shirin said.

Leah put the bags down as gingerly as she could. She shook out her hands, which had gone partially numb carrying the sack around for a half hour.

"Sit, and I will explain," Laran said, gesturing to the dining table.

"Explain what?" Shirin asked. Leah had only known the woman for a couple of weeks, but she could already tell when the woman was playing a bit. If Laran was going to break silence and read them in, then all the better.

Laran tapped through some commands on a panel by the door, then joined the Genrenauts at a pair of half-circular couches, surrounding a circular coffee table adorned by a three-tier board game that reminded Leah of Star Trek's Three-Dimensional chess, but with way weirder-looking pieces.

"Commander Bugayeva recommended your services, and her word carries great weight with me. I dare not use the local operators, as the walls have ears, so I put my trust in you. But that trust is as thin as a blade. Fall wrong, cross me, and you will be cut upon the razor." "We understand," Shirin said.

"Once we pass this juncture, your hearts are pledged to the service of the station." Shirin nodded. "So pledged are we." She looked to Leah.

Leah repeated Shirin's words, hoping that was the right thing to do. Laran nodded.

The ambassador took a breath. "Kaylin Reed has been kidnapped." Boom. There's the plot.

"I see," Shirin said. "How can we help?"

"Two blades will ward off doom and doubt. One must strike at darkness and cut through to truth, the other must deflect doubt and guard the light against twilight."

Shirin leaned to Leah. "Find out who did it, get her back, and keep the Alliance from falling apart in the meantime."

"Got it," Leah said.

The older woman gave a formal nod. "Such blades as we have are yours."

Laran pulled back a sleeve and tapped out commands on her wrist-screen. Hers was sleeker, more ergonomic, the screen curved to the shape of her arm, the bezel made of pearlescent coral or something that looked close enough.

"Then we begin with all haste."

Chapter Four:
Hands-On Information-Gathering

Roman tightened his grip on the Nbere rough, twisting his grip into the man's shirt.

"So you're sure that you don't know what merc groups came through the station, despite the fact that you say you can set me up with whatever crew I need. Seems like one of these things doesn't add up, doesn't it?"

King stood a meter to Roman's left, arms still crossed. "It's very strange. Seems like a proper fixer would know something like that. Unless he'd been paid to stay silent, and in that case, he's no good as a fixer to anyone else, since he'd become someone's lapdog, not a real Free Agent and rider of the fringe."

"Seems like," Roman said, his mouth just inches from the Nbere's elongated, whisker-filled ears. A part of him wanted to just rampage through the whole bar and interrogate the one guy left alive, but he'd play by this world's rules, and King's—less murder, more intimidation. "Now what are you, Do Mal? Are you a lapdog, or are you a rider?"

Do Mal's friend, a thick-set Yai, shuffled forward, but King headed him off, leaving Roman with the Nbere.

The Nbere's attenuated arms pinwheeled. The crowd around them had cleared out, no one interested in butting in. The Deep Dive was that kind of bar. You didn't come for the company, you came for the discretion. Which included leaving aggressive negotiations be, unless they involved personal friends. And it seemed like Roman and King were the closest this pair had to friends.

"So, maybe I did hear something," the Nbere said. "But I remember a lot better when my beard ain't yanking on my brainstem, you get me?"

Roman released some slack on the alien's beard, but kept his grip. "That jog your memory?"

"I'm jogging, I'm jogging!" the alien said. "I saw three, no, four crews come through over the last week. Three of 'em left today, one said they was staying around for another week, bleeding off credit before their next long run on the rim."

"And those three that left?" Roman asked, releasing some more pressure, letting the Nbere stand up to a stoop instead of a full crouch.

"There was the Dark Stars, the Widowmakers, and, which was it, Garro, Velocities?" "I think it was the Seventh Sons," the Yai said.

"The Seventh Sons it was! See, no hassle, no bother. So how about you let me go like a civilized ape."

"Ape?" King asked. Roman tightened his grip.

"Sorry, habit. Like a civilized and upstanding totally evolved Terran."

Roman let go, then turned to the bar, cupping hands in a low-tech megaphone. "Can I get some shots for my new friends?!"

* * *

Do Mal and Garro were, when not being threatened or browbeaten, rather friendly company. Roman realized he should have gone for the Yai first—he was far chattier than Do Mal.

"The Widowmakers like to gab, they does. Anyone with grease under their nails and a functioning set of ears, flesh or tech, can find out what they've been up to."

King leaned forward. "Especially when they have friends like you. What were the

Widowmakers talking about this time around?"

The Yai tipped back his third stout, belching. "Just some good honest smuggling. Heavy metals towing through the Gaan blockade."

Roman scoffed. "They're still blockading? I thought those lunks would have just swallowed their pride and accepted the tariffs by now."

"The Gaan are as likely to swallow their pride as I am to ask one to be my wife," the Nbere said. "Could you imagine that? Bearded lizard-babies thumping around making an abysmal racket with their trunks." He stomped his feet, wavering.

King extended a hand and steadied the drunkard. "And the Dark Stars? What's the word from them?"

Garro shook his head. "No, they don't talk. Uriah whips them if they gab outside the compact.

You gotta go direct to them to find anything out."

"Any Stars stick around more permanent-like?" Roman asked.

"Zoor retired from the Dark Stars last cycle, settled down with his Ethkar partner and opened a flower shop, if you'll believe it."

"Flowers?" King lurched forward, as if he'd just remembered something. "It's my anniversary! I need to get flowers, or my wife'll space me. Where's the shop?"

"Too far, friend. They set up on wheel three," Garro said, waving for another pint. "There's a half-dozen shops between here and there."

Roman kept on track while King worked the angles. "If we're going to find the right crew for our job, my client needs to know that we found only the very best."

"Zoor ain't the one to talk to, though. He can maybe get you an introduction, but not like I could. Me and Uriah are like this," Do Mal said, holding up a braid of his beard, wet with backwash from his beer.

"Soggy and matted?" Roman asked.

The Yai pounded the table, roaring. "A tongue on this one! How come I haven't met you in this hole before?"

"Just passing through, looking for work."

King watched the room, checking for prying eyes. The nearest table of drinkers had moved farther away, but that was more likely due to the Nbere's wild swings than anything they were saying.

Roman mimed drunkenly counting to three, mouthing the names of the crews. When he reached three, he asked, "And what's the other crew up to, Seventh Sons? What's their specialty?"

"Wetwork and banditry, son. You want someone bled or something stolen, you call the Seventh Sons. Bloody folk they are. Ain't no one a proper Seventh Son until they've been painted in the blood of a kill."

"That's right," the Yai said. "A clutch-mate of mine joined the Sons, vicious egg he was. He was going to meet me here, but they blasted out like a comet earlier today."

"He say why?"

"No, his beam just said he couldn't make it, that he'd be back in maybe a month."

"What a cutter!" Roman said. "I thought clutch-mates were supposed to stick together. Am I right?"

The Yai cheered at that, then again as the next round appeared.

Roman nodded to King. They'd have to keep tabs on this pair. They were leakier than the bathroom pipes in the men's room at HQ. Hopefully, Shirin and Leah were turning up good information on the higher-class side to go with their greaser gossip.

* * *

Laran led Shirin and Leah out, the three of them pushing their way through the sea of supplicants to the corner and around to another door. Two station security guards flanked the entrance. They nodded to Laran as she lifted her wrist-screened hand, which opened the door.

"Quickly, now."

Ambassador Reed's apartment was even bigger than Do-Ethar's, but this one was decorated with more familiar material—Terran art and artifacts, though alien affectations were still present— here a pearlescent vase with horizontal handles, there an incomprehensible musical instrument, and so on.

"Whispers have not yet reached the public, though the station staff knows," Laran said. "Without
Reed, the fragile Alliance will collapse."

"Shouldn't we be worrying about contaminating the scene?" Leah asked, indicating the room around them.

"The detectives have come and gone. Only the bedroom remains forbidden, for now."

Shirin slid into one of the floating chairs and patted the one next to her, which Leah took, holding back the lip curl of disdain that usually accompanied her response to being led around like a child. She was new to the job, not a toddler. "We received word six hours ago," Laran said, "when the guardian system returned after being struck down by a fell blow. They were silent as shadows, but they failed to disable the automated resets."

"The redundancies still on an alternating four-hour rotation?" The Ethkar nodded.

"Then the kidnapping had to have occurred between 1400 and 1600, judging by the camera data.
What does security say?" Shirin asked, leaning forward.

"Multiple assailants, all wearing working boots. All bipedal."

"So none of them were Gaan, though there might have been some Xenei as well," she said, listing off the possible races of the attackers.

"So it would seem. The shadows knew their prey, knew the terrain, there were no tracks anywhere else in the suite. They were well-informed, lucky, or—"

"They had her itinerary."

"Possible. The light of truth will scatter shadows, but dawn is yet hours away at best."

"What happens if Reed doesn't come back? Does the Alliance have a chance?"

Laran looked away, glancing back at the bedroom. "Without the sun, the system will spin out of control, the cosmos of consensus we've built will dissolve. A lesser alliance might be found between the Ethkar, Terrans, and some others. A dagger forged from the shattered steel that might have been a sword, but a dagger is of little use when hunting a Vren."

Leah hung "Vren" in her mental overhead-storage space, not sure if her cover would be expected to know. If she was, but went to her encyclopedia right away, Laran might twig to their deception. Instead, she did her best to sit still, not fidget, not ask follow-ups, and to generally ignore every inclination she had in the strange and marvelous place.

That part of the job she'd still have to get used to. But she wouldn't be new forever.

"When Laran's absence is revealed, the day's proceedings will begin to unravel almost

immediately. The day will devolve into distraction, deflection, and bribery to keep the ambassadors on-point. My team cannot preserve the nascent web alone. Tend to the web's more disagreeable nodes. As Ambassador Reed would say, we will 'plug holes with our fingers until the dam breaks.'"

Shirin nodded. "We're all yours. Just beam over the dossiers and any notes you have on who to speak to first, we can begin first thing in the morning." Shirin reached a hand out to Do-Ethar. "I know how long you and Reed have been working on this. We won't let it wash away like a sigil in the sand."

Laran stood. "It will be done."

"I have a colleague working this case with me," Shirin said. "He was once an investigator. I'm sure he'd want to take his own look at the room, if it would be permissible. I've gotten clearance from Commander Bugayeva."

"Bring him. May he shed light."

Laran and Shirin shared another gesture of greeting, which apparently doubled as "goodbye."

"Good luck, Shirin, and to your apprentice, too. Next time, perhaps you will allow her to speak.

I would be very interested to hear what she has to say."

And with that, Laran strode out, the door irising open and closed automatically. The Ethkar stepped into the waiting mob without hesitation, the commotion filling the room for just an instant before the door closed once more.

"Get on the line and beam the boys to tell them we're clear to scrub the bedroom. Then you can look up what Vren are."

"How do you do that?" Leah asked, hands thrown out to the side.

"Practice, newbie. Now let's get to it. King and Roman will be back from their slumming intel trip soon."

King and Roman arrived fifty minutes later, coming from the nearest wheel wing of the station.

Roman took video of the room while King sprayed an aerosol can around the room, stepping carefully in boots coated with plastic booties. Leah watched from the hallway. The spray stayed visible, didn't dissipate into the air. It just hung there, gray and passive.

Shirin sprayed the other side of the room, similarly tiptoeing in covered shoes. They'd have to empty two whole cans to cover a room this big. Luckily, that's what they'd brought. Not that the Quartermaster would be happy to see them return empty-handed. This stuff wasn't cheap, and the High Council wasn't made of money. Well, not endless amounts of money.

"These are versatile particles," King said, taking the expository role. "With stimulus from the wrist-screen, they'll react with various chemicals. Each spectrum covers a different type of search.

But they'll take a little while to change between types."

"So what will this tell us?" Leah asked. "Can we get genetic scans, find out what species the kidnappers were, what material their shoes were made of, Sci-Fi Sherlock stuff?"

"Basically. We're looking for as well-rounded a picture as we can get. I read the security report on the way over, and I'm not impressed."

"Why not?" Shirin asked.

"Station security has never impressed me here," King said. "Makes sense, since that allows the crimes to happen in the first place that move stories forward. But it doesn't make our jobs any easier."

"If this is normal, then why does it count as a breach?" Leah asked.

Finished with his scan, Roman stepped lightly out of the room to join Leah in the hall. "It's a breach because the forecasting team back home says it's a breach, and because our guts tell us it's a breach. Unless something else is going on and we're totally missing it."

"How likely is that?"

From in the room, King said, "More likely than I'm comfortable with. But bringing the ambassador back will stabilize this region, and that's better for this world's stability, regardless. And judging by the intel we got out of our chatty, drunk friends, my gut tells me we're on the right track." Roman pulled up a feed on his screen while the others worked.

Leah asked, "What are you looking at?"

The Genrenaut rotated his arm to show her. "News reports. Trying to sort out which of the local gangs kidnapped the ambassador. So far it looks like the Dark Sons are probably small potatoes for the job, but I can't count them out yet. How's forensics coming, King?"

"Just a second." King tapped his wrist-screen, and the versatile particles disappeared from sight. "We're coming up now. Leah, watch this."

* * *

Leah squinted as King tapped his wrist-screen trying to tell where the versatile particles had gone. King slipped the aerosol can into his belt, then pulled out a pair of sunglasses. "Up in three.

Cover your eyes."

Leah slipped the glasses on in a hurry, poking herself in the eye with the plastic earpiece before getting the shades into place just as King shut off the light, revealing …

Green. Tons of green, all in a cloud, catching the light that King's screen was putting out. But it was all undifferentiated, some kind of neutral.

King tapped his screen. "Infrared is first." The screen changed colors, and the particles in the air moved to the ground, showing footprints in cool blues and greens, as well as a residual shape on the bed.

"Signs of struggle here." He walked to a cluster of overlapping footprints. "I'd say … three attackers, and one more in the room."

"They threw her to the ground here, then she was pinned, probably hooded or gagged," Shirin added.

King and Shirin circled the heat signatures in opposite directions, leaving their own tracks on the floor.

The pair stopped, their eyes meeting for a moment. An understanding passed between them, and King tapped his screen. The color changed to blue, and some of particles pulled up off of the ground.

A group rushed to the doorframe and the door, spilling out into the hall behind her.

The lit particles settled on scratches and scuffs and shapes on the floor, as well as on the door, swung open into the room, and the door hinges.

"Door was kicked in, superficial scratches to the floor corroborates the struggle," King said.

"Now for the real lottery. Do we get any particulates, hair, saliva, or fibers?" Shirin asked, glancing up to Leah by way of indicating context.

The light changed to yellow, and the particles shifted again, some staying on the door, others moving to scatter along the floor like a dusting of snow.

Ew, yellow snow. Bad comparison, she thought. Like dust, she thought, reframing the sight.

Shirin looked to the door. "Residue on the door, that'll give us the boots."

"It's in the report," Roman said from the hallway. "Work boots, size twelve. Available a hundred different places on the station."

"We've got biological material all over the floor, but distribution looks like hair, dead skin. Did station security already take samples?"

"They're running them now. They usually take six hours on analysis, should be done before you bunk down," Roman said. "You?"

"King and I are going to head back to chase down more leads on the working class side."

Shirin turned to Leah. "And by chase down leads, they mean drink and fight until answers spill out of people's mouths along with teeth and blood."

Roman shrugged. "It works."

King said, "We tried a mission all-diplomacy style a few years back. Shirin called the shots.

And we almost let the killer get away."

Shirin raised a finger. "Objection. Extenuating circumstances. It was a brand new alien species. How was I supposed to know it was preying on the fears and hunger of the poor people living in air ducts?"

"And that," Roman said, "is why we cover all of our bases."

"It just happens that covering bases in the rougher parts of the station tends to be fairly hands-on and high risk."

Leah asked, "So a little brutalization and casual violence to see you through?"

Roman bristled. "Nothing casual about it. But we do what we must to the story back on-track,

Probie."

"I'm good, I'm good. Just, be careful, and don't whack anyone you don't have to."

Shirin shook her head. "The local security does enough of that as is."

King took charge. "We're done here. Shirin, you and Leah start first thing tomorrow. You'll have the materials analysis, and we'll send updates from the fringe if we get any leads."

"Okay, newbie, you're with me." Shirin walked toward the door, smiling with her whole body. "Let's go find ourselves an overpriced diplomatic district hotel and charge it to HQ."

* * *

Their quarters were literally a quarter of the size of the ambassador's suite, but Leah's own room was still as large as her entire apartment.

The door opened into a common room, couches and comfy seats, a wall-sized screen, and spacefaux-homey details like digital paintings of nebulae and a selection of plant life. Each painting was more science fictional than the last—from something that looked like carnivorous orchids to fiberoptic grass and a bush that had leaves made out of flattened rocks.

That was, of course, until Shirin started rearranging everything, enlisting Leah for extra muscle.

"We're going to be taking meetings here, which means doing a bit of no-cost redecorating."

Shirin repositioned the furniture to create a two-on-one chair-to-couch space, and moved another couch across the room to just inside the door. She pointed at the chair by the door, designating it as the "waiting area," and the couch-and-chairs section as the "meeting room." "Why not make them wait outside?" Leah asked.

"Some we will, others we'll want to see who we're talking to and for those people to see who we're about to talk to." Shirin tossed a pillow across the room, turning toward her bedroom. "A lot of diplomacy is managing public image, the interplay of information, who knows what, and who knows who else knows what they know." She paused as she went into the bedroom, then returned with a trio of throw pillows.

Shirin placed one pillow on the couch, then eyed the other two, one white-

and-blue, the other green-and-yellow-green. She tossed the white-and-blue into the same corner, and then set the other one in the lap of one of the chairs. "If we're going to help Laran triage this Alliance until the ambassador's back, there's a lot of confidence-building to be done, and we can save ourselves trouble by using tricks like this to offload some of the gossip workload onto the diplomats themselves."

"Through the power of interior design?"

"Design shapes the narrative. Setting is as important a part of a story as character and action. Constrain setting, and you constrain and shape character. Now let's strip your bed and get this couch a cover."

Chapter Five:
Friends in Low (Gravity) Places

The fiber and DNA tests came back just before midnight. There were more common fibers from working clothes, two sets of DNA not in the system, one human, one Nai, and an industrial cleaner that was used mostly on long-haul rim ships, used to create a lasting seal and protection against asteroids.

And so Roman and King found themselves in a seedy bar in the roughest level of the station's third ring.

Here, the station's organized crime world flourished, operating discretely and effectively enough that they had an understanding with station security.

Walking among toughs and mercs, people living on the fringes, Roman felt dangerously at home.

Fitting in here would be all too easy. But he'd have King to pull him out if he got too deep.

Which meant that everyone in the bar—literally everyone—noticed when the two of them walked in not wearing colors of any of the station gangs.

The bar was an old industrial facility, assembly lines turned into long bar rows, with wandering servers and a central bar at the far wall. The bar was maybe two hundred feet wide, and Roman guessed that there were around a hundred gangers and hangers-on present, just as the night was getting rowdy.

Roman claimed the first open space, which wasn't actually open. It was a stool beside a cluster of four gangers, all wearing red bandannas, then nodded at a server to get her attention. The server denied eye contact and kept going.

"Seats'r taken, rando," said a husky voice. An Ethkar woman with cut ears turned from the circle and loomed over him and King.

"Sorry, looked empty to me." Roman stood, hands up and back. "Not looking for trouble."

"Then why'd you come to a Dead Dwarf bar?" asked one of the Ethkar's companions, a short man with a torso like a keg.

"We're just looking for a quiet drink," King said. "We can go somewhere else." "Dawn smiles upon the prudent," the Ethkar said.

Roman read the scene. Too many to seduce all at once, even for him, and if they threw down with a brawl, they'd subsequently be thrown out.

Strike at their pride, instead. Roman adjusted his hat, preparing to go. "Damn. Guess that

Widowmaker was right, this place is shit."

The wide man bristled, blocking Roman's exit from the bar. "Widowmaker said what?"

"Met a Widowmaker. Ex-Widowmaker, I guess. He said this place was shit, but he was an ass, so I thought maybe it was something to see, he was keeping it to himself."

"Real contrary guy, you know," King said. "Like those Junai—they're always saying the opposite of what they mean."

"Dwarves nest, fuck the rest," the Ethkar said.

"If this is a colors bar, why'd the bouncer even let me in?" Roman asked.

"We'll take your money, don't mean we want you here," the wide man said. "Someone's gotta pay for these drinks."

Roman puffed himself up, eyes locked on the wide man. King held him back. "Cool it, Ro. We'll take our money and our action somewhere else." "Action?" asked the Ethkar.

"Yeah, action," said King. "Good action. Alliance is doomed, right? That makes a lot of opportunities for someone smart. I heard the Dwarves were smart. Fleecing people without offering service, that's just debris. We'll find someone else for the job."

The wide man dialed the aggression down a tick, then waved the server over. "What kind of job?"

"Big job went down on-station. You know about it, right?" King asked.

"Course we do," the wide man said. He didn't. Roman knew that flavor of puffing up, the need to be in on the joke.

"That was a choice grab," Roman said. "We find who did it, we've got some work for them." "Dwarves have many hands and more eyes, willing for the right price," the Etkhar said.

Basically, they could have done the job, or could do one like it.

A server stepped up, a small man with gray skin. The wide ganger took the beer off his platter.

"What'll you have?" the ganger asked Roman and King.

"Royal Deep, Sol back," Roman answered. "And a FUBAR for my friend." The server slunk away.

"So what's the word? You know about the job or not?"

"We know about the missing ambassador. Ain't nothing happens on Ahura-3 that doesn't make it to the Dwarves," the wide man said.

"'Cause it seemed like an outside job. My snitch says Security pulled DNA off the job, but they didn't get no matches," King said.

The gangers nodded. Anyone who'd been in organized crime on the station for this long would have been printed, their DNA taken for record in case they did something truly heinous, something bad enough that station security couldn't look the other way.

"We know some merc companies, maybe the type that could have done it. Some real deep voiders, you know."

"So out with it, then." King followed up his request with a chuckle, softening the demand.

"A stiff drink loosens lips," the Ethkar said.

And so they drank. This time, it only took an hour and three rounds to get the Ethkar and her friends to finger the Dark Stars for the job.

* * *

With the culprits identified, it was time for a trip to wheel three to talk to Zoor, the retired mercturned-florist and his Ethkar paramour.

Roman and King cleaned up for the visit, planning to lead with Good Tough instead of Bad Tough.

There were seventeen florist shops in wheel three. Only twelve were owned by humans or Ethkar, and of those, two had gone out of business but hadn't lost their station registry.

Which meant that Roman and King spent four hours making the rounds, crossing florist shops off their list, smelling of gardenias, fanar, gerry rasps, and an abundance of roses when they walked into the Twin Bloom.

The storefront was small, just a ten-by-ten room of displays and sample product, a glasscovered wall of more flowers, and a reinforced glass cash register, blocked off from the rest of the store by a reinforced door.

A smaller Ethkar woman stood at the cash register as they walked in.

The Ethkar greeted them, voice coming through on a PA. "The road swells to meet you, friend." "Greetings," Roman said. "I'm looking to have a few arrangements made for our friends.

They're receiving guests of all races, so it's going to be a pretty big job. Can you accommodate?" "My husband has the fastest hands you've ever seen work a pair of shears."

A man walked up from the back, entering the glass display area. He was around six feet, and despite his inoffensive white collared shirt and khaki pants, he still looked like a tough. His hair was short, only mostly covering the tattoos that extended up onto his scalp.

"That's great. She prepared a list." King held up his wrist-screen. "Can I beam it to you?" The woman wobbled her head in an Ethkar affirmative. "LAN handshake coming up now." King tapped at his screen while Roman studied the ex-merc.

"Can you have these over to the diplomatic wing by 1800?"

The man squinted at something above his head, presumably a screen. "That'll be tight," the man said through the PA. "But yeah, we can do it. Except for the whistala—we're fresh out." "I'm getting more in two days, if that will suffice," the Ethkar said.

"No problem. I can get whistala somewhere else. Delivery by 1800 for the rest?" The Ethkar assented again.

"Beautiful," King said.

Roman made a small gesture toward the man's tattoo. "Friend, I don't mean to dredge up old business, but your skin tells me you used to run with the Dark Stars." "Can't prove it," Zoor said, not facing the pair.

"It's just, word on the spin says that the ambassador is missing, and that the Dark Stars did the deed. Damn shame. Way we figure, if the Alliance had gone through, maybe that'd make it easier for Terrans and Ethkar to live together," Roman said, looking from the man to the Ethkar woman.

"That the case?" Zoor said, hands clipping and arranging flowers, assured but not quite unconscious in his confidence. He hadn't been at it too long. There was a difference between dexterous competence and the ease of thousands of hours of practice.

"I know someone people who could get the ambassador back, maybe salvage the Alliance. You've got a nice shop here, a nice life. Just as long as nothing happens to the fragile peace between the Terrans and the Ethkar. If you know anything about where the Stars might have taken her, you could do a lot of good, Zoor."

The man turned, brows narrowed, fear touching his eyes.

"You can leave now. We don't need your business," the Ethkar woman said.

"But you have our business, and we need your help," King said. "The Terran council has established a generous finder's fee for anyone with information about the ambassador's whereabouts," he lied.

"Shadows and vapor," the Ethkar said, calling his bluff. The station staff were keeping as tight a lid on the news as they could. Good for morale, maybe not as good for their immediate plans.

"Because they don't want to be flooded with void facts brought to them by opportunists. Our friends, the ones hosting the diplomats, they heard about the finder's fee. Five thousand credits.

That'd go pretty far out here on the wheel, I think."

The Ethkar hardened, pointing to the door. "Out."

Roman stepped forward. His kind recognized their own. So he'd tell Zoor what he'd want someone to tell him. "We need your help, Zoor. You got out of the Dark Stars for a reason. I bet you wanted peace. Stability. A life that didn't involve looking over your shoulder, didn't count on balancing favors and lackeys and alliances, always waiting for the other boot to drop." "Get out," Zoor said, shaken.

Out of the corner of his eye, Roman saw King give him the nod. So instead of leaving, he pushed it, riding that edge between conversation and combat.

"Sure, I'll leave. If you can look me in the eye and tell me that you didn't leave so you could find a way to make things grow, to create and preserve life instead of taking it by force. Getting out of that life isn't hiding. It's choosing to push against the death instead of riding the tide of blood. You want peace? You want a real chance at a life worth living? Kaylin Reed can bring both of those to the

station and beyond, but not with a bolt through her brain. Where would they take her?" The man's knuckles were white, fists clenched.

"I'm calling security," the woman said.

Roman and Zoor shared another moment that dilated into infinity. Zoor's body language showed anger, resentment, shame, fear, and finally hope. The ex-merc slumped, setting his shears down beside an arrangement. "No, Fela. They're right."

Roman smiled. Not as eloquent as the speech King had given him back in the wasteland, when he was on the end of his rope, but it was close enough.

Zoor continued. "There's a hideout in the rings of Aeros, just one jump from here. Anytime we bugged out of Ahura-3, we stopped there first. It's big enough to fortify, but out of the way of commercial traffic."

"How do we find it once we're in the rings?" Roman asked.

The man tapped his wrist screen. "The coordinates. But you keep me out of this, you hear? I don't want any of this getting back to the Stars. You're right, I got out for safety, for me and Fela. And I expect that finder's fee in our account the minute you get the stuck-up noble back.

"Your arrangements will be there by 1800. Now get out of here before I regret this and decide to piss in your flowers."

"Thank you, Zoor," Roman said. "It's not exaggerating to say that you may have saved the galaxy from war."

Zoor's tone changed. It was softer, uncertain. "Where do you come from?"

"The hell next door. Same shit, different quadrant."

"So what's it like. To really leave it all behind?"

"When I find out, I'll let you know." They walked out, and once they'd turned the corner, Roman leaned against the wall, took a moment.

King raised a hand, set it gently on Roman's shoulder. "Are you okay?" Pull it together, he told himself. We're not done here.

Roman stood. "I'm fine. Wasn't sure how that one would go."

King squeezed Roman's shoulder. "You did good. We're on the right track."

"Get Shirin on the line. We're going to need to call in some favors to get a ship. With guns. And a cloaking field."

* * *

Shirin woke Leah at 0505 the next day, already decked out in her diplomatic robes, a mug of coffee wafting liquid wakefulness as she walked into the newbie's room. Shirin had been up since 0430.

One advantage of aging was she found she could get by on less and less sleep, especially if it

was undisturbed by children jumping on her bed or the cat deciding that 3 a.m. was the time to flip out and run laps in the bedroom hall.

"Is privacy not a thing on Ahura-3?" Leah croaked as she emerged from her room.

"Not when the new kid on the block is late for her first day of diplomatic duty. Shower's all yours, we need to be out of here and over to Laran's offices at 0530."

"Give me that coffee and we're square," Leah said, shaky hand pointing at the mug.

"It's yours if you can get to the kitchen." Shirin turned and left the room.

Leah hopped to, padding into the kitchen fully dressed at 0523 as Shirin watched the clock, rewarding the newbie with the first pour from the fresh pot.

The pair made the short walk from their apartments to Laran's residence one level down, finding a small mob of robed and fineried aliens waiting in the hallway, talking among themselves in a dozen languages, gesturing with mandibles, multiplicitous arms, and so on. The mood was nervous, a bit impatient, but not panicked. The morning news feeds showed rumors of the ambassador's health taking a turn for the worse, but the update from Do-Ethar dispelled those with Ethkar flair:

"Rumors of the ambassador's health fading are but the contrails of cowards adrift without her guiding hand."

Shirin waved her wrist-screen at the door. They moved past the sound of several complaints and into Do-Ethar's quarters.

In the foyer, standing arms crossed in front of her, today's robes in red and yellow, stood the ambassador.

"One minute early, as usual. Bright morning. May the light of truth guide us, and the wings of triumph lift us up so that we might pierce the guard of doubt and dissent to achieve unity."

Leah leaned over to Shirin, "She's like a Lao Tzu MBA course."

Shirin held back the laugh that was building at the back of her throat. Even half-awake, the girl had a tongue on her. But it would be up to her to make sure the girl's tongue didn't get them spaced or tank the Alliance. This world had such a gigantic learning curve, with dozens of cultures and histories, alien technologies, and more. Shirin had gotten three months to study up on the world before she'd had to go on her first mission here. But a lot had changed in the Genrenauts' world, and they had to play the hand they were dealt.

Or find a way to sneak the ace out of their sleeve.

"Good day, honored friend," Shirin said. "We are at your disposal. How may we help?"

The ambassador wasted no time putting them to work. There were fifty appointments scheduled for the day, and Laran could attend to twenty-four at most.

Shirin and the Ethkar divided the appointments. Which meant that Shirin and Leah were assigned to the guest room and given half of the queue, told to stall and dissemble, but most of all, to not let anyone leave angry.

Their first appointment was a Yai merchant representative, the agent for a conglomerate that stood to make a great deal of money if the Alliance went through.

Shirin wore her diplomacy face, placating but firm. "I assure you, Lord Reeve, the ambassador will be well in time to conclude negotiations and preside over the signing. In the meantime, pulling your contract would be disastrous for all involved. Merely the time rewriting contracts would cost your guild hundreds of thousands of credits."

The Reeve moved her hands, weaving wrists and fingers through the air like a dance, then speaking, as if she'd thought the matter through with movement, then responded.

"But I have hundreds of ships across the system ready to begin trade, and without an alliance in place, I cannot guarantee their safety. With that many ships exposed, my pilots will revolt!"

"What routes will they be taking where they did not already have protections and agreements in place?" Shirin asked.

The Yai's hands waved back and forth, then oscillated up and down like a conductor.

"I ... I don't have that information in front of me. But this is an unprecedented commitment from my guild, and one that cannot be made on faith alone!"

"But any alliance is about faith, is it not?" Shirin asked. "If I recall my Endera-Na, it says, 'Two hands clasped fear not daggers, though they can see the hilts.'"

"Well put, Ms. Shirin. But while faith may shield against doubt, it does precious little against lasercannon fire."

"The ambassador is receiving the best care the station can afford. Give her forty-eight hours. By your accounts, most of the shipments will not be ready to load out until then, anyway."

The Yai thought a bit more, wringing her hands, then nodded. "So it will be. Please pass on my best wishes to the ambassador for her recovery.

"But of course. Thank you for your time, Honored Reeve."

The Yai stood, and the women traded bows, Shirin's a shade deeper.

Once the woman was out of the room, Shirin slumped back in her chair. "One down, twenty-five to go. Who's up next?"

"Ugn Fa, assistant to the Nbere ambassador. It looks like he's complaining that his boss is being seated next to the Gaan. He says they stink."

"This one will at least be easy."

"Why's that?"

"I don't give a crap about this complaint. He just wants to be heard." "Got it," Leah said, heading to the door to let the Nbere in.

Chapter Six:
Rescue Op

It had taken five hours, three calls, and a generous transfer of cash, but by 1600, Roman and King were strapping in to a Fader-7 HX with an after-market pulse cannon and a thoroughly illegal Ethkar cloaking system.

Commander Bugayeva pulled rank and got them jumped ahead in the flight schedule, cleared for departure at 1610.

Roman loaded the coordinates they'd gotten from Zoor, setting the computer's Navigation system to the task of plotting a course that would bring them to the hideout with minimal exposure and maximum speed.

"How certain of this lead are you?" King asked as they squared the gear away.

"It fits the region's tale types, and presents a good, rounded story—we go and fight on the rescue op while Shirin and Leah cover. This type of world pulls on me differently than n the rest of you.

We'll each have a couple of twists along the way, but my gut tells me we're on the right path." King nodded. "Then we're on the right path. Are we forgetting anything?"

Roman tapped a few more controls, then left the pilot's seat to grab one more crate from the docking area, dragging it inside.

"Almost. This here's our doorknocker." Roman patted the crate. Gently.

"That's not what I think it is," King said.

"Unless you outright say what you think it is, we have plausible deniability. You can call me reckless once we've gotten in and secured the ambassador."

"I'll call you reckless any damn time I want to. But if it works, it works."

"It'll work," Roman said. "I've had to lean into the Action Hero archetype, so let's use it. Keep me from going overboard, and let's sew this up quick."

King pinched the bridge of his nose, clearly not comfortable with the risks Roman was suggesting they take. "Finish up the start sequence. Let's get this disaster on the road."

* * *

Ten hours in, Leah wanted to throttle someone. Many someones. Gray people, green people, brainsin-jars people, and four-armed contrarian people.

Every meeting, Leah had to digest another lump of background information, political history, cultural context, species dimorphism, and beyond.

Possibly worse than the information overload were the dinners. So. Many. Dinners.

At 1500, they'd moved from Laran's apartment to a nearby restaurant, where they'd taken five back-to-back dinner meetings, each running around 45 minutes.

"Sharing a meal is a powerful social adhesive, not just for humans," Shirin had said when their partners for dinner number three walked into the restaurant.

Now, hustling to another restaurant for dinner number six, Leah's stomach sloshed like she was an overfull water cooler. Thankfully, one of the dinners had been nothing but tea (Nai), and another — the one with the Xenei guildmaster — just involved little fish being dumped into the guildmaster's fishbowl, whereupon the brain opened up a fleshy maw and gobbled the fish up.

Leah'd excused herself to the restroom, but managed to keep her three dinners down.

Tolerance, Leah, she told herself. Chances were, the Xenei would think human eating was just as disgusting.

"Can I just have water at the next one?" Leah asked, as plaintive as she could manage while keeping her food down.

"Of course not," Shirin said. "This next meeting is with a Gaan prelate, and he notices everything."

"Can we at least explain that this is our sixth dinner, and that when I say I really couldn't have another appetizer, it's not politeness, but physiological reality?"

"No."

"Also, how are you keeping up without hurling? Aren't metabolisms supposed to slow down when you get older?"

Leah was a half step behind Shirin, but she could see the older woman's smile move her hair. "I didn't eat anything for breakfast."

"You told me I needed to get my strength!"

Shirin turned the corner and stopped. "Yes, and you did. I've learned to portion out my strength. Plus, I dealt with this a lot growing up. You should see the dinner parties I went to as a teen. Five hours, twelve courses, and pots of tea so caffeinated you could practically see through time."

Leah caught up to Shirin and saw the new restaurant, which looked like a wallow. Actually, it was a wallow. A wallow with flattened stone disks beside muddy pools, Gaan servers carrying platters on their noses.

"Really?" Leah asked.

"Hey, at least here we get to recline. It'll be good for your digestion."

"But the mud! And none of that looks like food?"

"Keep your voice down. We don't want to offend. The prelate is there, third from the left. And don't comment on his size."

When in Rome, Leah recited to herself, putting on her polite smile as she followed Shirin through the less-muddy parts of the artificial wallow, making their way to the prelate, already on his side, covered in mud.

"Prelate!" Shirin said, throwing her arms open wide. "It's been too long."

The prelate snorted in response, trunk rising and waving in a more-than-passable imitation of a diplomatic wave.

It's just another improv sketch, she told herself, trying to stay cool as she sat down (in mud) to converse at length with a talking, nude, and self-bathing elephant-lizard-person.

Like you do.

* * *

The artificial floor only looked muddy. So while she was still lying prone beside a mud pit, the prelate half in the pit and still bathing himself, she was not herself asked to bathe herself or sit in dampness.

Luckily, Shirin was even more at home, charging ahead conversationally.

"But Prelate, certainly you can't be thinking of rescinding your endorsement. You and I both know what happened to the last prelate who stepped back on a treaty."

The prelate lifted a strip of barely cooked meat with his trunk and dropped it into his mouth. He spoke while chewing (which her wrist-screen said was a mark of trust and respect and should not be met with grimaces, despite teeth).

"Prelate Mevk's failures are his own, his time is his own. The broken promise here is Reed's, not mine. I will support a healthy alliance, but the Terran has let a simple illness waylay her from this historic agreement. How are we to partner with a people so delicate? How can I entrust Gaan lives with such fragile Terrans ?"

The Gaan were very proud of their toughness, they valorized it. Her dossier included a halfdozen Gaan sagas and when she'd glossed over the summaries, it seemed like they were all about persevering, stoicism, and the like.

She jumped in, tired of holding her tongue. "But doesn't that mean that Terrans know all too well the value of life? We live on a razor's edge, and so we empathize, we come together and gather friends so that if we fall, someone is there to pick us up. And we don't forget those that help us."

The Gaan snorted a huffing exhale. Leah couldn't tell if it was dismissive or something else.

"Well said, child."

Shirin jumped right in and took the conversational reins.

"Terrans' mortality is one of the major reasons we build alliances. We seek out those who complement our skills. We have many trade hubs, but a marketplace without goods is a crossroads without carts."

The Gaan chuffed again. Which meant he was still angry, or these were positive expressions.

"Of course, but surely you know this illness is just a cover for the ambassador's kidnapping. An illness is one thing, but if the crown jewel of the Terran's trade hubs is not secure, how am I to entrust my people to you?"

Boom goes the dynamite.

Leah snuck a look to Shirin, and that bomb shook even her still-as-deep-waters poker face.

There was no way they could have kept it all under wraps, but if the prelate knew, then word would be getting around. This wouldn't be the last they'd hear about it. And things would deteriorate quickly.

Leah wished she had enough room in her stomach for a drink.

To her massive credit, Shirin recovered. "And isn't it an indication of the potential of the Alliance that someone would go to the audacious lengths of kidnapping a Terran ambassador off a Terran station? That kind of boldness comes only from great fear."

This snort was clearly a dismissive one. "Or from great confidence. To know your target so weak that you can strike without reprisal."

"Without reprisal?" Shirin asked, waving a dismissive hand. "By initial reports, at least three of the attackers were killed in the attempt. And I have heard from Commander Bugayeva herself that she has her top agents hunting down the kidnappers even now. They will be brought to justice, and the Alliance sealed. When the story of this mighty Alliance is sung, do you wish to be the reluctant prelate without vision who was won over after his doubts, or the resolute leader of a proud people whose resolve never wavered?"

"Ever the optimist, Shirin. The galaxy could use more with your vision and your boundless hope. But my responsibilities are deep, and wading through them is far less comfortable than this fine wallow."

The prelate gestured to the pool around him with his trunk. "For now, I will stand by. The Xenei have said they will give the Terrans two days. That is enough time for your agents to retrieve the ambassador and show that they can protect their own people."

Two days to find the ambassador, get her out of the mercs' hands, and back onto the base. Leah hadn't gotten to the information about space travel yet, didn't know how fast ships could really move if they needed to get somewhere yesterday. She tapped out a note on her wrist-screen, another question to ask later. Her list was up to thirty-eight such questions. She'd have to do triage since their schedule showed no signs of letting up.

Shirin kept up niceties for a few minutes more, then the senior Genrenaut excused the pair and they departed, leaving the prelate to his luxurious wallow.

"Now off to a dinner party. They'll just have appetizers there, you'll be safe."

"Thank God," Leah said. "Two days? Is that viable? And what if the word gets out to everyone else? Will we be facing riots and shit?"

"Two days will have to be enough time. It has to be. The mercs only had about an eighteen-hour lead on Roman and King, and our informant said that the hideout was only a twelve-hour burn away.

The timing should line up."

"Which dinner party is this, again? There were like three."

"We start with the Xenei, then the shipwright's guild, and then we round the day out at Laran's small soiree for Alliance die-hards. At least we get to end the day with a friendly crowd."

"Remind me to pick up a stim habit before we come here next time. This is insane. My feet are going to fall off any minute."

"At least we're not making you wear heels," Shirin said.

Just a block's walk away (or what she mapped in her head as a block, since the station had branching hallways like no one's business, every hundred feet or so), they came across a thick crowd, all waiting in line for something. "Is this the party?"

"Yes. Oonar Th'Nal is a major information broker, and his parties are paid events—there's nowhere better to dig up information or trade favors. Today's was just announced three hours ago.

Oonar never misses an opportunity to capitalize on a crisis."

The crowd included several other Xenei, hovering anxiously on their classic UFO-shaped discs. Representatives of every race were there as well, the same Cantina-ready mix she'd almost actually started getting used to. There were more Xenei than she'd seen together elsewhere, and fewer of the pink race. A quick check of her wrist-screen reminded her that those were in fact the Nai, the hippiecommunist ones.

"Do I actually get to talk this time?" Leah asked.

"Of course. I'll need to go off and work my magic, and there's too much going on for us to not split up. Don't engage in any conversations where you feel you're out of your depth, and don't be afraid to lean into your character."

The pair rounded a corner and found the end of the line, more than two hundred persons deep.

Leah restrained a sigh. "How long is this going to take?"

"As long as it takes to introduce everyone ahead of us."

"At least I don't have to wear a ridiculously frilly dress."

"I thought you were more the Captain Tightpants type, anyway." "True story."

Chapter Seven:
Graveyard Pit Stop

Six hours into their flight—almost halfway to the coordinates Zoor had provided—Roman picked something up on his radar. They were flying around a patch of debris from a centuries-old battle, the mass of a wrecked behemoth carrier ship forming a gravitic biome. The ship was Ra'Gar, left over from the last invasion.

The shattered ship looked like an imploded grenade, all yellow metallic sheets and sharp edges. Around it floated wrecks of Terran, Nbere, and other ships, ranging from fighters close to the size of their own ship to mid-level cruisers, nearly half as big as the Ra'Gar behemoth. The last alliance had only brought together three civilizations, but from the reports of new Ra'Gar movements, it'd take a hell of a lot more to stop them this time.

"Radar ping, two hundred thousand klicks out. Looks fighter-sized, but it could just be hot debris or an asteroid." His adrenaline kicked in, ramping up his reaction times and making him giddy. He kept a lid on the giddy, as it unnerved his teammates. Even King.

King roused from the rack in the back room and made his way up to back into the copilot seat.

He blinked the sleep from his eyes and studied the readouts. "Could be, but let's not take that chance. How long will the cloak on this last?"

"Ten minutes, with a ten-hour recharge."

"What's the sensor range on commercial fighters?" King asked.

Roman sorted through his mental inventory of systems available. Every member of the team had their genre specialties, and this region was one of his. He could look up the information on the wristscreens, but if all he did was rely on the database, there was no reason to be a specialist.

"One hundred and fifty-thousand klicks at best. Unless they've got a satellite booster nearby, a sentry or the like."

"That seems likely. Come in under the sensor shadow of the debris so we can get a better sensor read. We don't want to break hearts before the final hand."

"As long as we can make it to the final hand. There's room for any number of traps in this debris field, boss. It's a great scavenger's hunting grounds."

King clapped Roman on the shoulder. "Then it's good that our best pilot's at the helm, isn't it?" "You're too kind."

"I have my moments."

"You could stand to be a little more kind and back me up on the sensor suite. Start on thermal and radioactive. Most of the traps big enough to cripple a ship run hot enough to give off a signature."

King flipped some switches, and several screens blinked off for Roman, popping up in the copilot seat.

Roman leaned into the controls, banking close around a wrecked Terran transport, lazily spinning head over stern in place, the same spin that had been born of its doom. Void-crawlers would have picked any biological matter clean long ago, leaving only the metallic corpses.

"Sensor suite extended to maximum," King said. "The ship is locked in a consistent patrol route, orbiting this location." King highlighted a point in space and swiped the display back over to Roman's screen. Free space on his screen zoomed in to show a sensor readout of the ship, its route, and a stable hull of something at the center.

"Any bounce-back?" Roman asked.

"Nothing yet. Coming up on jamming range."

"Shut them down before they see us. If the scout can rabbit and inform the rest of the Dark Stars, we'll be up to our ears in lead the moment we set foot on that station. But get us within range before the scout twigs and we'll be fine," Roman said, cutting main thrust and pushing the attitude adjusters, turning up to slope over a cluster of shattered fighters, keeping a solid chunk of the Ra'Gar ship between them and the solo fighter.

Roman turned and twisted and snaked his way through the ship graveyard until they were within sensor range, but shielded by the still-hot cores of a trio of frigates.

"I'll jam, you scan," King said. Their fingers danced across the consoles, lights blinking, alarms and acknowledgments beeping as they worked. Roman ran a deeper scan on the ship, pulling IFF information as well as ship specs.

It was a retrofitted freighter flying under Nbere tags, though he doubted that a Nbere was at the helm. The Nbere were happy to sell ship tags to anyone who could pay, so the void was full of "Nbere" ships. They were the Panama of space, and all an Nbere tag told you was the owner wanted anonymity. The IFF, however, was clearly spoofed, a weak cover proclaiming them as an Nbere messenger easily penetrated to reveal a Dark Stars IFF signal, running the same ping address as Zoor had indicated.

"It's a Dark Star, alright. Flimsy-as-hell IFF. They need a better tech."

"I think Zoor was their tech," King chuckled. "Jam is up, but I think they'll notice her right quick.

They've been spamming radar pulses like rats on an endorphin lever."

"Closing distance. Keep the jam up, and hold on to something."

Roman grabbed the stick again and floored the thrusters, punching out of the field of dead freighters and looping down out of the debris to make a hard half-Immelman and come at the fighter as it broke from its route and made for the jump node.

Roman pushed the thrusters to cut off the merc ship's escape.

"Weapons systems spooling up," he said, vocalizing the actions as he tapped through the menu to activate the lasercannon. Years of running with heavily armed packs and working around vehicular weaponry had prepped him to think nothing of saying aloud every single thing he did. There was a long while where he had to keep from announcing, "Brushing teeth," and "Taking a dump," which was fair, since several of his pack-mates took to doing just so, sharing every little bit of their lives with the squad out of a clownish perversion of group cohesion. Hellish circumstances made for weird traditions.

"They're rabbiting. Impressive speed for a ship that size. They'll lose us in …" King ran the numbers. "Five minutes. Let's hope that cannon we picked up can pick them off in time." "Ready to fire in five. Take the wheel?" Roman asked.

"Assuming Navigation control," King said, grabbing his control stick.

"Releasing control," Roman answered, wrapping both hands around the firing stick, , exaggerated curves around the hand and into the base, three buttons on top, wired to activate up to three different weapon systems. Roman had only bothered with the one, and hoped it'd have the range to pick off the merc before they could get to a jump point.

"Locking on," Roman said, holding the ship in his sights. As the targeting circles clicked into place, the ship started banking and juking, responding to the incipient lock.

"They're evading. Pursuit pattern beta," King said, matching their movements to the merc's.

King was rated for this class of ship, but Roman was the one with the real stick time. But when you were the top gun and the top pilot ...

"Sorry, boss, this isn't going to work. Resuming navigation. I'll have to dogfight them. Keep on

the jammer, in case they've got a copilot and try to get sneaky."

"Roger," King said, releasing the controls, slipping back into drumming on the console to work the sensor suite.

With piloting and gunnery back under his control, Roman leaned back into his seat and found his happy place. He'd logged more flight time than any active North American Genrenaut, though not nearly as much in the field as he'd prefer. The simulators couldn't quite match the way the G-forces work, never gave the full suite of randomness that a real sortie always brought.

Roman opened fire, without a lock, hoping to shoot into the mercs' evasive maneuvers.

But their pilot was no slouch, either. The merc ship banked and twisted and looped through and around his laser-fire. Roman followed a deep sloping turn, letting up on the stick and hoping for another lock, the merc ship flipped stern over prow and floored its jets, coming right for them.

"Bold," Roman said, hauling the stick to one side and firing the attitude thrusters, moving them off to the side as the merc ship unleashed a barrage through the empty space where they had just been.

"Come on, then. Show us that all of that simulator time was worth letting you slack on your readings," King taunted.

"Yes, your Majesty." Roman pushed forward, flying at a relative forty-degree incline to the merc ship, then tapped the attitude thrusters just so, a quick burst to turn and then stop, leaving him cutting through space at the same angle, but with their nose (and cannon) pointed down.

These ships were single-chair fighters, no cargo capacity. The ambassador would be held on a transport or freighter.

Which meant he didn't have to worry about fragging them.

Roman squinted, leaning forward and waiting for Just.

The right.

Moment.

He squeezed the trigger, and the pulse cannon spat out a tight trio. The merc ship tried to bank, but caught two of the blasts along the undercarriage. The ship went up like a firework, a genre concession given the fact that there wasn't enough of anything explosive in the ships to detonate.

"How's that for justification?" Roman said, righting the ship and looping around to confirm the kill and grab salvage.

"That'll do. Now, let's see if their IFF is intact …"

* * *

Leah waggled her head in her best aping of the Jenr manner. "But of course, your honor!"

The crowd roared. And while her crowd was a mere three people—all junior diplomats and attachés like her—it was the most welcome and acknowledged she'd felt since touching down on Ahura-3.

When in doubt, go with what you know.

It hadn't taken long to slot this dimension's races and cultures into existing material—everyone had stereotypes about everyone else, and most of the time, they didn't vary that much.

The Yai thought the Nai were lazy, the Nai thought the Yai were callous and greedy. Most people thought the Gaan were a little slow, the Nbere ambassadors were super-standoffish but had their secret proclivities, and only the Gaan didn't think the Xenei were unnerving.

Her colleagues, a Nai, a Gaan, and a Jenr, chuckled again, but softer, probably remembering themselves. Gut-busting laughter was apparently Just Not Done, even at cocktail parties that were, as far as she could tell, all about gossip.

Darei, the Nai, leaned in to the other women and said in a low voice, "Don't tell anyone I said so, but the Yai do that, too. But when they do it, they use both hands!"

That got more laughter, which Leah answered. Darei was the talker, which meant Leah didn't have to hold up the conversation by herself, which would be just about guaranteed to reveal the spaceship-sized gaps in her knowledge.

"We do not have such problems, but then again, just one trunk," said Haaja, the Gaan, gesturing with her prehensile trunk. Haaja, like the prelate, used her trunk to gesture, grip food, and to shake hands. It was all Leah could do to not flash back to YouTube videos of elephants rollicking on the beach.

On top of being dangerously amusing, Haaja was loose-lipped. "You just had dinner with the prelate, did you not?" Haaja asked.

"If by 'had dinner,' you mean tried not to even look at food, then yes," Leah said. "It was my sixth dinner meeting, and if I'd had one more bite, I swear I'd have exploded."

Ufa, the Jenr, crossed her lower arms. "We had the same. Every race with their own dinner times and customs. I wish the translators we use could let us all agree on one way to eat." "It's a wonder all of us diplomats aren't as round as a beach ball," Leah said.

"Beach ball?" Darei asked.

"Oh, you don't have beach balls?" Leah said, forgetting her mission more than a little bit. She set her drink on the railing to the stairs she and the junior diplomats had taken as their perch and held her arms open wide. "It's a plastic inflated ball this big, and you use it to play games on the beach."

"That would be very large for a playing piece," Haaja said.

"Do you have different colors to indicate the castes for Uga?"

"I've never played Uga on the beach, so I couldn't tell you. But as a kid, I mainly just kicked it in the water and splashed around, screaming with joy."

For lack of a specific agenda, Leah was happy to just hang out and shoot the shit with the three women. And she figured that having the ear of assistants to a vice-prelate, an ambassador, and a gray speaker would be useful over the next couple of days as diplomatic push came to shove.

Leah picked Shirin out of the crowd, then noticed the woman was heading right toward her.

And she looked pissed.

"Sorry friends, business calls," Leah said, picking up her drink again. She shook, hugged, and waggle-nodded to her new space-friends, then matched step with Shirin as she made a beeline for the door.

"What's up?"

"Emergency. Bhean, the Nbere ambassador, just blew up at Laran and said he's leaving the station to head home. We need to intercept him so that Laran can follow up and talk him down."

"And do we know where he is?"

"Somewhere between the Nbere sector and the VIP dock."

"So how do you delay an angry Nbere ambassador?"

"Very carefully." The pair turned into the hallway and headed for the nearest lift.

"Wait, did you say his name was Bhean?"

"That's right," Shirin said, her voice sounding uncertain.

"I know that one!" Leah rewound her memory to the conversation with her fellow junior diplomats. "He likes dancing boys. Jenr dancing boys."

Shirin stopped, and looked Leah dead on. "Where did you hear this?"

"From one of the junior attachés. She said that her boss arranged for some special kind of dancing boys to join them at a negotiation a while back. The guy was a total ass, except with those ...

she called them something."

"Verene?"

"That's it."

Shirin pulled Leah in and kissed her on the cheek, once again assuming the role of classy aunt. "You've earned your gold star for this mission, newbie. We've got some calls to make."

* * *

After a short jaunt out into space with the ship's EVA suit, Roman returned and sat in the copilot's seat, working on the IFF box while King kept watch as the autopilot continued them on their course for the Dark Star base.

The thing was well and properly slagged. He knew this dimension's tech, but that didn't mean he was a miracle worker.

"Three hours out. How's it coming?"

"It's not. The circuit board is half-melted, and I've got maybe a one-in-three chance of being able to strip the IFF without it breaking entirely."

"Any chance of just hooking it up as is?"

"This kind of IFF has to be slotted. Makes it harder to trick." "So that's a no."

Roman flipped the box around and eyed it from the other direction, holding a penlight on the connections between the board and the IFF transponder.

"Pretty much. I'll try to pry it out, but the problem is, we could slot it in and patch the Dark Star signal over our own, but if the transponder is slagged, we won't know until the mercs open fire on us or set off whatever traps they've got."

"So we assume it won't work, then celebrate if it does."

"Pretty much," Roman said, setting the box on his lap and reaching for the flat-head screwdriver.

Tongue peeking out of his mouth, Roman fiddled, pushed, and pulled, popping the IFF transponder out of the circuit board. He set the board aside and leaned over to pop open the control console.

"Keep an eye on our course. These small freighters can lose autopilot when someone's monkeying around with the transponders."

"That's not ominous, no sir," King said from the pilot's seat.

"I could just toss this thing out the airlock and declare that entire EVA a waste."

"You still get to log it on your chart."

"Almost a complete waste, then." Roman shone the light into a mess of cords. Even though they had fancy super-Bluetooth and wireless wearable computers, the innards of the ships on this dimension were a huge tangled hassle.

Just one of a hundred things about the dimension that didn't make sense, thanks to the uneven conceptualization of the genre world. Hi-tech, but with inconsistencies galore. Not unlike home. But where this region had hi-tech, he had "whatever you could cobble together from whatever you could salvage."

"Ready with the stick. Splicing transponder now." Roman reached into the morass, working by touch. He found an open space on a circuit board, then held the position as he twisted to the side, resting on his hip, and brought the hand with the transponder in to find the slot. There was no way he could get any light in there, so he worked by touch, rotating the piece and slotting it in. He heard the soft click, then leaned out and shone the light on it.

"Looks good," Roman said. Any problems?"

"Two hours, fifty-seven minutes. Nicely done."

"Save the celebratory shot until we blow by their security."

"Will do. Want the wheel back?"

"Need to shake out my hands. Why don't you pull your weight for a little while?"

"Remind me to never let you take lead on another mission unless I can help it."

"I forgot to remind you the last time you asked, so don't hold your breath. I'm going to take a nap."

Roman headed aft, rearranging his duffel into a pillow. "Yell if something breaks, okay?"

Chapter Eight:
Hide and Go Zap!

Just under three hours later, their ship reached the rings containing the Dark Star's station.

The coordinates placed the base in the middle of the ring, giving them natural cover and concealment from casual sensor sweeps and pursuit.

But with Zoor's coordinates, they practically had an invitation.

The yellow-orange planet overwhelmed their viewscreen, rimmed by a planetary ring. Seen from a distance, it looked like a rocky beach at the edge of a spherical sand castle.

Roman, back in the pilot's seat after his power-nap, eased the ship in through some outliers of the ring, knocked off-course somewhere along the line, but not out of the planet's orbit.

"Keep that sensor suite working. I need to know as soon as they see us. There'll be more than one ship this time, I guarantee."

Several minutes later, as Roman flew just above the plane of the ring, the sensors chirped positive contact.

King read the screen. "Three contacts, each around fifty thousand klicks from the base. All the same configuration as our last friend."

"Three? I can do three," Roman said, pushing the throttle a bit higher. Especially if the IFF worked.

"They're holding formation for now."

"Even if the IFF fails, they'll likely stay together, let me come to them. They'll know the rings better than I do. But we've got a few surprises of our own. Activating stealth package." Roman tapped through the menus, and their ship disappeared from all conventional sensors. "The outfitter said the cloak should hold for ten minutes. So I'm betting that means we'll get maybe five." "Sounds about right. You bought this from a Nai?" King asked.

"Yep."

"Five minutes it is. And we are four minutes, thirty seconds from the base's coordinates."

Roman held his trajectory, using a soft touch on the controls to limit their heat signature, only small bursts from the maneuvering thrusters.

As they came up on the first ship, its orbit bringing it within laser range, Roman said, "Taking the opening shot. See if you can jam the other two while we're at it."

King worked the controls, then made a constrained growl of frustration. "The rings here are going to make that a lot harder than around the ship graveyard."

"Do what you can. Laser spooling up."

Here we go. Roman moved one hand from the wheel to the firing stick. As soon as he started locking on, the ship would know. He led the shot, focused on their arc of movement, and shot without a lock. It was like hip-firing a sniper-rifle at a hundred yards. There were maybe three Genrenauts worldwide who could make the shot.

Roman was one of them.

The shot arced after the ship once it'd already turned its focus away, and snuck up on it, shearing off a wing. The ship went into a spiral and crashed into a nearby asteroid in the ring.

"One down. Now to see if we can pick up the other two in the confusion."

"They're transmitting an SOS back to base. Jamming is doing bugger-all. They know we're here."

"Copy that. Coming up on the second ship."

Roman started to line up his next shot. The angle on this one was no good for a manual shot, however; the deflection was too high. He'd need a lock, or he'd need to be much closer.

And so he waited as the ships cut through the space that separated them, his trigger finger waiting, whole body settling into the ship, the controls, the anticipation.

The second merc fighter broke right and started coming around at a different angle.

Right toward them.

"Stealth package is down," King said.

Roman gave a gallows grin. "That's the problem with pessimism. Even when I'm right, I still hate the result."

"At least it dropped now and not when you've just flown yourself into their crosshairs."

Roman banked and wove, moving into the ring to take cover as well. Now the fight would get truly interesting, the proximity of the asteroids limiting their speed and maneuvering. Moments like this were what he was born for.

"That's the spirit. Keep an eye on the other one for me, okay?"

"Third ship is at ten o'clock, thirty thousand klicks out."

And so they went into cat-and-mouse mode. Roman cut in and out of the ring, trying to throw off the mercenaries as he closed the distance. But the mercs played their home-field advantage, using hiding places and the cover from moonlets to throw him off.

He caught the second ship banking around an asteroid, trying to flank the Genrenauts, and sheared the merc ship in half with his lasercannon.

With one down, the merc ship vanished off of their sensors, finding a choice hiding spot somewhere else.

So Roman made for the merc base, weaving around and through the asteroid, the shattered portions of the planet that had been broken off but never truly lost to the yellow-orange body that loomed large above them all.

As they came around a large asteroid, time slowed as Roman saw the third merc ship, perfectly positioned to watch the corner. The mercs launched a cluster of missiles directly into their path. That same time dilation gave Roman the edge he needed to pound the attitude thrusters, giving them a burst of movement "up."

The twenty missiles passed beneath them, detonating an asteroid to their aft. But Roman wasn't able to re-fire the opposite thrusters in time to avoid slamming the top of the ship into another asteroid. The whole ship shook, making the never-fun sound of folding metal.

"Dammit," Roman said, banking to follow. He spat laser fire after the merc, but they got behind cover. Roman pushed out of the ring, settling the ship with a view back to the asteroids.

"What's the damage?" he asked.

"Moderate structural damage to the top of the ship, including the hatch. The next time we open the ship up might be the last, unless we can make some spot repairs. And the sensor suite is damaged. No more jamming, even if the ring wasn't in the way. Other systems are nominal. Though we won't be able to take another collision like that."

"What's our position relative to the base?"

"Two hundred thousand klicks out, with the last ship pinging somewhere in between." "I'm going to try to make a break for the base, flush the third one out of hiding." "Roger that," King said, working the sensors.

Roman raced along the underside of the planetary ring, chewing up the empty space, until they were within a minute's journey of the base.

And there was the third ship, poking out of the ring to get a sensor ping. The ship disappeared back into the ring, a spider beckoning a fly to come into its web.

Rather than that, Roman opened fire on the asteroids around the third merc ship.

The detonations and ricocheting from the laser fire started a chain reaction, ripples moving throughout that portion of the ring. The standard movements and positions of the asteroids spoiled, the home field advantage would be all but gone.

Roman pushed the ship forward, moving into the chaos.

"You are aware that this is a terrible idea, yes?" King said. "This will be a more chaotic killing ground than anything on our simulations."

"Then I'll be right at home," Roman said, leaning into his nature as a being of the Action genre. This region drew enough from that tradition that his narrative weight bent the universe to his will.

Sometimes.

And playing those odds was part of the entry fee. Roman scanned the field of vision, calculating the vectors, the future collisions, the rebounds, keeping the projected position of the merc base in mind.

And he threw their ship into the morass, once again becoming the hunter.

The third ship spooked, or got cocky, showing itself in a field cleared out by Roman's pool break maneuver.

Roman opened fire, and then kept on, spewing bursts and filling the void between them with death. The merc took a sharp dive to clear the field of fire.

As expected.

Roman hit two attitude thrusters at once, flipping the ship almost end-over-end.

"Warn me when you do that!" King said, one arm braced on the side of the ship. Out of the corner of his eye, he saw the senior Genrenaut looking a bit green around the gills.

"Sorry, boss." Roman took the firing stick again, narrowed in, and squeezed off another triplet.

And hit.

The cannon fire shredded the ship, leaving them alone with the disturbed planetary ring and waiting mercenary base, where he had no doubt the rest of the Dark Stars were armed to the teeth.

"Plotting a course to the mercenary base. You want to start pulling out the guns?" "As long as you don't pull another one of those Star Fury flips, we'll be fine." "Aye-aye," Roman said, saluting as King unbuckled and headed astern.

* * *

Shirin gave Leah the rundown on Verene en-route to catch the ambassador.

"The Verene are Jenr pleasure-dancers, trained the same way our geisha or courtesans were. Smart, inventive, and practically irresistible. In reality, more Jenr dynasties have been ruled by the concubines than the regents."

"Let's hear it for Verene," Leah said as the party packed into a transport tube.

"We've got to get Bhean to break down and indulge, first, and this one's all you—your plan, your execution. Just run it the way your new friend told you."

Given the fact that her friend had only said that the Verene were present and "attentive" during the negotiations, that left her feeling a bit out an airlock with a thin lifeline, but this was the job. Leah faded back to join the Verene.

The quartet of Jenr dancers chatted companionably, wearing sheer shoulder throws, their gray loincloths, slippers, shoulder capelets, and nothing else. Each one of them was a four-armed Adonis, sculpted abs, powerful arms and shoulders.

"Hey guys, thanks for coming on such short notice. We've got to keep Bhean on the ship, or the Insterstellar Alliance falls apart. I'm going to be the lure, so I need you to watch me and then act when you see your opportunity. Shirin tells me you're pros, so impress me. This isn't just about a paycheck, we're talking interstellar peace and all that good stuff."

The Verene nodded. One, who in boy-band shorthand she couldn't help but describe as the Bad Boy, said, "We've had assignations like this many a time, Terran. The labor guild stands to gain a huge amount of business with this alliance. We will follow your lead."

Leah winked at the dancers and walked ahead to Shirin. "I'm going over the top. You bring me back down if it looks like I'm going too far. Ready to be loud and a bit obnoxious?"

"Lead on, Probie."

* * *

Leah and Shirin caught the Nbere ambassador just as he was about to board his ship, retinue in tow. Shirin had paid off the station crew to delay the embarkation, which gave them time to pull into line behind them.

"Is the heating over-clocked in this sector, or is it just me?" Leah asked Shirin, her voice raised for the ambassador's benefit.

"Don't tell me this is your first time on a Pleasure Cruise," Shirin said, playing in to the bit.

"I've had private dances, but there's just so many muscles," she said, fanning herself.

The Nbere turned again to watch them and their retinue.

"What is the delay?" asked one of Nbere's retinue, leaning out of line to see the station staff talking among themselves, as if confused or conflicted about some point of order.

"If we have to wait much longer, I'll be tempted to just take them back to my quarters and have our own cruise," Leah said.

Shirin feigned scandal. "How could we?"

"What? They're paid for, and they're very eager." Leah put her hand on the bicep of the lower left arm of one of the Jenr. "This one auditioned for the job. He's very … limber."

"I do say, woman," the Nbere huffed. "Do you need to flaunt them in public so?"

The ambassador doth protest waaaay too much. The giant's face was flushed, his voice shaky.

He was a powder keg ready for a light. And in this case, the light was sexy four-armed blue boys.

"I'm terribly sorry, Ambassador," Leah said. "It's just, this delay is so frustrating, and with these fine specimens here, I feel like Tantalus. You know our story of Tantalus?"

The Nbere ambassador moved to the back of his party, putting him within arms' reach of the

Verene. "Of course. I'm well-versed in all Terran mythology."

"Then you must see what I mean. To have these kings among Jenr right. Here. At my fingertips, and to be held back by propriety?"

"I mean, well, this is …" The ambassador was well and properly flustered. Now they just needed to allay his fears while fanning his desire.

Leah felt a tall presence approach. And, cue the Boy Band.

"You sound so stressed, Lord Ambassador? We are here, and we are most. Definitely. Willing."

The leader of the troupe joined the ruse, leaning into Bhean and brushing one hand across the Nbere's beard.

The four of them knew exactly what they were doing. The Verene were members of the station's labor guild, which stood to gain a huge amount of standing and jurisdiction if the Alliance was sealed.

Ambassador Bhean melted into the Jenr's touch, then turned to his own attaché.

"Chane, delay my flight. This travesty extends to the Terrans' management of the station, and I won't be made to wait for my own ship. They can call on us when they've sorted out their idiocy."

Bhean extended a massive hand to Leah. "Now, madam attachée, I would ask to impose upon your hospitality while we find better things to do during this most egregious delay."

"I would never call a chance to partake of the finer things in life an imposition, Ambassador. My apartment is this way. I'm sure that these fine specimens can help us unwind."

Bhean and the Jenr went ahead, the ambassador's retinue hustling to keep pace. Shirin and Leah dropped back. Shirin offered a not-at-all subtle fist bump.

"Hook, line, and sinker," she said.

"Those guys know what they're doing," Leah said, pulling on her collar.

"Got to you, did they?"

"The downside of throwing yourself into a role."

"I'm sure." Shirin gave a knowing smile. The two women moved to the front, leading the party to their quarters in the diplomatic quarter through back channels that allowed for … discretion.

But these Hail Mary saves were expensive. If the boys weren't back when the deadlines they argued and bargained, wheeled and dealed for started to pop, all bets were off.

* * *

It seemed like the Dark Stars spent all of their money on fighters. The Genrenauts' ship approached the merc base unmolested, the gray-and-silver building standing out from the yellow-orange of the moonlet it rested on.

"Get that docking airlock open for me, kindly?" Roman asked, easing the ship in, bleeding throttle until he saw the way was open.

"About that," King said. "When we took the hit to the sensor suite, that's one of the functions that went down. We're not going to be able to just knock and get inside." Roman cracked his neck, adjusting and stretching in his seat.

"Then it looks like you'll get to fire up the torch and cut us a way in. Moving up for hard seal."

"Acknowledge close for hard seal. Readying docking tube." King worked the controls to extend the ship's docking tube. Their ship could create a seal on a flat surface, good for salvage operations where the docking mechanism or airlocks in derelict ships—or in this case, unfriendly hideouts— were not functional or not responsive.

Roman eased the ship in, keeping an eye out for laser turrets, proximity bombs, or anything else.

But instead, he pulled the ship up and nailed a hard seal on the first try.

"Piloting is a lot easier when no one is shooting at you." Roman grinned. "Not as much fun, though. Hard seal confirmed." He set all of the systems to standby, then diverted engines to sensors and climbed out of his chair.

King had the acetylene torch in hand, face-shield down. "Ready torch. Unless you'd rather." "Wouldn't dare dream of denying you the fun."

The docking tube reached out from the undercarriage of their ship, showing the hull of the stillclosed base door, worn steel probably twelve inches thick.

"Roger that. Torch going live," King said.

Roman turned away from the torch, pawing through his jacket until he found his welding goggles, which looked like classic swimming goggles, complete with plastic bands, but with blacked-out lenses.

He turned and watched the senior Genrenaut start to cut a yard-wide circle in the base's front door.

King worked methodically, neither rushed nor laggardly, completing the circular cut.

"'Ware the door," King said, letting the cuts cool for a few seconds. He reached to the center of the circle formed by the cut, then pushed with one arm, keeping his center of balance behind the cut. It wouldn't do to open the door and then fall right in behind it. Without a proper welcome, the airlock was probably depressurized or gravity-free.

The door slid and popped out the other side. A split-second later, it went 'thud' on the ground inside the base.

"Gravity normal," King said.

"Excellent. EVA firefights are a pain in the …"

"Yep. You going to retrieve that dangerous ordnance or what?"

Roman headed aft and unlocked the box full of explosives. It held a rocket launcher, three RPGs, as well as a handful of standard grenades and an assortment of station-grade firearms, high-caliber enough to take out humanoids, but not so high end that they'd punch through the Doppel-eisen steel hull of the base.

While Roman rechecked and recleared the guns, King pulled out the personal armor. The pair armored up, then strapped on the personal weapons, the rifles and hallway sweepers slung over them. It was enough firepower to clear forty mercs, though Roman hoped they'd only have to face half that many, and not at once. The Dark Stars weren't military, had never been military. With a good leader, they might be able to work five or so at once, but otherwise, they'd be solo gunslingers looking to pick a fight. But they were still looking at 10:1 odds in total.

Roman and King had been through easily fifty firefights together over the years, and could work as smoothly together as Roman had ever operated with a pack-mate back home. And King had another twenty years of experience on top.

But all of that just added up to make what they were about to do possible, but not anything resembling easy.

They didn't know how many mercs were inside, how they were armed, or where the ambassador was. They'd have to take the place room by room, and with only two of them, they had very little margin for error. Even tac vests were only good for so much protection in the field. This region of the Science Fiction world didn't have personal shields, so their super-kevlar was as good as it got.

Roman took the rocket launcher for himself and floated the munitions box down the tube toward the base.

"Start with the flares?" Roman asked as they hovered in the tube.

King leaned over the hole and tossed a pair of red flares into the base, establishing their new "down."

"Youth before wisdom."

"Bullet shield before senior operative, you mean."

"More like don't ever make the black guy go first on a story world," King countered.

"Roger that," Roman said, jumping into the base.

The flares illuminated a wide, open hangar, one drape-covered ship in the corner. The only other exit was a door in the far left corner, red lights above the closed door.

"Hangar is clear."

Roman continued to scan the hangar as he walked forward. He flipped on the under-slung light on his MP5, red-filtered light banishing shadows as he swept side to side. He held the RPG launcher over his left shoulder.

King thudded into the hangar behind him.

"You going to bring these RPGs, or just swing that thing around like a big metallic rod of compensation?"

"I'll have you know this thing makes a totally inappropriate but terrifying melee weapon."

"Save the sass for the mercs."

The room clear, King handed down the box of ordnance. Roman pushed the box along the floor with his steel-toed boot, the box making ear-assaulting metal-on-metal screech.

"Too cheap for the stealth package, then?"

"These come last. And they're not exactly sneaky weapons. But just you wait. Twenty bucks says these come in handy."

King countered with "Fifty bucks says they almost get us killed."

"You're no fun. Coming up on the door. Ready to breach?"

"Ready."

"Breaching."

Roman threw open the door and was met by the sound of gunfire.

"Here we go!" Roman said, and opened fire into the hallway.

Chapter Nine:
Knock Knock

Roman and King moved slow and steady. Rushing would just get one of them a bullet somewhere vital.

Instead, they moved room to room. Roman took point, grenades and flares preceding him.

He finally got to use the RPG to break open a hard-sealed bulkhead after working the console proved unresponsive. When the bulkhead blew, a flurry of gunfire came through the hole, sending Roman and King back to their firing positions.

In the subsequent report, he would fervently deny any claims by King that he had a "shit-eating grin" on his face.

Roman lobbed a stun grenade through the mangled bulkhead. He covered his ears as the grenade's concussive blast filled the hallway, then leapt into the fray with the launcher, swinging it around like a thick fighting stick. He clotheslined two dazed mercs and then spun the launcher around to jab it at the third's gut, doubling over and allowing Roman to deliver the KO with a snapping front kick.

He double-checked to make sure all three were out for the count, then whistled the all-clear.

King chided him. "You are completely nuts. This isn't your home world where you can toss weapons around like they're unbreakable . On this world …"

Roman shushed his boss, which was doubtless a bad idea, but necessary. "Don't say that. Doubt will make you right. We're in an action story, and Science Fiction is as much a setting as a genre. I'm the hero. My powder doesn't get wet, I've always got a bullet left in the chamber, and when I use improvised weapons, they don't break. Got it?"

King nodded. "You're the hero, hero."

He was playing fast and loose with the genre conventions, true. But there was a reason he'd picked up the rules of Science Fiction so quickly. Every genre had points of continuity, parallels with others. And on the world where he came from, he'd been able to use and abuse weapons more ridiculously than treating a rocket launcher like a baseball bat, and they always came through in the end.

Roman inspected the launcher, grinning as he found no dents or breaks. Still got it, he thought.

"When are we going to tell Leah where I come from?" Roman asked.

"Whenever you want. It's your story to tell."

"Not particularly relevant yet, is it?" "No, but it will be."

"Oh, I know. Just not very fond of only ever being known as That Action World Freak Who Didn't Die When He Was Supposed to."

"Mallery would hand you your ass on a silver platter if she heard you calling yourself a freak." Roman stopped for a moment, memories flowing in, steadying him.

"Remember what we're here for, why you do this. And then let's take that Hero luck and get moving," King said, head-nodding at the open hall.

The explosively opened hall had three doors, all arrayed on the right side. They were marked unhelpfully as 1, 2, and 3.

Roman brought the launcher and the explosives to the outside lip of the hatch, then joined King. He pointed to the doors. "There's no other way deeper into the base, so …"

"Looks like it's Let's Make a Deal time," King said.

They started with Door #1. King pulled the door back and Roman leaned around the corner to scan the room.

Door #1 led to a ready room, with four mercs, all in cover, overturned card tables and chairs giving them cover. Roman threw himself back to avoid the gunfire, which peppered the far wall in the hallway. King shoved the door closed.

"Next one?" King asked. They tried Door #2, and gunfire opened even before Roman got his head around to peek. He dropped to the floor for cover as King closed the door.

"Third time's the charm, right?" Roman said, squaring up with Door #3.

Actually, third time was usually something weird. But again, voicing doubt could make it real.

King opened the door, leaving Roman to do the quick-pop to scan the room.

Kids. The room was full of kids. And their parents. It was a nursery. Children and parents from a half-dozen races. All unarmed, up and fleeing for the back door.

And screaming.

"Gun! Gun! He's got a gun!"

Shit. Roman pulled the door closed. Something weird, indeed. Of course the mercs would have their families here if it was a base of operations. Just grateful that he hadn't just tossed a grenade in for good measure after seeing the first two doors.

King chuckled. "So, Door #1?"

* * *

Seven mercs and a few reloads later, they reached another hard-sealed door.

"I can head back and get the torch," King said, leading.

"Nope. I'm going to end the fight in one move." With a manic grin, Roman dropped his last flare in front of the sealed bulkhead, then moved back, and back, and back some more, until he stood a good fifty feet away, back through the hallway, the last room they'd cleared, and beyond into the hallway before that.

He had a clear shot all the way to the bulkhead.

"I see. You're really keen on getting your money's worth on this hardware."

"Old salvager habits. Use what you can find or barter or someone will take it from you."

"I'm liable to deny the request next time just so I don't have to see that disturbing smile on your face."

Roman loaded the second-to-last rocket in the launcher, tapped a command on his wrist-screen, then took position so that King was clear of the blowback. He used the flare to sight the shot, holding his breath as he locked everything into place.

"Blowback area clear," he said by rote, then "Fire in the hole!"

The launcher drowned the hallway in sound, and the grenade arced through the hall, the room, and the second hallway, hitting dead-on. The hallway became a fireball, which roared back into the empty room, then receded.

Roman lowered the launcher and reached for the last rocket. "Reloading."

"So we're going with the naked display of force negotiating technique, then?"

"Whoever ordered this wanted her ransomed, not dead. They won't kill the hostage when threatened. That's not how these stories work."

"But you do sure take glee in pushing stories right to their edge, don't you?" King asked, covering the door with his rifle.

"Makes them more exciting. Narrative gods will be happy."

"Keep it together, Roman. Don't go off the edge."

"No problem." Roman trotted down the hall with the loaded launcher pointed at the far door.

The flare hadn't survived the explosion, but there were dim red lights inside.

"Don't you come any closer!" said a human-sounding voice inside.

"I'm here to negotiate!" Roman shouted, words carrying down the hall.

"With a freaking rocket launcher?"

"That's my icebreaker." Roman was still advancing.

"Stop right there, unless you want the ambassador to bleed out on the floor."

"You don't want that, either. You want the big payout from whoever ordered the kidnapping. And unless I'm wrong, you don't get that if Reed is dead."

"Who the void are you?"

"A friend of the ambassador, that's all you need to know." Roman nodded to King, who moved softly forward, hugging the wall. Roman was their heavy combat operative, but King was the stealth master. And as long as the mercs were focused on Roman ...

"She ain't mentioned friends like you. I caught your ship coming in. You're Terran, but you ain't Terran Military."

"Just your ordinary pro-Interstellar Alliance patriot with high explosives and big brass balls. Who do you think will take your turf after this? Widowmakers? Seventh Sons?" Roman kept talking, full-voice, trying to cover up King's advance.

And as he escalated, the merc holding Reed would get angrier, more cocky. He'd step forward, move until he was visible from the door.

"Ain't no Seventh Sons gonna take our turf. When we space you and get our reward, we'll be the only ones spared the coming wave. It's gonna wash that Interstellar Alliance away so as no one will even remember it was so much as a glimmer in the ambassador's eye."

Roman heard the sounds of struggle, a woman's voice, gagged. And that would tell King what he needed to know about where Reed was in relation to the head merc.

King reached the far hallway, still twenty feet out from the door.

In an Earth Prime situation, this strategy would never work. But this was a story world, and tale types dominated here. Which meant that there was only one more trick left to pull.

King gave the signal. He was ready.

Roman shouted. "Blowback area clear. Fire in the hole!" But he did not fire.

Instead, a second and a half later, the sound of a firing rocket came from King's wrist-screen, recorded from the last rocket, doppled to sound like the rocket was coming in and flying into the room.

Roman saw figures dive inside the room, then caught King's shadow as he stepped inside the threshold.

A single gun report echoed through the hall back to Roman. Then King's voice.

"Should have given yourselves up. Stay on the ground."

Roman trotted ahead, tending to the launcher to avoid any accidental firing. The sleight-of-hand trick had been the last thing they needed, no time to blow a hole in the top of the station and suck them all out into space.

Another shot rang out, and a gun clattered across the floor.

"Anyone else feel like doing something stupid?" King asked.

There were no other sounds until Roman stepped up to the doorway.

"Coming in." He ducked into the final room and saw two dead mercs, another three cowering prone across the room, and a very tired-looking Ambassador Kaylin Reed kneeling beside one of the bodies. "Ambassador, are you well?"

"Well enough now. That was … bold. You have my most heartfelt thanks, and those of the nascent Alliance."

"Let's see if we can get you home on the double and remove the nascent part of that alliance, eh?"

Reed stood, keeping an eye on the other mercs. They didn't dare move. "A fine plan."

King addressed the mercs. "What shall we do with the three of you?"

"We was just following orders, we was!" said a sniveling Yai, curled up in a ball in the corner.

"As if that excuse has ever worked on anyone," Roman said as an aside to King. King focused on the Yai. "Who ordered the kidnapping?"

"It was the Ra'Gar!"

"Don't tell them, Fraal!" snarled another, a Jenr.

"They's going to kill us if they wants to, and I won't want to die on this crap rock in the middle of nowhere!"

"Snitch!" shouted the second merc. The Jenr went for his gun, taking a wild shot at Fraal. King put a bullet in the Jenr's chest, and the alien dropped his gun.

"The Ra'Gar. Do you have any proof, any digital trail?" Ambassador Reed asked.

Fraal pointed to the dead leader merc's wrist screen. "It's in Yarden's messages." Roman covered Fraal with his pistol while King covered the last of the mercs, leaving Reed to retrieve the wrist-screen. "What was the passcode?"

"I don't know! I don't know! But he wasn't never that inventive. I bet your smart techies could crack it."

"Let's hope so."

King asked, "What would you like to do with these two, Ambassador?"

The Ambassador leveled the mercs with a look of disdain. "Do you have room in your ship?"

"It'll be real cozy. But we've got ways to restrain them, no problem."

The ambassador drew herself up, regal despite ragged clothes, fatigue-mottled features, and unkempt hair. "Then they shall face justice. Bring them with us."

Roman closed on Fraal. "Yes, ma'am."

* * *

Back on the ship, King watched the ambassador emerge from the airplane-sized bathroom, far more put together despite walking in there with nothing more than a hand towel.

"Are the prisoners secure?" she asked, golden hair loose over her robes of state, which were somewhere between a cloak and an A-line runway dress.

"Yes, ma'am," King said from the copilot's seat. The prisoners had been searched, cuffed, and then locked to the bulkheads at opposite ends of the ship's back room. There would be no napping on the way back, but they weren't expecting a fight on the other end of this trip.

King did another visual circuit of the sensors as the ship arced through the void, five hours out from Ahura-3.

Behind him came the sound of pacing.

"There's not much to do other than wait, Madam Ambassador," Roman said. "There's a pulldown seat here." He gestured behind and to his left, where the emergency fold-down seats lined the sides of the ship.

"Thank you, Mr. Roman, but I think better standing. And as this ship is luxurious enough to have its own gravity, I will take that opportunity afforded to me to work on my speech. What of the Alliance? Is there still hope?"

King nodded. "That's what my colleagues just beamed me about. I'll sling the message to your personal."

"This will do. Thank you." The ambassador continued to pace, but her footfalls were calmer, steadier.

"Can we get you anything else, Ambassador? Food? A change of clothes?"

"I will manage, Mr. King. Thank you. Right now, all I need is the fastest ride home and this report your colleagues sent. I apologize if my focus undercuts my thanks, which are meant to be nothing less than overflowing. But celebration and reward follow success, not uncertainty."

"Yes, ma'am. Just let us know." King shot Roman a look, and the Afrikaaner tried not to laugh at his own boss's surprise. This from a man with a nearly legendary game face.

"Sensor sweep is negative on pursuit. Five hours to destination," Roman said, moving the conversation back into businesslike routine.

They'd done their part. It was up to Shirin and Leah to keep Ahura-3 from imploding until they could get Ambassador Reed back on-station.

He pushed Shirin's report to his earbuds for text-to-speech to listen without taking his eyes off of the space before them, even if the journey in front of them wasn't 99.9999 percent emptiness.

Which it was.

Just because science fiction usually skipped most of the flying scenes didn't mean that you got places instantly. It just means that good storytellers knew when to gloss over scenes. But he'd be there for the whole thing. He wasn't the hero of this story anymore. He was just the Ambassador's wheelman, now.

* * *

Leah had thought that Bhean was the last hurdle.

Oh, oh no. The night had just begun.

After Bhean and the pleasure-dancers it was Seeker De-van storming off to his hidey-hole on the second ring, swearing to never trust the Terrans again. They'd pulled him out of hiding with a highstakes Vrebak game and promises of an early hearing before the Insterstellar Alliance Trade commission.

And after that, it was Vice-Prelate Janan, who felt unloved after their dinner wallow with his boss. So they rushed back to the restaurant, back to the fake mud, and back to another gray-green Gaan fanning himself and Shirin talking more circles around the massive diplomat. And on.

And on.

Shirin and Leah finally turned in at 0400. Leah fortunately spent the last two hours of the evening tapping out their preliminary report to King and Roman after receiving the beam that they'd retrieved the ambassador. First they'd informed Ambassador Laran, then helped Laran get word out to the other principals, and then another two meetings to assure various players that the ambassador was, in fact, coming back. Here's her picture from their colleague's ship with a hard time-code, no seriously.

Leah face-planted on her bed at 0417 knowing full well that she'd have to be up again at quarter till six to be up and ready to receive Ambassador Reed and escort her to the meeting hall so that the grand Assembly could be gathered for the signing of the treaty.

The alarm came as soon as she closed her eyes. So fast that Leah pinched herself to make sure that this wasn't some kind of hateful dream.

Assured of what passed for reality in this sleep-thief of a story world, she threw herself in the shower again until Shirin "ahem-ed" loud enough to be heard inside.

And so it was, that despite all logic, and motivated only by space station coffee and a reminder that she was making better money than she'd ever seen in her life, that she got back into her diplomatic robes to face the world.

Epilogue:
Let's Try That Alliance Thing Again

Ambassador Reed stepped back onto Ahura-3 at 0713 local time, accompanied by King, Roman, and preceded by the two Dark Stars prisoners.

The prisoners were handed over to Commander Bugayeva, and Ambassador Reed was met by her counterpart Laran, as well as Shirin, and Leah.

Leah noticed that the ambassadors' greeting was very, very friendly, and filed that away with the thousand and one other notes she'd have to unload and process once they were back on Earth Prime.

They proceeded immediately to the Grand Assembly, where, thanks to the last night's epic bender of diplomacy and distraction, the principals for the would-be Interstellar Alliance were all present, the representatives and their retinues filling a room meant for fifty, with a long table at the center.

The language of the Alliance was unchanged. It was written out on a two-yard-long parchment, stacked seven copies tall. One each for the member races, and two for the archives—one to stay on Ahura-3, one bound for Terra.

Ambassador Reed gave a stirring speech, during which Leah fell asleep twice. That she counted.

But it worked.

One by one, the ambassadors lined up and signed their names in septuplicate (that's totally a word), then shook hands and congratulated one another and stood for a zillion pictures.

Once it was done, Roman gave the signal and the four of them filed out of the room.

Ambassador Laran met them just outside the docks, still wearing a crown of Gaan flowers that signified friendship or everlasting trust or something. Leah was too tired to check on her wrist-screen.

"I am in your debt, Shirin. A deep, powerful debt that I hope you will allow me to discharge soon before it weighs too heavily on me. Peace will bring such light into this galaxy that it will blind the agents of darkness."

"Speaking of agents of darkness, the mercs said they were hired by the Ra'Gar," Roman said.

Laran narrowed her eyes, poker face broken. "Unlikely. The Ra'Gar do not have such influence in this sector. More likely it is another force posing as the Ra'Gar. Regardless, Commander

Bugayeva's team will press the matter until the truth is out." "You'll keep me informed?" Shirin asked.

"Since you're not staying, I presume the standard relay will suffice." "Indeed."

"Once again, you have my thanks. Kaylin and my thanks, both." The Ethkar bowed. To the waist. Shirin led them in returning the bow, just barely shallower. Then Shirin wrapped the woman in a hug, and they made their final farewells.

Leah passed on Shirin's message to Bugayeva to get Zoor and Fela compensated for their help, hoping that between them they'd catch any exhaustion-derived typos.

All four of them were dead tired, so the return trip was very silent. And fortunately, no one threw anything at Leah when she napped the whole way back until the dimensional crossing. It'd be a long time before she could sleep through that.

* * *

"Two odd story breaks in as many weeks. I've got a bad feeling about this," King kept muttering to himself as they deplaned, finally back on Earth Prime.

Leah had Preeti call her a cab, trying not to pass out on the beanbag chairs while she waited. Shirin gathered her things to head home. King collected their reports and left to give his report to the High Council, and Roman wandered off somewhere.

After white-knuckling it to not fall asleep in the cab, Leah stumbled into her apartment at 4:23, dropped her phone on the couch, and then curled up under her covers to sleep for a day, or until King called to yell at her to come into work.

Either way.

Her mind refused to cooperate, still running a thousand cycles a minute, replaying her bizarre and wondrous experiences off-world, traipsing around having diplomatic adventures, eating otherworldly foods, memorizing several novels' worth of backstory and anthropological data all at once. But it had paid off.

Leah had two missions under her belt now, and she could barely wait for number three. It was exhausting as any five of the eighteen hells, but this Genrenaut gig was working out pretty well.

* * *

Marjana, the youngest nurse, stood watch at the nurse's station. Even slumped by long hours, she was nearly as tall as Roman. Today's choice of hijabs was orange, accenting her blue scrubs.

She nodded as Roman approached. "How was the mission?"

"We came, we saw, we exploded things. Mallery was missed. How's she doing?"

"Recovering and restless. She's pushing to get back on the rotation immediately. Maybe you can convince her to take some time."

Roman lifted a thumb toward her room. "She up?"

"Go ahead."

Mallery's room already showed her personality. Roman had brought over books and her trophies from her time Off-Broadway. Roman traveled light, but there wasn't anywhere Mallery went where she didn't leave a mark.

In a room with flood lights, Mallery would still be the brightest thing. She was everything his home world wasn't—kind, funny, and refined. Even clad in scrubs, arm in a cast, and her bottleblonde hair mussed with a serious case of bed-head, she was still poised.

"Hey there," she said. "How was the mission? Pull up a chair and tell me all about it."

He retold the story of their mission, filled in what he knew of Shirin and Leah's parts, and didn't spare the details about the lengths he'd gone to, how deep he'd tapped into his nature to get the job done. How he felt more alive on-mission.

Mallery reached across the bed for his hand. He offered it, and she squeezed it, reassuring him. He still fiddled and fidgeted as she talked. "You know what you're doing, and you trusted King to look after you when I wasn't there to do it myself. I think the RPG thing was a bit much, and that probably would have blown up in somebody's faces if anybody else tried to do it. But it didn't, and you pulled it out. If we're going to get through this story story system or whatever the Council calls it, we'll need to stick together, and we'll need you to be every bit of your badass self.

They talked for another half-hour, mostly Mallery updating him on the minutia of the HQ during the days they'd been gone. Even in a hospital bed, she still got all the gossip.

But still, Roman couldn't still his mind. He'd been living in condition yellow as long as he could remember. He could jog and read and listen all at once, and all that did was distract him.

But something was better than nothing. Far better. Nothing would let the memories come flooding through.

"Em?" His voice was shaking, his defenses down.

"Yeah."

"Tell me a story?"

Her carriage shifted immediately. This wasn't the first time, far from it. She squeezed his hand again, then let go and retrieved her eReader.

Roman closed his eyes, grabbed the sound of her voice and held tight, a life preserver in the choppy tides of his unease. He'd hold on, for her, for himself, for the team. He wasn't made for this world, but he'd learned to love it, even if he'd never quite feel at home.

END EPISODE TWO

Episode Three:
The Cupid Reconciliation

Chapter One:
The Comedienne Returns

Leah Tang hustled into Genrenauts HQ at nine-o-eight AM and snuck her way to the ready room, exhaling in relief at having escaped King's anal-retentive time-cop powers.

Strangely, no one else was there. This time of day at the team's ready room in Genrenauts HQ, the team would be in morning relaxing mode. The ever-multitasking Roman de Jager should be kicked up one table over, leaning back in his chair to an audiobook or leaning forward over a comic. Team lead Angstrom King would be pacing, a tablet in hand as he pored over reports. And Senior Genrenaut Shirin Tehrani would be reclining in the book nook, speed-reading a biography or history text.

Instead, the room was empty.

Leah left her bag and tablet on the table and stalked the halls. They weren't in Ops. Preeti and the other operators whiled away on their multi-screen displays, the big wall showing data feeds from all around Earth and from beyond, data recorded on various trips and sent back by scouting missions. The team wasn't where they usually would be, but she'd only been on the job for a few weeks, and maybe there was a monthly meeting or something that she was missing? Something she'd forgotten when she collapsed after swordplay night?

Leah froze, struck by a thought. She checked her work email and saw nothing about a meeting, just the same assortment of forecasting and scouting reports.

However, she did have a text message, from Shirin. Shirin was older, basically the mom of the team, but in practice, she was more like the cool aunt who always had good stories.

"Come to Medical."

Continuing, Leah rounded the corner and saw a crowd. The whole team—Shirin, dashing badass Roman, and King, the alternatingly stern and thoughtful Team Lead—clustered around their injured teammate Mallery York, freshly out of a medical gown and back in skinny jeans and a gauzy top, one arm in a cast. Leah had only seen the woman in her recovery room, wearing a gown, looking far less stylish than she did in the team dossiers.

All together, they looked like a totally odd but comfortable family of choice. Which made Leah the new foster kid—not yet adopted, still feeling out her place in everything.

Shirin noticed Leah come around the bend and waved her over. The team parted to give Mallery a clean view.

Mallery was just a hair taller than Leah, taller still with heels. She had bleach-blond hair in a progressive bob, and the kind of skin that looked like it would burn in the shade. *Heels already?* Leah thought, shuddering. One of the things that was not in the regs was a requirement to wear heels (unlike some jobs she'd had). Leah wore flats to work. And at home. Everywhere. But no, Mallery went straight from infirmary socks to three-inch heels.

Shirin made the introduction. "Mallery, I don't think you've properly met our new probationary agent, Leah Tang."

Mallery's face went from bright to incandescent. She threw open her arms, adjusting for the awkwardness of the cast. "Probie! Welcome to the team. Sorry I wasn't in any condition to give you a proper welcome earlier, what with the being shot and all."

So, if she's back on-duty, do I still have a job? Leah asked herself, even though King and all of the paperwork said that the position was ongoing, pending review after six months. Leah had been hired partially to sub for Mallery, and she was just settling into the role, but here Mallery was…

"I'm glad you're on your feet again," Leah said, politeness winning out. "How are you feeling?"

"Ready to climb the Great Wall, if it means getting back to doing something useful. I love reading and all, but we didn't join the team to become literature professors, right?"

Mallery talked fast, accentuating speech with one hand, the other arm held in a fixed position by her cast.

"I hope Roman hasn't been giving you too much trouble," Mallery said, placing a friendly hand on Leah's elbow. "He loves to play with the newbies.

I remember when I was new, he stole the batteries out of everything I brought into the office and replaced all of the romance novels on my eReader with spiritual self-help books. Serves him right that I spent the next month boring him to death with love languages."

Leah let the woman plow ahead, slightly awed. Some people were animated. Mallery was Pixar 3D IMAX.

"Fair's fair," Roman said.

King cleared his throat. "That's enough reunion. Let's get back to work."

Mallery chattered at Leah every inch of the way.

"How are you liking the job so far? I was so overwhelmed my first year. The reading lists, the training, and the missions. My first one, we went to the Noir region, and I was so excited to get to dig into the wardrobe. But newbies never get to dress themselves, so I got the stodgy spinster outfit. It was a gag, though, since I needed to be the Femme Fatale; we were getting a detective out of the bottle so he could solve the case, you see…"

And on she went. It was like she'd been storing up all of the words from several weeks of inactivity, and had to get them all out now.

Or maybe this was how she was all the time.

Leah took the conversational backseat, happy to let Mallery drive, sharing experiences from her days as a probationary Genrenaut. Leah tried to commit the pranks to memory, hoping to avoid or maybe turn the tables if Shirin or Roman tried to pull them out again.

Being the butt of every joke as the low woman on the org chart wasn't the most fun part of the job. On the other hand, it was a damn sight better than getting the side-eye from lifers at her last job, who suspected her of being an affirmative action hire. All for a reception job. *Thanks, Simmons & Sains!*

"So, tell me about your missions. I saw the reports, of course, but it was always so exciting for me to talk about my first missions. Did you really distract a gunslinger with a totally improvised bit on your first trip out? I was such a bundle of nerves my first mission. You should have seen me in that dress."

Mallery counted with her fingers, accentuated by a playful wink. "One, because it fit like a glove—Shirin is a miracle-worker—and two, I was so struck with stage fright, I might as well have been a freshman auditioning for a top ten theater program."

Mallery took a breath, and Leah jumped right in like it was a game of double Dutch, taking her turn.

"It was the only thing I could think of, really. The baddie had a hostage, right; I peeked through the kitchen door and saw Maribel, our heroine, all stalemated with the Black Hat, and I knew I wasn't a good enough shot to be sure not to hit his hostage, so I remembered that her brother had been using the stairs by the kitchen and made my way around."

Leah caught herself matching Mallery's speed, talking like someone was pumping the oxygen out of the room and she had to talk fast while there was still time. She stopped herself, then resumed at a slower pace. "I took the carafe of lemonade with me. I knew I was going to do something with it. I didn't want to just toss the thing at him; he'd probably flinch and shoot someone. I needed him distracted, so I just reached into my improv quiver."

"Improv quiver, I love it!" Mallery said, slapping her uninjured hand on her hip.

The rest of the team settled into their places in the rec room, and Mallery joined Leah at her table.

"Are you a coffee drinker?" Mallery asked.

"Only always."

"Great. Make us some coffee, and I'll think up some more tips for you before King whisks us away to some meeting about the socio-narrative implications of declining crop yields in Fantasyland or whatever."

Leah chuckled to herself as she made the coffee. Making coffee had fallen to her at her last job, and the one bit of continuity was both reassuring and disappointing. The last time she'd been anywhere near the top of an org chart was college, as captain of her improv comedy troupe. Of course, senior year was marred by the epic drama from when JD dumped Karen, then proceeded to try to sleep his way through the rest of the troupe. She'd had to boot him after he made a handsy pass at her after a Saturday performance.

So, that was a bonus to being on the bottom of the heap—other people had to do the firing, make the choices on behalf of the whole team, take the flak for a split-second decision.

King, however, came off as flak-proof, stainless steel in a pressed suit.

Leah was practicing the art of watching coffee brew when King walked into the room, holding his tablet like a conductor's baton.

"Eyes up, folks. We've got a breach in Romance. Scouting report is in your email; we're scheduled for lift-off in thirty minutes. Roman, pre-flight. Shirin, wardrobe. Leah, you help Shirin. Mallery, you're with me."

Somehow, Mallery got even more energetic, punching the air. "You're going to love this world, Leah. It's like an endless *Love, Actually*, only the queer characters actually get a place at the table. And women get to decide things for themselves. It's got problems, to be sure, just like romance here on our world." Mallery walked over and poured herself a cup of coffee from the freshly brewed pot as she continued.

Shirin beckoned, waiting by the door. "Come on, newbie. It's time to get ourselves some gorgeous Hollywood outfits."

King said, "T minus thirty, people," as the group disbanded.

* * *

The wardrobe was, by itself, the size of a small warehouse, with divided sections by genre.

"Is Mallery always like that?" Leah asked Shirin as the women unzipped roller-bag suitcases.

"She was on high-transmitting mode. She's just excited by new people. Don't worry; the shiny wears off after a couple of missions. Though I think she likes you."

Following Shirin, Leah carted the tied-together roller-bags past the SF, Noir, and Horror sections to the warehouse within a warehouse that was the Romance section.

Making their way past cotehardies and corsets, kilts and puffy shirts, they stopped at last among racks of clothing in the Contemporary Romance section.

"It seems like she likes everybody."

"She reads people at the speed King reads books. If she thinks you're good people, it takes a lot to change her mind."

Shirin punched in a key code, and a garage-door gate rolled up, revealing even more wardrobe options—two twenty-foot-long hangars filled with freshly pressed clothes. Tops, pants, dresses, suits, and more.

"She's ex-Broadway, right?"

"Born and bred, as she says. She comes on a bit strong, but it's reassuring. Like how you want cars to make sounds even when they're electric, just so other people can hear them coming?"

Leah nodded.

"Who curates these collections?" Leah asked, trying not to drool at the tens of thousands of dollars' worth of clothes in this one subsection of the room.

"Logistics tracks trends and styles, and takes our measurements to make sure HQ is constantly stocked with a selection to prepare us for a range of covers and scenarios off-world."

"They ordered ten worlds' worth of clothes to fit me in a week?" Leah asked, looking at the section with her name on it.

Shirin brought an armful of clothes on lines, stylish casual outfits for King—broad at the shoulder, long in the torso, in bold colors that went well with his brown skin, several shades darker than Shirin's. "They ordered them in a week, and then Logistics tailored them so that they looked custom, store-bought, and/or poorly fitting, depending on the type of covers needed. In the post-apocalyptic region, everyone's clothes are weirdly well-fitting, but in a way that looks ill-fitting." The senior Genrenaut racked the clothes on the hangars that flanked each room.

Leah took the clothes and started packing, remembering her days on the stand-up comedy circuit, fitting two weeks' worth of clothes into a single roller-bag.

"How often do these worlds, trends, or whatever change? It seems like Sci-Fi world pretty much stayed the way you know it, and has been like that for a while, alliance aside."

Shirin slid hangars along the line, picking through acid-washed men's jeans. "No faster or slower than the average feeling of a genre changes. Get a flashpoint story, and things change quick."

"I'm guessing you don't mean the DC Flashpoint," Leah said.

"No. Those hard resets haven't happened since I've been on the job. Plenty of landmark works, though. Rapid change, but not all at once."

"So, there have been hard reboots?"

"King just barely escaped a region-wide continuity wipe not long after he got started. Doesn't talk about it, though. Every contact we'd developed there forgot us; all of the missions we'd logged had been written out of existence."

Shirin handed a set of jeans directly to Leah. They had the cultivated mussy look, so there was no need for hangers. "These go in Roman's bag." Leah opened another roller-bag and started packing the jeans. "Written out of existence? That's not ominous at all."

"It's been decades since a world has reset like that during a mission, so if we're lucky, if it happens again, it won't be on our watch."

"Can I ask for flats again?" Leah asked as Shirin moved to pick through some smaller clothes. Seeing as she was three inches shorter than Mallery, she figured her odds were good of picking the timing.

"You can have flats, but we have to bring these, too." Shirin handed Leah a pair of sunflower-yellow four-inch heels.

"Just as long as I'm not expected to walk around the street in these things."

"Don't worry, dear. Heels only get caught in subway grates when it's dramatically appropriate," Shirin said.

"How long did it take before you always knew how to think in the right genre?"

"We already do it, every day. We tell ourselves what kind of story we're in, and we're often wrong, because life is mostly every genre, sometimes at once. These worlds, they make sense. Now, for a ball gown, would you rather go with black or something more daring?"

Leah sighed at Shirin's latest selection. "Ball gown?"

"Genrenauts' motto: be prepared, and expect drama."

"So, we're a TV network now?"

"Hush, newbie. Keep packing."

* * *

This was Leah's third time traveling to another dimension, and it was almost becoming familiar. Or would, if it didn't involve getting to travel in a freaking rocket ship. That would never get old. Or, at least, she hoped it never would. They sat strapped into the ship, which stood straight up like a NASA rocket. But instead of blasting off, the ship rattled, then slipped side-ways between dimensions, the view of the hangar roof replaced by technicolor strobes and the wiggly designs that she came to associate with their cross-dimensional travel. There was blissfully little turbulence, unlike some of the earlier trips.

Minutes later, they slipped from the in-between into a new world. Gravity was still down, the rocket point-up. The front viewscreen revealed the inside of what looked like the roof of a warehouse.

"Where are we?" Leah asked as Roman double-checked the instrumentation.

King gestured to the view. "We maintain properties on all of the story worlds where landing out of sight is impossible but spaceships are still not in-genre."

"So, is this our safe house, too?" Leah asked.

Mallery jumped in. "No, thank goodness. This place is drafty as all get-out, and even worse, it's in Long Island City."

"What's wrong with Long Island City?"

Mallery unbuckled and climbed out of her seat, descending the rails along the side of the ship. "It's so close to Manhattan, practically within a stone's throw, but the neighborhood is split between soulless industrial and far-too-ritzy condos, with barely anything left besides. No, the company maintains an apartment on the Upper East Side for teams to do their business."

Leah started to climb down after Mallery. Roman released the hatch, revealing the poorly lit interior of a mostly empty warehouse. They formed a baggage line to bring down the gear.

After a few minutes to lock down the ship and get their gear sorted, Mallery led them out. The warehouse was lit with motion sensors, and as they were walking through the vast room, one blinked on, revealing a medical station in one corner, and a whole lot of nothing else. She paced around the building a bit to test out the sensors, and to explore.

"So, this place is just for landing the ship?"

"Pretty much. Other worlds, we tend to lay in supplies and surplus gear. Here, most everything has to be contracted or ordered fresh," Shirin said.

"Flowers, chocolates, Jet Ski rentals, things like that," Mallery said. "It's wonderful. I feel like Cupid every time we have a mission here. There's a reason TV channels keep ordering matchmaker dramas even when they don't take off. Same reason why we have dating shows. The romantic impulse is undeniable."

"For many people," Roman said. "Some of us can't be bothered."

"Only those with cold, dead hearts," Mallery shot back, smiling.

"Just try to keep from going full Manic Pixie Dream Girl on the mission this time."

Mallery laughed. "No worries about that. It's not like I could play the suzaphone with a broken arm."

From the look on Roman's face, this was an old, toothless argument among friends.

King's smile confirmed Leah's suspicion. "Play nice, children. I'll get us a cab."

Mallery cocked her head. "I thought you said you couldn't get a cab in NYC even if you were wearing a two-thousand-dollar suit?"

King grinned. "On our Earth, yes. Here, anyone can get a cab in five seconds flat."

And so he did.

A half-hour of halting traffic on the Manhattan side of the bridge later, they reached the field office, which turned out to be a posh three-bedroom apartment on the fourth floor of a gorgeous building in Central Park East. Their previous trips had taken them to obviously foreign climes—the nineteenth-century American frontier in Western World, and deep space in Science Fiction World. The Rom-Com world was just…New York. The richest and prettiest possible New York, but still identifiable as the Big Apple she knew and feared for its inconsistent comedy club crowds.

The apartment had smart, modern furniture, a fully-stocked pantry, and enough knickknacks and fiddly bits to make for a fine cocktail party.

"Is this a field office or a superhero loft?" Leah asked, picking her jaw up off of the floor.

"Why, both, of course!" Mallery snaked an arm around Leah's elbow and led her through the rest of the apartment. Each bedroom had a different feel—one leaned eclectic NYC hippie with Tibetan prayer flags, herbs, and a peace-symbol blanket over the bed, one was super-literary-prep with wall-to-wall bookshelves, and the third was a hipster paradise, complete with ukulele, steampunky Victoriana daguerreotypes, and more.

"How does the Council pay for all of this? This condo has to cost a fortune."

"Oh, on Earth Prime, it would. However, every Rom-Com protagonist in films has a swank apartment like this, even on lower-middle-class jobs, so that's just how this world works. If I recall, the rent for this place is something like a thousand dollars a month."

Leah was aghast. This called for aghast. "My last apartment cost a grand a month, and that was in an only moderately shady part of Baltimore. This place should cost several times as much."

Putting her useless jealousy aside, Leah walked up to a double-wide window facing the park. The leaves were changing, making for a sea of rich oranges and yellows beside a crystal-clear lake. The view was postcard-perfect. And as a cherry on top, there was a couple rowing a boat in the lake, one carrying a parasol. And Leah could even make out a picnic basket. The energy of the place was contagious. Western world was cheesy and scary. Science Fiction was cheesy and a bit confusing. Rom-Com world was cheesy and delightful.

"Can I just live here and report to work using a spare ship or something?" she asked.

"No go," Mallery said. "Long-term exposure to a story world has an elevated chance of wrapping us up into the world's story. Worst case, you forget where you come from and become a local forever."

"Like, lose yourself in the Matrix kind of thing?"

"Basically." Mallery joined Leah at the window to share in the view.

"Has that ever happened?"

Mallery's expression darkened. "Yes. So we come, we do our jobs, and then we leave. Just like our New York. Nice place to visit, but leave before it makes you hard, like the song says." Mallery stared out the window for a long moment, hand wrapped in the curtains.

Then, in a sharp motion, she turned from the window and called through the condo.

"Assemble in the living room, please! We have a love story to fix!"

Chapter Two:
Meddling for Fun and Profit

Mallery gathered the team around a table. She had pulled a flippable school-style whiteboard from somewhere. On the whiteboard were a trio of bullet points and a header:

HOW TO FIND A BROKEN STORY IN ROMANCE WORLD

1) Dating sites
2) Major haunts
3) Gossip network

Mallery stood by the whiteboard, marker in hand. "Okay, so we know that the breach originated in this urban center. Chances are, we're looking at a recent breakup or missed connection. We're going to divide up the team to cover the three major sources of information for finding broken stories."

Mallery tapped the three numbered points in sequence.

"Roman, you'll get to work the dating sites. Use the back-end key I designed to get in and see who reactivated accounts in the last month, and feed some bait accounts into the algorithm to find some likely partner candidates. You'll also want to reactivate the bait accounts we have set up."

"Bait accounts?" Leah asked.

"We forge dating profiles using models from our own Earth, which we craft into archetypes that should attract romantic comedy protagonists—quirky but gorgeous."

Nice. "Got it." It was like *Person of Interest* but for romance.

Leah tapped away on her tablet, taking notes. Since Mallery was in the driver's seat for this mission, King's custom of requiring everyone take notes with legal pads was apparently suspended. King still took notes analog-style, sitting up, his legs crossed, but when Roman and Shirin pulled out their tablets, Leah followed suit.

Mallery continued. "Newbie, you're with me on major haunts. I'll show you how to pick up broken stories in the wild. It'll be fun. Hydrate now and decide on a cocktail of choice. Mixing your drink types is a rookie mistake, and I won't have it on my mission."

Leah chuckled, continuing to reset her brain to fit the story world—in Western World you had to watch your guns, so of course in Romance World you had to watch your drinks.

"That leaves Shirin and King on gossip networks," Mallery said. "Pick up contacts and see where social circles have gone off. Focus on Midtown in the publishing business, NYU, and the fashion industry, but let's not forget the sexy art jobs like architects and the theatre world. Most of our documented breaches in this territory are upper-middle-class, dating for less than two years. My analysis of latest reports from Scouting and Forecasting is in the mission folder. Text or email with any leads, otherwise we check in with progress tomorrow at nine AM. Any questions?"

Leah had questions, but they could wait until she headed out with Mallery. Her first mission, they'd known exactly where the story had broken, and her second, Shirin's contacts had put them on the trail within the afternoon. This was looking like it'd take longer. And even with an intimidatingly large organization supporting them, it seemed like this job always came down to fieldwork.

Find one specific unhappy couple in a city of eight million. No big deal, right?

Mallery walked past Leah, on her way to the bedrooms. "Suit up. Club attire."

Luckily, Leah had been allowed to pick out her own outfits, though Shirin had given her all of three minutes to do it, which was not nearly enough time to play with a several-thousand-dollar wardrobe of hand-or-at-least-algorithm-picked clothes.

Leah wheeled her suitcase to one of the bathrooms, which sported a full-length mirror. She'd been told to pack three everyday chic outfits, two club/bar outfits, a just-in-case ball gown, and exercise clothes.

Since the laws of dramatic progression suggested she save the fanciest clothes for later in the story, Leah went with her less risqué club outfit—black palazzo pants and a white tank top with a blue chiffon throw over it. The more risqué one was a pour-yourself-in-tight print dress that Shirin had pointed her toward when her other two choices were deemed "too tame." She reluctantly pulled out the yellow heels, hoping that there would be seats at the club.

Leah emerged from the restroom to see Mallery waiting, decked out in a black cocktail dress and an epic-level push-up bra. Her bombshell look was somewhat undercut by the cast, but only just.

"Whoa. That bra come with a permit?" Leah said.

Mallery stood proud, hands on hips, one stance allowed by her cast. "We're looking to get information. If people want to talk to my boobs instead of me, so be it. Now get back in there; we need to do makeup."

"I'm already wearing makeup," Leah said, already knowing she was doomed.

"Oh, honey. We're going clubbing in the Lower East Side. That's a full-face situation at least."

Crammed into the front bathroom, Leah became very aware of Mallery's presence. Her body heat, her breath. Suddenly, it was very warm in the restroom.

"Can we open the door?" Leah asked, moving a hand to the door and accidentally elbowing a very soft body part.

Mallery winced, covering up. "Geez. Careful there."

"Sorry." Leah opened the door, letting in some cooler air. It helped a little. "It's a bit cramped in here. Wasn't the other restroom like three times this size?"

"Yes, but we were already here. I'll finish up in the other room." Mallery sidestepped out, leaving Leah to catch her breath.

A minute later, Leah made her way to the master bedroom and its accompanying bathroom. She passed Shirin, who raised an eyebrow as she walked by.

Leah gave a defusing smile and a shrug.

The master bathroom was more than large enough to work comfortably. Mallery finished Leah's makeup, then did her own.

Leah felt like she was about to step onto a movie set, which made sense. Mallery had done her makeup better than she ever bothered to do for herself.

Her college improv comedy troupe had used makeup for shows, but this was a whole other level. Compared to her last mission, it was totally normal. Every world had its own levels of weird, and Leah could imagine the whiplash that would come with jumping between worlds quickly in back-to-back missions.

She imagined King barking orders in the ready room. "Okay, folks, put away the lasers and armor and suit up in your Elizabethan gear. Roman, don't skimp on the codpieces."

Gawking at herself in the front hall mirror, Leah asked, "So, where are we going first?"

"Red Rooster, then PopBar, and if there's time, we'll close out the night in the Meatpacking District at a place called Puzzles."

Leah sighed to herself. *Oh, New York. Home of aggressive crowds and highway-robbery drink prices.*

"We're out!" Mallery called to the rest of the team as she swapped her cell's SIM card to one of the cards provided in the safe house. Cell phones couldn't call across dimensions, but with a local SIM, they worked in the field just fine. "Text with any updates."

"Have fun," said Shirin.

At the same time, Roman called, "Don't go overboard."

Going out on the town with a fabulous ex-Broadway leading lady, prowling for love stories gone awry. What could possibly go wrong?

* * *

The apartment was abuzz with noise and preparations for fifteen minutes, then suddenly silent once both pairs had departed for their assignments.

Leaving Roman alone to get to work. He synced his phone to the room's speaker, listening to a podcast as he reset the desk workspace into a standing desk. The tech on this world was basically identical to that of their Prime World; all they had to do was swap out SIM cards and IP addresses.

Roman and sitting desks did not get along—too constricting, not enough chance to move around. He'd gotten the ADHD and dyslexia diagnoses not long after landing on-planet. Back in the Post-Apocalyptic Region of Action World, where he'd grown up, what passed for doctors didn't get that sophisticated. He had meds, but the harder he had to push himself on a mission, the more his story nature reasserted itself and reset his neurochemistry to its defaults.

Which meant that when he was faced with several hours of focus-intensive work, he needed every advantage he could make for himself. He tested his modified desk's stability, and when satisfied, he pulled up Persona and Matchmaker.com on his tablet, pacing the apartment, working individual case studies, while the main workstation crunched numbers.

Initially, Roman had been uncomfortable on this beat. After all, comedic romance in a cosmopolitan city was about as hard a contrast from the world he'd been born into as you could imagine.

Love was about as close to a universal as you could hope for. People looked for it even in the wasteland.

The first compile came back with no results. He set the next search to run and started another lap of the apartment.

This part of the job, the data-combing, match-selecting, turned out to be not that different from what he was already used to. Back home, he'd analyze people to see where the weak spots in a gang or community were; here, he studied them to find their compatibilities, the places where the sum transcended the whole of the parts.

Like these two he'd found on Matchmaker. Testimonial from a happy couple—Chiana and Aisha—met on Matchmaker right when Aisha was going to let her membership lapse—the timely email, a disastrous first date, a make-up date, and the testimonial ended with a picture of the happy couple, Aisha showing off a sparkling engagement ring.

The frisson of happiness for others put a spring in Roman's step, and he started another lap, setting the workstation to run another simulation.

With luck, the others were getting better results than the parade of fail he'd seen so far.

* * *

Red Rooster was a gay bar just to the northeast of the NYU campus, and was filled with the young and the fabulous. The DJ played Adele, Lorde, Prince, and the Spice Girls, mixed in with some alt-pop Leah had never heard of but would fit perfectly in a Rom-Com soundtrack.

The bar was already packed at seven PM, dance floor filled with bushy bears, beefcakes, and more, a half-dozen muscled men in tight shirts joyfully grinding together to the music. Women dominated the other half of the floor, burly butches alongside fineried femmes, angelic androgynes mixing here and there and everywhere. Neon drinks lined tables, and the bartenders were wearing almost as little as the patrons, muscle-showcasing V-necks on men, midriff-bearing tops on women, tattoos and piercings abounding.

Mallery strode right up to the bar and leaned forward, catching the attention of a Pacific Islander bartender with an undercut, wearing a black vest as her top.

"Can I get an amaretto sour and two dirty martinis, darling?"

The woman flashed a rakish smile and continued her whirlwind of activity, pouring, scooping, measuring, and sliding glasses back and forth to thirsty patrons.

The music pounded on as Leah joined Mallery at the bar.

"So, how do we do this?" She realized she was almost yelling, but it was the only way to be heard.

"Spotting broken stories is like sexing chicks."

"What?" Leah asked, her voice cracking.

"Baby chickens. There are people whose job…"

"Ah, okay," Leah said, getting the point.

Mallery continued, one eye on the bar, one eye on the dance floor. "They spend all day telling if chicks are male or female. At first, they all look the same, and you have to watch someone who knows how as they work. Then eventually, you just get a sense for it. Same thing here."

"So, you're just going to use the Force and find broken stories?" Leah asked.

The bartender returned with drinks, setting them by Mallery. Mallery presented a platinum card. "Let 'er ride," she told the bartender.

"The Force, and liquor as a social lubricant. Grab your drink and follow me." Mallery took a martini in each hand and forged into the crowd, drinks held high to avoid the crush.

Leah fetched her drink and took as a sip as she followed her teammate. Also, the drink was excellent.

Mallery worked the room like a pro. Shirin's method involved making everyone feel like they were old friends; Mallery was just the life of the party. She laughed, joked, flirted, all the while pumping people for information.

Even though she was following in the wake of a bombshell, Leah got several offers of drinks and varyingly obvious pickup lines herself, which she tried to deflect without offending anyone and engaging just enough to get some leads. It'd been a while since she'd been to a gay club for anything other than an evening out without dudes trying to pick her up constantly. Leah placed herself at around a "2" on the Kinsey Scale, so she appreciated the view from all sides of the bar before Mallery settled up and whisked her off to bar number two.

* * *

Mallery adopted a Long Island accent as she slid into the cab, Leah following.

"If you want to be an agent, you need to learn how to read a story. The stories are all around us, right? So, you want to look for stories in progress, read the difference between a lack of sexual tension between people and the comfortable ease that settles in with a couple that's been together for years."

Mallery dug a compact out of her purse and set about touching up her makeup. Seeing from the side instead of from the front, Leah could tell she wasn't actually applying anything. Just another part of the show for the cabbie.

"One of the big signs to look for is people being self-conscious, people who look and act like they're lost at sea, off course, you know? Those are the ones that are worth studying. The next question to ask yourself is "What's missing? Are they broken-hearted or just yearning? Where did their story go off track?

Mallery was playing around the edges, avoiding saying anything too blatantly weird, staying within the bounds of self-indulgent New York Arts People weird.

"This will do, driver." Mallery tapped a manicured hand on the glass. She paid with crisp bills, then nodded to Leah to slide out on the passenger side as cabs and cars beeped and honked, threading and honking their way down the street. The official paperwork said the Genrenauts were privately funded, but Leah guessed they may be getting some government cash, too. King was not very forthcoming with answers on the subject, and when she asked anyone else, they told her to ask King.

PopBar stood just down the street, red neon and black broadcasting the promise of delight to a darkening street. Fall coats abounded in the block-long line to get in to the bar.

"Looks like we're due for a wait," Leah thumbed at the line.

"Oh, please." Mallery passed Leah and walked straight to the bouncer, a tall Latino with an earpiece, a clipboard, and a tailored suit.

Leah caught a flash of a bill folding on the way between Mallery's purse and the bouncer's suitcoat, and the velvet rope opened magically. This earned them stares from the people in line. Some of appreciation, some of disgust.

Leah looked over her shoulder to the crowd behind them as they walked into the dim front hall, coat check on the right, music thumping from the left. "Do we get to throw money around like this on every mission?"

"They call them discretionary funds for a reason, my dear. This time, you look out for stories yourself. When you see a likely breach, I want you to tap me on the shoulder and lean in as if to say something, then tell me who and where. Let's see how your instincts are."

The interior of PopBar was more bistro than club, with tables and servers. The crowd was less edgy and less queer. Women sat on the interior spaces, straight down the line, with men on the outside, an assembly line of smartly-dressed couples at tables for two, some with appetizer plates, others just nursing drinks.

This wasn't just any restaurant setup, though. The tables were numbered. In the server's aisle by the row of numbered tables, a South Asian woman with a tight bun, a headset mic, and a slick blazer announced, "Time's up." The couples waved, shook, or sighed in relief as the men grabbed their drinks and slid down one setting, introducing themselves to the next woman in line.

"Speed dating, a prime locale for spotting people in broken stories." Mallery once again made a beeline to the bar.

"How do we tell the people in broken stories from the regular lovelorn at the start of their stories?"

Mallery surveyed the speed daters. Leah zeroed in on the body language, the conversational flow, anything out of order.

"It's different from someone at the start of their story—those folks are more likely to seem bland or listless. Someone with a broken story will be distracted, hesitant, off-balance. And if you're lucky, they'll look just a shade out of sync with the world around them. King says he explained that part. Any likely suspects?"

"The woman at seven isn't having any of it," Leah said, a gentle nod indicating a black woman with arms crossed, her eyes focused somewhere in the distance as a white man leaned forward, eyes on the woman's neckline, swishing his drink and talking with a wolfish grin.

"Yeah, but I'd peg that more on the guy's creeper look than anything else."

"What about the guy at one?" The Middle-Eastern man at the end table wasn't even looking at his momentary match. His focus was three tables down with the woman at four: white, hair pulled back, and librarian glasses offsetting a baby blue sweater.

"Good eye. They'll finish in twenty minutes or so. Watch for other potential breaches. When the speed daters take a break, the participants will fill out their cards, and that's when you'll swing by to say hello to lovelorn number one and see if you can tease out the story about his bespectacled crush. Got it?"

"I'm not good at chatting guys up on my own, let alone with a covert purpose."

"You could just lay into him, comedian-style."

"That's not likely to get me good answers either; he'd just bolt."

"It would be funny," Mallery said with a wink. "No, just ask him if he's okay, joke about the speed dating format. The story should fall out pretty easy on its own, if you're right about the breach. When someone's story is broken here, they're subconsciously looking for someone, anyone, to latch on to, to start another romance."

Well, that's not alarming at all, Leah thought, watching the awkward mark as his momentary match, a probably-Malaysian woman in a hijab, tried to carry the conversation.

Their drinks arrived, and Leah sipped ever so slowly at hers while Mallery worked the crowd. She moved more here than at the Red Rooster, the room more open. She walked the length of the bar, then turned and made her way back, setting her drink on the bar and picking up conversations one at a time with the singletons and their nursed drinks.

Leah watched her mark phone it in through three more speed dates, until he sat down at the table with the subject of his attention. The maybe-librarian gave a big sigh and buried her attention in the plate of appetizers before her. The man started talking, hands shaking, all false starts and clumsiness. He knocked over his own drink, spilling the wine on the woman's lap. The woman shot up and slid out past him, jetting for the bathroom. The man followed after her for two steps, but the hostess stepped up to stop him with an authoritatively raised hand. He watched for a moment, then turned and almost jogged out the front door.

And this is where you go after him, Leah realized. Abandoning her drink, she left the bar, trying to work in stealth mode as best she could.

The man leaned over a newspaper stand, hands still shaking. He looked like he was about to hurl.

Chapter Three:
Learning on the Job

"Are you okay?" Leah asked, voice cutting through the street sounds—the rubber-on-asphalt of cars, honking cabbies, and the clattering of shoes on concrete.

The man didn't respond.

She stepped up to his side and leaned into his field of vision, repeating her question.

This time he noticed her, righting himself and crossing his arms as if he was holding in his fear and shame.

"I'm just a dolt."

Leah shrugged. "I've done worse. Once, I had a date over to cook dinner together. Accidentally cracked an egg in my hands and dropped it all over his brand-new sneakers. And then, once I'd cleaned it off, I gave him a bloody nose when I stood up and clocked him with my head. He didn't call after that."

A twinge of a smile flashed across the man's mouth, and his body language loosened up.

Sadly, the story was 100% true.

"Whatever it is, I'm sure it'll be fine," Leah said. Remembering her mission, she added, "Do you need to talk about it? I'm happy to be a neutral party. I was always the confessional buddy for my friends in high school." Which was true, but she hadn't planned on saying it. She'd just switched into empathy mode and it'd come spilling out.

"I don't want to bother you with it. It's ridiculous," he said, looking down at his own shoes.

Leah extended a hand. "I'm sure it's not. I'm Leah."

"Hossan," he said, shaking her hand.

Hossan leaned on the newspaper stand, facing the street, looking away from the bar. "Sarah," Hossan caught himself. "That's her name, Sarah. She and I were designers working at Himalaya, perfecting their Also Bought algorithms. We started going out for drinks after work, and got to working on an algorithm for dating, wanting to use our skills for something better than selling people more useless crap."

"So, we left and started Cliq, turning the algorithm to dating. We spent all of our time together, pulling twenty-hour days laying out the basic code to underlie the algorithm. It wasn't long before we weren't just coding together. That part, that was good." Hossan blushed. "When we launched, companies came sniffing around almost immediately, with angel investments, promises, and expectations."

The heartbroken man watched the street, buses and cars dancing their honk-tastic cha-cha. "Sarah wanted to keep the company pure, let it grow at its own rate, but I got blinded by the money; I wanted to take over the online dating world all at once. We started fighting over the business, and then over little, ridiculous stuff. It got worse over the next six months, even as the site was exploding and the offers came rolling in."

Hossan pulled out a scribbled note on the back of a receipt. "Two weeks ago, she moved out of our apartment and left a note."

Hossan handed it to Leah.

It read:

"Hossan,

I'm through. You can keep the damned company. Buy me out, and then go sell your soul around town all you want.

Sarah"

Leah looked to see that Hossan was staring up at the skyline and the clouded sky. "So, now I'm here, and I just fell on my face trying to make it right. I don't even really care about the money. I just got locked into this competitive loop, trying to top everyone. I lost track of what made it special.

And now I can't say any of it. I look at her and all I can see is every wrong-headed thing I said when I was caught up in it all, and then I spilled my wine on her favorite sweater her dead aunt knitted for her, and made it all worse."

Well, hell. Maybe I can fix this right now and we can be back before midnight! Leah put a hand on Hossan's shoulder.

"I bet you that if you go back in there and say just what you told me, you'll be fine. Take a long breath before you start, and speak slowly. She knows you; she's got to know how you feel. The note tells me she's obviously more hurt by what you said than anything else, which means you can go in there and make things right."

"All I want to do is crawl inside a dark hole and forget."

"How do you think Sarah feels? She made this amazing thing with you, and then you got caught up in the business, not the beauty. Forget Cliq and convince her you care about her more than the money and the fame and everything."

This part came strangely easy. She had been the one her friends came to for help, since she'd always been the "funny one" in her group of friends, more often the third or fifth wheel than the leading lady in the romantic drama of the group.

Maybe that would come in handy this time.

Hossan looked back at the PopBar, drew himself to his full height, and walked back at the door, hands still shaking. Leah followed at a discreet distance, talking under her breath to Mallery.

"I've got Repentant Loverboy headed back in to make the Big Reconciliation."

Mallery responded over the earpiece. "I heard. Brilliantly done. You're a natural."

"Helps that I've had some experience with romantic misadventure."

"I could tell. Meet me at the bar and we'll watch this play out."

* * *

Mallery greeted Leah by holding out Leah's mostly full amaretto sour, her other hand wrapped around a glass of red wine.

The speed dating crowd had broken out into a mingling period, couples reconnecting and expanding on their conversations. Sarah stood in a corner, shields up with crossed arms and face buried in her phone.

"It's super-intrusive, but is there any way we can hear what they say?"

"We'd have to drop an omnidirectional mic with a power source somewhere nearby. Also, ten bucks says they make up."

"This is my story fix. Why would I bet against myself?"

"If you're right, I pay for the next round of drinks."

Leah chuckled. "You're already paying for drinks."

"Work is paying for drinks. You pull this off, and I slap down my own hard-earned cash to celebrate. It's a gesture; please take it in the manner it's intended."

"Sorry, of course." Leah just hoped it wasn't also some other kind of gesture. Workplace romance drama was exactly what she didn't need in this new amazing job. There was too much going on in her day-to-day to get distracted by hot coworkers, bombshell dress or no.

Leah focused on the couple in the corner.

Hossan's hands were shaking, but he kept solid eye contact with Sarah. He wasn't boxing her in, either. She had room to get out but wasn't even eyeing an escape, looking for help. They were really talking, and so far, there was no more spilling or klutzy ridiculousness.

Sarah set her drink down and took Hossan's trembling hand. Tension bled out of him and the couple closed in to kiss.

"Yes!" Leah said more than a little too loud for the bar's average volume. Apparently, everyone's attention was on the couple in the corner, and she got away with it.

Mallery turned to the bar. "Can you please send a bottle of champagne to the couple in the corner, and another round for us, please?"

"So, is that it?" Leah asked, heart racing.

"I hope so. We'll have to wait an hour or so and take readings again. There might be multiple breaches, or this might have been a story that was supposed to end badly, and maybe we've made things worse. Rom-Com can be a tricky region if you don't peg the breach right away—it's not like Crime World, where a breach means that the wrong people are dead. But the impact back home is just as bad. A while back, we—" Mallery stopped, interrupting herself. "Not literally *we*, but the organization *we* bungled a mission here by getting the wrong people together, it led to that insidious 'fifty percent of marriages end in divorce' meme back on our world."

Leah shuddered. She'd heard that statistic from more than one would-be significant other when they blew off her attempts to start a define-the-relationship talk. "How can we make things worse by making a happy ending?"

"Not all romantic comedies end in a happily-ever-after."

"Yeah, but like one percent, right?" Leah said. "I can think of about two in the last fifteen years."

"It's very rare, which is why I had you go for it. Let's hope this was the breach. Missions don't tend to go this easy. Especially not this year. More breaches and worse. It's like El Niño for making our job a pain in the ass."

Leah peeked at the couple. Awkwardly adorable, they were perched half-on a wide bar stool, totally wrapped up in one another. She flashed back to her own relationships, to foolishly patterning her life off of Rom-Coms for a semester, and the montage of heartbreak that had led to. She was probably too young to be jaded about relationships, but she was well on her way. But that didn't stop her from enjoying every second they spent in this world so focused on people finding love.

"Yeah, King and folks read me in about the storms and the breach rate. Any idea of why things have gotten harder?"

Mallery finished off her drink and picked up her backup, sliding Leah's new round over to her. "That's the question that's making the High Council twitchy and is driving Ops up the wall. Leading theories at the top are that this *is* the interdimensional equivalent of El Niño or a meteor shower, some kind of convergence or confluence of forces that we can't adequately read, accumulating in a way that increases dimensional instability."

"So, basically, 'We don't know; maybe weather?'"

Mallery shrugged. "That's for Ops and the Council to figure out. We're just the story plumbers."

"That makes it way less glamorous than our current fancy-outfit-wearing, cocktail-sipping existence would indicate."

"Oh, it gets far worse than this. Romance World tends to be the best, since the chances of gross bodily harm are pretty low. Though there was that brief crossover with Fantasyland where there were as many spells cast and dragons fought as there were long walks through gardens."

"Crossover?" Leah asked. "There's nothing in the documentation that talks about crossovers."

"Council regulations. They say crossovers are so infrequent as to be not worth putting into the official material. I'd have thought that King would have told you about those by now." The Genrenauts High Council was the founders and directors of the organization, which had bases all around the world. Of their team, only King ever talked to the Council, which suited Leah just fine. They sounded like a bunch of jerks, to be honest.

Leah took a sip of her drink. "They might have. My brain has gotten so full it spilled at least three times so far."

"Do I ever know that feeling." Mallery peeked at the couple in the corner. "Our work here is done. I'll leave behind a sensor to collect the readings. Do you want to hit the third bar to relax out the night, or turn in for an early day tomorrow, should your marvelous story fix turn out to not be the patch we needed?"

"This better be my last drink, if I'm going to be at all useful tomorrow."

Mallery made a comically mopey face, still impressing with her almost cartoonishly elastic actress skills. She dropped the look, tossing it aside as the joke it was. "Okay. Then skip the drink and just take in the city. I did mention it's a rooftop bar, right?"

"You didn't. Rooftop, eh?"

Leah imagined a shoulder angel and a shoulder devil. Her shoulder angel was dressed in professional slacks and a collared shirt in the manner of her style idol, Janelle Monáe. The shoulder devil was Mallery, wearing an even-more-exaggerated version of the woman's dress.

"Drink lots of water and get enough sleep! This is a job!" shoulder angel said.

"Rooftop bar! Cute coworker! New York!" said the shoulder devil.

I really hope I don't regret this, Leah thought, banishing the shoulder angel and devil.

"Let's do it."

Mallery lit up like a kid on Christmas. "Fantastic."

The senior Genrenaut turned to the bartender and called, "Check, please!"

Chapter Four:
Did You Get the Number of that Martini?

Leah woke up with a head full of mothballs, light piercing her eyes like lances.

For a moment, she didn't know where she was, but the residual smell of patchouli opened the window of memory, and reality came streaming in.

She was still dressed in her fancy club gear, which meant she hadn't bothered to undress after getting back from the bar.

The previous night came back to her in fits and starts. The sights, the sounds of pounding techno, and another round of drinks.

An imaginary Better Judgement shoulder angel appeared, shaking her head, dressed in the elaborate dresses her mother made her wear as a kid for Chinese cultural festivals.

"Told you so," the angel said in Mandarin. It had always been a know-it-all. And yet she never seemed to listen.

Her mission phone read 8:17, which was only fairly late. There was a glass of water on the bedside table. She glugged the water, then grabbed her towels and made a break for the shower.

One bracingly cold shower later, she wandered into the office/living room, wearing her gym clothes. She skipped makeup for the morning.

Walking into the room with the team assembled, she saw Mallery in trendy clothes and a full face of makeup.

"Good morning. Nice of you to join us," King said, tut-tutting heavy in his tone.

You're doing great today! she taunted herself as she slunk around the couches and took a seat.

The whiteboard was back, with a fresh message in two columns.

The first read:
STORY BREACH LEADS

1) Techie couple reunited by Leah
   Leah reports
2) Online dating pool
   Roman reports
3) Gossip pool
   Shirin reports

And in the second:
TODAY'S AGENDA

1) Follow-ups based on leads
2) Regular haunts

Mallery set her coffee down and tapped on the board with her marker. "Okay, let's get started. Word from HQ says that the story Leah patched last night was not our breach. We're going to hear from Leah first, since even though it wasn't the breach, patching a story is still a very exciting achievement, especially since she did it all by herself." Mallery tapped the other numbered points on the board. "Next, we'll get status reports and leads from Roman and Shirin, and then I'll assign today's tasks."

Mallery said, "You're up, newbie."

Leah wished for caffeine, wobbling to her feet to address the team at Mallery's prompting. She ran through the night's adventures, focusing on identifying Hossan and Sarah, inserting herself to give advice, and the PDA-tastic reconciliation between the pair.

"Nicely done," King said. "Next time, you can plant a mic on the subject so your team can listen and intervene if things are heading off base. When we ID the prime suspect couple, remember what you did here. Chances are, what we have to do will just be a bigger version of your story patch, though experience tells us that it usually takes more than a five-minute pep talk for a breach as far-reaching as this one."

"How far-reaching?" Leah asked.

"Filings for divorce in the USA and Canada have increased nine percent over the last month, and dating websites have seen a twenty percent increase in membership cancellations due to frustration."

Shirin piped in, "For context, the last time there was a breach in Romance, those numbers were three percent and twelve percent, respectively."

"Holy schnikes."

Mallery shook her head. "I'm sorry, dear, but I won't stand by and accept that as field profanity. We've got some latitude in our PG-13 rating; give it a proper *crap* or *hot damn*."

"Well, crap."

"There you go. Don't let a little hangover keep you from speaking with gusto." Mallery tapped the whiteboard again. "Now, to Roman, with some findings from the online dating site mines."

Roman was dressed in gym clothes, warm-up pants and a grey hoodie over white tank top. "We've sorted out a half-dozen candidates using Mallery's algorithms, and cross-referenced their hobbies and locations to find some likely places to run into them over the next couple of days."

Leah raised her hand. "Wait, how? Isn't that, like, ridiculously invasive?"

Roman looked to Mallery, then King. He shrugged. "This is what we do. If we fix their stories, we're helping them. The natural state in this world is Happily Ever After. In this world, people are _actually_ incomplete until they've found their match. If they aren't in story breaches, our making contact will be a momentary blip on their lives. No one gets hurt."

Leah looked around to the group. "And this doesn't bother anyone else?"

"It's this or rely entirely on serendipity to do our legwork for us," King said. "With the ripple effects we're seeing on Earth, these approaches have been sanctioned by the High Council and are entirely appropriate."

"Is it possible to log my displeasure without being insubordinate? Can I, like, fill out a form or something?"

"So noted," King said. "Roman…"

"As I was saying." Roman wrote out the six names on the whiteboard, beside the "Online dating pool" section.

"I've got likely haunts and plans for making contact in today's briefing email, along with relevant details for each candidate."

Mallery kept going. "Shirin, you're up with word from the wide world of gossip. Please, spare no detail. I do love these little morsels of story, even the red herrings. They are the relationship hors d'oeuvres before the main course of romantic reconciliation."

Shirin took the presenter position, spinning the whiteboard around to the clean back. Leah's stomach grumbled, which elicited a smile from the older Genrenaut. "Someone hasn't had breakfast yet."

Leah shrugged. "Meetings take priority."

"Some of us were up at six and got in a run and a breakfast before the meeting," Shirin said.

"And some of us had to shepherd home an inebriated probie at one AM," Mallery riposted before stepping back to let Shirin go.

There was no venom in the women's words, just the bantering barbs of long acquaintance.

"Shaking the gossip branches yielded a few choice bits." Shirin started writing on the whiteboard, breaking down their leads for possible plot threads. They'd covered this in her orientation—it was standard approach when a breach wasn't immediately evident—look for events and trends that stood out, then narrow down until you find your breach. If possible, use one plot to resolve another.

"Newspaper sources indicate Mercy Hospital admitted three people who were hit by cars after getting engaged. Two have been discharged; one is still recovering."

On the board: ENGAGEMENT RINGS IN HOSPITAL

"The Off-Broadway Achievement Awards are in five days."

OFF-BROADWAY AWARDS

"And a physical therapy company embedded in a gym that caters to the trendy urban professionals is advertising for two new PTs."

PT POSTS OPEN

"And lastly, millionaire actor Kyle Randal is hosting a gala tomorrow night. Randal is well known for being a lecherous skeeve, so there's a very good chance, given where we are, of women put into compromising situations which would then make for a creepy but in-genre meet-cute with innocuous guys."

SKEEVE PARTY

"Thanks, Shirin." Mallery tapped the board over the listed plot threads. "King and Roman, you go ahead and grab those PT jobs. The gym association gives us a good field base for a wide range of possible stories. Shirin, I want you on the algorithms today; see if we can cross-reference some of these findings and come up with intersections to narrow our search."

"Leah and I will hit the haunts. Two of them jog in the mornings in Central Park, so we'll start there. Updates by five PM for the evening meet-up, then we make plans for the evening."

Mallery paused as the team shuffled on the couches and seats, ready to move.

"Any questions?"

Leah, as usual, had many questions, but they could wait until she was talking to Mallery.

Starting the day in Central Park, served both of Mallery's agendas: reconnaissance and working through Leah's hangover.

Mallery trotted along merrily, gloves and yoga pants and a light fleece, hair held back in an exercise-standard ponytail.

Leah, meanwhile, huffed as she tried to keep pace.

"How are you in better shape than I am and you've just been in traction?"

"Because I was in marathon-running shape before my last mission, and you haven't been around long enough for Roman's fitness regimen to deform your life like a black hole. Also, it looks like your liver also needs some more training."

Leah huffed and puffed, pushing herself to catch up to Mallery. "I was stretching it. Next time I say, 'I shouldn't have another drink,' please don't pressure me like it's no big deal, even if it makes me out to be a spoilsport."

Mallery's face darkened. "You're right. I was just so happy to be back on my feet, I got a bit carried away. And then I had to carry you away!"

"Sorry about that. I hope I didn't inadvertently kick off any romance plots with random passers-by at the bar."

Mallery picked up the pace again. "No, nothing like that. You were very easy to take care of. Once we got back, I just left you with the glass of water and went on my way."

A moment passed. "Priority One is spotting the candidates from Roman's notes who frequent this park – Anna Grace and Jasper Montes, but also be on the lookout for other broken stories. So, what we're looking for," Mallery said, gesturing to the other runners on the trails, "is groups of friends, probably three of them, talking about relationships. They'll be running just a bit slower than everyone else, but they'll be talking a lot."

"Like we are," Leah said.

"Exactly! If I were a group of Genrenauts watching the scene, I'd definitely peg us as candidates. You'd be the romantic lead, and I'd be the wise, free-spirited friend, offering you advice about how you need to put yourself out there more."

"Got it," Leah said, pushing past the wall and finding something resembling a stride.

Focusing on the other joggers helped distract her from how not-in-shape she was. She saw solo runners in their own worlds, pairs jogging silently, love-birds in matching outfits jogging and stealing long glances at one another.

Then, Leah spotted a trio of women moving a clip slower, jogging in a shallow chevron formation, one of them a half-pace ahead of the other two. They moved along a trail that would converge a few hundred feet ahead.

"How about them?" Leah said, indicating the trio with a short motion, trying not to be too obvious.

"Good eye. Now we have to catch up. Let's get the lead out. Pain is just weakness leaving the body!" With that, Mallery poured on the speed, leaving Leah behind.

Sometimes this job was too much. On the other hand were the cushy salary, amazing benefits, and impossibly cool vistas. She kept reminding herself of the positives as she hurried to catch up with Mallery and the trio.

The center woman was a brunette white woman in her mid-twenties. Her friends were a shorter white redhead and a taller black woman, seemingly of a similar age. The women were still ten paces ahead, but they spoke loud enough to be heard. Or maybe that was just the world's physics giving them a break.

"…to get yourself back out there," the black woman said.

"One thing at a time." the woman in the center said. "I still don't know if I want to take the offer from the studio."

The redhead said, "You need closure. Go see him."

"Can we talk about something else?" the woman in the center said.

"No problem, Anna," said the taller woman. "We've got to get to rehearsal. Let's take the turn-off here and hit the showers."

The women turned off of the track, heading for the edge of the park.

"Back in a sec." Mallery threw up her hoodie, leaned forward and rushed ahead, sprinting to overtake the women. She pushed straight through the middle of the trio, jostling the women aside.

"Excuse me," the redhead said as Mallery rushed ahead then turned back around toward the center of the park.

Lungs heaving, Leah was happy to drop off the pace. She slowed and stopped at a bench, collapsing onto the cold wooden slats as Mallery looped around, heading her way.

The trio headed off, turning out of the park and out of sight.

Mallery slowed to a jog, then a walk, walking up to Leah sweat-sheened but still beaming.

"Good pick. That's definitely a lead worth following. I snuck a picture, so I'm going to shoot that over to the team for them to run through the algorithm for confirmation. The tracer I dropped in Anna's hoodie will let us keep tabs on her on the way to her gym and then home."

"Can I state again that this is kind of creepy?" Leah said.

"We're serving as donor figures in these people's stories. Like fairy godparents but with headsets and genre knowledge instead of magic wands and transforming rodents," Mallery said. "You're going to need to get over this if you want to stick with the team, newbie. If you've got a major problem, you should log it with King, but I can tell you now that it won't end well."

Mallery stretched her arms and legs, reminding Leah she should do the same. Her head spun as she got to her feet again, but her lungs felt better, like she'd dusted the curtains.

"King doesn't like wasting his time," Mallery said. "If he starts to think he's been wasting his time with you, it'll throw a pall over everything you do, even the good stuff like your patch yesterday. Hold on to those doubts until we get this story patched, and if you're still worried, we'll grab coffee and talk it through."

Leah's back cracked as she stretched, short of breath "It's just a big adjustment. All of this sneaking around and playing with people's lives."

"It's for the good. Not just the greater good. It's for individual people's good as well. Especially here. Ninety-nine times out a hundred, fixing a story means reuniting someone with a lifelong love. We're the guardian angels they never need to meet."

"I guess. It's still creepy."

Mallery made for the park exit, raising a hand to hail a taxi as soon as she was within view of the street. "You'll get used to it. Let's get back to the condo so we can shower and head back out to the next haunt."

"Can I collapse and die for a few minutes somewhere in there?"

A taxi rolled to a stop right in front of Mallery. Leah smiled at the story world magic.

"That's what showers are for. Come on, you're the youngest of us all." Mallery beamed, which Leah was realizing was pretty close to the woman's resting face. Some women had resting bitch face, but Mallery glowed. It was impressive. A little annoying, but impressive.

* * *

Leah didn't die during their pit stop, but she did spend ten extra minutes in the shower massaging her already-sore legs.

This time, instead of heading back out with Mallery, she got to stick around and work the data mines with Shirin.

"You've gotten a taste of finding stories in the field. Shirin can teach you about how the other half of the story is assembled," Mallery said, throwing on her coat, picking up a bright yellow umbrella from the front closet, and blowing a kiss to the pair of women before whirlwinding out of the door.

"That woman is a force of nature," Leah said, watching the door.

"She sure is. Just make sure you've got both legs planted firmly on the ground when she comes blowing by, or you'll get caught up in her storm system," Shirin said.

Now, what does she mean by that? Leah wondered as the older Genrenaut turned and moved to the workstation set up in the living room.

"Come on over, newbie. Now you get to learn how to do the real work." She waved her hand at the three screens arrayed like half a hexagon.

"We're tracking Anna, the woman you and Mallery pegged at the park, as well as digging into the cases in the hospital. What I'm going to have you do is run down any intersections between the candidates we've identified. We're assuming a straight pair based on the conversation, but don't automatically discount queer pairings – there may be something less obvious going on. Occam's Straight Razor has gotten teams in trouble in the past. Just because there are almost no mainstream queer romances in the theaters doesn't mean they don't have their own stories here," Shirin said.

"Glad to hear." One more point in this world's favor. Red Rooster was hectic and dazzling, but it also felt welcoming, validating.

"So, are you good to help me track down our unhappy couple?" Shirin asked.

Leah sat in the fold-out chair beside Shirin at the work station. "Where do I start?"

Shirin browsed over to a window open to Persona, the social network, which had its own problems with data privacy. "Mallery made a backdoor, so you can browse all accounts as if you were friended. I've cross-referenced three of the six hospital sweethearts with Anna already; I want you to run down the other three."

"We have her name and a picture."

"So that's where you start, assuming she uses her real name on the site. If not, search for people named Anna connected to the patients' accounts, and you'll need to go at least one degree of separation based on closest friends and family members."

"So, I get to spend all afternoon Persona-stalking these people?"

"It could be worse. You could be interviewing for a job like King and Roman. You ever want to get Roman upset, tell him he has to wear a tie."

"Noted. What are you going to be doing while I'm doing this?"

"Two things. One, resting my eyes. Too much time in front of LCD screens gives me a migraine. Two, I'm going to spend the rest of the afternoon in the gossip magazines and on local discussion groups to keep an eye out for any rumblings, especially about Kyle Randal's party."

"Please tell me we won't have to go," Leah said. "I had my fill of frat parties when I was actually in school."

"Jury's still out on that one, I'm afraid. If we have to go, it'll likely be you, Mallery, and Roman. King is not especially fond of this world. He prefers the dramas."

Leah nodded, and Shirin took up position on the couch, reclining with a book by her side.

Shirin left Leah with the trio of screens all filled with browser windows, a zillion tabs open between them.

She plugged in the earphones sitting by the workstation, cued up some techno, and got down to the social hacking business.

First up, Kevin French.

Leah browsed through all twelve-hundred and thirty-eight of Kevin's photos, keeping an eye on tagged names and untagged faces. Persona did its damnedest to fill in every possible bit of data, but some people resisted. She kept the photo of Anna that Mallery had taken at the ready, using it plus her own memory to try to filter through the pictures and look for a match.

Once she finished the pictures, she started over, sorting through any friends named Anna. And after that, she trolled the woman's timeline, checking for anyone who might look related, or who might look like they could be either of Anna's friends.

All of that took a good half hour. She put an X next to Kevin French and moved on to the next name, Oliver Brown.

Three hours of eye-straining, mouse-scrolling mundanity later, she hit pay dirt.

Theo Long, candidate number three. He was Han Chinese (judging by the clothes he wore in old family pictures - Leah could tell one of her people), in his late twenties, with hints of worry lines at his brows. He didn't have much of a Persona presence, but in the handful of pictures that he had up, Anna Grace was in fully half of them. There were pictures of the pair dancing in a studio, some kind of ballroom, from the look of it. Dinners, drinks out with friends, and more. Nothing in the last three weeks, however. The last two posts on his Persona account were a post from his mother talking about how Theo was going to be getting out of the hospital soon, how attentive (and pretty) his doctor was, and then one from Theo himself, with a picture of him walking out of the hospital with a crutch.

There were some wrinkles.

Theo's Persona page said "Engaged," where Anna's said "It's complicated." And Anna's page had pictures of Theo, but they'd all been untagged.

Leah gestured Shirin over to take a look. "That's a red flag for us if I've ever seen one." She laid out the connections in several tabs across the multiple screens, then scooted aside to let Shirin look at the results.

"I think you've got a winner here, newbie. Write it up and send it out to the team. They'll do a first-contact pass today, then we meet up to run down their story tonight so we can start building the patch."

"Can I take a break first?" Leah asked. "I kind of got in the zone, and I think your headache came back to the computer so it could hang out with me."

Shirin patted Leah on the shoulder. "Sure. But don't wait too long. Mallery is out there spending HQ's money, and King's the one who has to write expense reports this mission."

"Got it." Leah stood and walked over to the couch, flopping facedown to shield her eyes.

And promptly fell asleep.

She woke up, not having meant to sleep. Checking the clock, she'd been out for all of five minutes, just long enough for her arm to go numb and for her to be totally disoriented.

King stood in the doorway, arms crossed. "Shirin tells me that you found a match. Let's not make the team wait anymore on that report, shall we?"

Leah leapt from the couch to the workstation in a single bound, which was tricky, since she had to scale the couch to get to the other side in order to reach the workstation. She managed not to fall over, but only just.

Within an hour, the team had come back from the field and sat in the living room, ready for the report.

Her report.

Don't screw this up, her teammates' eyes said, all watching, waiting.

It's just another story. Tell the story, Leah, she told herself, and began.

Chapter Five:
Meet Bachelorette Number One

Leah pointed to the board. "So, our lead candidates are Anna Grace and Theo Long. Mallery and I saw Anna this morning, jogging with friends in Central Park. I dug through the Persona pages of the six people admitted to hospitals with engagement rings over the last month, which led me to Theo Long."

It was like her hands were asleep—she couldn't help but be incredibly aware of them and feel awkward. During a set, she had the mic as her woobie, could focus her body language on working the room, shifting the mic, and so on. She tried to use the dry-erase marker in the same way, but then it ended up looking like she thought the marker was a mic, which was just silly.

Roman swiped through the report on his tablet. "These Persona pages tell a pretty messy story."

"Sure do," Leah said. "So, I figure we need to get in there and get both sides of the story, then start working on a way to make a happily-ever-after, right?" She looked to Mallery, who nodded.

Mallery stood. "Thanks, Leah. I can take it from here. King, you and Roman will make contact with Theo. See if we can't get him to do PT at your gym, and if not, we'll see about tweaking his insurance so that he ends up there anyway. In the meantime, get a tracker on him and see if you can't manufacture a meeting to get yourselves into his life, bro-style."

"Bro-style?" Leah asked.

"Doing that emotionally-repressed around all other men unless you're drunk because only then is it okay to cry because the Patriarchy sucks. You know, bro-style."

"Got it."

"Leah and I will make contact with Anna, posing as a Wise Lesbian Couple so we can get her side of the story. We've got her tracked to her home, so we just need to pick up the trail when she heads out to dinner or drinks or whatever tonight."

Working the archetypes was standard procedure—fill an established role and it was easier for people in story worlds to fit you into their life without question. Since Shirin had told Leah a couple of days before that Mallery was very out as a lesbian in real life, not as much would be acting.

"Wise Lesbian Couple?" Leah asked. "Shouldn't it be Anna's Gay BFF if we're in a Romantic Comedy?"

Roman cut in. "I'm the one who does Gay BFF, but I'll need to work with Theo. Can't work both threads of the story at once."

"Gay BFF isn't in my repertoire," King said. "Never got the hang of it. Veers too close to Magical Negro, and I hate that shit."

For a moment, Leah was back in her comedy troupe, people arguing over roles. The familiarity was comforting, even if she felt a little bit out in left field as the others talked about their specialties and preferences.

"Why can't we just use a PPM to change up our appearance and be able to play multiple roles?" Leah asked. The Personal Phase Manipulators allowed the Genrenauts to disguise their appearance and voices.

King shook his head. "PPMs are very expensive, and hard to replace. We've lost three already this year in missions gone wrong. Council's keeping them on reserve."

Mallery made the move-it-along hand gesture. "More's the pity. They're dangerously fun to play with. Shirin, you're on logistics duty. Coordinate between the teams, feeding information back and forth. Mostly, I want you designing our Grand Reconciliation. Tomorrow's party will be too soon and has too high a skeeve factor, so look farther ahead."

Mallery looked at the board, taking it all in. "We'll probably need to go to extra innings on this one, so King, let's get ready to make our appeal to stay for, say, nine days? I think that'll be enough time to lay in groundwork. Assuming this story can actually be fixed."

"HQ has been denying extension requests left and right, especially since..." King said. "Let's see if we can't make it six days. We'll reassess at five."

"That's fair. Okay, everyone know what we're doing? Leah, you're with me. We have to get our covers sorted before we go visit our Leading Lady."

"Roger," Leah said.

Walking back to the master bedroom, Mallery launched right in.

"So, for this story, we're going to want to insert ourselves into Ms. Grace's life as seamlessly as we can, but not in such a big way that we leave a hole when we leave." Mallery turned into the bedroom and threw open the stand-up dresser, revealing her wardrobe as if it were an arsenal. Which, really, it was.

She pulled down three dresses, stacking clothes together, arranging and rearranging. *This is why Mallery's bag was twice as full as anyone else's*, Leah realized. In Sci-Fi or Western World, Roman brought the big bag of guns. Here, Mallery had her wardrobe.

Absently inspecting one of the dresses, Mallery continued. "If there's one thing Shirin goes overboard on, it's making herself indispensable. I read the report from your trip to Azura-3. She's pushing the boundaries of long-term involvement there, and we won't need to be as blatant with this one."

Mallery held up a dress, looking in the mirror. "That won't do with this hair," she said under her breath, then continued. "We're going to do a drive-by fairy-godmothering. We should be tourists instead of New York residents. That gives us a built-in departure."

"Sounds good," Leah said. "Can we be visiting from somewhere that doesn't require accents? I can only do Minnesota and Chinese. Never got into the impersonations part of comedy."

Mallery chuckled. "That's fine, darling." She dropped into a Georgia accent, thick as molasses. "I'll go big with mine and it'll draw the attention. So, who shall we be? Honeymooning actresses? Hippies on a food tourist adventure, adventurous enough to go to the Big Apple but not rich enough to fly to Kazakhstan?"

"I like the actress idea," Leah said. "It's high-status, so it'll grab attention, and it will cover for a good amount of the story talk. We can get meta on it, helping her fix her story within her 'real' world."

"Let's not get too close to the nose there. That can throw things off. Actresses it is. How did we meet?"

"Working a TV show together. No, auditions! We were rivals for a role but went out for coffee after encouraging one another. Neither of us got the role, but the consolation prize was pretty nice."

"And that's how you'll tell the story. Just like that." Mallery looked over her shoulder to Leah. "Now, what are we doing in NYC?"

"Museums and taking in the Broadway shows before they go on tour. You're looking to get into musical theatre, since you never got to put your triple-threat chops to sufficient use in Hollywood."

Mallery rolled with it. "I got frozen out of the high school musicals, since they were all about the White Girl Soprano, and I, alas, am a mezzo."

"So, you've got the song-and-dance chops to back this story up?" Leah asked.

Mallery launched into a waltz, holding her dress as her partner, dancing backward as she sang a song from *My Fair Lady*.

"Song-and-dance chops, check. That makes me the comedienne?"

"Indeed. Hollywood takes you as exotic, but roles for funny women that aren't white are pretty thin on the ground."

"Also, I'm not that thin."

"We needn't focus on that. You're lovely." Mallery looked in the mirror. "I'm barely thin enough for Hollywood, and I put in twenty hours at the gym every week. The only person with more time logged there is Roman."

Mallery found her outfit, then took to helping dress Leah, continuing to weave together their backstory. Mallery was not quite as hands-on with the makeup this time, thankfully. Plus, the air was on in the bathroom from the start.

Properly snazzed up and armed with a solid-enough backstory, Mallery loaded the software for the tracker they'd slipped into Anna's hoodie and they headed out to hail a cab.

"No Ultra?" Leah asked, figuring they'd use the super-convenient but ethically suspect app-based car service.

"Never Ultra," Mallery said, her face sour. "Plus, we never have to wait for a cab, remember?" Mallery whistled and waved a hand, and a yellow checkered car turned the corner and rolled up to a stop in front of their building.

"Every Little Thing She Does Is Magic" played in Leah's head as the pair climbed in and headed out to intercept their Leading Lady.

* * *

The GPS placed Anna in Times Square, which earned a small sigh from the cabbie, who was probably about to get off shift and would have rather not picked up a fare that would require him to drive into and out of a clusterfuck of traffic one more time.

Mallery dove straight into character, the Georgia coming back out. It was smooth enough that Leah wondered if this was the woman's native accent, one she'd rounded out toward the Central Ohio Valley default.

Mallery followed her GPS, looking like a capital-T Tourist—head down, ignorant of the flows of people, leaving Leah to watch out for her.

Except even the distracted bit was an act. Mallery wove through the crowd, looking like she was going to bump into people but never managing to do more than brush by their jackets.

All the while, she chattered, loudly.

"Ain't this the most amazing thing, Toni?" Leah was Toni, Mallery was Susan.

"Remember to look up, Susan. Can we get a picture at the top of those stairs?"

"But everyone gets a picture there. I want an authentic experience, something that really says I get New York, not 'I followed the guide book.'"

If they wanted that, they wouldn't be in Times Square to start, but Leah decided to hold her tongue there.

"There's a Disney store!" she clapped with feigned excitement as Mallery turned in that direction.

They wove and wound their way through the pedestrian-dominated street, hand in hand, eventually turning out of the super-touristy area into the Broadway theatre district, ending up in front of a side-street building with a dance studio's sign hanging on the second floor—ALWAYS EN POINTE DANCE STUDIO.

"Looks like our heroine is somewhere in this building," Mallery said.

"Her Persona profile listed her as an instructor at a dance studio; I think it was this one."

"It was this one, yes. So now we go in and talk our way into the class. We want the authentic New York dance experience. I'll carry you through the class."

"Does everything we do have to be about you being amazing and me bumbling through?" Leah regretted how hurt she sounded even before she was done asking the question.

Mallery turned and dropped all vestiges of her character. "Sorry, newbie. Rom-com couples are studies in opposites. Contrast hides who we really are. They'll see the bumbling and ignore who you are behind it. We need to be just enough in Anna's life to make a difference. It's far better if she remembers us as that wacky pair of actresses, not as the people we really are. Or even the people we aren't really."

"Got it. Lean into the stereotypes. How naggy are we?"

"Newlyweds, so not very. I'd say a two out of ten."

"But sassy," Leah asked, worried Mallery was going to somehow bleed all of the fun out of the characters.

Mallery beamed. "So sassy. At least eight out of ten. Shall we?"

* * *

The studio was narrow, no more than twenty feet across, but long, with mirrors along the entire wall opposite the windows. The dancers were all dressed in black, no pointe shoes, no socks. Leah guessed jazz or modern, probably jazz, given Broadway.

Which of course meant that their makeup could stay, but the wealthy-women-about-town outfits had to go.

Anna Grace stood in the studio, listening to something on earbuds. Her hair was back and up, head bobbing to the music.

Mallery kicked off her shoes in the lobby, walking past a half-dozen women getting ready, and entered the studio. Leah avoided tripping on her shoes as she rushed to follow.

"Hello? Are you Anna Grace? I'm Susan Mallery; this is my wife, Toni Tang." Leah had complained about the alliteration but Mallery countered that it was both adorable and appropriately ridiculous for a Rom-Com.

It could have been worse. In Hollywood, it could always be worse.

Anna looked the women over. "Hello. What can I do for you?"

"We heard about your class from a friend, Jamie, who moved out to Hollywood a while ago? We met at an audition. She was always going on about how amazing her classes with Anna Grace were, so when we decided that we'd come and visit the city, she said, 'Oh you just have to go take a class with Anna.' Isn't that right, Toni?"

"Precisely. I never really got into dancing, but Susie here, she's dancing reality show–level. I keep telling her to try out; it'd be a good platform-builder."

Activate Super-Cute Lesbians act! Leah thought.

Susan poured it on a bit more until Anna relented and let them audit the class. They changed into their gym gear and barefoot on the cold floor, joined in when the Fosse started.

Leah stumbled her way through the class, while Mallery was on the beat the whole time, fierce and loving it, even with the cast locking one arm into a permanent chicken wing.

After class, Mallery used some kind of social-force-of-nature magic to convince Anna to grab coffee with the two of them, leading the way to a theatre-crowd cafe around the corner called the All-Nighter.

"How did you get into show business?" Mallery-as-Susan asked, her Georgia accent holding.

"I grew up in Queens, and my parents took me to see shows when I was a kid. I bounced around between a few different majors, racking up music and acting classes before settling on a finance degree. Got me a steady but soul-crushing day job."

"I know how that is," Leah said, not having to act as Anna took a sip of her coffee. Their Leading Lady continued. "Off-Broadway roles started lining up, and I was able to go part-time, then quit the finance biz altogether, thanks to the studio. Heck, I was even offered a spot as a partner in the studio. That was unreal," Anna said, twitching as if shaking off the idea. There was more than that behind the move, if Leah was on the mark with her people-watching.

"Anyone special in your life?" Leah asked, diving right in. Mallery had warmed her up enough, and this sure as heck looked like an opening.

Anna leaned back, head against the booth, which told Leah she may have misfired on her timing. A microexpression wince from Mallery corroborated her failure.

Mallery jumped in to cover, "Oh, Toni, let's not pry."

"No, it's fine. It's just..." Anna said, looking for words.

"It's complicated?" Leah volunteered.

"Yeah. I was seeing this guy; he was sweet, super-organized, he planned these incredibly thoughtful dates, and he loved the theater. Loves, I guess. But then, and this will make you laugh, he proposed six months into our relationship, the day after I was offered partnership at the studio."

"Oh, my." Mallery took a sip of her drink, shifting in the seat. "I assume from your tone that wasn't a good thing?"

"It was just...I mean, we'd only been together for six months, and Theo's down on one knee, and I've never lived in one place more than a year since I went to college. I didn't like to be tied down. And now, with the studio and something I can almost be unashamed to call a career, and the ring, it was all just too much."

Mallery put her hand on Susan's for a moment. "Oh, honey, don't I know it. Toni here's like this Theo, I think. She loves to organize everything, loves to know answers to questions before they're asked. It makes my life livable, but sometimes you don't want to be tied down, am I right?"

"Totally. And then it gets even worse. I come back after leaving town for the weekend to sort out my head, and he's been in a car accident."

Leah tapped into the refreshed sympathy and dialed it up as best as she could to feign the shocked reaction she should have, covering her mouth and nose with her free hand.

"Oh no," Mallery said. "Is..."

"He'll be fine, thank god. The car wasn't going that fast, and he fell well, the doctors say. He's in PT now. I was on the plane when it happened, and no one picked up when I called. I turned straight around for a return flight, but I got caught in a weekend's worth of cancellations. I went straight to the hospital when I got back, but his doctor said that he didn't want to see me."

Leah shared a quick look with Mallery, wishing for telepathy. That's what the debrief was for. She wasn't the biggest Rom-Com fan ever, but this definitely sounded like breach-worthy levels of weird. Would a guy that just proposed really turn her away like that?

Anna looked down into her coffee. "So I left, deleted his number, and pretended that it never happened. Which is super-mature, right?"

"You both went through a trauma; it's understandable," Leah said, leaning into sympathy while thinking that Anna's extreme reaction was probably fallout from the breach. Breaches weren't just one break in the story, like the accident. They snowballed, like people leaving town in her first mission or the diplomatic implosion on Ahura-3.

Mallery followed up. "How long between the accident and when you went to visit?"

"I was gone when the accident happened. So, like a week. No, five days. He'd just woken up, and I wasn't there. Can you blame him for not wanting to see me?" Anna's eyes went red and puffy as her emotional fortitude crumbled. Normally, eyes didn't do that so fast. *Must be another story world thing*, Leah thought.

Mallery took Anna's hand and squeezed. "He went overboard with the proposal, sure, but did you tell him about the partner offer?"

"I did, and that's when he proposed! He said the timing was perfect, that everything was coming together just how he'd imagined it."

"That is a bit off." Leah had no idea where Mallery was going with the conversation. So she tried to answer like an actual friend.

"It is," Anna said. "It's like I didn't even get a say in my life. He fit the story he'd been telling himself in his heart or, more accurately, the story he'd been raised to tell himself because his family told him to, and I was the missing piece, the perfect adornment to his perfect life."

"Did you tell him that?" Leah asked.

"Of course not. It's just how he is. He likes things to go smoothly, and I go with the wind. We made it work for a while. I'd helped him be more spontaneous; he helped me be grounded. This was just way too much, all at once. I've been reeling ever since."

"How long ago was all this?" Mallery asked.

"A couple of weeks now. Theo's out of the hospital, and I...I don't know what to do. The easy thing would be to forget about it, try to figure out if I want to stay here and teach dance for the rest of my life, if that's something I can handle. He made his choice, right?"

Anna looked out the window, at the marquee of a theatre across the street. "Being a partner at the studio would limit what kind of and how many shows I could audition for. It's trading possibility for certainty, but not the certainty I wanted."

"You like the studio; you obviously like the people," Leah said.

Mallery jumped in, answering for Anna. "Of course she does. They're delightful. Loveliest bunch of ladies I've ever met."

"You haven't been up against them in an audition," Anna said, an absent chuckle reaching all the way to her eyes.

Mallery cocked her head. "Fair point. So, what can we do to help? Do you want to play hostess and show us all of the cool sights of the city and distract you from the life drama?"

Leah caught the ball and ran with it. "We're excellent distractions. Susan here can hold a room for an hour just talking about her makeup regimen. Now, if I let a makeup artist do my face like they're used to, I'll end up looking like a geisha doll. Asian faces paint different, and not many makeup folks know how to work on faces that aren't white."

"No one can do you justice, my dear." Mallery leaned over and took Leah's face in both hands, planting a big, Roger Rabbit smacker of a kiss on her lips.

All of a sudden, it was very hot in the cafe.

211

Leah leaned back and fanned herself, leaving Anna to clap in delight.

"Oh, you're so cute. How do you stay spontaneous after being together for so long?"

Mallery favored Anna with a smile. "We're actresses, my dear. We wake up as different people every day. Just find a way to make that work for you. Shall we be off?"

Leah managed to nod. Or maybe it was just more swooning.

"This was great. I mean, I unloaded all of this drama on my friends already." Anna stood and donned her coat. "They've been through the ups and the downs, and it's good to get a fresh perspective."

Mallery put on her own coat with delicate grace, keeping eye contact with their mark. "Well, we're here for about a week, give or take."

"Susan likes open return tickets."

"I'm like you, my dear. I like to keep my options open." Changing the subject, Mallery asked, "So, when will we see you next? There are a million and one things to do and see here; I'm simply overwhelmed. I could use some spontaneity."

"I just don't know where to start," Leah added.

Anna looked between the two of them. "Well, I don't have class tomorrow…"

"Excellent. So, we'll pick you up at, what, eight? New York theater folk are late risers, yes? I've gotten used to five AM call times, myself, so it'll be lovely to sleep in."

Mallery manifested a business card out of seemingly nowhere and handed it to Anna. "Cell and email are the best. Shall we pick you up here, or do you live elsewhere?"

"I live down in the Village. Why don't we start at Union Square and find our way from there?"

"Which one's Union Square?" Mallery asked, as if the whole room would answer her.

Leah put a hand on Mallery's shoulder. "I know that one. Southwest corner, at eight?"

"Sounds good," Anna said with a polite smile.

"So lovely to meet you, darling." Mallery went in for European air kisses. Anna agreed, looking only slightly less shocked by the gesture than Leah had been when her teammate had planted one on her lips.

They let Anna leave first. When she was out the door, Mallery hopped over to the next chair so that they faced each other instead of sitting thigh-to-thigh.

"That went splendidly. We'll have to work on our conversational rhythm a bit, but you're a good improviser. King said as much, but chemistry plays such a big part, you never know."

Mallery topped off their glasses of water from the carafe. It seemed like they were going to stay for a while. "We've got plenty of time to come up with ways of steering the conversation more adroitly tomorrow, and maybe even working in a chance to get Anna and Theo in the same place to start to reacclimate them."

Maybe if I keep her supplied with water, she'll solve the whole case by herself, Leah thought.

"I think this one is going to take a few steps," Mallery said." It seems like they were almost, almost back together, but this car accident, it's as severe a breach as I've seen in this world. Given what's gone on the last six months, I shouldn't be surprised, but still."

Leah took a long breath, letting the barrage of words roll over her. "Yep. Got it. Shall we get back to the team? Also, dinner?"

"Got your appetite back, I see?"

"Well, I jogged five miles today, when I usually run zero miles, so yes, I'm hungry. And as you said, there are a million and one places to see, most of them amazing restaurants. Please tell me the fancy genrenauts business card extends to expense dinners."

"Oh, but of course. We'll have family dinner most nights that we aren't in the field, and if folks don't feel like going out, delivery. The food here is amazing; it all looks like it was made by world-renowned chefs and plated by food photographers. Just you wait."

"If you're going to keep talking, we need to eat now."

"Hold your horses," Mallery said, cranking up the Georgia. "Let's get back to the condo first."

This is my life, Leah thought as they paid, left, and caught a taxi, again in a matter of seconds from Mallery whistling and raising her arm.

My amazing, confusing, totally screwed-up life.

Chapter Six:
The Glamour. The Marvel. The Paperwork.

Roman sat at a chic desk at the corner of the gym floor, sorting through client charts. In reality, he wouldn't need to do any substantive work with other clients, as he could farm them out to other PTs. They were there for Theo, and he was due for his first appointment at the gym any moment now.

It had taken some finagling, with King and Shirin tag-teaming the computer systems to rearrange Theo's insurance and make it so their gym was the only place where his physical therapy would be covered.

A severe and beautiful white woman walked in. She had midnight-black hair and wore a lab coat draped over business wear. She held a clipboard, like she'd just walked off of the set of *Grey's Anatomy*.

"Are you Gregory Roman?" she asked from ten paces away.

"Yes, may I help you?"

"I'm Doctor Andrea Thorsson, and I'm here to talk to you or someone about why my patient was reassigned here when I'd referred him to, and he'd already started, physical therapy at another practice."

The hell? Roman thought. He put on a "what can you do? "face to stay in character and rolled forward. "I just got the referral and saw him on my schedule. You didn't have to come down here yourself. Should have taken it up with the insurance company."

Dr. Thorsson scowled. "This is quite ridiculous."

Roman shrugged. "Insurance companies, right?"

A hobbling Theo Long walked in the door, with the assistance of a crutch. He said, "Doctor Thorsson, it's fine. The insurance company says I should go here, I'll go here. It's the treatment that matters, right?"

Theo looked thinner than his pictures, his smart clothes hanging a bit loose on his frame. He was put together, but not severe like his companion. Also, there wasn't supposed to *be* a companion. Why was his doctor accompanying him to PT? He was glad King was out of sight; it'd keep another member of their team in reserve. Roman started to think of how they'd investigate her but refocused on the now.

Roman extended a hand to shake. "We'll take very good care of Mr. Long."

They had a staredown for a beat. As he watched her intensely, the doctor blurred slightly at the edges, out of focus with the world around her. Which meant she was connected to the breach, tied in more substantially than he'd imagined. That'd explain the odd behavior. The doctor was caught up in the story.

"Well, don't get too cozy," Doctor Thorsson said. "I expect he'll be out of your hands very soon. I'll be here if you need me," she said to Theo.

Roman turned the doc's comment back around on her, all smiles. "Sounds good to us. We love getting clients back on their feet as quickly and safely as possible."

Before she left for the waiting area in front, the doctor gave Theo a significant look, and more pieces clicked into place. He'd need to update the team as soon as this scene was done.

Roman extended a hand to Theo. "I'm Greg Roman, I'll be your therapist. Shall we take a seat and get started?" He moved to engage Theo and block off the doctor from the conversation, trying to minimize her role in the scene. A twinge of guilt ran down his spine as Mallery's voice called out the macho power play for what it was. However, he didn't see a way to preserve the connection without sidelining her. Social engineering wasn't his forte.

He kept one eye on the doctor to fill out his report to the team. They'd need to run down her connection to the story.

Then they'd need to disentangle whatever her dynamic was with Theo. While trying to rekindle his relationship with Anna, and actually doing physical therapy so he's ready for the reconciliation? Mallery needed to hear about this as soon as possible. First, the scene at hand.

Roman led Theo to a pair of chairs along the wall of the gym. The man set aside his crutch and sat in the chair, wincing as he went.

"So, your referral says you're looking to recover range of motion and strength in your left leg. Can you tell me about the accident?"

"I was crossing the street on Eighth Ave, and a black compact car comes careening around the corner, driven by some blonde woman in a hat. It hit me here," Theo said, gesturing to his left hip, "and kept going. I went flying, people say like ten feet, and landed weird on my leg. People say she didn't even stop, just drove off. New York, man." He shrugged. "Anyway. I was in traction for several weeks, and now that I'm out, I'm here."

"You got lucky," Roman said with his best smile, trying to build rapport. "Why don't you hop up on the bench here so I can see what's what."

Roman rolled out some paper and Theo climbed onto the bench, sitting with his legs over the side.

"What do you do for work?" Roman asked, testing Theo's range of motion. He'd never actually studied physiotherapy, but a lifetime of dealing with his friends and comrades' injuries let him fake it pretty well. "A lot of physical activity?" He stopped when he felt resistance and saw Theo wince.

"No, I'm an architect. Desk jockey. I dance on weeknights and weekends, though. Or I did, I guess."

"Before the accident?" Roman asked, betting that wasn't the answer but still baiting for the info.

"Yeah, that, and. Well, just before the accident, I had a bit of a blowup in my personal life."

"Oh, sorry to hear that. Rough timing. On your back, please." Roman gestured to the bench. "Any chance of putting things back together?"

Theo leaned back, easing the descent with his elbows. The guy was not in great shape. They might have to go for a low-physicality reunion plan if he didn't start making strides soon.

"I don't know. My fiancée, or she was going to be my fiancée. I proposed because I was so happy for her that she'd gotten offered this great job." Theo was going red. Roman stopped for a moment, let his client-slash-lead catch his breath. "It seemed like things were finally coming together for her. If she wasn't worried about her future, she'd be open to the proposal, but instead, I spooked her and she left for the weekend. Haven't heard from her since, not even after the accident."

"Oh, man, that's harsh."

"Yeah, I just don't know what to do. I mean, are we even together? Is that what happens when you blow a proposal? It's not something you can take back."

"Well, just like this leg, it's not going to get better if you don't work at it.

Extend your foot as far as you can go without pain," Roman lifted the man's upper leg, watching as it reached seventy degrees of rotation, then Theo gasped and stopped.

"Okay, we'll definitely have to work on that."

Roman continued to run Theo's leg through its paces, drawing on the many, many hours he'd spent in physical therapy himself, while he started to workshop solutions, trying to anticipate questions from his teammates. They'd look more into Theo and this Doctor Thorsson.

"Okay, on your feet. Let's look at how you walk."

"This is going to hurt," Theo said.

"I know. I'm right here. I've been through this myself. We're going to make this better," Roman said with genuine warmth. He liked this guy and really hoped they could actually help. He'd been born to help, even if he was used to solving problems by punching people and blowing things up. Here, he could help just by being there for someone at the right time, and that, that was pretty fantastic.

*　*　*

When Theo left, Dr. Thorsson guiding him out, Roman and King caught up over "paperwork" and headed back to the loft. Leah and Mallery had returned from their assignment just minutes before.

"I think the Doctor is a genuine factor," Roman told the team. "Definitely worth looking into. My guess would be False Fiancée, but there's a chance she and the boy are supposed to end up together."

Leah jumped in to clarify. "So, by False Fiancée, we mean like the person that the romantic lead shacks up with when the hero and heroine are estranged, who is perfectly wonderful on paper but is never actually the right match. That kind of false fiancée?

King answered. "Or the hero or heroine's partner at the start of the story, the one who is either nice but boring or actually quietly or not-so-quietly abusive-slash-demeaning."

"So, Not the One," Leah said.

"Precisely."

King paced. "If she's not a False Fiancée and he's supposed to end up with the doctor, then why'd we get dispatched for the breach?"

"Exactly. It might have been the accident. But maybe the world is self-correcting with the doctor."

"How often does that ever happen when we're on-world?" Roman asked.

King shook his head. "Never when we need it to." He looked at Roman's stack of files, brought back from the PT clinic. "You going to up those notes and get them filed?"

Roman made a small grumbling sound as Leah and Mallery went to another room. "Why do we have to do the paperwork if we've farmed the clients out to real physical therapists?" he asked.

"Part of the deal. They dictate notes, we file them."

"Fair enough." And really, to do otherwise would cause more ripples, if small ones. He put in his earbuds and cued up the recorded notes of the PTs, stopping and rewinding to get every word precisely right, but not nearly as much as if he'd been asked to transcribe one text to another. The joys of dyslexia.

However he did it, he'd do it right. They were guests in this world, and part of their job was to leave as few ripples as possible, and only the right ripples.

It didn't matter if these people were bound up by universal rules that he saw as being tighter, more restrictive than his own, whether their world felt like just another story to him and anyone from Earth Prime. These people's lives were their own, and he'd spent enough time in war zones made by power-hungry warlords to want to propagate any of that if he could avoid it. They couldn't avoid it entirely, so he'd try to minimize the damage.

Rewind again and get it right. The meeting could wait.

* * *

The team assembled at an Italian restaurant around the corner from the condo. Leah barely caught Mallery slipping the server a twenty to get them a table tucked away in the back corner, with instructions that the servers were only to visit every ten minutes.

They caught up and plotted over pasta so amazing that Leah was afraid that she'd died and gone to story heaven. It was like a troupe meeting from her improv days, but with less intra-group drama and way better food.

The five of them sat around a circular table, digging into the food, family style.

"The thing that's got me worried is the doctor here," Shirin said. "She's clearly part of the breach—ripple or instigator. Get her out of the equation, we're looking at a two-day-fix, maybe four at max, depending on how quickly we can put together a reconciliation moment."

"Agreed," Mallery said. "Our first priority is figuring out where the Doctor fits in this equation."

"Once we find out where she practices, I can go in as a pharma rep and get a read on her," King said. "Try to trip her up if I need to."

"Would that be Sexy Pharma Rep?" Mallery asked with Groucho Marx level eyebrow-waggling."

King chuckled. "If that's what it takes."

"When in Rome, right?" Leah added, very happy to join in on the opportunity to have a laugh at the boss's expense while he was in on the joke.

Mallery continued. "That's settled, then. Roman, you tail Theo and see if we can't find out when he'll be out with Dr. Thorsson and vulnerable to an interruption once we take her measure."

Mallery clapped. "Now, enough with the shop talk. I need to catch up on all of the office gossip from while I've been gone. Shirin, you're up."

Chapter Seven:
Only Tourists Look Up

Mallery was expecting the Empire State Building, or maybe a trip down to the Statue of Liberty.

Instead, when Mallery and Leah met Anna for their day of sightseeing, she just started walking down the street.

"The best way to experience New York is block by block, on the ground level, the way New Yorkers do," Anna said, gesturing to the bustling city around them. "More New Yorkers use the subway than cabs; more walk to work than drive. The tourist things, those you can do on your own. The real magic of the Big Apple is in the moments that come up organically."

"First stop, New York bagels," Anna continued.

Walking up to a Jewish deli, they found a line out the door and down the street. They chatted in line, Mallery and Leah trying to angle the conversation around to topics that could help nudge her toward reconciliation, but Anna wasn't having any of it. She headed off all conversational advances, coming back around to talk about the city. Anna knew a surprising amount about the city's theatre history, though since Leah didn't, it was hard to tell if this was actual history or Romance World history.

Either way, the bagels were delicious. Steaming hot, with schmear that melted as it hit the bread. The shell was slightly crunchy; the center was soft but chewy.

Leah had to take a moment to savor. "This alone is worth the price we paid to get here," she said, covering her mouth as she chewed.

"So true." Mallery's accent firmly in place. "So, what's next?"

Anna walked on, already done with her bagel, fingers licked clean.

"Now we walk around Bryant Park and do some people-watching."

Since they weren't getting anywhere on their conversational agenda, Leah assumed they'd just back off and work on building rapport. They'd reached their limit of allowed personal prying, and now they had to build up trust to the next threshold.

So, they talked about everything and nothing, Mallery guiding the trio through an increasingly elaborate backstory about "Toni" and "Susan's" lives in LA. Mallery was seriously a machine. Wind her up and then she could just go, and go, and go. Leah thought of herself as good on her feet. She'd maintained backstory while reacting in-character and trying to steer the conversation around to a particular topic, all while subtly communicating to a colleague what should come next...but even her improv experience couldn't prepare her for this level of con-artistry.

Because that's what it was, ultimately. Even with the best of intentions, they were still habitually lying to the woman and manipulating her. And they'd only known her for hours, instead of troupe-mates she'd known for years in improv.

Leah had only spent this much time with a couple of people from story worlds, and never this long with someone who wasn't already on board with (at least a version of) the Genrenauts' plan. It wasn't yet a long game, but it was something different.

The day rolled into a highly filmable montage of the city—street vendors, parks, weird little shops so specialized that they were almost too cute (thank you, East Village), and more.

They took an extended break to eat lunch at Anna's absolute favorite burger joint, which also served cupcakes in a combination that was as delightful as it was unexpected.

Every step of the way, Leah had to keep up the Honeymooners act, and it was getting to her. Feigning intimacy with someone you'd just met was one thing. When you clearly had chemistry? And were on Romance World? That was something completely different. There were signals, and hotness, and kissing, and Leah was going to need to check some regulations here really quick.

Five hours in, Anna started to open up again, giving Leah a blissful distraction from her ambivalence.

"So, what do you want to do next?" Mallery asked.

"I thought we could relax here for a little while longer, then I could take you on the High Line, then put you on the ferry to go see the Statue of Liberty."

"What happened to 'The real New York is the everyday New York'?" Leah asked, keeping her tone light.

"Of course, but you still want to see the Statue of Liberty, right?"

They nodded.

"Plus, I have to get to work for my afternoon classes, and I have to prep for an audition tomorrow."

"An audition? For what part?" Leah asked.

"A chorus role in a revival of *Oklahoma!* It'd be a steady paycheck. They're guessing they'll get at least a year out of the run."

"Do you like the show?" Mallery asked. "Not that I'm biased. I have nothing against Oklahoma. It's North Carolina I can't stand," Mallery said, winking.

"It's fine. If the show doesn't last too long, I can apply for something else. I just—it's funny, I just want some kind of control over my life after all of the last month's whirlwind. Normally, in this situation, I'd go running away from certainty, but…"

"Certainty comes with control," Leah said.

"Yeah. And life's been pretty out of control. In other people's control. My bosses. My…" She paused, sorting through her choice of words. "…Theo, his accident, his family."

Mallery put her hand on Anna's. "I know what you mean. So I'll tell you what my friend Lance told me when I was freaking out about the idea of proposing to Toni."

"This story is good," Leah said, even though she was pretty sure Mallery had just made it up in her head.

"He said: 'Honey, you can't control everything in your life. Usually, you can control very little. So why not be smart about the things you can control? You don't know that everything is going to work out with her, but you know how you feel, and you damn well better know how she feels. So, either that's enough or you accept you're so scared of getting locked in, you'd rather just float on the wind, hoping that somehow something even better comes along. And darling, that don't happen every day. Ask yourself—is she worth the risk? If so, then that's all the certainty you're going to get and all you need.'"

Leah sniffed back a tear. *Damn, the girl was good.*

Anna squeezed Mallery's hand, then leaned back in her chair.

"And…" Anna asked.

Mallery sighed, beaming. "I ran to Toni and never looked back."

Leah leaned over and gave Mallery a healthy peck on the cheek. If she'd done any less after a story like that, it'd just have been weird.

Anna took another long breath. "I have to call him."

Leah shifted in her chair. "Really?"

Mallery squeezed Anna's hand again. "Of course you call him. You call, you talk, you meet somewhere, you remember what it's really about."

"I have to head out. Thanks so much for the chat," Anna said.

"It's the least we can do after all of your hospitality," Mallery said. Leah nodded her agreement and watched as Anna got up in a rush, throwing on her jacket and reassembling her purse, and nearly rushed out of the restaurant.

Mallery waited until Anna was out of sight, then raised her hand for a high five. The resulting hand slap sounded like victory.

"I'll call it in to Shirin so she can let Roman and King know," Leah said. "By the way, that story?"

"I know."

"That's the reason why you get the big bucks."

"The benefits are really what does it. Let's have a round. There's a bar just a block south of here with some great whiskey."

"Shouldn't we get back?"

"Waiting here means we won't have to grab a second cab to get back out into the city to make whatever our next move is. It's just strategic thinking." Mallery's smile was half-imp, half-wolf, and all pleased.

"Uh-huh," Leah said, standing.

"Remember to get the check," Mallery said, chuckling on her way out.

Leah sighed. At least the story was looking up. Fingers crossed they'd be home by dinnertime tomorrow.

* * *

Late the next morning, King put on his best smile as he waltzed into the hospital. He had a pad of scratch-off lottery cards tucked in his suitcoat pocket, and trailed a cart of medical samples in a pristine rolling briefcase. The samples were all placebos and the boxes were a year old, but they were essential props for his cover to get in to see Doctor Thorsson.

He'd cased the place hours earlier in casual clothes and a big coat, looking disheveled and unkempt. And then, he waited. It'd taken all of ten minutes of eavesdropping on the receptionist Susanne—a black woman of about his own age—to find out what leverage he'd need to get past her. He picked up the scratch-off cards on the way back to the apartment, then returned shaved, showered, and decked out as a Sexy Pharma Rep.

The room was half-full, people waiting in a cube of chairs surrounding a coffee table with stacks of months-old magazines.

Susanne was the main hurdle. Get the reception staff on your side and you could get in to talk to anyone. On Earth Prime, this would all be far harder, but in a Rom-Com, genre tropes permitted preposterous things left and right as long as they were in the service of a story. King was banking on the fact that Dr. Thorsson was important enough to the story that he'd be able to pull off this scam…with the right prop.

King strode up and greeted Susanne. She wore a bright floral print dress and had tightly curled hair. She paused her conversation with a colleague sitting behind and to her left to greet King. He made a show of reading her nametag and started.

Trusting his gut, King switched out his work-default Ivy League accent for his native Baltimorean. "Miss Susanne, I'm Victor King, with Inspiria Tech. How are you today?"

The woman's express grew a shade less tired. "Getting by. What can I do for you?"

"Just making my rounds, you know. I got some samples for Dr. Thorsson. She in?"

Susanne turned and looked behind her, to a duty board or a break room or something. King didn't have a good angle. What he did have was the scratch cards. He slipped the cards out of his suit coat and laid them on the table, subtly and not noticeably sticking out from under some dummy pharmaceutical papers.

In a low voice, King said, "A fellow rep said this was your game. And I did tell my wife I'd quit." He said, winking. King didn't pride himself on his charm offensive like some on his team, but he did alright.

Susanne slipped the scratch-off tickets off the desk and down out of sight, nodding with vague approval.

"She's not here just now, but you can wait."

"Any recommendations on how to talk to the doc? This is my first time around here, and it's always easier when I know how folks like to operate."

Leaning in, Susanne spoke softly. "Normally, the doc's cold. Efficient, doesn't hang around for socializing."

"That's too bad." King matched her low volume. "You sure there ain't nothing you know to help a brother out? This beat is rough."

She looked at him for a hard moment, taking his measure. "There's this patient of hers. Handsome Chinese boy. Got her all twitterpated, taking vacation days for the first time I've ever heard. She'll need to get her siddity self calmed down a bit before she can be happy. Maybe this boy will do it."

King nodded along, letting her fill the air. A moment passed, and Miss Susanne added. "She doesn't like anybody wasting her time, you understand?"

King nodded along as she spoke. "I'll have myself a seat, then. Thank you kindly." He gave an appreciative smile and returned to the waiting area, filing away Susanne's commentary. The way Roman described her protectiveness at the physical therapist's made him think *False Fiancée*, but if Theo was helping her come out of her shell, changing her way of being in the world, maybe the story was fixing itself. He'd need to talk to her directly and see what his instincts had to say.

* * *

Around a half-hour later, Susanne cued King and buzzed him through to see Dr. Thorsson. He rolled his cart back and tucked a placebo-tastic packet of Vialita-C (imported from Earth Prime, where Vialita had a wider product range) into his suit coat.

Dr. Thorsson stood beside a file cabinet, looking over patient charts as he walked in.

"I have a patient waiting. What did you give Susanne?"

Blunt as a mace. Got it, King thought.

He defused with a smile. "A gentleman never tells his secrets." He drew out an Inspiria business card (printed in the safe-house) and presented it to the doctor. She did not take it.

"I'm with Inspiria. I've got some Vialita-C samples to drop off, and a special gift from the company. As you probably know, we're co-sponsoring a gala this week, and we're extending an invitation to prominent physicians in the area. Mr. Randal would be pleased if you could join him."

King replaced the card and pulled out the invite (also forged, off a copy shared on Pictogram), setting it on the cabinet beside the doctor.

The doctor's smile was that of an indulgent predator. "Thank you. You can leave the samples and I'll use them when I can. Now I really have to go."

King's story senses were going wild. The doctor and her clothes looked slightly wrong, like they were in an overexposed picture, even more so than he'd expect with the brutal lighting.

Roman was right, King thought. *She's tied up in the breach in a big way.*

King presented his business card again, and social pressure won out as the doctor took the card and slipped it into her lab coat. King waited as the doctor exited and turned right, deeper into the hospital, allowing himself a small exhalation of relief.

The tracker was in place, so they'd be able to follow her as long as she was wearing the lab coat. Plus, they'd be able to piggyback onto any phone calls she made. It might only work for a few hours, but every variable they could eliminate made their work that much easier.

He'd been expecting a little more give-and-take—usually when you came in repping big pharma, most doctors would at least give you the time of day. The question then was why.

King nodded to Miss Susanne on his way out and then closed down, making his presence small as he left the hospital, avoiding anyone else.

Once he hit the street, he tapped off a quick message to Mallery and then hailed a cab.

* * *

When Theo came in for his next session (this time without the doctor), Roman took the opportunity to dig deeper into his side of the story.

"How are you doing in getting around day-to-day?" Roman asked as he led Theo through slow stretches.

Theo winced, still early in the curve of rebuilding his strength. "Not too bad. I feel pretty useless, but now that I'm getting used to moving more slowly, it's not too bad. Could have been much worse."

Roman switched Theo to another exercise and continued the small talk. "That's the spirit. Are you already back to work?"

"Yeah, mostly. I'm telecommuting this week, then back in the office next week."

Then it was time to get into the meat of the conversation. "So, this Doctor Thorsson, she seems very hands-on with her care."

Theo's reaction was mixed—mostly it looked like uncertainty. "Yeah, she's been great—stayed with me from the operating room to ICU and recovery."

Roman didn't know many doctors that would escort their patient to a PT gym, but this was a story world. And she was part of a breach.

"Are you sure her interest is strictly professional?" Roman stood and led Theo over to the leg press, setting it for the lowest weight "I don't get many doctors escorting their discharged patients around to physical therapy."

"She offered to give me a ride," Theo said while struggling, pressing slowly, "spare me the subway trip"—his leg trembled on the third rep—"so I wouldn't show up to PT already exhausted." After the third, he exhaled hard. Not quite there.

"Let's stop there for now and get some ice on that leg. Taking time outside of work to give a patient a ride. Does that strike you as odd behavior for a doctor?" he asked, not caring how obvious of a leading question it was.

"I mean, I guess? I try not to question generosity."

Theo pulled an ice pack out of the freezer and set Theo up with the electrical stimulation, ice over top. Theo flinched at the ice, then settled in, leaning back and relaxing.

"What if it's more than generosity? I saw the way she looked at you on Monday."

Theo got a deer-in-the-headlights look. "Really?"

"Totally. So, what are you going to do about it?"

"I don't know. I mean, the accident was like a day after I proposed and my girlfriend responded by leaving the country. I've got a lot on my plate already."

He'd take some nudging, then. Remembering his profile and Mallery's report, Roman adjusted his approach. "Maybe it's just me, but I hate that kind of ambiguity. The not knowing. I want to be certain where I stand."

Theo closed his eyes. "Yeah. Anna hasn't been in touch since she left."

That's not what Anna said. Another note for the debrief.

"Think it over. She's probably holding back because she doesn't want to pressure you. If you're interested, even one date with the doc might be enough to tell you whether the attraction is mostly leftover positive 'thanks for saving my life' feelings or something deeper."

"Am I going to be charged extra for this therapy?"

"This one's on the house. But next time, we start on the comfy couch and you tell me about your parents. Let that ice work for another ten minutes or so, and then you're done. Good work today. Let me know if you need anything."

With that, he let Theo be, not ready to push any harder. He'd already been incredibly forward. This part of the work wasn't his specialty; he didn't have the nuance that the others brought to bear. He could play a role, especially in the SF or Thriller regions, but pulling other people's strings here in Romance? Not nearly so much.

Roman took one more appointment that day, working off the chart to handle the bare minimum work load to not instantly get fired even in the "no one is ever really paying that close of attention to your work" rules of this story world, which would work as long as he avoided eye contact with Benjamin, that Adonis of a senior PT with abs that had nearly led to Roman dropping a five-pound weight on a client's foot. Assuming he could stay focused, Roman might need to coach Theo through at least one more session if they couldn't get the plot moving on their patch in other ways.

News of King's scouting mission and Mallery's success came through during the appointment, so Roman cut out at three, catching the subway back to the condo. The tracker they'd placed in Theo's shoe was still showing him at home, so they'd be able to arrange a chance encounter later on, but not without a plan.

* * *

Back at the condo, Roman changed out of gym gear into everyday wear. He joined the others in the living room, where Mallery was holding court. They'd ordered in Italian from the restaurant they'd visited the night before — lasagna, gnocchi, spaghetti, cannoli, and more. Leah was seated on the sofa chair, a good foot farther back than it had been that morning. Odd.

"Our Leading Lady is on board," Mallery said. "I pulled out a Friend Monologue, and it looks like it's done the trick. She said she'd call our loverboy today. We can monitor the situation and hope it resolves itself, or double down and try to create the reconciliation moment."

Roman shook his head, doubtful. "Theo's tracker has him at home. Unless he's out with different shoes."

"Couldn't plant it in his wallet?" King asked.

"Never had a clear shot."

"Well, we've got Anna's phone number now, so I can track her GPS," Shirin said, standing from the couch and moving to the workstation.

"And as long as the doc keeps her lab coat on, we've got her tracked as well."

"I'm still nervous about this doctor," Mallery said. "Theo and Anna's accounts don't line up. Did Anna really call him? If so, what happened to those calls?"

"Think the Doc's got that much sway over him?" Leah asked. "Or maybe she messed with his phone, deleted the calls?"

"Hard to say," King said. "She was pretty forceful, and it fits the tale type."

Mallery shook her head. "We need more on her. Did you get her card, any body language cues?"

King crossed his arms. "She was closed off like a North Korean border. My best read is that she's either just a controlling workaholic. Or she's gone into protective mode about Theo, working his case extracurricular."

"Extra-curricular," Leah said, elbowing King to accentuate the joke.

Mallery scoffed with amusement. Roman managed to restrain himself, as King was not amused.

Roman's phone rang. He pulled it out of his pocket and looked at the number.

"Is this her?" he asked, showing the phone to King, who nodded.

"Gym sounds," Roman said, giving the phone another ring. Shirin slid over to the computer and pulled up an audio file. It played the indistinct sounds of grunting, metal on metal, and fast footfalls on treadmill rubber. King put the phone on speaker and set it on the desk.

"Fairness Gym, this is Howard King; how many I help you?"

"This is Dr. Thorsson. I wanted to let you know that I've cleared things up with Mr. Long's insurance, and he'll be returning to his proper physical therapist. I'm sorry for the mix-up," she said without a drop of sincerity.

She really couldn't leave things alone, could she? Thorsson didn't even have the authority to be making those calls. Pushing back would pull her into the forefront of the story even more. They'd need to find a way to sideline her entirely, and this wasn't the time.

"Not a problem, ma'am; we're here to help. Please give our best to Mr. Long and wish him a speedy recovery on behalf of all of us at Fairness Gym."

"Goodbye," the doctor said, then hung up.

"Well, she's lovely," Leah said, gushing sarcasm.

Mallery stood. "This is heating up. I think we may need to go for a Hail Mary. Anna's not going to be ready for a surprise reconciliation if we spring it on her."

Mallery shook her head. "And..."

"And that means we need to do some shopping. If you approve."

That smile meant she approved.

Leah looked to King and Shirin. "Keep tabs on our leads?"

"Of course. GPS and phone taps are still up and running, so we should have some warning.

Leah laughed, going whole-hog on the glorious zaniness of the genre, hand-in-hand with Mallery. "Let's build ourselves a Hail Mary makeover in a bag."

"Spend sensibly!" Shirin called halfheartedly.

* * *

Thanks to the wonders of story timing—where people always entered scenes right as something was about to happen, in order to avoid dead air or page time—Mallery and Leah were just setting their bags down from the shopping trip when King shushed them all, turning up the mic on the computer and leaning his head in, closing his eyes to help focus.

Theo's voice came through the speakers via the bug King had planted on the doc.

"Hello?"

"Hi, Theo. This is Doc…Andrea. Andrea Thorsson."

Behind him, the team jockeyed for position to listen in.

A pause for a moment, then Theo's voice again. "Oh, hi. Is everything okay?"

"Everything's fine. This is…It's a personal call. I wanted to see how you were doing, if you needed anything."

"Her game is weak," Mallery said, interrupting.

"But she's going for it," Roman added.

King shushed them.

"…fine. I get around okay, but I have a newfound respect for anyone trying to get around this city with a cane or wheelchair."

"I could imagine." A pause. "So, Theo. I also wanted to ask if you might want to have dinner sometime. With me."

Another pause. "Oh. Sure!"

"Excellent. I'm free tonight. Say, seven?"

"She doesn't waste time," Mallery added.

"Tonight is fine. What do you like?"

"What about that pizza place you mentioned? Pizzeria something?"

"Trio. Oh, sure. They know me there." King picked up a hint of doubt from Theo on that one.

"Excellent. I'll make a reservation. See you then!"

The doctor had grabbed the opportunity and run with it.

"Respect for her hustle," Mallery said.

"That does mean we need to move," Shirin said.

"Hail Mary time?" Leah asked.

Mallery grabbed herself a fork-full of cold spaghetti from the table, took a bite, then pointed the fork at Leah. "Newbie, you're point on this operation. Shirin is the wild card, since she's not in either narrative, but you can use any of the rest of us if you can stitch the story together. We interfere with the doc's potential to have a big moment with Theo, open his eyes to how much of a controlling neatnik she is, and how much he misses Anna's free spirit."

Mallery gestured to her plans on the whiteboard, which showed football-esque plays, lines and Xs and Os, but for plays like THE CLUMSY WAITER and THE HAIL MARY. "We take this two by two," she said. "We need to be ready to approach in any configuration. Roman, whatever you had planned for interference, let's bring it along. Maybe we can't bring it home all at once, but we need to head the doc off before she can deepen the breach."

"I've got the outfits." Leah said.

"Pack some spare clothes for both of us, too. I expect we may need to commit some alcohol abuse to escalate the situation."

Leah frowned. "More drinking?"

"She means spilling booze," Roman said.

"Where is our Leading Lady?" Mallery asked.

Shirin checked the screen. "Headed downtown, probably on the E train."

"Let us know when it looks like she's back on the street. No sense in chasing her around the city through the subways. Not that I mind a good game of subway tag, but if we can get this one in the bag by tonight, that'd be groovy."

"Groovy?" Leah asked.

Mallery shrugged. "It fit the moment. Come on, let's get cracking."

* * *

Anna's GPS went still ten minutes on the road, so Mallery and Leah checked her apartment first.

She wasn't there.

Leah decided to improvise, and they started trekking around the neighborhood, checking at the studio. They left a voicemail and two texts with Anna during their rounds.

"Any more than that is excessive," Mallery said. "She should be answering by now."

And yet nothing. Roman settled in across the street from the pizzeria, with Shirin waiting in the wings for the doc and Theo's reservation.

"I've got movement on Anna's GPS!" King called through the comms.

Leah sighed in relief.

"That mean's she's back in the apartment or will be soon."

Unfortunately, they were a twenty-minute walk from the apartment, and it was closing in on seven.

Mallery stepped out to the street and whistled. "Taxi!"

Ten seconds later, they were off.

* * *

At six forty-five, Shirin put on her I Am Supposed to Be Here face and strode straight toward the side entrance to fast-talk her way into Pizzeria Trio to assert herself as a server. The place was as chaotic as any story-world restaurant during the pre-show dinner rush, which meant everyone was distracted. She caught enough gossip on the way in that by the time she made it all the way up to the hostess, a tiny olive-skinned woman with big eyes, she had her story in place.

Shirin affected a broad Long Island accent. "I'm here to replace Susan."

The hostess froze for a second, processing. "Who are you?"

"I'm Sherry. Her neighbor's aunt. She called in, then asked if I could cover for her. I mostly take catering work, but she figured you could use the help. You want it or not?"

She focused her full presence on the tiny woman, who was maybe twenty-two. Shirin had been slipping on identities like outfits since before this girl was born. While the hostess considered, Shirin pegged Theo in her well-trained peripheral vision. Their Leading Man wore a dapper vest that was a bit big on him. He was doubtless down a few pounds after the accident. He fiddled with his hands and took a long sip of water.

Finally, the hostess relented. "Yeah, okay. Here's the menu, specials are on the board in the back. Orders go to Joaquin."

No restaurant on Earth Prime would work this way, but on a story world, where an active breach had just walked in? Force of personality went a long way. The story breach had its own narrative gravity, and the restaurant was caught up in it. Shirin rode the turbulent tides into position. She had thirty minutes, maybe an hour before the server came to her senses or the manager caught wind of what was happening. Hopefully, it would be enough.

"Doc is incoming," Roman said over the comms.

Shirin looked up to see Doctor Thorsson walk in. Just in time.

The doctor's hair was done up and back, and she wore a curve-hugging little black dress with a deep V neck. In Rom-Com terms, this was coming out swinging.

"Doc's here and not pulling any punches," she said under her breath, grateful for the earpiece's sensitivity.

Shirin put on a smile and hit her first table, keeping an eye on the pair but giving them time to settle in before her first pass.

Theo stood to greet the doctor as she arrived. Their energy was halting, awkward, his body language cueing uncertainty, hers uncertainty and hope.

They had a very short window to intervene. If this date went well enough, the breached narrative might grab hold of the two of them in a powerful need for relief, for resolution.

All that would do is make the breach permanent—it'd scab over and the ripples would continue. Less, but never quite the same as if they reunited Theo and Anna.

She placed her first table's drink order with the bar and checked in on the girls.

"Hurry," she said over the comms.

* * *

Mallery told the cabbie to hurry, but the taxi couldn't go any faster and avoid an actual collision. Their driver, a chatty Grenadian woman by the name of Karla, alternated between gesturing in frustration at other drivers and relating her life story to Leah and Mallery.

"There she is," Mallery said, pointing out the window. "You can stop here, please."

Mallery paid the driver while Leah hopped out, bags in hand.

Anna was walking down the street with a slice of pizza for dinner in classic New Yorker walk-and-eat fashion—slice folded into a V for ease of eating.

Leah waved from across the street. "Anna!"

Their Leading Lady had on casual wear, just enjoying a stroll. *Her hair was wet. She must have been taking a shower or something,* Leah thought.

Anna crossed the street, jaywalking flagrantly through the congested traffic.

"How are you doing?"

Anna, still caught a bit by surprise, shrugged and said, "Living the glamorous life, as you can clearly tell. Sorry I missed your call. Just needed some downtime."

"Of course. We were thinking of going for pizza ourselves. Care to join us? I mean, if you want something a bit fancier. That looks great, though."

Anna shrugged and dumped the slice in the corner garbage can, which was not quite to the precarious refuse-mountain stage.

Mallery joined the party by hugging Anna. "So good to run into you. What are the odds?"

"That's New York for you," Anna said. "So, dinner?"

"We were thinking of going to the place you recommended, Trio Mio or something?"

"Pizzeria Trio," Anna said, slightly less than enthusiastic, from her voice.

Mallery snapped, "That's the one. You were right," she said to Leah.

Leah gave a fake-gloating smile and turned. "You said it was on Seventh Avenue, yes?

Just like that, they were off, Anna pulled once more into Mallery's enthusiasm storm. Leah helped, but Mallery was gale force all on her own.

"Drop back," Mallery whispered through comms. Leah let the pair drift ahead and reported in.

"We've got Anna. Three blocks out from the restaurant."

"Good," King said. "Shirin, what's our status?"

"Some sparks flying here for sure. I can try to interrupt their flow, stifle conversation."

"Agreed," said King, audible since Mallery had the volume turned up. "We can be there in ten minutes if you need extra actors."

"Not sure that will be enough. What's Anna wearing?"

"Comfy casual," Leah said. "Not exactly the outfit for a big romantic gesture."

Ahead, Mallery told Anna, "You know, we should totally go shopping. I bet we're the same size. I found some great stuff just this afternoon."

"She's laying the groundwork for your plan," Shirin said. "You just have to find a restroom to use."

Leah was so engrossed in the conversation, she nearly missed the turn onto Seventh Avenue.

King hopped back in. "Once she's in, you'll need a plan to get the doctor out of the way."

Mallery dropped back to grab Leah and pull her forward. "You tell Anna about that time in Culver City with the rabbi. I forgot to call for reservations."

Which was a weird premise but far from the weirdest she'd been pitched in her improv days. Leah started making a story up to distract Anna while Mallery dropped back. Leah heard the team chatter continuing, which was incredibly distracting as she tried to BS on the move.

"Leah's plan means we'll have Anna in the right outfit to make our move. Newbie can play the klutz, and I'll agitate to get the doctor to reveal herself. King, I'll want you in my ear as we go in case you have ideas of where to provoke her. Roman, good to backseat from your position?"

"No problem," Roman said. "I can be inside within a minute."

"King said, "Shirin's already in place, so I think we'll be fine as long as she doesn't get made by the manager."

"Got it. I'll get my earpiece in and leave my phone on in my pocket," Mallery said. "Any questions?"

Leah dove back into relating her story to Anna.

I'll take that as a yes, Mallery thought. *You got this, newbie.*

* * *

The three women walked into the restaurant, Mallery in the lead. Leah nodded to Shirin as Anna froze for a second and then not-so-casually walked right back out again. Leah made a "one second" gesture and followed.

"Is everything okay?" Leah asked as they clustered on the sidewalk.

"It's fine," Anna said.

"It's clearly not," Mallery said, her voice more supportive than critical. They had to handle this scene with absolute care. Leah's instant makeover idea was solid, but this was still a Hail Mary move. Forceful, and honestly, they were doing it without a lot of set-up. Shirin's help would make it possible, but chances were, the Doc wouldn't step aside without a fight.

Anna pointed. "Theo's there. He's sitting at a table with some gorgeous woman." In any normal world or situation, Anna would be totally right to GTFO. They'd been fanning the flames, building the tension, and done everything they could to make this a big-finale scene. Anna wavered at the edges, flickering, the jagged edge of her broken story flaring up.

Leah tried to peek in the window, playing along. "Oh, damn. Should we go somewhere else?"

Mallery cut Leah off, building the scene's energy. "No, we should eat here." The affirmation built the scene, got the blood going.

Leah was getting a hang of the tag-team dynamic, switching back and forth between the role of foil and supportive friend, controlling the conversation and heading off doubts even before Anna could express them.

Leah said, "This is your favorite restaurant. Plus, what better chance to talk to Theo and sort things out?"

Anna was losing her nerve. "While he's on a date with someone else? And while I look like this? Plus, when I tried to call him, the number was blocked."

Mallery countered. "You don't know it's a date, do you?"

Anna was certain, playing into their move. "He's wearing a vest. He doesn't like wearing vests to work. Also, I saw her neckline. It's a date."

"All the more reason to go in there," Mallery said. "You've got to fight for love."

"Do I?"

"You do, you do." Leah said, aligning herself with Mallery to reinforce the argument.

"I'm going to need some wine first. I'm dressed like crap."

Leah put on an "I have the best idea" look. "Well, we just happen to have gone shopping. And Susan here is basically your size, so we can go and do a quick-change while she holds down the fort!"

Mallery clapped in genuine appreciation of Leah's hustle, while also playing along. "Perfect! I'll check out the bar and make sure we have a table." She leaned in to whisper instructions to Leah, covering it with a kiss on the cheek. "I'll be your smokescreen cover you for the change. Don't let Theo or the Doc see you."

The women stood, and Mallery whispered more instructions. "When we go over, you'll spill something on the Doctor. We may need to interrupt more to drive the doc over the edge."

Then Mallery adjusted her dress, cracked her back, and thought to herself: *You own this room.*

She strode toward the bar, activating Bombshell Mode to draw as many eyes as possible while Anna and Leah scurried off to the restroom.

* * *

Leah watched Mallery charge off.

"Is she always like this?" Anna asked.

Leah caught this moment on the front end. She gave a happy sigh. "Yep."

Leah offered her hand back to Anna, the other holding the shopping bags. "Let's go get your boy back."

And so they went.

Chapter Eight:
The Hail Mary

Shirin got them a table with a clear view of Theo and the doctor's table.

Mallery left the group, walking over to "check out their bar," aka "scope out the pair for herself."

Yep, Anna's quick-read was dead-on. The Doc was going all in.

Which is why it was good that Mallery was still the interdimensional champion at the five-minute makeover, even without help from the genre world. Anna now wore a show-stopping silver dress and a basic everyday makeup look, her hair snazzed up with the simplest of quick braids.

Mallery caught Anna's attention. "Remember to breathe, dear."

Shirin approached and filled their water glasses. Mallery gave a silent prayer of thanks that it was about as hard to fake your way into being a waiter in the Rom-Com region as it was in the Heist region of Crime World—which is to say, not very. She and Leah could catch snippets of Theo and the doc's conversation through the earpieces.

"Can we get some wine, please?" Anna asked.

Shirin nodded.

"Hold on, Anna," Leah said. "They're still on their entrée; you've got time."

"But they've seen us."

Mallery poured her smile on thicker. "That's fine. Let her sweat."

Anna peeked over her shoulder. "I don't think she's sweating."

Leah took a sip of her water. "Not yet, but soon."

They kept watching, Anna sipping and sipping, finishing her first glass of wine before their bread was gone.

Mallery peeled the crust from the last piece of bread, eating it one bite at a time. "Do you know what you're going to say?"

"You can try it out on us," Leah added.

"I can't overthink it. I'll freak myself out. I just need to go over there and start."

"Do you want us to go over with you?" Leah asked. "We can be your excuse to say hello."

"That. That might be good. At least you can keep me from running for the door."

"I don't know; I think you're in better shape than either of us, Ms. Always En Pointe," Mallery said.

That got a chuckle from Anna. "They're finishing up. We should go now."

* * *

Leah, Mallery, and Anna slid out of the booth. Anna took a breath, then walked across the restaurant, weaving through tables and past servers toward Theo and the doctor's table. The doctor clocked them first and adjusted herself in the seat, her face unreadable.

At least this is unlikely to end in gunplay, Leah realized. No one was going to die here, since this world didn't have shootouts. The stakes here were no less powerful. If they failed, thousands, maybe millions of relationships on Earth would crumble and people around the world would give up on finding love. Then, they'd all get fired. Good to not forget that part.

Anna started friendly. "Glad to see you out and about!"

Theo's response was hard to read. He eased his way to his feet, setting the napkin on his place setting. Desire, hurt, and uncertainty passed over his face in turn. "Still coming along, but it beats a hospital bed."

The doctor coughed, poker face intact. *Not subtle, are we?*, she thought.

Theo gestured to his companion, "Anna, this is my friend, Doctor Thorsson."

The doctor stood, offering a hand. "Ms. Grace."

Anna met the doctor's hand and shook it. "Yes," we spoke on the phone when I called about Theo."

The doctor faked confusion well. "I'm sorry, I don't recall."

Here we go, Leah thought. Would Anna insist, breaking social niceties, or let the lie stand?"

"Like I said on the phone, I appreciate everything you've done for him.

Doctor, Theo, this is Susan and Toni, some friends of mine visiting the city."

Nice, Leah thought. *Roll the correction into a compliment—a perfect riposte.*

Theo's look of confusion deepened. That was an opening if she'd ever seen one.

The doctor gave them a territorial smile, keeping Leah and Mallery at bay. "Charmed."

"We've heard so much about you, Theo." Mallery-as-Susan cut through the doctor's stare and went straight in to hug Theo. She watched his leg as he shifted in surprise, keeping pressure off. Subtlety in everything even as she was brash.

Leaving her to play the understated counterpart to round out the experience. Leah offered a hand to shake once Mallery had released Theo.

"What brings you two here?" Mallery asked, gesturing to the restaurant. They'd drawn some attention already and would probably get more before all was said and done.

The doctor's gaze could have pierced Kevlar. Not that anyone in the situation could easily say, "We're clearly on a date, and you're intruding."

No one had any weapons, but this was turning out to be no less a combat than the shootout in Western World. Every look, every word was as calculated as the swing of a sword or pull of a trigger.

Theo filled the tense silence. "I wanted to thank Dr. Thorsson for everything she's done, and she suggested dinner here, since I mentioned it when I was in traction."

"I'd heard about the restaurant since I started as a resident, and this was a perfect chance to celebrate." The doctor wrapped an arm around Theo's, staking her claim physically as well as verbally.

This kind of jockeying for relationship position was infinitely easier to parse up close when you weren't the one in the middle of it—hormones and anxiety giving you tunnel vision and making your tongue feel like dried leather and ash.

"Of course," Anna said. "Theo and I came here all the time. In fact, this was where Theo proposed to me."

SHOTS FIRED. SHOTS FIRED, Leah thought.

The Doctor tensed. "Oh, really. I hadn't heard."

"Theo, could we talk for a minute, just the two of us?" Anna asked.

Yes. Go, go! Leah thought.

The Doctor didn't let go. "Anything you want to say, you can say to me."

"Now, dear, I think that's Theo's decision, isn't it?" Mallery asked, all smiles and Georgia charm.

All eyes were on Theo. "Of course," he said. "Do you want to step outside?"

"No need, darling. The doctor is welcome to join us at our table while you talk here," Mallery said.

Leah raised with her slightly overfull glass. "We've got wine."

The doctor doubled down. "Theo, this is really…"

Shirin walked by, giving Leah the opening for the pick. Leah shifted her weight left to right, bumping Shirin's tray. She recoiled from the bump, guiding her hand and glass to slosh forward and out of her glass.

Right onto the doctor's dress. Bull's-eye.

Leah dropped her glass, spilling more wine on both the doctor's and her shoes. "Ohmigod, I'm so sorry."

Shirin disappeared as quickly as she'd come, her job complete.

"Oh, dear. Honey, let's get you two cleaned up." Mallery and Leah double-teamed the doctor with apologies and aggressive helpfulness, making for the restroom, leaving Theo and Anna on their own.

Okay, hon. We cleared the way. Now it's all up to you, Leah thought.

* * *

Shirin went to make a gesture of cleaning herself off. Mostly, she kept one eye and both ears on the lovers, finally alone together again.

Anna led off, but her confidence was waning. She broke eye contact and looked at the table, down at his leg. "I tried to visit, but your date said you didn't want to see me."

"She what? She said that you didn't come. That they called you and you didn't answer."

"Not at first. I was out of town, then all the flights back were delayed and then cancelled. I spent seventy-two hours in an airport trying to get back to you." Anna looked up, searched for eye contact. "You put a big ball in my court when I really didn't want anything else big and amazing and scary to think about."

Theo wrung his hands but met Anna's eyes. "I thought it was the best time, that now that everything was coming together for you…"

"I know. It was just…"

A moment. "It was too much at once," Theo said. "I'm sorry. I didn't mean to scare you. I just knew how excited you were to make a change, to have a path that gave you freedom and security. And I thought I could be part of that."

"It wasn't about you or about the ring. I had to process things one at a time." She took a breath. "I'm taking the partnership."

Anna pulled a box out of her purse and knelt. The diamond caught the light from the candelabra overhead, glittering bright for the whole room to see.

"That's not all I want. Will you be my partner, Theo Long? Do you think we can still do this? Because I really hope the answer is yes." Tears welled in Anna's eyes, her voice shaking but not breaking. "And I can't promise that I won't need to be random, I can't promise I'll be tidy, but I do promise that I will love you every day."

A hundred thoughts must have gone through Theo's head in that moment, doubt and hope, self-conscious uncertainty and love.

But in the end, love won out.

Theo took the ring and Anna's hand, helping her back to her feet as he steadied himself on the chair.

"Of course. Of course I will."

Shirin coughed into her collar, then said, "We have reconciliation. Time to clean up," transmitting to the team. Then she smiled and started planning her exfiltration.

* * *

Dr. Thorsson waved them off of her when they got to the bathroom. Mallery positioned herself by the door, making a big gesture out of dabbing Leah's shirt, the two women blocking the doctor from being able to get out.

"You utter, complete klutz!" the Doctor said, dabbing furiously at her shirt and leggings.

"I'm so sorry," Leah said.

"It was an accident, Doc. No need to raise your voice. My poor Toni's out a pair of shoes that are at least as expensive as that top."

Dr. Thorsson adjusted herself, looking in the mirror. "It's not about the shirt."

"Oh, what, the boy?" Mallery asked. "Honey, you've already lost. These two would already be engaged if it weren't for that wild driver. Your Florence Nightingale act was never going to work."

"It wasn't an act," the doctor said. "He's the first decent guy to cross my path in years. He needs structure, support."

"Let's let Theo decide what he needs, okay?" Leah said.

The doctor made for the door, stopping just inside Leah and Mallery's personal space bubble. "If he's going to decide, I need to at least be there."

"Give them a minute to sort things out, then you can go out there and break things off like a responsible adult."

"Actually, do you swing both ways? I've got an ex out here. I think you'd get along fabulously," Leah said, remembering a preppy lawyer from the online dating reports they'd run.

"I don't need to be set up. I need you to step aside so I can save Theo from making the wrong decision and ruining his life."

Mallery looked sideways to Leah, as if to ask telepathically, "Think she's worked up enough?"

Before Leah could answer, Shirin's all-clear came through the comms. Leah nodded.

"Why don't you go back out there and see what's really happening?" Mallery said.

The doctor pushed past the pair and shoved the door open, heading back into the restaurant.

"Are we done?"

Mallery flipped back to her normal accent. "Assuming the doc doesn't actually haul off on someone, I think so," she said, offering a hand to Leah. "Sorry about your shoes and tights."

"We do what we must. Besides, it's not like I get to keep the clothes when we go home."

Mallery winked. "Well, we're not supposed to."

"Oh, really?" Leah said as the pair returned to the dining room.

They turned the corner and Leah saw all she needed to see.

Theo and Anna, kissing, arms wrapped around one another. A bling-tastic ring shone from Anna's left hand. The doctor stood by, fuming.

Mallery reached out a hand to the Doc's shoulder, conciliatory. "I'm sorry, hon. It's like we said."

The doctor looked over her shoulder, started a snarl, then gave up. Sniffing back a tear, she made a beeline for the door, snatching her coat from the coat rack on the way out.

Leah crossed her arms. "Now I kind of feel bad. She was a controlling witch, but…"

Mallery nodded. "She wasn't evil. Just not the One. I changed my mind. She should look up the Brooklyn conceptual artist. Like you said. Study in opposites."

"Wrap it up," King said through the comms.

Mallery paused for a second. "Roger that. They're kissing, and she's wearing the engagement ring. I think we're clear here. I'm going to do an exit formula, and then let's head back to the condo and wait for the all-clear."

"Roger that," Shirin said.

Mallery headed for the hostess. "I'll get the bill; you see if you can catch Anna's attention to wave goodbye."

Mallery set off toward the hostess's stand, hips swaying, every bit the perfect social manipulator.

Leah took her eyes off of Mallery and walked up to Anna and Theo, who had come up for breath.

"We'll leave you two," Leah said. "I assume you've got some catching-up to do?"

Their goofy smiles told her all she needed to know.

Anna gave Leah a big happy sobby hug. "Thank you, thank you both. I wouldn't have come inside if not for you."

Theo extended a hand. "Thank you."

"It's our pleasure. Susan fancies herself something of a matchmaker."

"Susan" returned and they had another round of hugs, Theo looking on, half-dazed with surprise and joy.

Mallery squeezed Anna's hand. "You have my card. Don't hesitate to email. Anytime."

Leah added, "She's not great at answering the phone."

"Guilty as charged. Take care, you two. And so nice to meet you, Theo."

Another few minutes of circling a conversational ender, Anna and Theo never out of physical contact for more than a few seconds, Mallery and Leah left the restaurant and high-fived outside.

And all around them, the world exploded into pheremone bombs and mete-cutes.

Two storefronts down, a pair of Latinas kissed beneath a lawn umbrella.

A Native American man in a suit ran down the street, tie loosened, stopping in front of a Black man in a tux. They melted together into a joyful embrace.

Doctor Thorsson walked down the street, despondent, then bumped right into a tired-looking but gorgeous white man in scrubs looking at his phone. They picked themselves up together, and when their eyes met, Leah could swear she heard fireworks.

In the restaurant above, an Eastern European man in a blazer knelt beside his table, holding a ring out to a Middle-Eastern man, who started crying tears of joy.

Across the street, two white men and a Korean woman, each following an Airedale terrier, each with their nose buried in a book, crossed paths. Their dogs circled and barked themselves into a knot, entangling their owners as well. As they got the dogs in order, their hands touched for a moment, electricity passing between each, first in one pair, then another, then all three watched one another with starry eyes.

All around, the world exploded into Rom-Com moments, like it'd been bottling it up for a week and was now bubbling over everywhere.

A car passed Leah and Mallery, Just Married scribbled on the back windshield.

Mallery sidestepped to the curb, getting ready to hail a cab. "I think we can call that the all clear."

"Can I try this time?" Leah asked.

"Of course."

Leah stepped up to the curb, brought a hand up, whistled, then waved her hand.

Not three seconds later, a cab turned the corner and rolled right up.

"I could get used to this," Leah said as they climbed into the cab.

Epilogue:
An Extended Denouement

The five Genrenauts raised glasses with amber liquor, shot-glass pours from King's victory flask.

"To another successful mission." King raised a toast around the condo's dinner table. They'd all changed into their fancy clothing to celebrate.

Leah decided to sip her drink this time. Roman and Mallery slammed theirs, movements synced with the air of ritual.

"If HQ has given the all clear, why not head home tonight?" Leah asked.

King shrugged. "Dimensional disturbance. Preeti says the storm will have passed by morning."

"Well, that's convenient for us. Another night in the big city!"

"Another night here, at least," Shirin said. "With the mission done, we don't have any need to leave the condo." She leveled a look at Mallery. "Don't want to cause any more ripples than we have by running roughshod over the city for the last few days."

"I have no idea what you're talking about. It was all for the mission," Mallery said.

Leah asked, "Do missions on story worlds that match up with Earth Prime's time frame usually involve this much felony wiretapping and cybercrime?"

Roman nodded. Mallery shrugged.

Shirin answered, "Not always. We use whatever tools are available to fix the breaches. Chances are, no one will ever know we did all of this."

Mallery winked. "I'm very good at covering my tracks."

"Which for a chatterbox is quite impressive," Shirin said.

"It helps that my approach in 'covering my trail' is actually to DDoS every system I've touched by dumping terabytes of Lorem Ipsum on them."

"Really?" Leah asked. She saw Mallery's look and knew the answer. No, not really.

A thought struck Mallery, and she set her drink down. "Before everyone gets too trashed, we need to put the place back in order for the next mission. Reset tasks are in your inboxes."

They finished their drinks and set about the packing. The schedule from King said they would be out of the condo at six AM, which was cruel, though Leah knew she could expect the chance to sleep all day once they got back.

This Genrenaut thing was wreaking havoc on her sleep schedule.

The last task on her prep list was to sort out the wardrobes with Mallery. The mission leader stood out on the balcony, loose robe rippling in the wind, a glass of wine in one hand.

"You did well, newbie," she said as Leah closed the door behind her.

"Thanks. Privacy concerns aside, this was really fun."

"Living the high life on the job certainly never hurts."

"No, it really doesn't. Is it like this on other worlds—Action, Thriller, Crime?"

"Action sometimes, not as much with the others." Mallery continued looking out at the city.

"Are you okay?"

Mallery turned. "It's fine. I just have the silly problem where I miss a place before I leave it."

Leah walked over to join Mallery on the balcony. The moon illuminated the city in grayscale, assisted by the thousands of lights atop buildings, in the park, and beyond. Central Park West buildings faced her on one side, and the skyscrapers and office buildings in Midtown loomed to her left. To her right, the city sloped down from giant scale into Harlem and beyond.

"It really is pretty magical."

"You'll do marvelously in this job, once you get used to the way we do business. Your hands aren't always clean, your life is never boring, but we're literally saving worlds and tend to do so while having more fun than any other job that has a claim to such heroics."

"So, King won't be benching or dismissing me now that you're back in action?"

"Was that what you were thinking would happen? He'd been considering you for weeks. We need all hands right now. You keep doing the job, and you'll be fine."

One worry down. Zillions to go, she thought.

"Does it ever get lonely?" Leah asked. "It seems like it'd be hard to keep a relationship going with this job. Shirin can do it, but I don't know how I could." Leah studied Mallery, whose gaze was fixed on the park.

"You get used to it. The team is like a family. Doesn't leave a lot of time to yourself, though. There's always another book to read, film to re-watch, or report to absorb."

Leah stepped up beside Mallery, taking the view in for herself. "That why you're taking the time now with this?" She waved to the city.

"How could I not?" Mallery took a big breath of night air. "The most romantic city in any world, glittering on a chilly night. The perfect time to curl up with someone."

"Are you offering?" The words came out before Leah could even know what she was saying. She hadn't even been thinking it.

Leah's breath quickened and time slowed as Mallery processed what had been said.

Mallery leaned over and kissed Leah on the cheek, then took a half-step back. "Let's try this conversation again when we're back on Earth Prime and don't have the universe pushing on us."

"Yeah. That's. Uh. Probably for the best."

Office romances were one thing when you worked for an insurance company. When you spent sixty-plus hours a week together and had to be counted on to save one another's lives in alternate dimensions, it was entirely different and *wow, remember how great of a kisser she was and is that cinnamon?* Leah thought.

"I don't know what came over me," Leah said. "We were talking, and it just came out."

"The rules of the story world don't just apply to the folks who were born here. Part of the reasons why we don't stay on-world too long at any one go."

Leah walked back into the bedroom. "We should get to packing. Or I, yeah, I can pack."

"It's okay. Nothing to be embarrassed about. Try to get some rest when you're done. You did good work here. It's been fun."

Mallery nodded, tying her robe closed and crossing to leave the room.

After the door shut, Leah stopped and just breathed for a minute, getting her composure back. When that didn't happen, she got to work anyway as all the feelings came rushing back again—embarrassment and excitement and affection and uncertainty. Ten minutes of mental chatter and thinking in circles later, she had the bags packed. She assumed Mallery's position on the balcony, looking out on the city and trying to focus on the parts that made sense, the things that worked.

They'd succeeded in their mission. She'd learned about another world, the technology they used to find breaches and speculate how to fix them. She'd found, diagnosed, and patched a story breach all on her own.

And possibly complicated her job forever, all in one impulsive sentence that she had absolutely zero memory of clearing at her mental checkpoint of approved speech.

She'd never expected Romance World to be one of the dangerous ones.

END EPISODE THREE

Episode Four:
The Substitute Sleuth

Chapter One:
Cross-Training Day

Two months into her job as a Genrenaut, Leah Tang had learned to expect the unexpected. Most jobs had a routine, even if that routine was "random things will happen." That had been the rule at her last gig receptionist-ing; she'd had to deal with oddball callers, walk-ins of senior partners' exes, and more.

At Genrenauts HQ, a morning might begin with a four-mile jog, interpreting dimensional stability reports, or a pop quiz about TV upfront trailers and their cultural implications.

Or in this case, a wake-up call at six AM from her phone's You Are Always On-Call For Work app. She'd scurried into the HQ as fast as possible.

Now let's just hope Mallery doesn't see me before I can put on some makeup, she thought. Things were awkward with the team's comedienne after the two of them had shared a Rom-Com World–derived moment of tantalizing Almost Something at the end of their last mission.

As she walked into the team's ready room, only King and Roman were present—a small consolation prize from fate.

Angstrom King wore a suit coat with cravat and ascot, looking entirely too posh for six-something in the morning. Roman de Jager wore his Versatile Dress Units, the generic basic clothes the Council approved for a variety of story worlds. He was jogging on his treadmill, one earbud in, his attention doubtless divided between the conversation and some audiobook. Roman was the poster boy for multi-tasking. She imagined the slogan—*Get Caught Multitasking.*

"Probie," King said. "Tell us about the process of auditioning for an improv comedy troupe."

Leah had largely stopped responding to King's non sequitur questions with 'What?' and instead just rolled with it.

"What do you need to know?"

"HQ just assigned us a mission, despite the ongoing dimensional disturbance. It's a softball—recon team traced a minor breach to a comedy team in the Police Procedural region of Crime World. We're deploying for a quick fix."

When a breach erupted in a story world, it started to cause ripples back on Earth. Which was why the Genrenauts even had a job—fix the breach, stop the ripples, protect Earth.

For Crime World, the ripples were pretty simple—more crime. Shootings, robberies, and more. The teams responsible for the various regions of Crime World had a high clearance rate, which was why the overall crime statistics had been going down over the years, not up. If they screwed the pooch, that dropping rate would rebound.

She'd had seen the scare tactics projections of what would happen if a team stuffed a mission. They ranged from fracas to unmitigated disaster.

Leah nodded, leaping to the challenge. "No sweat. I'll roll in to the team and sort things out in an hour. I was a team captain in college, as you'll recall from your somewhat invasive recruitment research."

King adopted the grin of the knowing professor. It had to be one of his favorites. "Oh, I recall. But that would be too easy. This is a softball breach, so I'm going to take the opportunity to help you develop your Masterminding skills."

"So, I'm going to wear a fancy Bond Villain suit and play the baddie? Please let that be it." Leah's mind launched into a ridiculous montage of knock-off spy villain hijinks, complete with sexy hench-people in Lycra.

Leah heard Mallery York before she saw her, the telltale clicking of the woman's heels turning the corner into the room. "We'll have to save that for next time, though I do love the titles in that region. Last time I got to be a marchessa." Mallery smiled as she passed into the room, wearing several layers like she was about to head out into the snow.

With a full face of camera-ready makeup, Mallery was either more of a morning person than Leah or used High Council super-tech to be made up at all hours. More likely, she'd just gotten a taxi to work and put on makeup along the way. Leah tended to avoid that approach after an incident with lipstick up her nose. The memory made her wince.

"Alas, no. You're going to be coaching Mallery as she auditions for the troupe that lost their prop bag, except a family heirloom ring."

"What incompetent excuse for a comedian would put an heirloom ring in a prop bag?" Leah asked. You never tossed anything into a prop bag you couldn't stand to do without. Or at least, do without becoming stanky as hell and covered in unidentifiable muck.

Leah continued, "Also, who would steal a junk bag but leave an actually valuable ring?"

"That's the breach, as far as we can tell."

She narrowed her eyes at King. "So, you're going to bench me when my actual specialty comes up and I could score a slam dunk?"

"We'll be using your specialty. But every operative is required to be prepared to serve multiple functions during a mission. You'll mastermind this patch while I show you around the region to help you start to develop some contacts. Crossing in T minus twenty minutes. Help Shirin get us squared away. And pack for a blizzard."

Leah looked briefly to Mallery. The comedienne was packing a makeup and disguise kit. Leah angled for a moment to talk with her before they went into the field, before yet another genre's rules would be pushing and pulling them around like puppets. But King and Roman were in earshot, and if she was supposed to help Shirin Tehrani—the other member of their team—pack and get to the ship in twenty minutes, there wasn't time for anything.

Including freshening up.

Dammit, boss.

* * *

Mallery led the team into the Police Procedural region field base with a "'ta-da" for Leah's benefit.

Here, they maintained a two-bedroom lofted apartment in a neighborhood on the rise, again more affordable due to Story World financial logic.

Mallery walked into the center of the living space. "Now, I'll admit that this place doesn't measure up to our last field base." Part of it was the genre world itself—even the glossier version of Crime World they occupied here wasn't as bright and inviting as some of their other bases.

She gestured to the wall, with team photos in frames against exposed brick, then the super-modern fixtures in the kitchen. "But I've done my best.

I've added personal touches for everyone—an elliptical and a gun rack for Roman, a comfy reading chair and four-monitor work station for Shirin, typewriters and a teak desk for King, and a full vanity for me. Makeup and disguise work, of course. We'll have to get something here for you. What would be fun—maybe some comedy props, remind you of your roots? Or a writing desk? I would have gotten to it earlier, but…"

Mallery waved with her still-cast-bound arm. So many things she'd fallen behind on. And missed out on getting to know Leah. They'd gone straight into the Rom-Com mission with hardly any time to get to know one another, then she'd pushed Leah into an intimate linked cover. What did she expect would happen, on that world of all places?

They'd talked since coming back, but hadn't had That Talk. She didn't always have That Talk. Sometimes she got to dive straight into the confusing joyfulness and then come up for air later on to discuss what was really going on. Mallery wanted to give this dynamic some time to breathe, reevaluate and see if there was real chemistry outside of the gravity of Romance World. They'd settled into the electrifying holding pattern, each seeming to wait for the other to make a move. It sucked, honestly.

And if Mallery's radar was working—and it was always working—then there was potential. Yes, potential for team drama and what King called "operational inefficiency" if things went poorly, but fear had never kept Mallery from following her heart. Or much of anything else. The unlived life isn't worth examining, after all.

And now they were back in the field and paired up again. But this time, it was in Leah's specialty. That'd be good for Leah, more for her to hold on to, more to work with. When Mallery had been recruited, she hadn't really gotten her feet under her until their first comedic mission, a farcical case of mistaken identity. So many slammed doors, so much wordplay.

And unlike this region, so little murder.

"This place is amazing." Leah beamed, looking up to the lofted area. "I live three times as fancy on these contemporary missions as in my apartment at home. And that's the new, badass-Salary-enabled place, not my old rinky-dink hole in the wall place on the east side."

"Thank you. Some people," she said, casting a faux-mocking glance at King, "don't appreciate the morale boost that attentive design can produce, but why can't we have fun while we're working? With a job like this, we have to remember not to lose our sense of joy."

A jerk of a voice in Mallery's mind hijacked her train of thought. *But just wait until something goes wrong. Who's going to get hurt this time?*

That voice had gotten stronger since she got hurt in the shootout in Western World, had been her bedside companion throughout recovery, even when Roman came to visit. Mallery gave the voice the vaudeville hook and focused on the moment.

It'll be an adventure, right? Mallery told herself, trying not to let the nerves show.

King rolled his suitcase to an ottoman and started unpacking with practiced precision. "That'll do for the tour, Ms. York. Everyone get squared away quick. We're diving straight in to on-the-ground recon. Leah will brief Mallery, and then we'll move to first contact."

* * *

Leah unpacked at warp speed to give herself time to freshen up, but tried to do it in a way that wasn't too obvious. Just a basic natural look and a soda out of the fridge, shotgunned just as King called the team to assemble at the dinner table, an eight-foot-wide twenty-first century version of the Round Table, complete with cushy chairs and a circular touchscreen computer in the middle. Mallery slid into a seat to Leah's left with a smile, the comedienne just as pressed for time.

"How can I get one of these for my house?"

"You don't. Proprietary Genrenauts tech."

So the Council did own tech patents. Another puzzle piece clicked into place. She restrained herself from playing around with the table's OS, making a note to do so later.

Everyone pulled out their tablets, and King began.

"Briefings are in your inbox. Council did flag this as a breach, even if it's minor. The Second City Irregulars' prop bag has gone missing. However, the heirloom diamond ring that stays with the bag did not disappear. Smart money says that's our breach. The ring belongs to Lauren McGill, the longest-running member of the troupe."

Leah opened up the case file, paging through background dossiers and the police report.

King continued. "Police filed the report, but our sources say there's little chance it'll get assigned resources. The troupe has turned on one another and is coming apart at the seams. Two members have already quit."

"Hence the audition slot we'll use to get Mallery in," Leah said.

"Precisely."

"I've seen things like this happen. Hell, I've been in it. You spend that much time being other people and yet nakedly yourself with a group, it becomes this big weird knot of intimacy and uncertainty."

Leah pointedly did not look at Mallery during that part. That'd be a bit too on the nose.

King continued, laying out the case like a police captain who was also a professor in a seminar. "Normally, there'd be almost a 100% chance that this was a prank pulled by one troupe member on the rest, a take-your-ball-home kind of thing. But if this is pinging our breach alarms, then there's got to be something else to it, something out of genre. What are some ways that theft stories break?"

Roman twirled a stylus while he swiped through the dossier. "Low-hanging fruit would be that the ring was supposed to be taken, but they forgot it."

Shirin jumped in. "Or that it wasn't even a theft—it was an accident—someone grabbed the wrong bag, or it got thrown out by the janitor."

King took over once more. "The police not investigating makes sense in the real world, but here, there's any number of plots that could start with a theft and end in murder, putting it right into the core of the genre. That's one thing we'll need to look out for. Which also means that Mallery will be going in armed and ready."

Mallery patted her bag. ".22 caliber bodyguard, a girl's best friend in Crime World."

King gestured at the two more senior team members, "Shirin and Roman, you work the case from the outside in—get me information on the police record and a history on the troupe—their venues, reviews, rivals, etc."

Then at Leah. "Leah, you brief Mallery on what she'll need to know to ace the audition, then meet me downstairs. We have some scouting to do."

Watching King's expression—neutral, authoritative—Leah swallowed the full plate of questions and objections about the way this mission was playing out.

If this was going to be a training mission, then pushing back would just make her seem obstinate or afraid. Eventually, she'd need to just know things. Which required asking questions. But at the right time.

"Get to it," King said. The team broke, leaving Leah and Mallery at the table.

She turned to the comedienne and psyched herself up. She'd kick this mission's ass, prove herself to King, and keep from embarrassing herself in front of everyone. Especially Mallery.

If I can't do this around Mallery, I should just quit and then ask her out. And if I quit, I can't afford the amazing apartment and pay off the rest of everything.

So, just do it.

A moment passed, and Leah pushed through her resistance and started talking. "Comedy troupes are looking for two major factors when adding to an existing troupe: they want to know that you can hack it and that they can get along with you. You've already got the acting chops, so what I can do is give you a breakdown of some popular improv games we used for auditions."

"Got it. Then, when I'm in the spotlight, it's down to reading them and seeing what they want."

"Yep. They'll probably ask for credentials, so we'll need to work up some believable fake comedy experience for you. I assume we have the same hacker-y tech on this world for fake IDs and all that jazz?"

Mallery cracked her knuckles, spinning the tablet around into a demi-laptop. "Boy, do we. Crime World means we can hack from here to the Pentagon and back before dinner break."

Normally, that would be kind of disconcerting, but they were doing it for good reasons. The heroes in Crime stories broke all sorts of rules in order to save the day, and it's not like they were actually cops. White hat hacking was a whole different world from a cop breaking regs left and right.

"So, games-wise, here are the top three I'd expect to see…" Leah broke down several improv games, focusing on her screen to avoid staring too deeply at Mallery. Of course, the reflection in her screen meant that she could do both without being a creeper. Much of a creeper.

Leah stopped, confirmed that there was no one else in the room. Good. She closed her eyes, and took a long breath. "Should we have that conversation now or later? Because I'm distracted as hell and it seems like this is the mature thing to do. So, I figured I'd at least ask so it wasn't hanging over us like a Romantic Tension Sword of Damocles."

She opened her eyes to see Mallery's face gone serious. "We should. I'm sorry I didn't bring it up earlier. It's probably better to do on Earth Prime. This mission shouldn't take more than a couple of days, so we won't have to wait long. How about a half-hour after we get back? Even if it's late. We can hit the commissary and then find a place to talk in private. There are some pretty delightful hidey holes I use when I need to get away."

Yes. This was sensible and mature and responsible. It didn't help them in the short term, but it made sense. Leah cursed herself for not having done this before they deployed, as now they'd be treated to another mission's worth of uncertainty, but this was a plan. They had a plan.

"So, like I said, they'll probably throw these games at you..." Leah wrapped herself in the familiarity of improv and put Damocles out of mind for the time being.

It was a good plan. But Leah had learned on the job that your first plan almost never survives contact with reality.

Chapter Two:
The Big Re-Con

Chicago was earning its name as the Windy City, ripping Leah's hat off of her head every thirty seconds. An hour into their reconnaissance mission in Crime World, she was regretting the choice of a fedora over a less stylish but more secure beanie.

Two paces ahead of her, King leaned into the wind and snow. He was bundled up in a beanie, a thick tan coat, and double-layer mittens-over-gloves.

Around them, people struggled against the storm, coming and going from jobs, to homes, wherever the background characters in a crime story headed when they weren't in immediate danger of being killed and weren't plotting murder themselves.

Though the red-faced guy across the street looked more than a little ticked off at the policewoman writing him a ticket for parking in a no-standing-when-there's-tons-of-snow-you-jerk spot, his car a small hill in the grey-and-white mess the storm had made of the street.

"In here." King ducked into a coffee shop, much to the relief of Leah and her numbing fingers. She'd left the Upper Midwest to get away from frostbite (and her family), and yet here she was, back in the land of deadly winters. Baltimore's winters were worse than its latitude should have warranted, but Chicago winter, especially story world Chicago winter, was a whole other level of cold.

The coffee shop was a local indie joint, pleasantly disorganized and nonstandard. All of the tables were full. Teenagers packed in seven people to a four-top; obligatory writers with their laptops; neighborhood folks meeting up for a drink; and probably homeless people taking refuge from the storm in the corner, keeping out of everyone's way.

King veered left and homed in on a table just as its occupants stood to leave, cutting off a trio coming from the counter, steaming drinks in hand.

"Claim the table; I'll get drinks," he said.

"Well played. Can I get a mocha?"

King returned with her drink and a black-as-the-void coffee.

"So, what have you observed so far?" Leah felt like she was back in college, meeting with a professor for an independent study. Which, considering King's academic background, was only fitting.

She took a sip of her mocha and let the heat seep all the way out to her fingers and toes, stamping her feet to force them to remember how to feel sensation.

"Mostly, I've observed the cold. Also, everyone seems like they've got an angle; significant glances, muttering to themselves, looking over their shoulders. Everyone's a suspect or a target or both. So, how often do story-worthy crimes happen here? Or is this region spread out over the whole world?"

"Each sub-genre has a region of the Earth. Police Procedural stretches from Chicago all the way across Pennsylvania, then down to DC and up to Boston. Cozies rule in the suburbs and in the Caribbean, Thrillers dominate Europe, and so on. In some genre worlds, the regions are more distinct from one another."

"Will I ever get caught up with all this inside-baseball research and skill-acquisition crap?"

"Eventually. There are a lot of moving targets in this business; things come at you and you have to learn to move with them." King sipped his coffee, cultivating the look of the reserved, unflappable team lead. The kind of leader who knew all and directed through expertise. King was a story-heist conductor who could dive into the pit and wail on sax if he needed to. That's what you got when you worked a job for what, twenty years?

"On recon, we walk the streets, take the pulse of the area, get readings with the sensors we brought, and make the rounds with on-world sources to stay abreast of major events, stories that have come and gone unbroken."

"Recon. And how do you, do we approach these people? *Hi, I'm a concerned citizen; solved any interesting murders lately?*"

"Every operative has their own specialties; they cultivate contacts."

"Shirin and Commander Bugayev, Mallery and her bartenders."

"Indeed. This is my beat, so we'll be checking in with my contacts in the precincts and PI firms. I've know some of these people for decades. Your cover…"

"I'm the newbie. Junior PI, learning the ropes. Same as every world. I assume at some point, I get to be a grown-up and decide my own covers?"

That got her a sliver of a grin. "Won't be too long now. Your review comes up in a couple of months. And so far, you're doing great. Keep your mind and ears open, and don't be afraid to take initiative. And don't forget your other responsibilities for this mission."

Because writing material was so easy while actively doing something else. Leah had learned to take notes in the in-between moments, but it was hard to have any in-between while keeping your eyes peeled. She watched for the little differences in how people behaved in his world versus others. More people looked over their shoulder here, spoke in hushed voices. But it also seemed like there were more arguments. Something it had in common with Romance-land. All of these different axes of narrative, the bones of story that went into the soup of story.

Her story-senses were getting better, but slowly. The others could ID people with broken stories by sight, seeing them as just a shade out of sync, or discolored when compared to the world around them. But so far, Leah mostly relied on the experience granted by a lifetime of consuming and studying stories to put her on the right track. The team assured her that her story-vision would get better with time.

"How do you decide when to do patrols? How often? Is it a High Council thing or your discretion?"

"A little bit of both. Every team has a beat. We keep informed about the active and recurring stories in our genres. Teams also give input on when breaches are likely to hit, and schedule recon missions."

King gestured to the room. "It'd been a while since I visited, and there have been some strange readings beyond the minor breach. This way, I get to introduce you around and give you something to balance while you work on the material for Mallery."

"And you're sure you don't just want me to join the troupe? That'd be a way to be hands-on, to take initiative."

King was unimpressed. Still getting nowhere with that. And thinking about writing for Mallery led to thinking about Mallery. The end of the mission would come soon enough.

Office romances: an unending source of drama, even when the romance was barely more than hypothetical, a momentary slippage as she'd been caught by the genre's undertow.

Was that really it, though? Leah's cheeks grew a welcome warm thinking about her teammate.

She shook the question off and focused on the moment. "So, what's next? Check with one of your snitches?"

"Yes, but don't call them snitches. I don't use CIs the way cops do."

"But you do have snitches."

King's shrug said "of course." "This is Crime World, after all."

Leah still found it weird to talk shop this openly on a story world, but she'd learned that people on these worlds tended to shrug off conversations that didn't pertain to their active storylines, especially when some cover was available—the din of a coffee shop, car horns on a street, and so on.

"Next, we head to the local police precinct. The captain is an old friend of mine. She'll catch us up on what's gone down in the last few months. And any weird cases show up while we're there…"

"We con our way onto the cases and check for breaches. This the same precinct that bounced the troupe's case?"

"Same precinct, different team. Homicide is always its own team." King gestured to the coffee bar. "Best top off your drink. It's a twenty-minute walk to the station."

Leah narrowed her eyes at King. "We're right on an El line. Why walk?"

"You end up waiting for ten minutes just to spend three minutes on the train. Walking's better. Plus, more chances to overhear people."

King stood and took Leah's cup, headed for the counter. Fair. If he was going to make her walk, the least he could do is top off the drinks.

"If you weren't my boss," Leah said. "I'd have some very unflattering things to say about that world view."

"I'm a big boy; I can take it."

"Unflattering things!" she said, raising her voice above the din.

* * *

Leah's feet were numb again by the time they stepped into the precinct, but the cold was forgotten as Police Precinct Archetypes bounced back and forth in front of her like superballs. First was the tired and disinterested desk sergeant who waved King past without looking up from his crossword puzzle.

Then the tattooed and leather-clad suspects resisting every step of the way toward lockup, the Polish and Irish cops yelling back at the outraged suspects, and the white boards covered in pictures and documents.

This was a Modern Cop Show precinct, more open office with team clusters, less the bullpens of the old 70s cop shows.

A woman walked up to King. She wore a gray suit with an emerald shirt. She had warm brown skin and curly hair—Leah pegged her as probably Filipina. The woman offered her hand. "Mr. King. Good to see you."

King met her hand with a healthy shake. "Detective De La Cruz, good to be back. This is Ms. Leah Tang, a junior PI I'm taking under my wing. Thought I'd make introductions while I called on Captain Franklin. She around?"

"In her office, as always," the detective said. The woman offered her hand, and Leah shook it.

"Pleased to meet you, detective." Leah nodded her head at the general chaos. "Looks like you stay busy here."

"Sometimes, it seems like I'm here for weeks at a time." She didn't look it, though. Like in the Romance world, most anyone who was anyone in a story world was default beautiful. Hollywood "average" was the law of the land.

King made his way to a closed-door office in the back of the room.

"Well, I hope you get some time to relax soon," Leah told De La Cruz, leaving to follow King.

"Not likely. Just waiting for my sleepyhead partner to arrive so we can get back to a case."

They waved farewell and walked deeper into the precinct, stopping outside an office.

King knocked twice on the door, then opened it without waiting for an answer.

The room was meticulously maintained, books and files and folders all neatly arrayed on shelves flanking both sides of the office. The room smelled faintly of cedar and sported a pair of aloe plants atop file folders.

Behind the desk stood a striking black woman. She had light brown skin, relaxed hair, wore bifocal glasses and a pantsuit.

"It's been too long, King." She stepped out from behind the desk and hugged the senior Genrenaut in a way that lingered a shade longer than you'd expect from friends. Unless Crime World was also Touchy-Feely World. If this was the standard-cable Crime World, then maybe so.

"Good to see you, Nancy." The woman returned to her chair, which looked like it had come straight out of the Staples discount aisle—same as the rest of the chairs in the precinct.

King took a seat, introducing Leah as his new apprentice.

Leah shook Captain Franklin's hand and sat. "It looks like you've got a busy precinct, Captain."

The captain gave Leah a proud nod. "And the best officers in the state to work it. Thanks for coming by. Your good luck paid off again, King. I've actually got a few minutes before my next meeting."

All seated, King pulled out an old-school yellow legal pad and a fountain pen. Leah took that as a cue to pull out her own notepad. She'd prefer to use her phone, but King was a stickler. Said that studies showed memory creation was more effective when cued by handwriting.

One of the many things Leah had learned over the last couple of months was that her handwriting was terrible. She'd been typing since she was four—why bother getting good at handwriting? But King was right—her recall on the hand-written mission notes was better than she expected.

"So, what has been going on here since I was last in town?"

Captain Franklin shrugged. "A few high-profile cases, some entanglements with the governor, and some trips through sub-cultures to root out jilted lovers and inheritance-seeking relatives. The usual. Detective De La Cruz has been picking up most of the weird cases, her and that PI boyfriend of hers."

"She's still seeing DeeZee?" King asked. "I gave that six months, to be honest."

"I took the under on that pool, myself. De La Cruz works harder and longer hours than any of my detectives, but DeeZee helps her keep perspective. He's a pain in my ass more often than not, but they deliver results."

King turned and explained for Leah's benefit. "DeeZee is a professional gamer-turned-PI. Unconventional, but as she said, he delivers results."

"Got it." So this was another "He's a Quirky Specialist. She's a Serious LEO. They Fight Crime!" pairing. Not surprising, given the TV zeitgeist.

Networks and cable were full of quirky brilliant heroes from odd backgrounds paired up with tough, beautiful and/or handsome, complicated LEOs, whether they be cops or Feds. And the two inevitably fell in love, even if it took seven seasons for them to admit it and the show fell apart afterword because the writers couldn't translate will-they-won't-they tension into a dramatic healthy relationship.

"Any unsolved cases giving you problems? Departmental shake-ups coming down the pike?" Leah asked, figuring they should probe for potential breaches while they were there.

The captain's body language told Leah the question was a dud. "Our closure rate is top in the city. And the commissioner loves us. Other precincts are more glamorous, but before I took this post, the place was a wreck."

"But not as bad as the seventeenth back in the day, right?" King grinned, and the captain returned the warm expression. More shared history.

"Captain Kowalski spent more time in his cups than at his desk. And the sergeants were no better."

And so the pair turned off onto memory lane, trading stories for fifteen minutes, tidbits about recent cases laced through their reminisces like veins of gold in a mine. Leah took notes about the cases and tried not to write down too much of the gossip being passed between the pair. Instead, she took the chance to observe King with a peer.

Probably an old flame first and a peer second, from the way their body language was vibing back and forth. Leah bet it had been a while, especially with the ring she wore, but there had been something between them. And this after King's ten-page memo about not fraternizing with the locals unless it was mission-critical.

All of King's memos were around ten pages. Dude could make anything into a lecture.

As the clock in the captain's office ticked past noon, Leah turned and looked out to the bullpen.

Detective De La Cruz hung up her cell phone and set it on her desk, her eyes wet. She curled up in her chair and buried her head in arms and knees.

Uhoh.

Chapter Three:
Man Down

Leah pointed to De La Cruz's cube and said, "I think that's probably worth your attention, Captain."

Captain Franklin looked over Leah's shoulders, and sad recognition played across her face.

She went to her detective.

"DeeZee has been shot," the captain said on her return. "He's in critical condition."

Detective De La Cruz joined them. "I want this case, Captain."

Of course she did. Whenever a case was personal in a police procedural, there was always some convoluted reason why the detective could stay on the case despite a clear conflict of interest.

Leah watched for the story to deform illogically to allow De La Cruz to work the case.

Except, the captain's response was, "Absolutely not. You're on indefinite administrative leave, starting now."

Leah looked to King, wracking her brain for a Crime story when a personal case had gone this way without the appeal working. Something to bring up with him.

"Captain, I…"

The captain hardened. "It can be a suspension if you'd rather, Detective."

"No, sir."

"Go look after your guy."

"Yes, sir." De La Cruz did that thing that cops and military and other folks with tons of emergency training did, where they locked it down and got their calm back. Wasn't universal, though. Roman rode his emotions like a surfboard.

"Thank you, sir," De La Cruz said. "I'll call in when I have updates."

"See that you do. Chen and McWilliams will want to hear as soon as there's news. Dismissed." Leah took them to be the friend cops, the other team that would work another part of a case—the cases that would all too often end up being related, thanks to the laws of narrative conservation.

The detective nodded to the group on the way out, picked her coat off of her chair, and hoofed it for the stairs.

King turned back to the captain. "So, who's going to catch this hot-potato case?"

"DeeZee isn't a cop, but he's family." She considered for a moment. "Feel like getting your hands dirty, gum shoe?"

"We're at your disposal."

"Good. Meet me in the briefing room in ten minutes."

King stood and the two shook hands.

"Come on, Probie. I'll fill you in on how these folks work."

* * *

King claimed the briefing room immediately, closing the door for something resembling privacy to talk things over with Leah.

"So, who is this captain to you," the rookie asked. "Old flame? What happened to 'the Regs forbid nonessential fraternization?' And why didn't she let De La Cruz work the case? The detective always gets to work the personal case."

King took a long breath. "I'll answer all of those at once. Captain Franklin wasn't born on this world. She was born on ours."

Understanding played across Leah's expression. "So, she what, got trapped here?"

King faced back out toward the bullpen, keeping his memories in check. "Twenty years ago. We were here together on a mission working a case—the rest of our team was off working another breach in the region. We worked and worked, and just could not close the case. We ran down three red herrings, and by the time we had the killer in our sights, we'd reached the end of our one week on-world. Nancy was so deep in the story that she wouldn't leave."

He paused for a moment, remembering that cold, rainy day, the last conversation they'd had as he ran the preflight check. She wore red and the ruby earrings he'd gotten her the Christmas before.

She'd folded her arms that way she always did when she'd decided and there was no changing her mind. "I have to see this through. And if I don't, the breach will be out of control by the time you can come back. I stay here, and hundreds, maybe thousands of people are spared the ripple. This is what we're here to do."

"Then I'll stay too," he'd said. "We'll start over here, make our own stories."

"The case only needs one. Go live your life. But don't forget about me."

They'd shared one last kiss, interrupted by his alarm. He'd cut it as close as possible, and had the book thrown at him when he got back.

King let the memory fade and turned to face his newest recruit.

"I came back with the rest of the team as soon as they'd let me—a week later. By the time we got there, the case was solved and Nancy had been enrolled in the police academy with a letter of recommendation from the commissioner. The story had her. She'd forgotten her home, where she came from. Our cover was as PIs, so that's what she thought she was. And now she's as much a part of this world as anyone."

"Shit, boss, I'm sorry. But what about bringing her back?"

Memories bubbled up again, conversations late at night on the stoop of their row house about what they'd do if they were ever stuck on a story world.

King shook his head. "Recovery from dimensional sickness has a very low success rate. Nancy knew it. She made her choice, and if I took her from this place and brought her back, even if she survived, I would have been violating her wishes."

Nancy told me, "I'd rather live a story than die trying to get back. It's still living." King spoke with practiced ease. He must have repeated this speech a thousand times. "Those worlds, they're as real as ours. Just more focused. Limited. And God knows my life was already limited before I signed up. But this time I'm making the choice."

King wiped his eyes, then straightened. *Plenty of time to feel sorry for myself later.* "What's most important right now is this case. And piling a second breach on top of the first one, even if the previous breach was small, means we've got trouble on our hands."

He'd seen it on De La Cruz's face as soon as she walked in. She'd gone out of sync with the world, flickering around the edges. Smart money said the same would be true of DeeZee when they saw him.

"With DeeZee out of action, this department is short a wacky specialist. It's how the precinct operates. They need a weird outsider with strange insights to solve the bizarre cases. Chen and McWilliams work the by-the-book kinds of cases and play second unit on the big stories."

King waved to the precinct, the rows of desks. "But there's so much of a thirst for these stories that the region's mandate has broadened, and the precincts with them. They've gotten more and more elaborate—bigger CSI teams, more Special Victims cases, and here, with DeeZee and De La Cruz, the oddball cases requiring off-the-wall thinking, almost a crossover with Cozies, though not in the same manner as Crossover Zones. This is more of a fully integrated sub-thread of the genre." He gestured out toward Detective De La Cruz's desk and the captain's office. "With the Odd Couple Duo, women get to be powerful cops, but the story boxes them in to Strong Female Character archetypes, and the wacky specialists balance them out."

"I'm your girl," Leah said.

Good. Confidence, no hesitation.

"I mean, stand-up comic turned PI? It practically writes itself."

"But that's not all," King said. "The whacky specialist needs a handler, a by-the-book, driven detective. This will be more trying than anything you've done yet. We'll have to keep one another afloat. The specialist goes off the wall, but their stern partner goes the other way, becomes uncompromising, harsh. By diving into a role this hard, with the strong history with the captain, there's a risk of me getting in over my head."

And diving into the role definitely isn't a defense mechanism to help keep your distance with Nancy, he told himself. He was old enough to own up to his bullshit. To himself, if not to his team. But it was the right call. For the mission, for her, for all of them.

This was no laughing matter. Well, her jokes would be. But this was heavy work. You dove into an archetype with every fiber of your being, and sometimes it got its hooks in you, left a mark. Every time he came back from Post-Apocalypse world having worn the mantle of the Max, he felt his world get a bit grayer, found himself expecting the worst a bit more often. But it also gave him an edge. There was power in wrapping yourself up in a story, but it always came with a price. Roman was *still* paying that price, still exploring who he was outside the role.

"We have to keep each other level. When we're not neck-deep in investigating, make me take a breather. Get me thinking about Mallery's case again; be the uppity new kid. And whatever you do, do not let us stay here more than seven days. In fact, it's best that we get out in six."

He couldn't make Nancy's choice. The team needed him. "I'm going to call this in. Shirin and company will stick with their mission. And don't think this lets you off the hook there."

Leah rubbed her arms. "Somehow, this is all very serious now."

"Comedy is just drama with a greater emotional range, newbie. There's a reason why some of the greatest actors the stage and screen have ever known started as comedians."

That line met with great approval from his rookie partner. "So, I treat this like a USA or TNT show, except I need to keep you from going off the method deep end."

King nodded. "Here comes the captain. I'm stepping out to tell my secretary we're on the case, got it?"

Her body language said yes. While her confidence was still developing, Leah had always been quick to adapt. Throw her a curveball and she adjusted on the fly.

Let's just hope it's enough to handle two cases at once. We're not exactly working with a full roster right now. The ever-full medical wing back at HQ jumped to mind, and he put it aside.

One thing at a time.

* * *

The number-one thing Leah had learned on the job so far was to roll with the punches. Sometimes literally, but not too often, so far. Fortunately, four years of improv comedy made her as light on her toes as a ballerina. But, like, a short third-tier ballerina that mostly stood in the back. Fortunately, no one had asked her to do anything en pointe yet.

The captain passed King as he left the room to call in the mission.

"Hi, Captain. King just stepped out to check in with his secretary, tell them we're on the case."

"Understood. Let's get started."

Leah helped the captain pin the pictures, email print-outs, and other materials to a corkboard. Every piece that Leah put up, the captain corrected her or added a comment, but Leah was used to being countermanded, overridden, and otherwise pushed around, and not just as a Genrenaut. The last time she'd stuck with something long enough to get seniority was the improv team, and even when she was team captain, she'd never been the star player. *Damn you, Gary Walker,* she thought, remembering the superstar transfer who had dominated her senior year. He could barely organize a stack of three apples, let alone a team. But how the audiences loved him.

King walked back in as Captain Franklin stepped back from the board, doing that cop thing of staring at the case materials to force it make sense. Mentally, she filled in the "thinking soft rock" music that accompanied the scenes on TV.

"Vic's name is Dwayne Smith, chef at Lake Effect, a high-end restaurant near the lake on Clark. DeeZee is a regular customer there, so it made sense for De La Cruz and him to take the case. Smith was found in the oven at Lake Effect this morning when the owner came in early to do payroll. No signs of struggle outside, but we got three inches last night, so who knows. The body had been cooking, probably since close. Doctor Lombardi will run the autopsy later today."

"They cooked him? Overnight?" Leah made a yuck face, exaggerating her reaction as she went for both gallows humor and wackiness. "Did they at least set a timer? Use some air freshener?"

King made an act of ignoring her clowning but gave her a wink out of the corner of his eye. "What's been done already?"

"Uniforms were on their way to secure the scene, and they found DeeZee in the alley. Lucky bastard. Paramedics say if he'd been there much longer, he might not have made it."

King got them back on-track. "Was anyone leaning on the restaurant? Rivals? Mob? Any enemies?"

"The owner, Adnan Refai, bought Lake Effect from Oliver Balicki about five years ago. The place is part of a line restaurateurs that broke from the mob back in the thirties. The Salvatores have had designs on the place for years. But they're staying squeaky clean. Plus they've got a handful of Aldermen in their pockets."

King jumped in. "Looks like the Mob angle is the most likely. Not exactly promising." His voice was more gruff, and he was moving more sharply, more severe. Like he was playing to an audience thirty feet away, in a room with only two other people, both within arm's reach. *And so it begins*, she thought. He'd be one extreme, she the other.

In Leah's previous missions, the Genrenauts had built identities to blend into the story worlds. They'd slid into archetypes with slight adjustments.

What King was doing here already felt different, the way he talked about it. He'd never looked worried about taking a role before. And his carriage was already different—stiffer but with more aggressive motions.

Fear crawled up her back like a big-ass spider.

Leah picked up the thread from King. "We could be the people that finally put them away!"

The captain and King both gave Leah a look that said *Good luck with that, kiddo.*

She pivoted. "Anyone on the staff have motive to go after Smith?"

"Good question. We'll bring that to the staff."

King said, "We'll need to run down all of these eventualities, plus investigate DeeZee's attack for any possible connections. For now, we need to get to the scene of DeeZee's shooting."

Leah hopped off the table, playing it broad. "Lead on, Captain." She waved toward the door, topping it off with a wider smile than would ever be appropriate in a police department. She added on a two-finger salute for bonus over-kill.

* * *

Lake Effect was located in a rich neighborhood—Leah could tell because the roads were spotless, plowed, and salted, all of the sidewalks similarly clean.

Caution tape surrounded the alley, and the captain's car was the third police vehicle on site. On the way over, King had kept up the act, filling the captain in about various cases he'd solved across the country. Thanks to her homework, she recognized all of them as cases from TV procedurals—*Castle, White Collar,* and *Lie to Me.*

They laid the groundwork to paint a picture of King as having become more hard-edged, more the man he thought he had to be for them to solve this case. The captain's body language shifted during the trip as King laid out this new version of himself. Or maybe it was just the story's momentum taking hold, wrapping the captain up in this new version of the narrative.

Their shoes and boots crunched on fresh-packed snow as they approached the crime scene, the uniformed officers snapping to attention as they noticed the captain approaching.

"Good morning, Captain," said a fresh-faced officer, who seemed to have run the scene before the captain arrived. "What brings you out into this weather?"

"We believe this may be related to the Smith case." The captain nodded over her shoulder to the Genrenauts. "You remember Mr. King, and this is his associate, Ms. Tang."

The officer nodded. "Mr. King."

"Officer Rodriguez."

"It's Sergeant now, actually."

King offered a handshake of congratulation, and then followed the captain under the police line to the scene. There wasn't much there. Some blood in the snow, marked with a numbered tent-stand. There was an indentation in the snow around the blood, the place where DeeZee had fallen. A dusting of fresh snow covered the packed base, filling in the indentation without altering its shape. Nearby, the snow was melted in a splatter pattern. The edges were stained brown, a cup-holder and two spent coffee cups nearby with their own evidence tent.

Living in the Upper Midwest, Leah had learned to read snow. Some days, that was all there was to do. She never expected it to come in handy for work.

The senior Genrenaut crouched down by the blood spatter, looked from the blood up and away.

"Judging from the silhouette and the blood splatter, I bet we're looking at a shooter from the roof. One of those two buildings," he said, pointing to a pair of two-story buildings behind Lake Effect, sharing the same alley. Both granted a clear view of the alley.

"How can you tell that just from a splatter of blood?"

"I've been doing this for a long time. Like I said, expectations for CSI evidence have been corrupted by the stories. Another team was on the beat, couldn't patch the breach well enough. So now it's been building over time, and now Earth Prime has unrealistic forensic expectations for real cases, real trials; they're through the roof. But here, we can get all the detail we need."

"That's a why explanation, not a how."

"The way the blood comes off the body tells you how fast it hit and lets me guess at where. Also, I see an indentation in the snow on the lips of the roofs of the buildings, there and there."

King pointed up, and Leah squinted, shielding her eyes from the drifting snow picked up and whirled around by the wind.

"Yeah, but how do we know that was the shooter?"

"Hunches, kid." King stomped down the alley, giving a wide berth to the evidence tents. "And decades of training."

Leah followed King up a fire escape and onto the roof. "What are you looking for now, boss?" She remembered her role and kept spitballing. "Clue particles? Recollections of old cases that I weave together to create a web of speculation and unsubstantiated claims that we use to catch the criminals until they screw themselves over by confessing? Will we have to torture people here? I'm not down with that. Just because TV shows do it…"

"That's enough, rookie. And watch where you're stepping." King held an arm out to stop Leah from wandering forward. She stepped back and matched his gaze, looking down at a hole in the blanket of snow. It had been mussed at the edges.

"What's this?"

"Spent casing. It discharged from the gun and arced into the snow." King shuffled sideways, still eyeballing the hole. "Which means that the killer fired from about…here." He said, pointing to a space with powder over packed snow.

King kept going. "The tracks here are layered, so the shooter was here for a while. They were disciplined, didn't pace, but in this weather, even someone trained would need to keep moving to stay warm."

"Can we pull tread prints or something from this? Get a shovel and pull the whole sheet of ice out, put it in a flat-bed cooler, and haul it off to the CSI techs?"

"More comedy speculation on top of the banter," King said. "We need to play up the archetypes more."

"Aye aye, cap'n. So, this scene is about a would-be killer so dedicated that they wait in the cold. What are they thinking while they're waiting? Maybe they're smoking, they've got to be doing something with their hands. If they don't smoke, no cigarettes around, right, and they've got medium-sized feet, wearing what, boots of some sort? The heel there looks pretty prominent, but it's a smaller heel. It's a woman! Totally a woman's boot imprint."

"Very good. Keep going."

Leah got to pacing, talking with her hands like she'd seen from a dozen different wacky TV investigators. "So, our would-be killer was chilling up here. Either waiting for DeeZee or waiting for someone else, and got spotted, maybe? Crime of opportunity and necessity. What's the official term?"

"It would be a crime of necessity. Opportunity would be if our shooter already wanted to kill them and got an unexpected chance. But if she was here waiting for someone, maybe Smith's killer, then DeeZee walked by, spotted her as she hid. He started to pursue, knowing as a PI that he could get away with trespassing onto a crime scene if it were in pursuit of a suspect…"

"Is that legal?"

"No, but it's in-genre for his type of PI."

"This scene makes me think Mob hit. How do we approach it if the mob's involved? Do we get to go eat Italian in a dimly lit restaurant, keeping our backs to the wall and having tense, super-subtextual conversations with dudes in three-piece suits over red wine while trying to avoid spilling red sauce on our fancy clothes? I didn't bring fancy clothes."

Leah looked over and saw that King had started down the fire escape, leaving her to vamp.

He called up after her. "We'll get to the Mob later. For now, we interview the chef and his staff, confirm alibis, et cetera."

Leah rubbed her arms as she stepped down onto the fire escape. "Anything to get out of this cold."

Being in this region, she felt like she had a bull's-eye painted on her back. *Being here too long could make a body paranoid.* For good reason. Apparently, you never knew when you were going to go from detective to victim.

* * *

The inside restaurant was way upscale, wearing its class trappings with pride—black-and-white photographs, massive wine selection displayed in glass-covered lacquered racks, and more.

Executive Chef Adnan Refai greeted them as Sergeant Rodriguez walked them in. Refai was a slim Middle Eastern man, probably late forties, a dash of gray in his pulled-back hair. He wore a charcoal suit with a burgundy-collared shirt, and had two earrings in his left ear. He was slick without coming off as smarmy. But maybe that was just the grief. He looked pained, shocked, eyes still wide.

"Thank you for coming so quickly. It's…it's horrible. First Dwayne, and now DeeZee…Is he going to make it?"

King repeated what Rodriguez had told them, positioning himself as the authority in the situation. "We haven't heard back from the hospital, but paramedics said that he should make it."

They walked back into the kitchen. All but empty, it felt hollow. And the body on the floor made it all the worse.

Dwayne Smith was burned all around, and the room smelled foul, even with industrial-grade cleaner. He'd been white-guy pasty once. Not anymore. Now he was charred.

"You said you found him in the oven?"

"Yes. I couldn't bear to leave him like that. But I wore gloves. He was my right hand, Detective. A good man. Not always the easiest to get along with, but gifted. Innovative."

Leah tried not to retch.

Tried.

And failed.

She looked around, desperate for something to hurl on that wasn't incredibly expensive kitchen equipment.

Fortunately, there was a bucket.

She hit the deck, clinging to the bucket for another few moments.

Yep, there goes another one.

After the second, she pushed the bucket away and averted her eyes. Not the first dead body she'd seen, but it was only the second. And the first burn victim.

"Rookie, are you going to be okay?"

"Can we go back?" she asked in a weak voice, pointing toward the dining area.

That's not embarrassing at all. Totally not mortified. But it was in-genre. She was the rookie, not hardened like King. At least she was screwing up appropriately.

King nodded. "I'll come back to check the body. Is there somewhere we can talk?"

Chef Refai led them out and they pulled the chairs down at a four-top round table. King flipped open his patented legal pad and said, "Why don't you start from the beginning. You came in early to do paperwork."

"Yes. It was just before nine. I walked through the dining area, into the kitchen, on the way to my office. I saw that the oven was on and rushed to turn it off. Gas, you know. I didn't smell any gas, but I did smell something far worse."

People. Leah gulped again.

"How was Smith's body arranged?" King had it locked down. All business. How long would it take her to be able to stay cool? Or was he already that deep into character?

Refai's face was a mask of horror. This guy was not used to seeing death.

Maybe less used to it than Leah. "The rack had been pulled out. He was stuffed in." Refai's voice cracked, and he shook. "Stuffed in like a rag doll. Who could have done this?"

"That's what we're here to find out," Leah ventured.

King said, "We'll need to interview all of the staff. Especially anyone who was working last night."

"Of course. I'll call them in. But I don't hire criminals, Detective. My people are dependable. Most have been with me for years, even the busboys."

King ran through the script. "We need to cover all of the bases. Was there anyone who might have had a grudge against Smith or against the restaurant?"

"Like I said, Dwayne was not always the easiest to work with. But he was always professional. He is from Chicago, like me. The Salvatores, though. They've been hounding me to sell the place ever since I bought it, and before, they tried to buy it from Oliver Balicki. They never outright threatened me, but it was always implied. If I were a betting man, I would say it was them. They killed him and then they took a shot at DeeZee to try to scare you off. He is a detective, like you. Not officially police. Safer to kill."

"Not that safe. Especially if he survives. I'll go take a closer look at the body now." King turned to ask Leah, "You okay to come along?"

She tried to put on a brave face, and then her stomach roiled again. "I'll look around the restaurant for other evidence?" she volunteered.

King sighed, walking off.

Doing great so far, she thought.

* * *

King and Leah interviewed all of the staff that had been on the night before. Refai promised to have the rest of them come in to the precinct later that day.

Mostly, they got the same story. Smith was hard to work with, very demanding, but incredibly inventive and precise. He wasn't well loved, but he was respected, even admired.

And then they got to Ricardo Hernandez, the other head chef. Hernandez was Latino, in his late thirties, wide-shouldered and in good shape. He was as grief-stricken as the rest of the staff, words coming slow through emotion.

"Did he have any enemies? Anyone who would want him harmed?" King asked.

Hernandez looked up, as if searching his memory. "No, not really."

Leah jumped in, following the cop script from TV shows. "Think back to the last couple of days. Anything out of the ordinary? Weird visitors, problem customers?"

Hernandez nodded, his face lighting up. "There was this thing yesterday. I was outside taking a smoke break, and Smith was talking in the alley with this woman. Tatiana. She's a regular here. She grew up in the neighborhood, used to run with a bad crowd, until the Salvatores left her out to dry. Now she scrimps and saves and comes in to have one nice lunch a month. Yesterday was her day. Talk with her, and I bet you'll get to the bottom of this."

King shared a look with Leah. That was a lead if he'd ever seen one.

"That's very good to know. One last question, just to be thorough. Where were you last night? You said you clocked out at eight…" King trailed off to let Hernandez take over.

"I went out for a drink at Sal's, halfway between here and my building. Got home at nine thirty, then I was in for the night."

"And who can corroborate that?" Leah asked, following the detective script.

"My wife, for one." A beat. "We have a doorman, too. They've got cameras and everything."

King filed away a note to check the footage and talk with the doorman.

"Thank you, Mr. Hernandez; that's all for now. You've been very helpful." Hernandez stood and they shook hands.

When he was out of earshot, Leah said, "That Tatiana chick sounds like a good lead."

"She does. We'll follow up with her and run down the alibis this afternoon. First, we should go check in on DeeZee." He held up his phone. "Captain texted and said he's in recovery."

Chapter Four:
Emergency Exposition

Leah hated hospitals—they smelled like death and surgery and hours of stressed waiting on bad news. She was getting used to it, thanks to having a medical wing built into Genrenauts HQ, but that didn't stop her from flinching when she stepped into the oxygen-heavy, antiseptic air of Chicago's Our Lady of Grace.

Remarking the signs on the wall, Leah asked, "Won't he still be in surgery or recovering?"

"Not in this world." King chewed up the tile floor, his gait less "confident investigator" and more "ha ha ha, I have longer legs than you"—at least, that's how Leah was taking it as she hustled to keep up. "We need him to be awake to move the story forward, so he will be."

DeeZee's room was on the third floor. It was already decked with balloons and flowers. The TV in the corner was hooked up to a next-gen console. Beside it was a small stack of game disc cases with taped-on labels. A controller sat on the bed next to the detective.

The ex-pro gamer looked run down, his white skin extra-pale, hair slicked back with sweat. He had thick bandages from his abdomen up and over his right nipple. He was still out, IV set up on the near side of the room.

Detective De La Cruz sat on the bed beside DeeZee, face teary, as anyone reasonable would expect. She was being a person, not a stony extension of the state's will.

King and Leah stood in the doorway, not wanting to intrude.

"May we join you?" King asked, hat in his hand.

Leah took the respite to de-winter a bit, taking off her hat, untying her scarf, and stuffing her gloves back into her voluminous, Doberman-training-grade coat.

"Please." The detective waved them in.

King's footfalls came soft. Leah tried to match his tone and calm down the wackiness a bit in recognition of the serious situation.

On the bed, DeeZee stirred, shifting and then wincing. Right on time.

"What the frakking frell..." He saw the detective, then the two visitors, and his eyes went wide. He looked down, grokked that he was in a hospital. Leah caught him processing, doubtless going through what had happened.

"Melissa?" he asked. His tone said there were a half-dozen questions baked into that one word. *What happened? Is everything okay? Where am I?* and more.

Detective De La Cruz squeezed the PI's hand. "I'm here, Dee. You're going to be fine. They got the bullet out, no major organs damaged. Your amazing luck continues, to the surprise of no one."

DeeZee raised his free hand a few inches off the bed. "A winner is me." His gaze passed to King and Leah. "Hey, King. Who's the newbie?"

King nodded. "This is my new junior associate, Leah Tang."

"Nice to meet you. Those game boxes don't look quite regulation—are they previews?"

DeeZee managed a grin. "I'm still an honorary member of a team of game streamers; friend hooked me up with his press copy once he'd had his fill. Haven't gotten to try it out yet. Strangely, my plans for today got derailed."

"About that, Mr. DeeZee." King brought them back on topic. "We're investigating the shooting, with the captain's blessing. One of my brotherhood comes under fire, I'm not about to stand by. We'd like to take your statement, if you're up for it."

King drew out his legal pad, and Leah quick-drew her phone to match. She reminded herself to choose the phablet option next time she had an upgrade. But only if she could get one that could hold on to its stylus.

"Yeah, sure." DeeZee pulled himself up to a seated position, "Can I get some water?" Leah slid over and offered the man the waiting cup of water. Detective De La Cruz's mask of worry relaxed, probably due to the combo of DeeZee waking and the familiarity of taking a witness statement.

"I was getting coffee for the team so we could work the case. Melissa and I, we're on the Dwayne Smith murder case. Or were, I guess."

King nodded.

"I live just around the corner from Lake Effect, and Melissa's favorite coffee shop is two blocks west of there. I passed by the alley and something twigged my radar. Being a lifelong gamer, you learn to trust your instincts, right?" he asked.

Leah chuckled internally at the concept of Gamer Detective. Plotlines unspooled in her mind, threatening to run around with her attention. She reined it back in.

"So, I looked into the alley and caught a flash of movement up high. I ran in, keeping the coffees level to avoid taking a latte-and-Americano shower. I looked up just in time to see the shooter on the roof of one of the buildings forming the alley. Looked like a woman, white. But that's all I could tell. And then…" DeeZee tapped his chest, then winced at what he'd done. "And that's all I've got."

"That confirms my findings from the scene. Is there anything else you remember? Something in the alley? Was the shooter holding anything other than the gun? What color was her hair?"

DeeZee's eyes went flat, like he was thinking. He slumped. "Mana sink like whoa. Is there a meds button or something?"

Detective De La Cruz grabbed the cord and pressed the button. "Can't find the right button on a controller? You must really be out of it," she said with loving mockery.

"Thanks, hon." He was too out of it to respond in bantering kind, apparently. DeeZee lay silent for a moment, breathing as the medication flowed.

They waited. King was patient when he needed to be. When he needed you to have done something ten minutes ago, he was less so.

"Her hair was dark, but I don't know if she was holding anything else. The gun was probably black. Her coat was. That's all I've got, sorry."

"That's very helpful. And rest assured we'll catch this shooter. We're helping the department with the Dwayne Smith case, as well. Captain gave Detective De La Cruz as much leave as she needs. The captain looks after her own, and so do I."

The detective piped up. "Captain Franklin has ordered a protective detail; the first officer should be here within minutes. We're safe here. And anyone coming after you has to go through me." Her grin was endearing, but also a bit intimidating. She was not kidding around.

King drew out a business card and left it on the bed, sparing DeeZee from having to reach out for it. "Call anytime. That way, you both can rest. Especially you, Detective."

De La Cruz popped her back and sighed, a crack showing in the Stalwart Protector armor. Leah imagined she'd been there the whole time since she arrived, maybe even sitting in that exact position, paralyzed by worry and the possibilities. Worrying about friends was one thing. Add romantic love to the mix and it was a whole extra level of heart-wrenching.

Advantages of being single, I guess? And that brought up thoughts of Mallery again. She channeled that straight into her other task and pulled out her phone to jot down notes for Mallery's skit. *Use her skill with accents. Maybe a riff on Legally Blonde?*

She followed King out of the room, his feet at the edge of her vision as she thumb-typed.

They stepped out into the cold before Leah realized she needed to re-winter. But she'd gotten rolling and kept brainstorming as she donned her scarf and gloves.

Okay, but what's the twist, she asked, pondering both her skit and the case at hand.

* * *

King watched snow fall as they sped back to the precinct in a cab. Even snowfall had patterns. Follow the wind, gauge the size of each snowflake, and you didn't have to be a chaos mathematician to guess where they would land.

But something wasn't adding up there. A second breach this quickly after the first? And that much bigger? Something was off.

On their way back from the hospital, Preeti had passed on reports of increased dimensional turbulence, a storm brewing between worlds. If it got much worse, it'd cut their comms to HQ, maybe even delay their return.

Leah broke his worried contemplation, spitballing. As she should be. Thoughtful Detective often became Maudlin Detective if left to their own devices. He'd need to be careful.

"That's two votes for a woman as the shooter," Leah said. "You think she did both hits? Killed Smith and stowed him in the oven to throw off suspicion, and then took a shot at DeeZee when he spotted her?"

"Could be. We'd need to know why she was back at the scene of the crime, though. And who she is. We haven't got nearly enough to build a useful profile, so it's back to the precinct. Narratology says that there will be some evidence available, and it'll set us on the path to a suspect."

"This region is that schematic? You can just beat it out, step by step?"

"Campbell isn't the only one who pegged a formula. I've watched probably a thousand hours of procedural detective shows. Thing is, this case is strange. The breach means that we're dealing with a double crime, so the pacing could vary. But checking in with the captain is good police work, and it's narratologically indicated, so that makes it a no-brainer. And it gives you time to send over your skit to Mallery. Her audition should be almost done."

"And you're not just taking us back because it means getting to see the captain again," Leah said, a big dollop of intimation in her voice.

The beginnings of a smile touched his cheeks. Involuntary. The archetype work already had him off-balance. Anywhere else, he'd be fine. But here, the stakes were different.

Leah didn't follow up with any of the hundred questions she doubtless had buzzing around in her mind.

But most of those were not questions you asked your boss less than two months on the job, even in as close working conditions as the Genrenauts.

"I'm not some lovesick kid. I made my peace with this a long time ago. I moved on."

Liar, he thought. He'd done his best, but there was a part of him that would always live here, with her, frozen in that last moment.

King cleared his throat. "I'll need you to focus on riffing and extrapolation when we get the lab results. Blue-sky thinking all around. Don't filter yourself."

Leah saluted. "Aye aye. By the way, I like this mission. People should get murdered here more often." She stopped herself. "That came out wrong. I like getting to be me but at a louder volume, and solving wacky crimes and being a part of a buddy-cop duo."

"Your interest has been noted. You'll need to test higher to get a Crime specialization on your roster, though. Enthusiasm and a sharp tongue don't get you that far outside this region."

On the street around them, a school let out, yearning figures standing across the street in coats with collars drawn up, each staring intently at a kid coming out of the playground. Estranged parents, most likely, each a potential suspect or victim.

The whole region was divided up into three types of people—potential criminals, potential victims, and people caught in the middle.

When the cab pulled up to the precinct, Leah all but leaping out of the car, clearing the grey-white slush beneath the curb.

Leah continued to chatter on their way in, leaning into her role as King found himself talking less, grumbling more, and getting a very bad feeling about the whole case.

* * *

It was an audition hall like so many others. Just a bit more dramatic. Everyone walked out either beaming with triumph or crushed with sorrow.

Mallery had auditioned for roles that were more of a stretch, but always within her discipline. And taking on covers with the Genrenauts was different—that was slipping into a whole other person's life. Here, she was just an alternate-universe version of herself, a Mallery who had tacked a different direction in college.

"Number seventeen!" a bass voice called from inside.

But ultimately, it was still comedy.

She strode into the room, head held high.

Ten minutes later, she had a time and date for callbacks, and instructions to bring in three scenarios to run and a monologue to show off her chops.

Leah's instructions had been right on. They'd had her work with props, play off of the remaining troupe members, and at the end, they'd asked personal questions, trying to embarrass her. As if. She'd stared down death on a half-dozen worlds. Comedians, even good ones, weren't quite the same level of stress. And the whole time they were auditioning her, she was reading them. They were nervous as a baseline. Some were angry about it and trying to take it out on anyone they could; one was just going through the motions, her mind somewhere else.

And the fourth was acting excited about everything and everyone, probably overcorrecting for the others. She knew that move from personal experience. She called it the Everything's Fine, I Will Make It Fine, and Shame on You for Not Being a Team Player If You Admit That Something's Wrong move. She'd learned it from her aunt. Not the most mature, but it had its uses.

When push came to shove, Mallery didn't take any options off the table.

She'd left trackers in the glossy headshots she'd given the troupe with her resume on the back. She'd also snuck a camera on the door coming in. That should give Roman and Shirin GPS signals they'd need to track the troupe members over the rest of the day, plus an eye on the studio.

Once she was out of the building, she called it in. "And we're in. Leah, I'm going to need a monologue and three skit scenarios for four players. That doable?"

Mallery nodded to a waiting Roman across the street, who dumped his newspaper in the trash can and trudged his way across the snow-laden street to rendezvous.

"Hey, good job!" came Leah's voice over their in-ear comms. "And yeah, no problem. Just let us get done with the morgue here."

"Have fun talking to the dead."

"This isn't that kind of story region, right?"

"Just screwing with you."

"Cut the chatter," King said, and that was that. Mallery rolled her eyes at the team lead's wet blanket-ness and picked up the pace, excited and nervous to brainstorm with Leah again. But the sooner they wrapped up the mission, the sooner they would get out of the in-between place. Sometimes, in-between was fun. She'd drawn out the in-between place on purpose a few times, reveling in the frustrating uncertainty, mined it for pathos.

But that was a long time before. Her brush with death had given her a lot of time to reflect on life. How much time she'd wasted in gray areas. Now, she wanted more certainty. For both their sakes, and for the mission. When things were unclear, people got hurt. Right on cue, a passer-by bumped her still-recovering arm, sending lances of pain up and down her arm. She swayed and put a hand on Roman to steady herself, gritting her teeth.

Certainty. Certainty was good.

"Those comedians are a rat king of tangled emotions," she told Roman, comms off. "Let's get untangling."

* * *

Leah had never been to a morgue, but since this was a TV-land morgue, it was exactly as she'd expected. Dimly lit, very empty, and incredibly clean. The room smelled of Freon, metal, and latex. It was operated by a single ME, one Doctor Consuela Lombardi, a curvy Mexican-American woman a hand shorter than Leah. Doctor Lombardi's dark hair was pulled back into a Gordian knot of a bun that must have taken twenty minutes but looked amazing.

Doctor Lombardi pulled back a sheet revealing the body of Dwayne

Smith, a wound at the back of his head.

Leah's stomach started to riot, and her throat clenched up. She took a step back, raising a "one second" hand. The ME handed her a bucket. But this time, she didn't need it.

"The oven had nothing to do with it, as you can see." She replaced the sheet. All of the burns were post-mortem. Lack of abrasion or frostbite on his front suggests he fell back, not forward."

Leah jumped in. "What could cause that kind of wound? A club? Baseball bat? Mobster with a baseball bat is a thing, right? Evil White Sox fan?"

"Other way around. This is the south side, Sox territory," the doctor said. "But as for the weapon, I don't think it was a bat or wrench. The shape of impact doesn't match."

"Were you able to pull any fibers or particulates from the victim's clothes or the wound?" King asked.

Leah noticed the distancing language, the short shot of the wound. Happily, this story was apparently echoing the less-gory parts of the genre as opposed to the "how extreme can we get in the violence we show on TV horse race that the networks and especially premium cable shows carried out.

Which led Leah to wondering. Were they really just in a case-of-the-week structure, or was something else going on there? Some way that theft at the stand-up troupe could connect with this crime. Most of the odd-couple detective shows were episodic, but the cable shows had been going serial, drilling into one case for a six- to thirteen-episode arc. Something else to ask King.

"So, what kind of shape was the weapon or whatever?" Leah asked, flipping through her mental Clue Rolodex.

"Circular, maybe two inches wide," the Doctor said. "From the angle, he was falling as he hit or it hit him."

Something caught in Leah's mind. She drew her phone and scanned through the pictures she'd taken at the crime scene. A half-dozen shots in, her phone showed her a two-inch round a copper circle covered with snow on the alley wall opposite the door to Lake Effect.

Leah handed the phone to the ME. "Could it have been this?"

Doctor Lombardi zoomed the picture and then nodded. "Quite possible. If he slipped and fell backward or was pushed into where that pipe juts out…CSI didn't bring in any scrapings like that; they must have missed it."

Leah saw her opportunity and dove on it like a hungry five-year-old on a plate of cookies. Drawing her sunglasses, she flipped them open and, putting them on, said, "Sounds like the forensics team needs to get their CS eyes checked."

A *YEAAAAAAH!* sound played in her mind.

Nailed it, she thought, pumping her fist.

King nodded slightly in appreciation. Or at least, that's what Leah told herself. But he moved straight on. "We'll head back to the crime scene and take a sample. If we can measure where the pipe was, we can estimate where he was standing and, from there, how tall his killer was."

The ME considered. "It'll be hard to be precise without knowing exactly how Mr. Smith was pushed or fell and hit his head on the pipe. But it should be able to give us a range."

"Thank you, Doctor Lombardi; you've been very helpful." King drew his gloves from his pocket and turned for the door. His phone buzzed.

Reading the message, King said, "Captain wants to check in. Says she has some leads for us."

Leah took her sunglasses off again (they were inside, after all) and waved awkwardly to the doctor. "Thanks for giving us details about a tragic death, I guess? What do people say to thank you without it being morbid?" she asked, her mouth moving faster than her brain, no doubt thanks to playing the archetype. Possibly cosmic backlash for her bad pun. But King had the stoic nod cornered, and if she was going to be the whacky investigator, so be it.

The doctor said, simply, "They say thank you. And you're welcome. Good luck."

The role was coming more easily, like when she'd downed a pair of energy drinks before a skit where she played a frenetic meter maid during the apocalypse.

But the question might quickly become: could she stop herself when she wanted to?

Leah pulled out her phone to jot down some more ideas for Mallery's skit as she scaled the stairs after King and up to the bullpen.

Where they were greeted by yelling.

Chapter Five:
Escalation

The captain's voice filled the floor as they walked in. King recognized that tone. This was Nancy's rage voice. And given how long her fuse was, this had to be something big. Playing the paired archetypes with Leah was helping him keep himself together—it wasn't like Post-Apocalypse World where he was all alone, fighting tooth-and-nail to balance between invoking the archetype and not going off the edge. Leah's presence reminded him of the mission, kept him from falling into Nancy's gravity.

Which was substantial right now, as the captain continued barking orders like an XO in a war zone. "I want cars there in ten minutes and another three minutes after that. And get me the director of the hospital on the phone five minutes ago. She better have godlike insurance, because I am going to have someone's head for this."

King steadied himself on a nearby desk. The whole room was off, like someone had run the place through a grainy blue filter.

The breach was escalating. Again. It was rare for a breach to spread this quickly, but given their last few months, he should hardly be surprised. With the rate of breaches across every story world, "weird" was increasingly the new normal for the Genrenauts.

This precinct was usually on the chummy side of the genre. But the filter was straight out of a gritty cop drama, the kind where the line between cop and vigilante was razor-thin.

He made a note to read the rest of the team in, get their take. His mental to-do list shifted, items rearranging on the fly. Check in with Preeti, get a read on the disturbance. Have her run a comparative analysis of disturbance vs.

the escalation in this region.

He pinged HQ, but the disturbance cut off his voice line. He sent a text message, calling for receipt confirmation.

If the storm was getting worse, that could impinge on their return timeline.

The captain continued to hold court as he pieced the situation together.

"King, glad you're back," Nancy said. King and Leah wove their way through the beehive-busy bullpen. He already had a good bet as to what happened, but needed to let the scene play out.

Nancy rolled her shoulders back, tension playing across her face and body. Angry, she was like a caged wolverine. "Some asshole took a shot at the officer outside DeeZee's room. The place is on lockdown, and I've got cars converging on the hospital. That shooter is not getting away." She raised her voice again. "Do you hear me! No one gets away with taking a shot at one of ours!"

King looked over his shoulder to catch Leah moving slowly through the crowd. She didn't have the years of experience force-of-personality-ing her way through scenes, and to a normal person, a room full of agitated cops being yelled at by their boss would be rather intimidating.

"We'll head right over," he said. "See what we can see."

"No go, King. My people are going in because it's their job. This is no place for civilians."

King crossed his arms, settling into the gruff detective archetype, feeling the flow of the scene and going with it. "I've seen more action than your ten-year sergeants, Captain."

"But she sure hasn't," Nancy said in Leah's direction. "And you're not on my insurance."

Even twenty years on, Nancy wasn't as hidebound by genre limitations as folks who were born on this world. She fit into the genre's rules but didn't use as limited a playbook. Usually, this was great, as she was more open-minded.

But it also meant that where another captain would have said, "This is highly irregular, but I'll allow it," she dug her heels in. It was the smart call, the right call for a real police captain. And that sensibility did her officers credit, helped keep them safe and close cases. But sometimes, her real-world senses could end up working against her, causing breaches all on their own. She both stabilized the region and put it into jeopardy. Not enough to justify pulling her out and risking a fatal case of dimensional sickness. So far. King didn't want to think about what he'd do if that order came down from the High Council.

In his heart of hearts, he sometimes wished that one day, she'd remember who she was in one of those breaches, would remember him, and would come home safe.

Poison hope, he told himself. The kind of hope that sneaked up on him in the hour of the wolf to gnaw at his resolve.

But her logical response to the case threw a major monkey wrench in his plan to track down this interloper and write them out of the story permanently.

He could press the issue, play the personal connection. Someone would need to investigate the hospital crime scene. Someone on his team. He'd send Roman. De Jager could adopt a federal cover, or infiltrate another way.

Leah slid into position beside him, derailing his train of thought with her well-cultivated energy.

"Where do you want us, then? Lombardi ruled out the oven, said it was blunt force trauma to the back of the head. We were going to head back to Lake Effect to try to suss out exactly how Smith was killed, maybe clarify the profile."

The bullpen emptied out as officers scrambled to their cars. Nancy threw on her own coat. "You do that, King. I'll call you when we have the shooter and you can get second crack at them."

"Second?" Leah asked. "What about…"

"Second."

King shot Leah the back-off signal. She got the message.

A part of him pulled toward Nancy, toward going all in, leaving the team behind, to bet everything on the case and see it through, no matter the cost.

To be with Nancy again. He could do so much good here, working cases side-by-side once more. All he'd have to do is let go. He'd spent decades holding on, holding on so tight.

Let go, a voice whispered in his ear.

"Boss?" Leah asked.

King cracked his knuckles and focused on the rookie's voice.

The pull faded. He looked at his ex-partner once more, and said, "Give em hell, Nance."

The captain's smile was fierce, a lioness on the prowl with her pride. "Always."

King unburdened some of his worry on their way back to the street. "This is getting worse by the minute. When a breach escalates, it's usually because the same force or happenstance that caused the original breach created a snowball effect, continuing to derail the story. Like a shooter continuing to hound their target. If the shooter had killed DeeZee, we'd be looking at a hard breach. Permanent damage. The world would force another partnership to fill the gap, and the ripples on Earth would be massive. We cannot let this escalate again."

Leah went pale.

"I'm bringing in more assets on this." King set Roman on the case on their way out, with Shirin running interference and backup. This breach had become their priority. Mallery could handle herself, even injured.

As they stepped out into the snow, the gritty-cop-drama filter gave way once again to the softer cinematography of cable and prime-time cop shows.

Something else to go into his mission report. Breach signs manifesting this way, for an entire precinct? Probably something to do with the way Nancy resonated with this dimension. Slightly off kilter, magnifying and muting narrative flow with her personal story gravity.

Escalating breach or no, sidelined or no, they'd run this case down until it was finished.

* * *

Back at the alley outside Lake Effect, Leah and King found the pipe without difficulty, leading to King going full-on PI, bringing out a tape measure and jotting down trajectories and arcs in his notebook.

"And what should I be doing?" Leah asked as he worked.

"Work on the profile, free-associate. But mostly watch my back."

"Watch your back. Got it." Leah paced the alley, keeping King in view while watching her exits. Her training hadn't included courses in "Bodyguarding Detectives Absorbed in Thought" or "How to Spot Snipers in a Snowstorm," so she just made it up as she went, trying to hold on to the sense of fitting in the moment, the story momentum she'd been tapping into.

When she fit in, it was like driving in lanes carved into a road by carts over decades. Easy to stay on track, unless you needed to do anything other than just follow the beaten path.

A few minutes later, King closed his notebook and looked up.

"So?"

"Our killer is probably between five-ten and six-one, give or take boots."

"Pretty tall for a dame," she joked in a Bogart voice. "Think her legs go up to here?" Leah set a hand at her rib cage, all but dropping her conversational filter. "Which should make it much easier to run our profile, right?"

King pondered. "Unless the first killer and the shooter aren't the same person. Why up close for Smith and from up there for DeeZee? Did they not know Smith's timetable? Crime of opportunity or something?"

"We still don't have enough information. After we bring this data back to Doctor Lombardi, let's get De La Cruz's case files and try to build a suspect list out of local hoods, run the mob angle with Tatiana as our main lead. Preeti's confirmation message said that the disturbance is getting worse, so they're going to pull all of the field teams as soon as windows appear. If we don't move fast, we may have to scrub the mission."

"And then what? We come back when the storm clears up?"

"Presumably," King said, heading to the street. "Ops is calling this the biggest dimensional storm in years. Once the eye comes, we bust out of here, but we may not be able to turn around and catch this breach before it's grown again. And that means a lot of spillover."

Leah stomped her feet to get her blood pumping. "So, let's put the pedal to the metal and wrap this up."

With the intensity of the blizzard, walking the three blocks back to the precinct was no easy feat. They passed several taxis, wheels sludging through the weather at a fraction of a mile an hour.

By the time the pair stepped into the precinct, King was pretty well livid. So, Leah went into full-on jester mode, trotting out material from her stand-up sets.

Which would normally work. King liked her comedy; it was part of why she'd gotten the job, after all. But that was normal King. Not Gritty Detective King.

Gritty Detective King's idea of stress relief was rooting around Detective De La Cruz's desk until he found a bottle of rum and then taking a long. Long. Drink. Straight from the bottle.

Oh great, we're into full-on Chandler-ian Alcoholic Detective mode. Just. Freaking. Great.

If she hadn't been motivated to close the case soon, she sure was now.

Chapter Six:
Herrings, Aisle Three

King tore through the case files in a controlled panic. Every moment they didn't close the case was another inch closer to failure, to danger, to cascading ripples across the world. It had been years since his team failed to clear a case, storm or no storm.

He took another swig from the bottle and opened Detective De La Cruz's dossier on the local mob enforcers.

Spinning the file around, he jabbed a finger at a portrait. "We go through the notes and lineups and pull out anyone five-ten and above. Look at stomping grounds, priors, and MO. We should be able to pull together a short list and go knocking on some doors. I'm betting that we have twelve hours or less to solve this case."

"What about Tatiana?"

"We'll start with her. But I won't leave any stone unturned on this. We can't be sloppy."

"What about the prop bag?"

"Small potatoes. Forget the training day; this is the real priority." He felt anger creep into his voice. *Don't take it out on her.* He softened. "What were you doing with the phone?"

"I was looking up Yipe! reviews of Lake Effect—try to get a sense of whether there were any disgruntled customers, someone likely to snap. You'd be surprised at how detailed and personal the negative reviews get on there, and I figured in Crime World, they'd be a great place to look for suspects."

Smart thinking, newbie, he thought. "Well done. Mallery has her algorithms for Romance World, and we have our sources, but in this region, it's still pretty old-school unless we're talking CSI tech."

King reached for the bottle again, then stopped himself.

Couldn't get too deep into archetype, not yet. He needed to be synced up with the genre to close the case, but not so wrapped up in the tropes—or booze, for that matter—that he lost control.

This time around, it looked like their time constraint was the storm rather than the one-week window, but working the case this hard meant there was the chance of going too far in. Responsibility to the team came before the mission. Dead Genrenauts fix no stories. Losing another team member here…

King shook the thought off and pulled over another file.

Keep it together, King, he heard in Nancy's voice. She had always been a rudder, and now that he was back in her orbit, she could do so again. Even though she'd long before changed what course she was plotting.

"Nothing's fitting. They're all too tall or too short. Easley's our best bet."

* * *

Leah opened Tatiana Easley's file. It was thick, a half-inch of paperwork about priors and numerous Polaroids over the years. Well, maybe not Polaroids, but whatever company was printing the 8.5x11 photos these days in Crime World.

A mug shot showed a thin woman with hooded eyes and stringy hair. Tatiana Easley was a Chicago native, references to a thick juvenile file closed when she hit eighteen. Five-eleven, multiple arrests for burglary, and an eighteen-month stint upstate after a bust of a Salvatore family money-laundering ring.

"Looks like the right kind of loser."

"And we've got a last known address—three blocks from Lake Effect. She could have gotten there and back without being noticed."

"So, we don't want to dig further on anyone else?"

"We need to move the story forward. I'm betting we get at least one red herring, then an escalation at the hospital, and then maybe we can find the real killer. But if we don't run down these story beats fast…"

"That reminds me of something," Leah said. "Are we sure this is a one-and-done episodic plot? The way the breach formed, the comedy troupe's theft, the oddness with the layered case. What if this is like a HBO or BBC-style serial mystery? Or what if that's happened with Nancy? A case so big, you can't solve it in one episode's worth of time?"

King folded his arms. "The serial cases tend to come with their own feeling. There's no killer's note here, but with the Mob angle, there is the potential for an arc plot—bring in the small fish, work your way up. And when we were in the precinct, the filter was off; it was more gritty. I don't think that's the case here, but it's a fine insight, thinking about format and structure. We're going to work this like it's episodic; that fits this precinct, and the restaurant and food wars angle tells me that we're still on track. With Nancy…you could be right. Sure didn't present itself that way, but I did miss the end of the story. Maybe I thought it was a two-parter and it was more a TV movie, that middle ground between them."

"Who works the serial cases, then? Different team?"

"The LA office, mostly. They get around the time limitations by rotating through the team, splitting up the story threads, beating the slow story on its own terms. But that's not us. We need to move fast."

"Got it." Leah stood, reaching more for her coat. Her toes had barely warmed, and if they were going to come back there sometime soon, she was going to have to start packing power bars or something in her coat. They hadn't eaten since the cafe.

She rubbed her hands for warmth. And maybe bring some of those hand-warmers her great aunt sent her every Christmas.

"Any chance of grabbing food on the way? Maybe something to soak up that whiskey?" she asked, trying to help.

"It's rum. I'm fine. I'll eat once we bring Easley in for questioning. We'll need an officer present for that."

"And we'll be able to bring her in without a badge?"

"That would be vigilantism. Highly frowned upon." King smiled. She knew that smile. That was a Bad Cop smile.

"Is this a plausible deniability thing where I don't want to know what you're doing?" Leah looked around the mostly empty room. One officer in the corner plugged away at her computer, and the janitor had passed by a few minutes before. Everyone else was at the hospital.

"On Earth, it would be. Here, you need to know the tricks of the trade." King tapped a pocket. "I nicked a badge years ago and had our props department make me a copy. It won't hold up to a lawyer or paperwork, but it looks plenty real in person."

"Fair enough. Why don't we skip transport entirely and just walk this time?" Leah asked. Her fingers and toes ached at the thought.

"Agreed." King looked sideways at the bottle, picked it up.

"Really?" she asked, immediately wishing she hadn't.

But instead of slipping the bottle in his coat, he stuffed it back in the detective's drawer. "And don't worry; I'll replace it later."

"Don't take that as a reason to need to finish it."

"When we get these bastards, there will be plenty of reason to finish the bottle."

"I'm down with that. Shall we go visit Ms. Easley, then?"

"After you, newbie."

Leah steeled herself for another walk in the snow. Considering that it was still late spring in back on Earth Prime, this was not easy. It usually took her a good week to get used to winter, even after spending the first eighteen years of her life in Minnesota.

She bundled up tight, raised all of her collars as high as possible, and the wind still felt like a scythe through her bones when she stepped outside.

King trudged ahead, his gait somewhere between a determined walk and jogging.

This better work, she thought. *Before we get frostbite. Or worse.*

* * *

Mallery and Shirin tracked the comedians for several hours. They went to respective homes, all within several miles of the theater. With the blizzard, staying put wasn't a surprise, but it didn't give them much of anything else to work with, since the theater camera hadn't shown anything but an empty room for hours.

Roman had peeled off to make a run by the hospital per King's orders.

This case had escalated in a big way. Less pressure on Mallery to nail the callbacks, but it did mean that King and Leah were in real danger, and the unpredictability gave Mallery goose bumps. And not the happy kind. It'd be just like a story universe to kill off a potential love interest just as Something was about to happen. The insidious bullshit of Bury Your Gays. Especially given the last year of TV.

None of that kind of thinking, she told herself. That didn't help anyone.

She had to focus on what was in front of her.

Poor Shirin caught the blunt of her nervousness. She'd talked the woman's ear off for an hour, trying to burn off the nerves. Instead of being in the thick of it, she was running the B plot. The world had pulled a bait-and-switch on them, and it was hard to not wonder why.

"You ever heard of a breach spreading laterally like this? And that quickly? Or is this a double event?"

"Hard to say." Shirin continued to work the screens, several linked monitors analyzing dimensional storm data that Preeti had gotten through, others keeping track of the comedians. "This year has been one exception after another. It's getting hard to see where the new status quo lies, if there even is one. On the team and off." Shirin punctuated the last bit with a subtly raised eyebrow.

I'm going to pretend I didn't see that, Mallery thought, and plowed right ahead. "With this blizzard, I don't know if we're going to get anything useful out of the chuckleheads. Maybe I should escalate somehow, press the issue with someone and see what shakes out."

"We don't need any more variables at this point, I imagine. Maybe this thread dies down and we focus on the other one. If we're supposed to be prepping for emergency evac, that doesn't sound like the time to be running new plays, does it?"

"No, but I'm feeling pretty wheel-spinny here." She gestured to the screens and their still-unmoving readings.

"Not back two months, and she's already climbing the walls. They can't all be love stories. I've got everything under control here if you want to work on your material or pack us up or take a walk around the block. Or call Leah."

Again with the knowing suggestions.

"A walk sounds good. I could use some fresh air."

"Don't wait for too long. Frostbite and all. We need you with all your faculties." Shirin wiggled her fingers and smiled.

Mallery bundled up and got all the way to the corner before the cold started cutting her to the bone.

She thought good thoughts for Leah and King out in this cold, running around after murderers. On the one hand, it'd be good to get out of this blizzard as soon as possible, but on the other, she'd been enjoying working with Leah on a more even footing.

On the last mission, she'd been leading Leah around, having her play second fiddle as part of Mallery's grand romantic opera. That kind of power imbalance was a garbage way to start a relationship. Just ask most anyone who ever shacked up with a professor. Start with one person uphill like that, and it was real damned hard to level things out. Authority and experience become power and expectation, and then came the questionable consent and worse.

The wind picked up again, and Mallery scurried back inside, teeth already chattering.

She looked back out into the cold and mouthed another prayer for her teammates to come back safe. And not just the one she was thinking about dating.

* * *

Leah could barely feel her toes by the time they got to the five-story apartment building, but it was marginally warmer inside and substantially less windy (though not without a draft, thanks to the poorly-seated window frames in the stairwell).

King gave instructions in a low voice. "Here's how this works. You watch my back while I talk to Easley. Keep an eye out for anyone who might be watching us, and make sure if she tries to break past me, you trip her up so she doesn't get away."

The team lead tromped up the stairs, tracking slush on top of slush, the carpeting on the stairs already stained nearly black, the original tan barely showing at the edges. "And if she goes out the back, I want you to head back down these stairs and try to head her off at the street. You've got the holdout pistol, but don't use it except in self-defense. Use the baton if she's getting away and you're in reach."

"She's got almost a foot on me, most of it legs. Seems like catching her is not a likely thing."

"I'm just running down the eventualities so you don't get caught flat-footed. If you're chasing her, think laterally. Be the wacky detective, not the cop. Got it?"

"Got it." They reached the fourth floor and King changed his gait, feet falling soft.

Leah stood a half-step back from King and widened her stance, ready to move in any direction.

Adventure, excitement, hypothermia. All of this and more await you in the Genrenauts! Fortunately, it also came with a sweet salary and benefits package, and, when they weren't wrapping themselves in self-destructive genre tropes, a pretty cool set of colleagues, including one of the very few bosses she'd actually hang out and drink a beer with.

King pounded three times on the door, then waited.

Leah leaned back and forth rather than fiddle with her hands. One hand waited above the extending baton (super-illegal on Earth Prime, but effective in close-quarters combat), the other inches from the mace in her coat pocket.

The door opened a crack, revealing a woman with dyed-red hair and pale features. A chain lock held the door closed, exposing just enough to show the woman looking King up and down with a big dollop of suspicion.

"What do you want?"

"Tatiana Easley?

"What. Do. You. Want?"

"I'm Detective King, CPD. This is my associate Ms. Tang. We'd like to ask you a few questions."

"I didn't do nothing. Go away."

King's voice was bored, with a tinge of exasperation, nicely inflected. "Ms. Easley, the terms of your parole clearly state that you are to cooperate with police."

"Told you I didn't do nothing. What do you want to know?"

"Where were you from two to five AM, day before yesterday?"

"Sleeping. I went out drinking, came back here with friends, and we woke up after noon," Tatiana said.

"Did you know this man?" King asked, holding up a picture of Dwayne Smith. Pre-dying, thankfully.

"Don't know. I see a lot of people. He's what? In trouble, or already dead?"

"The latter, I'm afraid. Can we step inside to talk?" King asked.

"No. I don't got to invite you in."

"Then we can talk in the precinct, if you'd like."

"I don't know this guy, I didn't do anything. You shoot straight on what I have to do to honor my parole, and I'll do it. Otherwise, buzz off."

"We need to verify that you were here the entirety of the time period during which Mr. Smith might have been killed."

Leah watched the hall, turning her head to look for observers. For the moment, at least, it seemed like Tatiana's neighbors were happy to leave well enough alone.

"And what reason you got to suspect me?" she asked.

"Aside from your track record of armed robbery or your association with the Salvatore family, which has a generations-old bone to pick with the family that owns Lake Effect?"

Tatiana's tone changed. "Wait, Smith—the chef? That guy was harmless. Why would someone want to rub him out? He made a mean steak frites. I ate at Lake Effect when I ran with the Salvatores. And since I got out, too. The chef doesn't hold it against me."

Why would they do that if they were rivals? A keep-your-enemies-closer thing, maybe. Mobsters worked the neighborhood and family angles hard, after all.

"That's what we hear, ma'am. And if you want to see his killer brought to justice and the heat off your back, all the better. Come with us to the precinct to answer a few other questions, and then we'll send you on your way. And the Salvatores will doubtless hear that you helped get them off our radar."

"Fuck the Salvatores. They left me out to dry." Tatiana looked down at King's pad. "I'll give you your names."

"It'll be best if you come with us, ma'am."

As Tatiana adjusted, Leah saw behind her into the apartment.

Most importantly, she saw a canvas bag beside a couch, with an inflated dinosaur sticking out of the mouth of the bag.

She whispered to King. "Bag behind her. That dinosaur was on the list of stuff in the comedy troupe's bag."

Tatiana pointed a finger. "You got something to say, say it to me."

King nodded inside. "Ms. Easley, can you tell me where you got that bag and the inflated dinosaur?"

Tatiana looked behind her, blinked, and cocked her head.

"Dammit."

"You'll want to come with us. And bring that bag."

"I don't know where that came from. Must have been a friend. We was up late, you know? Sometimes he crashes with me."

"We have reason to suspect that is stolen property. Bring it."

"You got twenty-four hours to hold me before you charge me with something. I got work to do. Here I am, trying to go straight, keep my head down, all that good-citizen crap, and you pull this crap."

"This crap is about a robbery. Bring the bag."

"Yeah, yeah. I know the drill." The woman closed the door, released the chain lock, then opened again. "Let me get my coat. It's cold as shriveled balls out there."

"That's got to be the bag, right?" Leah asked as they waited.

"Or a red herring. Good eye regardless. We'll need to run down all of these leads. First, back to the precinct. You call in one of the comedians to verify the bag; I'll start interrogating Easley. Smart money says that the captain and company are back by the time we get there, and then we'll grind files for a while until we get a better lead. If we're really lucky, Nancy will have caught the killer and we'll be able to just stand by in the ship until we get the all-clear."

"How long does Preeti think the window will be?"

"Not certain. I'd bet on less than an hour. Which means we stay close to the precinct and therefore the warehouse."

They'd landed in one of the Genrenauts' many empty warehouses rented to allow their ships to land and then go into camouflage mode. On this world, the ship was disguised as a massive pile of crates under a tarp. The warehouse was close to the FOB, or as close as they could get. Even here, the warehouse districts weren't terribly close to the upscale apartments.

Tatiana emerged in a giant fur coat, handing the bag to King. She locked up her apartment and said, "This better not take long." Leah went first, then Tatiana, with King taking up the rear, keeping an eye on the suspect.

Leah kept very upright to minimize the chances of slipping on the stairs and breaking her everything tumbling down the narrow stairs.

This time, they took a cab, one of the two-row hatchback deals. Tatiana sat in the front seat next to the driver, demanding her space.

King and Leah sat in the back, the team lead watching Tatiana like a hawk. An underfed, possibly buzzed hawk.

"What about your catch-up with the captain?" Leah asked in a low voice. Thanks to the plastic divider, Tatiana shouldn't be able to hear them. "Shouldn't you be going out for dinner or something—keep up appearances or the like?"

"I try not to get too close when I come back. It sets the wrong expectation. She's married now."

"So, you come back and just make significant glances at one another all mission and then jet off."

"How many exes do you have, Probie?" King asked as they reached the bottom of the stairs, bundling up.

"A few. None that I talk to anymore."

"Exactly. Now imagine what it's like to have to see them again and again, and to know that if the dice had fallen differently, that they'd have been with you your whole life. And then see how comfortable you are hanging out with them socially and keeping secrets from them for their own good."

"Gotcha. Anything I can do? Should I ask to tag along and help protect against angst or something?"

"I'll be fine. With this case, there's no room for error, no time for social calls. It'll happen anyway, might be essential for solving the case, but I should be able to keep from lingering. Just keep me relatively sober until this is all done."

"Yeah, what's with that?"

"Archetype bleed-over. The version of Detective I'm performing is frequently cross-indexed with the Alcoholic PI."

"Gotcha. And how am I supposed to browbeat my boss into not drinking, exactly?"

"Distraction, mostly. You don't want to get into too much of a groove, not for too long. Extended-flow states make it harder to come back up for air."

The car pulled up to the precinct and the cabbie rattled off their exorbitant rate. Traffic was still moving at a trickle. But King had said they weren't going to try to walk the whole way there and give Tatiana a million chances to bolt.

"I can see why you and Shirin have been doing this for decades," Leah said, sliding over once King had paid. "Seems like there's always another layer to this genre onion."

"Work at it long enough, and you learn to manage the tears," King donned his hat and stepped out into the cold as Tatiana power-walked up the steps, apparently eager to be done with them.

Raymond Chandler, eat your heart out.

Chapter Seven:
Wacky PI, Grumpy PI

Tatiana cooperated all the way to the interview (aka interrogation) room, then clammed up like she'd forgotten how to talk. The captain and most of the squad were back, though Franklin had tripled the detail at the hospital, just to be sure. King spent a good fifteen minutes getting the breakdown from Roman of what turned out to be a very boring lockdown of the hospital. By all reports, Nancy had gotten into a shouting match with a very short and very loud hospital administrator.

Apparently unsatisfied by that encounter, Nancy had taken over the interrogation, since King wasn't actually a cop. Leah would be watching them from the room behind one-way glass.

The captain put both hands on the table. "We're talking to your friends about two nights ago, but we still need to know where you were this morning between eleven and eleven thirty."

"I was out, doing errands. I got a life to live, you know. Trying to, at least, since I got out of lockup."

Nancy pinched the bridge of her nose. She only did that when she was frustrated. And if she was frustrated there, it meant they weren't getting anywhere. But even if Easley was a red herring, he needed to run down every angle until the next plot beat emerged.

King checked his watch for the fifth time in as many minutes. The phone on his hip was set to buzz if any word came through from HQ, and he'd partitioned part of his brain to will the phone not to buzz, not to pull the plug on their mission.

He repeated the captain's question. "Can anyone verify where you were this morning between eleven and eleven thirty? If they can, and your alibis check out, you'll be free to go and return to putting your life back together. But here's the thing. I think you didn't kill Dwayne Smith, but you had every reason to take a shot at DeeZee."

"You're damn right I'd have reason to shoot DeeZee. But I didn't. Wish I had. Joystick-loving tool. Thinks he doesn't owe anything to the neighborhood. We went to the same school, you know. He hit the pro circuit and disappeared from the streets, suddenly too important to look out for the kids who schooled him in *Halo* when he was too young to be able to play arcade games without a milk crate."

"When was the last time you saw him?" King asked.

Tatian scrunched up her nose, thinking, still frustrated with them. "I dunno, maybe a month ago, at the restaurant? He was there with his hottie detective girlfriend, being all cutsie."

"That's interesting, because we have a witness that puts you at the restaurant yesterday, and we know DeeZee is there all the time?"

"I was there yesterday, but I didn't see him. I went in, had my lunch, and left. I talked to Angela, the server. That's 'bout it."

So now we have conflicting accounts, King thought. They'd need to loop around again with Hernandez.

King tugged at another line of questioning. "Almost two years you spent upstate. Eighteen months nursing that grudge against DeeZee and De La Cruz for ruining your life, or whatever lie you told yourself about why you got caught."

He knew he was monologuing but leaned into it. The faster they could push through this scene, the better. "But here's the thing. They busted you on laundering, but it could have been far worse. You have another chance now. If the comedians confirm that this bag was theirs, that's a petty larceny charge. Not good with you being on parole. But if you are the one that shot DeeZee, I will make sure that you go away for a long, long time. So, if you did it, you need to confess now and roll on the Salvatores the way you didn't when they left you out to dry."

King watched Easley, trying to read her small movements, to catch the moment where she broke or gave something away, pointed them at the real killer, something.

Easley said nothing, so Nancy escalated, pounding on the table. "Tell us, Tatiana. You knew DeeZee, came up together. You resent his success, especially since you had to work so much harder to get a mere fraction of what he got, all because he was good at games. If you did it, I'd understand. But if you give us nothing, we can't give you anything. Not another chance, not protection from the Salvatores."

"I didn't fucking do it, okay?" Tatiana shouted, scooting back and standing out of the chair, finding the wall behind her. "The bag, yeah. I went to their show, and I get these moods, you know? Get a thrill out of stealing little stuff. Pack of gum, pair of socks. Used to shoplift when I was a kid; still do the little stuff here and there. I always take it back. More fun to sneak things back in than to take them in the first place. I took that fancy ring out and left it. Only thing worth a damn in that bag. Charge me for the bag if you want, but I didn't kill the cook, and I didn't shoot DeeZee. So, all you're doing is yelling and wasting your time."

King looked to Nancy, who nodded. He turned and walked out into the hallway, then around to the observation room, where Leah stood hunched over her phone.

"Not interesting enough to hold your attention?"

Leah held up her hands, placating. "You can cool down the routine, boss. It's just me."

King took a few long breaths, slowing his pulse. She was right. The case couldn't wait, but he had to keep his edge.

"What do you think?" she asked.

"This solves the first breach, but I don't think she's related to Smith or DeeZee."

"She's the connection between the two cases—there's no other angle."

"What if the breaches aren't connected?"

"It makes too much story sense that they are. This region, the two cases always end up connecting in the end."

"What if we already had our connection, and she's the red herring for the murder-homicide case?

King gave her a doubtful look. But the doubt wasn't just for her. Maybe he was being too reductive, looking for the easy win so they could get back home.

"I kept digging. Think I have a lead." She presented her phone.

Leah displayed a set of Yipe! reviews for Lake Effect. One mentioned hearing shouting from the kitchen, another mentioned two men talking in the office, their voices carrying as the reviewer used the restroom. The third talked of a Latino chef storming out just a week before, followed by the restaurant owner (whom the user knew due to a feature in the Tribune).

Together, they made for a huge red flag that all was not well in Lake Effect, and pointed a suspect finger at Hernandez.

King nodded in appreciation. Smart thinking. Initiative, lateral thinking. Exactly what he was hoping for. "Good work, Probie. Let's get the owner on the line and start asking some questions. Someone is covering something up, and I'm betting we've got our murderer."

Leah pumped her fist, beaming like she'd just won the lottery.

The kid was getting better, learning how to bring her instincts and perspective to each world, fitting its expectations while still keeping her distinctive point of view.

But first, they had to make sure this lead was legit. Which meant it was time to head back to Lake Effect.

* * *

The restaurant was still closed, Refai fending off questions from the media.

This time, they stopped at a table and just sat, sparing Leah the kitchen and flashback memories of hurling.

"Thank you for meeting us again. We have some follow-up questions, if you don't mind."

"Of course. I hope this means you have a lead?"

King nodded. "My colleague Miss Tang was going through some reviews of the restaurant and found some curious accounts. We were hoping you could put them into context and tell us what was going on in the kitchen over the last few weeks."

Leah pulled up the screenshots she'd taken of the reviews and presented the phone to the Chef. It felt both weird and awesome to be presenting Yipe! reviews as a lead in a murder investigation, but this was her role, after all. She was fulfilling it as much by being a millennial digital native as by being a wacky comedienne. She could imagine the junior staff writer pitching the plot beat in the room to the eccentric Luddite showrunner. Technological savvy was presented as basically magic on cop shows, especially when deployed by The Youth.

Chef Refai read the reviews, then set the phone down on the table, lips pursed in thought.

"I did not want to tell you earlier because of my investors. They said if anyone found out about the announcement early, it would tank their chances—competition for restaurant real estate is no joke in this city. I decided a few months ago to open a new restaurant. Downtown, with an ultra-hip aesthetic—more affordable but still catering to the modern gourmand. But I cannot manage two restaurants with the same care I give one—the new bistro would demand all of my attention. Over the last few months, I have been observing my two head chefs—Ricardo and Dwayne. I had hoped to make my selection before anyone found out about the bistro. But rumors multiplied, like they do, and word got out. Instantly, Ricardo and Dwayne began competing, trying to one-up each other with more and more grandiose specials. It got...heated."

Biting her tongue, Leah let the obvious joke pass her by. *Don't interrupt the exposition that helps you close the case,* she heard an inner version of King whisper.

Adnan was a gesticulating talker, his hands moving as fast as his words. "And so last week, I offered the position of executive chef to Dwayne, and he accepted. Which left me with the unhappy duty to let Ricardo down easy. Dwayne's vision is"—he caught himself, sighed—"was just stronger, it was more Lake Effect. But Ricardo was hired six months before Dwayne and thought the position should have been his by seniority. If I'm looking after the best interests of my restaurant, how am I to choose seniority over vision?"

"You should have told us this the first time, Mr. Refai. Withholding information in a murder investigation...."

Adnan shook his head. "I know. But the stockholders told me that if news got out, in any way...and how could Ricardo have killed Dwayne? They were rivals, but Ricardo is a good man. He is not a murderer."

King set down his glass, looked with remorse at the half-eaten steak, and sighed. "Your trust in your staff is admirable, but we'll need to ask for his home address. Is there anything else you've been holding back for your investors?" King's voice was short.

Refai pulled out a pen and wrote an address on a Post-it note from his coat pocket. "No. That's everything."

Chapter Eight:
Express Delivery

Ricardo Hernandez's apartment was a fifteen-minute walk west from Lake Effect. Leah struggled to keep up with a power-walking King.

The team lead's phone buzzed ten minutes into their walk. He read the message, then made a frustrated sound and held the phone back to Leah. She grabbed it, trying to focus both on the slushtastic ground so she didn't lose her footing and the phone to read the message.

> *Break in the storm is coming. From the next message, you will have no more than thirty minutes to return to your ship and get off-world. The next break is not projected for ten days. Respond immediately if you need extraction.—Preeti*

"Shouldn't we head back?" Leah asked.

"The time counts down from the next message. We've still got a bit of a buffer. And we're so close to closing this case."

"Where we're going is like twenty minutes from the warehouse. That's cutting it pretty close. Can't we send the info to the captain and let her solve it? We need to rendezvous with the others."

King's voice grew hard. "We are going to close this case, rookie. You and me. It's got to be us. If we punt this back to the precinct, the breaches will keep growing. We'd see a crime wave across the country, maybe beyond."

Leah gulped. "And you're sure this isn't just the archetype talking? Very sure?"

King shook off her doubt like a dusting of snow. "It has to be us, Leah. We're nearly there. But text the information to the captain regardless. Her contact information's in my phone."

Leah was very glad for the capacitive touch gloves that had come with this world's gear, tapping out the message about Ricardo, their conversation with the chef, and the pair's plan of action, attaching the screenshot of the Yipe! reviews that she'd forwarded to King. The phone made the *bwee-doop* sound of a sent message, and she took three quick steps, catching up to King to pass the phone back over his shoulder.

Ricardo Hernandez lived in a condo building, #27 by Chef Refai's notes. This meant they only had one flight of stairs to scale.

King flashed his bogus badge to the guard, along with a fierce Takes No Shit Cop look, and the guard buzzed them in with haste.

"Same deal as with Tatiana. Be ready for him to make a break, got it?"

"We're really going to chase after him if he runs? In the murderific weather? I nearly ate it twice on black ice just walking over here."

King stopped and turned to Leah, his expression softening. "We can do this. Believe it, and we can do it. You've done great, and we're almost home. Got it?"

"I've got a bad feeling about this."

"Overruled. Let's get moving."

"You might not mind getting stuck here, but the rest of us don't have someone tying us here, boss. We have to remember the bigger stakes."

"Your objections have been noted, rookie. Stick with the plan and we'll out of here faster."

If we get out at all.

This round of shivers wasn't from the cold.

But King had the experience, and they were so close to a breakthrough. King drew his gun as they scaled the stairs. Leah left hers in its holster. She'd put in twenty-something hours in the firing range since joining, but the gun still felt like an alien artifact strapped to her hip.

They found condo #27, and King slid up beside the door, gesturing where Leah should stand, behind and slightly to his side, cutting off the hall behind them. He held the gun high by his head and knocked with his free hand.

"Ricardo Hernandez? This is Detective King, CPD."

Why would they knock?

Well, they didn't have a warrant. Even in a story world, where police procedure was loosey-goosey at its best, they needed a warrant to just go barging in. But if they knocked and the response was something suspicious?

Then they had TV-level probable cause. And there was still a chance that Hernandez was innocent, that Tatiana had done for both crimes.

Leah heard shuffling from inside, then the howling of wind, as if through an empty window.

"We're coming in!" King shouted, turning and kicking in the door. Leah had learned, trapped in the bathroom during Chinese New Year, that even a big strong dude like King (or her uncle Ronnie) could take a dozen tries or more to kick down a door.

But this was a story world, and King was a protagonist. The door cracked and splintered open, revealing Ricardo Hernandez climbing out the window to his fire escape, a suitcase in one hand.

"Down to the street, cut him off!" King barked, charging into the condo.

As she turned and headed toward the stairs, she heard the familiar buzz from King's phone.

Shit.

"We gotta go!" she shouted, heading for the stairs.

"Stick to the plan!"

Shit, shit, shit.

They had to close the case, but they had to get home. There was no way they'd get a cab or an El in time, and the ice was getting worse. But King wasn't going to back down.

So instead, she took the stairs as fast as she possibly could, half-sledding down the rail as she did her best to keep her balance and head Ricardo off before he could hit ground level.

* * *

King was through the apartment and out the window in a flash, tucking his legs up to hurdle through the window and catch himself on the fire escape.

Below him, Hernandez dropped off the second-floor fire escape, tumbling into a stack of trash bags covered in snow, doubly cushioned. Hernandez was up and off, moving fast. The chef was in good shape and wore boots made for moving.

Barely thinking, King hopped the rails cartwheeling his arms and shifting to make sure he landed flat, distributing the impact.

He hit the trash with a soft and then notably harder impact, exhaling as he landed.

Remember to thank Roman for helping with the practice, King thought. Just one of the man's myriad Action Hero skills.

Time was of the essence, and of course, Hernandez was running the opposite direction from where he and Leah needed to go to get back to the ship. If he didn't catch Hernandez in four blocks, they'd have to run the entire way back to the ship to have a chance of getting off in time.

Even an emergency evac would cut it close, since the rest of the team couldn't just buzz them for a drive-by pickup like they could on the Science Fiction World or other locations. The PPM was good enough to mask their ship as a helicopter, but the engines didn't allow for that kind of extraction. They'd need a pickup hook, which he did not have.

King ran the numbers and possibilities as he dodged around joggers, put-upon laborers, and the other unfortunate folk who were out and about in the blizzard that had all but stopped car traffic. Hernandez juked right, started across the street. A car hit the brakes and came sliding toward them, forcing King to either wait, risk getting hit, or run past the car to cross.

Instead, he bargained that his archetype had the chops to bolster what would otherwise be a terrible idea, and take another page from Roman's book. The car was only going ten or so miles an hour. He jumped, folding in his coat, and slid across the hood as the car honked and skidded to a stop. King found his feet with only a quick shuffle to catch his balance and continue.

It wasn't up to Roman's standard, but it'd do. Hernandez was only twenty feet ahead.

"Leah!" King shouted, not able to spare the time to spot her, wherever she was. "Headed west on West Chicago. Go north on Wells and head him off!"

But with Leah's stride disadvantage, he had to assume that the job of catching Hernandez was going to fall to him alone.

Solve the case and endanger your crew or give up to protect your newbie and endanger hundreds, a calculating, pragmatic voice echoed in his mind.

He rejected the dichotomy and pushed on, picking up his pace and trusting in his Gore-Tex boots to keep his footing even as Hernandez slid across a patch of black ice on the sidewalk.

Even on Crime World, some people were crappy neighbors and neglected to shovel their sidewalks. Sometimes it was even intentional, an attempt to cause an accident. King slid across one patch, and then bounded over one that Hernandez had caught.

The chef looked over his shoulder at King and turned at the crossroads.

King checked his watch as he dashed to the corner. Twenty-three minutes to get back. He was cutting it obscenely close. Even if they made it back, the Council would not be pleased.

So, if he was going to get dressed down, he might as well secure a successful patch to show for it.

King grabbed a fencepost and took the corner at speed, launching forward and picking Hernandez's gray jacket out of the crowd as the man turned into an alley.

The alley's driveway was all ice. King slid uncontrollably, and stopped himself with a huff, crashing into the far wall of the alley. His vision shook as he pushed himself off the wall, settling from three images into just one, a panicked man jumping and flailing for the raised ladder to a fire escape.

"Freeze!"

Hernandez saw King, then flailed harder. He caught the lowest rung of the ladder and started hauling himself up, more in shape than King had expect from a long-suffering restaurateur. *Plot twist, or another part of the breach?* He filed yet another detail away for his after-action analysis.

Not fast enough. King tackled the man off the ladder. The pair went skidding and sliding across the alley, rolling in muck until King stopped them. He grappled into guard position, straddling the chef.

"Stop. Now. Why did you run? Is it because you lied about Tatiana, because it was you that killed Dwayne Smith? And now you're, what? Skipping town with the mob payoff?" King nodded at the briefcase askew on the wrought iron landing of the fire escape.

"It's not like that! I didn't mean to kill him!"

King's phone buzzed again. Twenty-minute warning. They'd have to run the whole way back or catch a miraculous and probably-dangerous cab ride.

"But you did, didn't you? Tell me what happened. You have one minute, or your life is going to get far, far worse." King pulled a pair of handcuffs out from his belt and cuffed Ricardo, tying the cuffs to the leg of an overladen Dumpster.

"It should have been me. I should have gotten the executive chef job. I'd been there for longer; my menu was more commercial. But that jackass Refai gave it to Smith. And then the woman, she came to me, got me all fired up."

"What woman?"

"That tall woman. I didn't get her name."

"What did she tell you?"

"She bought me drinks, listened while I complained. My wife, she doesn't listen to me complain anymore, says I complain too much. That just complaining never makes things better unless you do something about it."

"What did the woman tell you?" King asked, keeping his pulse down, resisting the urge to lose himself in the scene, to cross the line into brutality the way TV cops did so frequently.

"She said it wasn't fair. That I should confront him. And then I did, and he slipped, and I panicked. I didn't kill him, you understand! I was just so angry, so I shoved him. He shoved back, and then the next time I shoved him, he slipped. There was so much..." And with that, Ricardo broke down, the emotions overflowing. He was responsible, but he wasn't a cold-blooded murderer. No way he took the shot at DeeZee.

"King! Drop!" Leah shouted.

King trusted his instincts, trusted his teammate, and hit the deck. He covered Hernandez with his body as they hit the slush, muck and cold slapping his face while a shot rang out. The bullet hit a couple of feet from him.

King slid behind the Dumpster and drew his gun. He heard Leah behind him, at the mouth of the alley. And at the dead end, standing over the lip of the roof, was a tall woman with dark hair standing beside a chimney. The instigator.

"Cover, Probie!" King reached his free hand out to Hernandez, trying to pull him behind the Dumpster. King popped a quick pair of shots off at the tall woman, but she saw him coming, took cover behind the chimney. She peeked around the chimney and took a quick shot, an expert-level move—no time to aim or calculate, just pure training and instinct.

And she hit.

The bullet hit Hernandez in the gut. King took the corner to open fire again. But she was already leaving, her rifle up from firing position, rolling out of King's field of vision. She was bugging out.

She was some kind of pro. What would call for a hit woman? The mob? Using this as a wedge for something?

Time slowed as King put all the pieces together. Both cases were solved, but only one was resolved. The shooter would get away, or he'd strand himself and Leah here permanently. He weighed the options, smelling Nancy's shampoo against the crispness of the snow, the moisture in the air against the coppery tang of blood.

She'd been made; she'd need to reposition. Pursuit was too risky. His duty was to the mission and to his team.

He checked Hernandez's pulse. Already slowing. King didn't have the training to save him, couldn't even keep him alive long enough for the ambulance, which would take at least fifteen minutes to get there in this weather.

He saw the two choices unfold before him in fast-forward. Chase the shooter, close the case. Get his team trapped. They become a team of oddball detectives. He stays with Nancy.

He fails his team. Fails the Council. Breaches multiply. And then everyone loses.

And the other path. He chooses his team, leaves Nancy behind again, and keeps going.

King looked at Leah, remembered his responsibilities, and decided. He kissed his fingers, touched them to Hernandez's head, and said a quick prayer for the accidental killer.

He stood, holstering his gun. "Back to the warehouse!"

Leah was shocked, visible breath coming fast. Her conditioning was questionable. But there was no other option.

"Run, rookie! Now!" He pointed, picking up speed while watching the ice. They slid back into the street and started hauling ass toward the ship.

At a slow and ice-laden run, it would take them ten minutes, leaving them maybe eight minutes for takeoff and crossing. It might be enough. It'd have to be enough.

Leah's running gait picked up behind him, and he pulled out his phone to call in the murderer. The victim. The dead.

"Nancy, this is King. The job's done, but there's a lot of blood. You'll need to send a team."

* * *

When King had pitched Leah on the job, he hadn't mentioned that she'd be sprinting through a blizzard with giant ice patches, racing against time to avoid getting trapped on Murder World in Wacky Detective Town.

Leah huffed and puffed, trying to keep up with King as they booked as fast as they possibly could back toward the warehouse containing their ship and its rapidly diminishing window of return.

King had called it in, gave Nancy just enough information to come for the body and declare the case closed, plus his best heads-up description of the Tall Woman. The bullets in the alley (and in Ricardo) should give them the link to DeeZee's shooter, and with luck, they'd be able to track her on their own. Or if not, they'd come back when the storm cleared and work that case, too.

Right now, Leah's job was to keep running, not slip and fall and crack her head open, and to trick her lungs and legs into continuing to function.

"How far?" she asked, panting. "Because I'm still not a big fan of the sprinting thing. I'm more a power-walking or jogging kind of girl. Didn't wear a sports bra, you know?"

Wacky Comedian Lack of Filter is still going strong, she thought, laughing at herself.

"One mile!" King called at a full voice. His movements were smooth, practiced. He also had an eight-inch height advantage on her, much of it in his legs.

"Tall people and your cheating giraffe legs!" she answered.

King didn't dignify that with a response. Instead, he turned on the comms. "All hands, check in!"

"This is Roman. We're standing by at the ship. Launch sequence spinning up. Projections show you cutting it right down the wire. Do we launch and intercept?"

"Negative. We are coming to you." King poured on the speed.

Focus, she thought. *You've been jogging, doing Genrenauts-brand CrossFit, and eating better. Mostly. Sort of. Commissary pizza had to be better for her than take & bake DiGiordanellos, right? Totally.* Her train of thought kept rolling down the tracks even as she tried to get back to the moment.

King scattered people with shouts of "Police", shoving aside those who didn't listen, the few folks still out and about in the still-raging blizzard. Something to do with the dimensional storms. Probably. Maybe?

Leah was happy for her stompy, mostly comfortable boots, keeping her pace and praying that they could keep avoiding the ice patches.

She thought back to the coaching Roman had given her to improve her running gait. *Breathe in, breathe out. Keep moving. Regular, consistent. Smooth.* Her mind flurried off to thinking about the case, putting the pieces together, and ridiculous pop culture references, gobbling up her attention…

Until she caught a patch of ice and went ass over teakettle, landing hard on the small of her back.

"Aaaaooowcrap!"

King skidded to a stop, his hand appearing from nowhere. Leah flailed for purchase, watching the world bobble like she was a doll. King held her hand and started moving. She followed. She moved forward, and the world kept shaking, and then a bit less.

And less, and she was back.

Still running. Always running.

Her lungs burned like she'd sprayed lighter fluid down her throat and then swallowed a torch. Like the circus.

Keep it together, she told herself, biting her lip and keeping on keeping on.

They turned the corner and Leah recognized the warehouse.

"Almost there, rookie. Stay with me."

But the end was in sight. She could make this. Totally. But as they ran, she felt her body slowing, like something was pulling against her, increasing her drag. It had to be fatigue, but her imagination spooled out a dozen weird science-fictional reasons—she hadn't fulfilled her role well enough, or the story was still unsolved and it needed her to stay, or the Tall Woman had caught her with some kind of weird grappling hook.

But it was none of those. She made it to the warehouse door, which King had opened and dashed inside.

The room was mostly empty—the thirty-foot-tall tower of the ship, disguised as covered boxes, the field cache in one corner, and the emergency shower beside it. The hatch was open, and Shirin stood in the airlock, beckoning them in.

King was in the cockpit by the time she reached the base of the stairs, Shirin and Mallery cheering her on. The world was still a bit wobbly, and her stomach felt like it'd been ripped open and then stuffed with buzz saws, but she kept going.

"Strap in," Shirin said. "It's not going to be an easy trip out of here."

"I'm coming, I'm coming," Leah waved a hand at the senior Genrenaut. And then totally whiffed the next rung, leading to her smacking her forehead on the ladder.

Way to look awesome in front of the team.

"Screw this world; let's get out of here!" Leah righted herself and climbed up into the ship. She and Shirin pulled the hatch closed and spun the wheel to seal it, then split up to climb the pair of ladders, one on each side of the ship's interior. Leah took the nearest seat, then strapped in, her heart (and back) pounding.

Strapped in, she faced up, like an astronaut in a rocket. Only they'd be going sideways rather than up. Sort of. Leah was still not super-clear on the exact physics.

King stared at the controls, not moving.

"King. We have to take off," Roman said.

He didn't move. "We almost had her. She was right there."

Shirin opened up the comms.

"Mid-Atlantic actual, this is Mid-Atlantic Three, taking off."

"We read you, Mid-Atlantic Three," Preeti said through the radio. The signal was already scratchy, like a weak Skype connection. "You have three minutes. Three minutes. The latest readings are with you."

"You hear that, King? We need to take off!" Roman repeated.

"Should have seen it earlier. She got the drop on me like a green flatfoot."

Shirin waved Leah up toward King. "He's getting lost in the role. You have to talk him out of it. He'll recognize you before any of the rest of us. Play the dynamic."

"You have one minute," Roman said.

"Not helping!" Mallery added.

Leah unstrapped and climbed up the ladder. Roman was in the copilot seat. She leaned over from the ladder, crowding her teammate.

"King. Boss. The case is over. Closed. We kicked everything back to Nancy, and now we have to get home."

"I should have stayed," King said, staring into the distance.

"She made her choice. That's what you said. Now you have to make yours. We all leave, or we're all stuck here. I don't want to stay; neither do Shirin, Mallery, or Roman. You're Angstrom King, Genrenauts team lead. Remember? You stay here, we all lose."

King looked at her, still locked in a steely gaze. He blinked, leaned back, and then looked at the controls.

"We're in the ship."

"And we need to leave. Can you fly us out?"

"Yes. I'm back. I'm here." He looked to Leah, then to the team. "Let's get out of here."

Leah hustled down the ladder and got back into her seat.

"Roman, you've got my back on copilot. I start to slip back into the archetype, you take over. Shirin, you have our path?"

"Affirmative. Let's go home."

The ship lurched forward. Leah leaned over to watch as Shirin studied the screen. Shirin gestured to her right. "Twenty degrees right and fifteen degrees down."

The head Genrenaut adjusted, and the ship's nose dipped and banked. Leah held on to her seat as she watched Shirin's console, trying to exert some control just by knowing what was going on.

Shirin called out the next set of directions, "It curves gradually to the right and down, then cuts left seventy degrees over five hundred meters, then up twenty degrees." She typed like the wind, feeding King verification on the degrees and slopes for the best path through the storm. Shirin called the turns and King took them. He was a more deliberate pilot than the others, almost more robotic, but not really; where the other two took joy in the flying, he just did it. Zen-style. No-mind, no distractions. Frosty.

Which, given how fast Leah's heart was racing, was a great counterbalance, averaging the team's heartbeat out to something vaguely functional.

All the while, Roman barked out the structural damage, hull integrity, and their progress across dimensions. And Mallery kept the line open to Preeti.

"Up ten degrees, left thirty!" Shirin called as the path through the tube veered.

"Halfway there. Two minutes. You've got it, you've got it," Preeti said through the comms, voice still scrambled.

King banked again, and Shirin called out the next turn, They'd found her groove. Another three turns came and went, and Leah blinked, double-checking to make sure she was seeing the screen correctly.

Shirin called "Hard dive, ten left. Now!"

King slammed the stick forward, taking them into a high-g dive.

"Come on, baby, hold together," she told the ship.

"We can't hold this turn for very long," Roman said, his patented calm straining.

"Almost out!" Mallery added.

Shirin called the next turn. "Left seventy, then down twenty-five immediately."

The turbulence increased, Leah's teeth chattering like she was back in the Chicago winter.

"Ninety right, thirty up on my mark. And…mark!"

King made the turn, and the ship rattled its way through a patch of dimensional chop.

And up, and out, and then…nothing.

Leah looked at the screen, then Shirin. "We good?" she asked.

"We're clear," Shirin confirmed.

Cheering came through the radio. Leah joined in with a whoop of her own.

"Now bring her home," Preeti said.

"Roger that, Mid-Atlantic Actual. Tell the commissary to get me some burgers ready." King looked down from the nose of the ship and gave Leah a for-reals smile. "And a pizza."

"Copy that, Mid-Atlantic Three," Preeti said. "Prepare for docking."

As Preeti guided them in to dock, Leah's rode the last of the adrenaline high back to thoughts about the case. And about her whole time with the Genrenauts. The Tall Woman's face crept back into her mind. Then she jumped to her first case. To Shirin's report about the mercs and the Ra'Gar connection. And to Theo's story in Rom-Com world.

Lightning arced across a dozen points of data and memory, and Leah gulped.

She had to talk to King. As soon as they landed, he was out of his seat and giving orders.

She shrunk back, dismissed the idea. *It's ridiculous*, she thought.

Then, *No, screw that. Worst case is I'm wrong and he chews me out. But if I'm right…*

She unbuckled and hurried to chase after the team lead. She'd speak her piece. She'd earned that much, at least.

Chapter Nine:
Consequences

King unsnapped the restraints and slid down the ladder, hitting the floor of the ship with a metallic *clang-thud*.

He turned to Roman. "Work with the crew in getting the ship cleared. Chances are, that turbulence rocked something loose."

The action hero looked at the smoldering, dented ship with a smile. "You think?"

The ship would be fine. It had to be. They had even fewer ships to spare than crew.

King's mental to-do list started spinning like the old flap displays at train stations.

File the mission report, ward off flak from the Council, debrief the team, put in the redeploy request…

"Boss?" Leah asked, hustling to catch him as he tore his way across Ops, toward their ready room.

"Yes?"

"I've got a bad feeling about that last mission."

He raised an eyebrow.

"Yeah, no kidding, right? I mean a specific bad feeling. It okay if I toss a theory at the team?"

Interesting. He had his own ideas and questions to process. Maybe her theory fit into it, maybe it didn't. Maybe it was residual wackiness from going so deep into archetype. "Sure. I've got to report in; that gives everyone a few minutes to grab some food or drink before the debrief. Gather your thoughts."

"It might be better if I pitch this before your report."

"The Council doesn't like to be kept waiting."

"Would they like it more than having you call them right back and say 'Oh, by the way, everything about that last mission report might be wrong?' Because that's what I'm thinking."

He stopped.

"Your gut telling you this?"

"My everything is telling me this."

"Then you're pitching the theory now." King pulled out his phone and called Roman in from the hangar. "Emergency debrief in the ready room."

He looked to Leah. "Let's hear what you have to say."

* * *

No stress, just maybe your job on the line, Leah thought, facing the assembled team.

Her mind raced back through the last mission. And the one before that. And the others. Every one a puzzle piece. Pieces she didn't even know were pieces, were even the same puzzle, until minutes ago. But if she was right, they needed to hear. Hell, the High Council needed to hear, though hopefully King could be the one to face them.

Shirin had melted into her comfy chair, Mallery sat with a power bar, Roman was stretching on a yoga mat, and King stood, arms crossed, watching her.

She wiped off the white board and started.

"Okay, so this might be totally off base, but here it is. Every mission I've been on, something's been off, right? Mallery's western posse bit the dust— we had the wrong hero. Then one of the bandits pulls some serious moves and gets away. Who is she?"

Gentle nodding from Shirin, blank silence from King.

"Then in Sci-Fi World, the gang kidnaps the Ambassador but no one can trace who hired them. Shirin said it would be incredibly unlikely for the Ra'Gar to have done it, so who? The report says it'd have to be someone that knew the Ahura-3 station well."

"Then in Rom-Com, we have a weird story breach after Theo gets run down by a driver. And all he remembers? Tall woman, dark hair. And the doc's mysterious stranger that told her to go for Theo? Then our mysterious hit-woman just now—tall, dark hair, moved like a pro."

"All circumstantial, newbie," King said.

"What did your shooter look like?" Roman asked. "How like a pro did she move?"

"Studied. And totally in control of the situation. At first. She put Ricardo up to the first murder, and then she took a shot at DeeZee."

"And she had the chops to sneak a weapon into the hospital and get past CPD to try to seal the deal."

"So, we're talking Big Deal villain, right? Some kind of heavy? So, we've got an uncommonly competent henchwoman in at least two missions, and weird instigations of story breaches in another two missions."

Shirin piped in. "This whole year has been off, though. More breaches, and stronger ripples at every juncture."

"What if that's because we've got a rogue element? Someone else moving across the dimensions?"

She let that sink in. Mallery and Shirin sat forward; King's arms had uncrossed. Roman was uncharacteristically still.

Leah asked again. "What if someone else got ahold of our tech?"

King cracked his knuckles.

"So, do you think I'm right?" Leah asked. A bit too much hope ended up in her voice. She felt all alone, on the stage again. But this time, her audience wasn't hecklers. It was colleagues.

Shirin bobbed her head, as if considering. "I think it's possible. Highly unlikely, but possible."

"Maybe it's a part of one of the breaches," Mallery said. "The same character from one world ended up on another. I don't know about the Ahura-3 mission, wasn't there, but the others? It's possible."

Roman nodded. "That henchwoman's moves were impressive. Patrols and sources haven't turned her up in any other stories since we left. You'd think a major character like that would recur."

"Roman, excerpt me your portion of the report for Leah's first mission. Shirin, I want your full analysis on the Ra'Gar's capabilities and what it'd take to set up that kidnapping. Mallery, pore over your case file too."

King looked straight at her.

"I think you're probably wrong."

Ouch, she thought, trying not to flinch.

His face brightened. "But I'm incredibly impressed by your performance on that mission, and if there's one thing I've learned over the years, it's to trust your team." He looked at the other members of the team. "I'll present the team's findings to the Council, raise the possibility. We can put an APB out for this tall woman, clue the other teams in, see if we can spot her elsewhere. Good money says nothing comes of it, but this was a good call."

"Thanks, boss."

"Thank me when we have the Council's response. Get me that material in five minutes. I'll start apologizing for the delay."

* * *

This time, the Council barely made him wait to call in. He didn't have a full written report, didn't even know what to think about everything that had happened.

What if Leah was right?

A rogue Genrenaut, perhaps, someone who had jumped ship and replicated the technology to cross dimensions? Or maybe someone from a technologically savvy world had replicated the Council's discovery and taken it into her own hands to travel the worlds and make changes?

The implications were staggering. If she knew how the multiverse worked, she could cause untold damage.

King was still organizing the reports from their last missions when the call light came on. The team had thrown everything together in ten minutes, but it was still rough, loose clusters of hunches cobbled together with scant data.

But it was too big of a question mark to let pass unsaid.

He queued up the packet, ready to send during the call for maximum effect. The High Council had a flair for mystery and drama, so he'd speak their language if it helped them take his assertion seriously.

Behind him, the servers and processors whirred as the connection was established, The panoramic screens before him lit up, going from flat dark to the organization's logo, worlds identified by genre circling Earth Prime. Then the image cross-faded with the live feed, showing the Council chamber room as five figures stepped forward into overhead light, casting them in shadow.

"King. You cut that return very. Very close," said Gisler, always the central figure.

"The breach was sealed, and I got my team home safe. And we've formed a disturbing hypothesis."

"First, your report," said D'Arienzo, to Gisler's left.

King gave as cursory an overview of the mission as he could without prompting the Councilors to ask him to elaborate.

"And Ms. Franklin?" Gisler asked as she came up in his report.

"No signs of remembering her tenure as a Genrenaut, nor any memory of me outside of the story world."

Gisler bade him continue.

King finished the report, underplaying elements about the Tall Woman until he was done. He tapped send on the email he had prepped, sending the reports to the Council.

"This Tall Woman, who we believe shot DeeZee and shot at me, who I saw kill Ricardo Hernandez, we believe she is the same woman who was a part of Jack Williamson's posse during our last mission to the Western World. Even with a PPM, her build and movements were too similar to be sheer coincidence. She matches Roman's report, and matches the description given to our team during our mission in the Romance world, a description of a tall woman behind the wheel of the truck that injured Theo, causing the story breach.

King adjusted his stance wider, weathering the glare of the Council. "Given this recurrence and her actions, I have good reason to believe that this woman is a dimensional traveler, crossing between story worlds with her own agenda, possibly diametrically opposed to our own. I would ask that all stations immediately enact a BOLO for this woman and bring her in, given opportunity."

The Council members shifted, looking at their displays. King waited, hands held behind his back, letting them absorb the information on their own. This would only work if the evidence convinced them, if the reports painted the picture he believed they painted.

"And you do not have proof that it's the same woman." Another Council member, on the far left. The voice was a middle alto, and he'd never been able to get a read on the Councilor's gender.

"No, Councilor. But we have three independent accounts across three worlds, each placing a similar woman at the scene of a breach."

Gisler gave a dismissing wave. "This evidence is all circumstantial, stitched together into a patchwork tale thanks to your admittedly valuable imagination, and animated by your need to make this increase of breaches into something you can fight, instead of the reality of our situation."

"If you see this woman again," another Councilor, female, said, "and can obtain incontrovertible evidence that she has traveled between story worlds, then bring it, and her, back to HQ. Until then, you hold the line."

D'Arienzo cut in. "Debrief your team and stand down to ready status. When the storm clears, we may need to send you out again if further breaches have emerged."

And with that, the call dropped, and King was alone once more.

Instead of their doubt stoking his own, it siphoned the life out of it. The Council was very slow to act, and over this last year, that conservatism had run right up against what he thought needed to be done. He and the other team leads had practically had to beg for permission to recruit more operatives.

If his team believed, and the Council didn't, he'd take his team's side. Running down all of the options and discovering Leah was wrong wouldn't help her ego, but it would help them all sleep soundly.

He clenched and unclenched his fists, then turned and walked out to return to his team. If it was evidence they wanted, then evidence they'd get. And when he saw the Tall Woman again, he'd get some real answers.

Epilogue:
Wave Form Collapse

A few minutes after King headed off to give the report, Leah caught Mallery's attention. She nodded out into the hall, and the comedienne returned the nod.

Leah went first, taking a right out of the ready room and walking down the hall. She pondered where to hide that would be private but not suspicious. The women's bathroom wasn't private enough, not without sneaking into a toilet stall or something equally ridiculous.

How would they do it in Rom-Com World? she thought. That didn't help, since in Rom-Com World, you had privacy whenever you needed it, unless the story said you didn't.

She settled for leaning against a wall, futzing with her phone. A minute later, she spotted Mallery out of the corner of her eye.

Three times she tried to say something, eventually getting out "Where's a good place to chat?"

Mallery pointed down the hall, confident. She was always confident, strutting even with a broken arm. "Requisitions, I think. All of the teams are in, and the others got back hours ago."

They walked in silence, Leah's face getting warm as the tension thickened like sauce in a pan. They'd been simmering the whole mission, not that they'd seen each other much after she went off with King for the short-lived scouting segment of the mission.

The lights were off in requisitions, so Mallery led them into a quick right, then a left, until they came to an alcove with furniture. She navigated by the light of her phone, then pulled a lamp off a shelf and plugged it into one of the many outlets located on the stations themselves.

"No reason to take stuff twenty yards away to test it, right?" She clicked the lamp on, taking them from spooky phone-lit to intimate mood lighting. "Very handy." She pulled down a foldout chair, handed it to Leah, and then grabbed one of her own. They set up their chairs and sat.

"Okay. So."

One side of Mallery's mouth twinged toward a smile. "So."

A moment of silence passed between them. Leah got up the gumption, shook her head, and started. "I feel like this has gotten really built up and I don't even know where to start, honestly."

"Let's start with I'm sorry. I should have said something earlier."

"Blame enough to go around on that. So, let's throw that out."

"Done."

Leah brushed hair out of her eyes. "That night, I didn't even remember thinking what I said before I said it. I didn't mean to make things awkward."

"I pushed you right into a couple-y cover when we'd barely met. That and being your first time in that world, I could have guessed."

"You're that irresistible?" Leah asked, raising an eyebrow.

Mallery laughed. Full-voice, unselfconscious laugh. "That's very fair."

"But it came from somewhere. I think you're pretty awesome. And that mission was amazingly fun. Even if much of it was pretend."

The comedienne's smile broadened. "It was."

"So, that's my..." Leah looked to her left, reached up to a shelf, and pulled out a bedside table. She set it down between them.

"That's my cards on the table," she said, miming the action as she spoke.

"Well played." Mallery took a second, exhaling. "I like you, too. Just about no one can keep up with me when I'm in whirlwind mode, and you handled it like a champ. I like the idea of a girl that can give me a run for my money. Someone I can learn from."

"I don't know about running," Leah said, recalling their Central Park jog, "but I've got plenty to share."

"A few more weeks of Roman's workout regimen and we'll both be right as rain."

"So, that's a yes? Or the interest of a yes? Also, will we get fired?"

Mallery waved the question away. "King's a softie about this stuff. You probably saw that when he was with Nancy. He plays all gruff, but he's got the soul of a poet underneath those layers of tweed and regulations. Plus, Shirin's already caught wise."

"Really?" Leah asked. "But we've barely talked since the last mission."

"Exactly. I talk to everyone, all the time, often to excess." She shrugged, again full of confidence. "It's clear I don't dislike you, so the other option…"

"So, Shirin already knows, we probably won't get fired, and we're both interested. Where does that leave us?" Leah asked, doing her best to be all mature and grown up in this conversation that was light-years from the other start-of-relationship or define-the-relationship conversations she'd had. *Is this what grown-up romance looks like?*

Mallery stood out of the chair and offered Leah a hand. "I think that means we can stop trying to be all cautious and responsible and go back to finding our own way."

Leah's cheeks got warm again, blood flowing to her head as she stood. She took Leah's hand, feeling her warmth, her smooth skin. She squeezed and said, "Then how about we blow this popsicle stand and grab some dinner? I could murder some bao right about now."

"We disappear now, King will be grumpy. But after debrief, yes. I think that's a fabulous idea. But first," Mallery said, leaning forward.

Time slowed down as the light played across Mallery's face, on her cheek, her nose, and her lips. Mallery gave Leah a brief peck on the cheek, chaste enough for even a prudish family reunion, but it was for her, Leah, not Mission Leah. And it was the beginning of something.

Leah exhaled, then shook out the electrifying feeling that was zipping up and down her skin.

She pulled herself back a half-step and started to disassemble the little room they'd made. "Damn, girl. Those chops with the Romance specialty?" She fanned herself.

Mallery gave an exaggerated wink. "That's why I'm the Love Queen."

Leah took Mallery's hand once more. "Love Queen? Oh, I'm using the hell out of that."

Mallery squeezed Leah's hand as they approached the doors leading them back toward the rest of HQ. "You good?"

"I'm good."

And so they returned to the team.

* * *

King returned a few minutes later and passed on the bad news—the Council hadn't bought Leah's hypothesis.

"But we're going to stay on the lookout. We see anyone that might even possibly be that Tall Woman, we move to capture and interrogate. Understood?"

They all nodded. Leah and Mallery in side-by-side chairs, both sipping at hot chocolate and dipping their toes in the tub Mallery had filled with hot water. Shirin gulped down chai, having turned down the chance to share the tub. Roman was back to his treadmill, warming up in his own way.

The rest of the debrief passed all too slowly as feeling fully returned to Leah's feet and giddiness led to stealing short glances sideways at her teammate.

They weren't being subtle, but who cared? It'd been quite a while since Leah'd had anyone to be giddy over. The stand-up scene didn't exactly give her the best dating pool. She'd set herself a rule of no dating fellow comics, which had cut out a pretty big swathe of the people she interacted with outside of work.

King dismissed them, heading off to write another report.

Note to self, she thought. *Turn down offers to be a team lead. Too much paperwork.*

Shirin set her tea down and said, "So, Leah, tell us your part of what happened in the chase." It was a good idea—collate all the information they had. But she hadn't asked it like that. She'd asked it like she wanted to hear a story.

Roman had returned to his jogging, but his earbuds were out—he was listening too.

Leah sat up and put her chocolate aside, rising to the challenge. "So, we knock on the chef's door, while outside the storm was raging...snowing like I'm back in Minnesota *snowing*-snowing." The women leaned in, intent.

She played out the story, summoning every detail she could remember, editorializing along the way, basking in the attention.

Somewhere along the line, she'd become part of the team, like really a part. Not just the mascot or the probationary screw-up. But one of the Genrenauts.

Leah smiled, and continued the story.

END EPISODE FOUR

Episode Five:
The Failed Fellowship (Part One)
The Shadow of the Night-Lord

Prologue:
No, Seriously, Read The Prologue This Time

Fantasy World—Heroic Region
Narrative Diagnostic 4071.514.3

DARK LORD RISES...YES
CHOSEN ONE RAISED IN SECRET...YES
HEROIC FELLOWSHIP ASSEMBLED...YES
CHOSEN ONE WIELDS MAGIC ARTIFACT...YES

From In-World Surveillance:

Theyn Lighthall held the Sun-sword aloft, catching the weak rays of the spell-shrouded sun in its crystalline facets. The blade drank in the power of light, refreshing its arcane power.

He swung at a unit of skeletons armored in darkened steel. The light shattered steel and bone alike. But then the purple smoke of the Night-Lord's necromancy flowed out and found three lifeless bodies of Fallran soldiers. The smoke seeped into noses and mouths, and then the bodies began to twitch, rising to un-life.

"Forward!" he shouted. Around them, armies raged, trebuchet and catapults spitting death up and down the walls of Ran-var Castle. The free people of Fallran fought for their beloved kingdom, but the Night-Lord's forces were buoyed by dark magics. Ran-var, the shining jewel of Fallran, had withstood sieges for a thousand years, only falling to an invader once. The same invader that now turned its might against Theyn and the forces of light.

It was up to Theyn and his companions to breach the walls and cast down the Night-Lord.

Standing atop the battlements, threescore and ten skeleton warriors yet stood between Theyn and the inner sanctum.

To his right: Ioseph Bluethorn scattered the warriors with arcane winds, beard and robes flowing, the azure gem atop his staff glowing with starlight.

And to his left: Nolan Sanz, the greatest swordsman Fallran had ever seen. His longsword cleaved through the crowd like a scythe back home cutting wheat.

Theyn checked over his shoulder and caught a glimpse of Alaria Vendar. The thief dodged and weaved through the melee, cudgel cracking bones and smashing skulls, each stroke a masterpiece. She was a moving poem, as beautiful as she was dangerous.

A roar filled Theyn's ears, and not a moment later, Xan'De crashed through the skeleton ranks with his rune-blessed axe. The bells in the foreigner's mane sang as he hewed the spell-animated army with swings that could fell a tree, punching and grappling with his other two arms.

Theyn charged forward into Xan'De's wake. He led with his shield. It was proofed against dark magics but not enough to break the animation spell with a simple touch. Still, it was enough to shove back or decapitate the undead legions as the heroes carved out a path forward.

Theyn cut them down and more rose to take their place. The herd was thinning, but the creatures continued crashing in on him like waves on the shore of his village.

Alaria burst through the ranks and joined him. They caught up to Xan'De, and together, the three broke the skeletons' formation and reached the entrance to the tower.

Hundreds of feet above, dark clouds shot through with purple lightning surrounded the tower spire. The Night-Lord awaited.

Ioseph stayed behind to hold the hordes back from the tower.

They climbed ten flights to a landing that should not be there. Another of the Night-Lord's spells.

The floor was filled by five giants, each wielding a club larger than Xan'De.

The four remaining heroes fought as one, cutting the giants' hamstrings and dodging their mighty clubs. Xan'De bisected the last giant's eye with his axe but fell poorly, and his leg was crushed beneath the giant's head.

"Go on, my friends. The Fenxi will restore my leg in time. Bring me the

Night-Lord's head!"

And so they pressed on, ever upward.

Twice more, they came to chokepoints, and twice more, Theyn's companions stepped forward to intercept the Night-Lord's forces so that the others could press on.

So it was that Theyn was alone when he reached the top of the tower, Sun-sword in hand, blessed with purpose and the hope of the land.

He kicked the door open, revealing a small room lit only by witch-fire in shades of purple. At the center of the room stood the Hopestone, the greatest artifact in Fallran, which the rightful kings had used to protect the land and maintain balance.

The same stone which had been stained dark, now used to animate the countless undead creatures that held the nation in their grasp.

The Night-Lord stood on the balcony, hands raised, tenebrous energy flowing between him and the corrupted gem.

"The time has come, Night-Lord! Your reign of darkness is at an end!"

The Night-Lord turned, face masked by hooded robes. He extended a pale and wart-laden hand.

His voice was raspy. "At last, the Sun-sword. Surrender the blade and I will let your companions live. Fallran will thrive under my power. It is my destiny to rule, and no deluded hero shall stand in my way, sword or no."

Theyn pointed the sword at the Night-Lord, gathering the power to strike the tyrant down and end the war.

"Fallran will never choose you, Night-Lord. This ends now."

"How right you are," the Night-Lord said.

And then, without warning, a blade slid into Theyn's back.

Panic and confusion crossed Theyn's face as he crumpled to the floor.

He'd come so far, done everything right. He was The Chosen One. He bore the Sun-sword, forged from the same crystal as the Hopestone itself.

His mind drifted to that night of the new moon, when Ioseph had read him the prophecy, said that he, Theyn, had a special fate. An ancient prophecy said that he was destined to save Fallran from darkness.

Theyn tried to turn, to face the being or construct that he had not seen, that had clutched victory from his grasp and dashed hope upon the rocks to be shattered and washed away with the bloody tide.

He reached forward, trying in his last moments to fulfill his destiny, to make Ioseph and the others proud.

But instead, he collapsed.

The sword clattered to the ground, and he drowned in eternal darkness.

DARK LORD DEFEATED…NO

SUMMON NEW CHOSEN ONE?

From the files of Angstrom King
Charlie Team—Mid-Atlantic
Recruitment records—Candidate—Leah King
Recorded at Comedy Corner in Baltimore, MD

Leah Tang:

My fantasy is discovery. New races, new kingdoms, new magics. I loved that when I opened a fantasy book or found a new author, I knew I was in for a tour through someone's imagination.

But as I grew up, I realized something that was incredibly rare in fantasy: people that looked like me.

In most fantasies, an Asian girl like me only shows up as a topless witch in need of rescue or killing, with snakes crawling over her boobs. And that is just not my scene.

My fantasy is less about the whips and the PVC, more about self-actualization and hope. And you know what? That's just as sexy to me.

In my fantasy, Asian girls can do anything we want. We can be fighters, wizards, and rogues. We can save the day and fall in love with the person we want, not be depowered or married off as a prize for the square-jawed hero.

When I was a kid, I read so much fantasy that I was convinced I was the Chosen One. My parents yelled at me for introducing my friends as my Sidekick or my Nemesis. Because heroes in fantasy can do it all—they learn magic, pick up languages in a montage, and become master swordsmen in a month on the road headed from their village to the Dark Lord's tower, winning the heart of the elven princess, and besting the champion swordsman from the pointy-hat-wearing pseudo-French kingdom along the way.

So, when I was eight, confident that I was the Chosen One, I decided to begin my heroic skills acquisition. I spent six months awaiting my parents' tragic death with Wednesday Addams-level fascination.

Thankfully, they lived, and I forged on un-orphaned. First, I tried to become a master alchemist. My parents bought me a My Little Scientist kit, but even after eight weeks, all I could do was almost blow up our garage. My older brother's bike is still stained mad-

scientist red, more than fifteen years later. Whatever; it's not like he was using those eyebrows.

So, I gave up on alchemy and focused on riding-every good fantasy hero can ride, right? Except it wasn't fourteenth-century England, and I wasn't royalty, and my parents unsurprisingly did not accept my argument, in a bad British accent, that if they didn't max out their credit cards on horse-related expenses, that an evil wizard would rule the world.

And that's when I knew. Sword fighting. Every good Chosen One knows their way around a sword. So, I guilted my parents into enrolling me in a fencing class, and I tell you what. You have never seen someone happier than ten-year-old me running around with a kid-sized epee pretending to be Aragorn or Inigo Montoya.

I practiced and practiced—stayed with it way longer than anything else. Even got into some tournaments. I got all the way to the finals in my division.

And you know what happened?

What happened is I got my ass handed to me six ways from Sunday by a kid from Iowa that had been fencing since he was four.

I was fuming after the bout. But my parents made me go congratulate him. He introduced me to his parents, and guess what? They were farmers. And the kid? Adopted.

You never choose *to be the Chosen One. You just* are.

And you know what? That kid sent me a friend request two weeks ago. He's headed to the Olympics.

But even though I never won a tournament, I found something I loved even though it was hard, even though I would never be the best. Those stories made me believe in myself. That's what fantasy means to me.

But I tell you what—if you come across a farm boy and an old wizard, shiv them, take their horses, and go make your own destiny.

Chapter One:
The Best Kind of Training

To qualify as a full-fledged Genrenaut, Leah Tang had to pass competency tests in a dozen disciplines. Every week, she took a new exam, and when the results came in, King adjusted her training. He'd assign yet another ridiculous or seemingly impossible task, from plotting out how to create three romantic meet-cutes in a small suburb on a fifty-dollar budget to tracing the narrative evolution of Hurt/comfort fic from its origins as Get'em fic in *Star Trek* fanfiction into its many permutations in twenty-first-century fandom.

King wore the mantle of professor well, but there was a reason Leah'd left academia—there was only so much info cramming she could take in any one day. Or week, really.

But then, sometimes, there were days like today.

Today's skill was fencing.

King and Mallery met Leah in the training room, which had guns of all genres and time periods on one side, complete with shooting lanes and Danger Room-like obstacle courses.

The other wall held an armory that could outfit twenty warriors from around the world and send them into war. Norman chain shirts, Italian plate, Mesoamerican hide armor, Japanese O-yoroi, shields from all over, and swords.

So many swords.

Leah honed in on a schiavona, polished basket hilt catching the institutional lights of the room. It practically begged to be used in daylight.

"So, which of these do I get to play with today?" she asked.

"Whichever one you like," King said. "You've tested into the highest level of proficiency for the Fantasy genre, and your profile shows you're quite experienced in swordplay. Let's see it." He pulled down a feder sword, a practice longsword.

As far as Leah could tell, about half of the weapons on the sword wall were live weapons with real edges, the others training gear.

She left the schiavona and grabbed another feder. Taking a cut-and-thrust sword against a taller opponent using a longsword was not her idea of a good time.

"Is that your best weapon?" King asked.

"If you're using a longsword, it is." Leah swung her blade to get a sense of its heft. In her hands, the hilt was long, good for the push-and-pull that made longswords the terror they were.

Dungeons & Dragons got longswords all wrong. They painted the image of a weapon weighing over five pounds and yet meant to be used one-handed, with a short sword or shield in the other. Real longswords were efficient workhorse weapons that weighed three or four pounds at most and were best used in two hands.

King put the longsword back. "If you're going to the Fantasy World, what weapon do you bring?"

"Aside from a Wand of Plot Convenience?"

Mallery jumped in. "Stepping into most spellcasting roles in Fantasy World takes about a year of training in theory here, and then another year worth of field time to get really comfortable. I'm rated in Cleric and Bard, but I don't even touch Wizard. Shirin's got that one covered quite nicely, and I prefer tabards to cloaks. Better draping."

So this wasn't about matching styles, this was "show me what you've got." Leah considered the wall and traded the longsword for an espada ropera, a blade good for cut-and-thrust. Her fencing club was hardcore into longsword, but she'd always preferred the Iberian styles. She drew the weapon and saluted. King nodded and matched her with a Pappenheimer-hilt rapier. His blade had more hand protection; hers had a thicker blade. It'd make for an interesting fight.

They donned vests and masks, and squared off. Mallery watched from the side with a cup of tea. Leah tried to avoid catching Mallery's eyes. Less because she didn't want to look at the comedienne, more because she didn't want to be distracted.

Leah and Mallery had gone out for dinner after their last mission. Then again during their comp time, and twice a week since then. That plus moments stolen in hallways and when no one else was around, it was getting pretty…something. Not serious. Serious was when work came hammering down on them. It was fun. They were having fun.

But just right then, Leah needed to focus. She took her stance, angled halfway between profile and squared-off. King matched her with a more back-weighted stance. Italian style—not surprising. It was calculating and dominated by setting traps. But she had gravity on her side, since her guard started higher than his.

She advanced, covering his weapon and feeling for his response. He disengaged and threatened her face. Leah cut into his blade and exploded forward at an angle. The blades covered her advance, and her point struck the big man inside the shoulder.

King pulled back and saluted.

The mask couldn't hide Leah's grin. After months of floundering as the newbie, they were finally back in her wheelhouse. She'd given up on swords for a while after that ill-fated tournament as a kid, but come college, it was her escape from the incestuous world of the improv comedy. And now that she was a Genrenaut nearly 24/7, fencing was the one hobby she had left.

King was methodical and very efficient, no wasted motion. But Leah had youth on her side and won a couple of bouts on pure athleticism. *Have to thank Roman for his workout routine,* she thought.

Several touches later, Leah was up 3–2, with one pass where they'd both taken kill shots. She'd failed to clear King's blade while entering, and they both ended up skewered.

"Good. Switch." King tagged out after the fifth pass, and Mallery took his place, a longsword over her shoulder.

If there was one thing movies and TV had taught her about sword fighting, it was that fencing was an A+ vehicle for flirting.

But could they keep it subtle with King around?

Leah kept her sword but adjusted her approach. Mallery had a shade of reach advantage thanks to her height. But while her arm was out of its cast, the doctors had told her to take it easy. This barely qualified, but it did give Leah some ideas of how she could both protect Mallery from injury and score more touches.

"Naturally, you must expect me to attack with de Rada?" Leah tossed out as they began to test one another's defenses.

Mallery grinned, picking up what Leah was putting down. "I find Meyer cancels out Rada."

Leah kept her movements short, using thrusts to counter Mallery's powerful cuts, cuts to turn aside her long-range thrusts. Leah danced around the mats as Mallery turned up the aggression. With one arm still weak, her winds and lever actions were weaker, giving Leah the opportunity to break or interrupt the comedienne's moves.

And all the while, they spiced up their bouts by trading modified quotes from *Zorro* movies, *Lord of the Rings*, *Hero*, and more.

She nearly lost her edge a couple of times, chuckling or flush from the sight of Mallery's legs in a lunge or the look of concentration on her face during a bind.

Leah called a break not because she was tired but because she needed to cool off. They were at work, after all. Probably wouldn't do to be rolling around on the mats in anything but actual wrestling positions.

The next bout, Leah kept the flirting-with-quotes game up until she found her moment. Mallery dominated Leah's blade with a heavy parry, giving the smaller woman an opportunity. Leah raised her sword into a hanging guard and launched forward, wrapping a hand around Mallery's wrist. Leah twisted Mallery's wrist and swung her sword to chop into the back of Mallery's helm.

"Nice!" Mallery said, hugging the smaller woman. Through the sweaty armor, Leah felt the taller woman's curves, their bodies fitting together with sweat and sensation.

Keep it cool, Leah, she told herself. They could pick this up later, after work.

"I've seen enough," King said. "You said you've been practicing on your own. Take two hours a week here on top of that. I'm sure you can convince Roman to spend time behind a blade."

"Roger that, boss."

"Just because he's done doesn't mean I am," Mallery said.

Leah looked to the door and waited until King was out of earshot.

"I need a break to cool down. I about melted into a puddle just then."

Mallery winked an audacious stage wink.

Leah pulled her helmet off and took a long slug from her water bottle. "First, I did not know you were that good with a sword. Second, I definitely need to bring you to my fencing club."

Mallery removed her own helmet, some of her hair slicked to her face, the rest tumbling free.

This is just hitting all of my buttons, Leah thought, accepting the reality of this marvelous day. Here she had the advantage of experience, though with the Genrenauts' kind of work, Leah guessed that more of Mallery's experience was practical than sparring.

"If I'd known crossing swords would be this much fun, I would have begged King to do it long ago. Though I would've had to fight one-handed."

"So. You want to go another round?" Leah asked.

Most of an hour later, when both women were happily soaked in sweat, nursing nascent bruises and headed for the showers, the breach alarm filled the training room.

Leaving the blades behind, the pair raced toward Ops.

King stood by their handler, Preeti Jandran, at her station. Both were intent on the many screens and the story they told.

"What have we got?" Leah asked, eyes racing across the screens. She was still hopped up on adrenaline from sparring, which was now transitioning into twitchiness. She usually went Giddy > Twitchy > Ravenous, and in short order. She'd need a black bean burger or massive protein shake before too long, or a nap. The adrenaline had fueled, then displaced her libido, which was good for keeping up standards of professionalism and not causing a scandal.

"Fantasy World-Heroic Region," Preeti said. "The Stats department is showing personal leave spiking by ten percent overnight, and a four-percent increase in depression diagnoses nationwide."

"Nationwide?" Leah asked. It was one thing to know the way that story breaches impacted their world, but seeing the numbers unfold in front of her eyes was something totally different.

"So, we gear up, yeah? Cloaks and swords and staffs are go?" Leah asked.

Preeti shook her head. "Council hasn't given any deploy orders. This storm just won't let up."

The dimensional storm that had nearly screwed Leah and King's detective mission was just the first of a whole system, grounding Genrenauts crews around the world off and on for weeks.

"When is it going to blow over?"

"Forecasting doesn't have a good answer for that yet. Three days, maybe four?"

King crossed his arms, disapproval clear on his face. "Which will amount to as many weeks on-world. Time moves faster in that region. The stories play out over months and years."

"That's a lot of time for a breach to get worse," Leah said.

"It is. For now, shower up and work with Shirin to get our gear ready. I want us to be prepped to deploy the minute we're cleared."

Which meant that they'd be sleeping on-site for the next few days. Leah spent less and less time at home, to the point where she was regretting upgrading to a larger apartment. She could get by with a studio as long as it had a proper bathtub and a good internet connection. But since Contrast Cable & Internet still had a city-sponsored monopoly, she'd have to settle for the tub.

HQ didn't have single-capacity bath tubs, but they did have some pretty amazing showers. Leah and Mallery behaved on the way in and out, despite the lingering glances and energy built up during the fencing.

If they were on-call for several days running, there would be more pent-up tension than just romantic. It could get really antsy in their ready room.

The shower helped her focus but didn't wash away any of the worry. Since she'd joined the Genrenauts, the dimensional storms and the rate of story breaches had just kept ramping up. And if they couldn't deploy for this mission, if other teams were grounded as well, it'd all come to a head real damn soon.

* * *

Leah came back to Ops and found King still standing at Preeti's side, reading the screens.

"Any change?" she asked, still drying her hair. Mallery was still changing, in all likelihood. Advantage, shorter hair.

Preeti shook her head. "None of our projections show this storm clearing up anytime today. I have to stay here, but you two can go do something else."

Leah gestured out of Ops. "Come on, boss, let's stop hovering over the nice lady."

King sighed and flexed his fingers—a sign of frustration, as she'd learned. They returned to the ready room, where Shirin had already claimed her traditional spot in the bowl chair with a huge book in her lap.

Roman was running all-out on the other treadmill, zoned out to wherever it was he went when exercising.

Leah had come to learn that of a Genrenaut's job was waiting. But not just any kind of waiting. Active, responsive waiting. The kind of waiting where you had to be totally committed and active, but also ready to drop everything and move at a moment's notice. Like firefighters, she imagined.

It wasn't a skill that came easily to her. She loved to lose herself in a good book but only when she knew she could forget the world. Waiting to deploy here was like trying to read on a busy commute, standing up while crammed into a bus like so many sardines.

Leah puttered around for a few minutes, trying to decide what to do. Facing seventy-two hours of downtime where she couldn't go home was paralyzing. She had an infinite amount of work to do but the leisure to choose the order she did it in.

So, she started by curling up in the new comfy chair she'd requisitioned and diving back into the romantic comedy she'd been reading about the accountant and the chef. Which was totally not also functioning as a way of trying to process her feelings for Mallery. Nope. Not at all. Nor was it about giving the two of them something else to talk about than the more mundane work small talk.

Not that Genrenauts small talk was that small. The Genrenauts took the long view, played the high-stakes games. Even their water-cooler chatter had big implications.

"How's that inter-dimensional tune-up coming?"

"Not bad. You done assessing the worldwide sociopolitical implications of the Oscar finalists?"

"Yeah, next year's going to be rough. Expect a three-percent increase in self-satisfied man-children. We'll need to keep a real close eye on the No Means Yes crowd."

Mallery joined the group a few minutes later, once again made up but wearing Comfy Girl–style yoga pants and a sweatshirt. She picked up her eReader and took the seat beside Leah. They toasted with their eReaders, smiled, and got to reading.

Leah and Mallery had found that reading was the best way to stay focused on work and not one another during downtime. It was the thing that would let them sit side by side and be in one another's company without being too obvious.

Shirin had already found them out, but so far, King hadn't said anything. And the longer they could keep it like that, the better. Probably. It could be that whatever she and Mallery had would fizzle out in another few weeks, and they'd settle back into being colleagues, and life would move on.

But if things went the other way, it'd be better to go to King with something more serious than the Getting To Know You phase they were still enjoying.

Or so they'd decided in one of their delightfully-not-too-stressful check-ins a few days back. Leah had been in relationships where any discussion about the relationship itself would take all of the air out of the room. And others where they'd talk, but it'd be incredibly difficult to get the other person to open up.

Usually, this was with guys. Thanks to BS gender norms, guys were far more likely to have underdeveloped emotional intelligence. Some learned the score, figured out how to say what they wanted instead of just flailing around and trying to take what they should be asking for.

Leah let that train of thought roll off into the distance and got back to her reading.

Hours passed. Several hours later, King rejoined the team and took a seat, lost in data and reports and projections or the like on his tablet.

Chapter Two:
We Are the Waiting

Two days later, they were still waiting.

Leah had logged plenty of time on mission prep with the entire team. Fantasy-world history with King, some more flirty fencing with Mallery, hand-to-hand with Roman, magical theory with Shirin.

The whole team had also spent time sparring with some Genrenauts from Mendoza's squad—Deanna, a Horror specialist, and Ernie, a historical buff.

All of that still left them with lots of downtime, since they still weren't allowed to leave HQ. She'd made a huge dent in her reading list, though new titles appeared as soon as she crossed one off her list.

And she and Mallery had eaten lunch together and taken several walks around the HQ, joking and sharing stories from their respective histories on the stage.

And while they waited, the bad news kept rolling in. Social indicators got worse and worse: Depression diagnoses continuing to spike, productivity dropping, and more. King relayed reports that other Genrenaut bases were detecting breaches in their territory worlds but were just as unable to plot a course through the storm. And so, HQ kept their hands off the deploy button.

Come five AM the third day since the breach was spotted, King called the team to attention.

"This is ridiculous. I'm stepping the team down to on-call status. Everyone go home and get some real sleep."

He said that looking more or less at Leah and Mallery. They were at the middle of the team, but it was hard to not be paranoid.

King stayed behind with paperwork, but the rest of the team rushed to their cars to head home, Shirin first of all.

Walking out to the cars, Mallery caught up to Leah.

"Hey, want to hang out some now that we're free? I was about ready to pull the fire alarm just to get some time alone."

Mallery looked at her, expectant and hopeful. Her eyes held promise and hunger. She imagined what a not-restful but very relaxing evening in Mallery's company would be like, and goose bumps ran up her arms and down her back.

When she was younger and more likely to drown herself in a new romance, she'd have jumped at the opportunity to blow off steam together. But she'd put together enough self-knowledge to know her needs right now, and they were boring and solitary.

"I'd love to, but I'm totally wiped. I need to stare at a wall and be a hermit for a while; sorry."

Mallery failed to hide the disappointment, but she nodded. "I get it. I could probably use some time to myself too. Tomorrow?"

"Tomorrow. Either we'll be on-world and have fun things to do, or we'll desperately need to get away from HQ again."

Leah gave Mallery a just-slightly-too-long-for-friends hug and then turned off toward her car, trying not to regret the decision to be a responsible grown-up.

She barely remembered the ride home.

Leah was torn from sleep by the on-call alarm, sitting up with a start in a room that still smelled like stir-fry. Every Genrenaut had to use the alarm app for their phone or carry a pager. Since she didn't relish living in the 1999 version of office life, she chose the app.

It was midnight. She'd had four hours of sleep at home. Better than nothing. Plus, the alarm wouldn't come unless they had clearance to deploy.

She also had a text from Shirin.

Meet me outside.

* * *

Leah dressed at light speed and headed down to the street, where a red-eyed Shirin met her in the typical family-of-four minivan. They picked up Mallery on the way and arrived at HQ to see that King and Roman's cars were already on-site.

King met them in the front hallway. "Good evening. The storms have let up enough for us to deploy to Fantasy World. Shirin, you're on gear. Leah, help her. Mallery and Roman, see to the ship. Our window is very short, so we have fifteen minutes until lift-off."

And with that, King turned and headed toward the ship.

Leah imagined "Yakety Sax" playing as the rest of the team set about their tasks, though really, everyone was speedy but organized. Even her, happy to say. By now, she knew the score, got what a crossing entailed. And deploying meant she'd get to use her sword skills in the field, albeit with drastically more danger.

Her journey to the Genrenauts had started, at least as far as she knew about it, with her stand-up set about fantasy those months earlier, and now she was finally getting a chance to see the world up-close. Dragons and sorcerers and farmboys and evil advisors, the whole shebang.

Watching as Shirin retrieved the crew's gear for the mission, already laid out when they got the breach alert, Leah imagined the crew in full *Dungeons & Dragons* adventurer kit, saving the visual to compare against reality. Chances were that King would not end up wearing a Kirby-level winged helmet, but she could dream.

The gear for Fantasy World was heavy enough that they had to use a cart to haul it down to the ship, but Shirin and Leah made it aboard with a minute to spare.

HQ was quiet but not empty, since Ops and Tech were already on a three-shift rotation, currently in the graveyard shift.

"Prep for takeoff," King said from the pilot's seat. Leah and Shirin strapped in, five of the ship's six seats filled. She sat on the bottom row, an empty seat beside her.

"Mid-Atlantic Actual, this is Mid-Atlantic 3 taking off," he said, and hit the dimensional thrusters. As soon as they kicked on, the ship began to shake. She'd been through turbulence, and nasty turbulence at that, as part of her last trip home from a story world, moving through the first break in this dimensional storm system. The ship rattled, lurching back and forth and left and right and every other direction. The disturbance was so bad, they didn't hear the customary response from Ops acknowledging their takeoff.

Leah locked her eyes on the viewscreen, which showed a psychedelic cascade of colors and flashes of light.

"Are you sure we can get through?" Mallery asked through rattling teeth.

Leah kept her mouth shut for fear of biting her own tongue off.

"We'll be fine." He looked to Shirin, who would be playing the role Leah did on the way back, watching the flow of dimensional disturbance.

"Twenty degrees to port, eight degrees down."

Shirin called directions and King steered.

Not being in the navigator's seat meant that the pressure was off for Leah, but that also meant she didn't have anything to distract her. She held on for dear life as the ship dived and swooped and juked around the roughest parts of the storm.

She regretted the power bar she'd devoured in the car, since it was now threatening to rush up her gullet and take her for a ride on the Tilt-A-Whirl.

Interminable minutes later, the ship broke through the storm and sailed easy for a short time before appearing in a forest grove, the viewscreen pointing up into a purple-tinged sky.

"That could have gone smoother," Roman said, taking the lead for Understatement of the Month.

"We got here, at least. But we're nearly three weeks behind on whatever this breach is. Gear up on the double so we can get into town and figure out what's happened."

King and Roman threw on cloaks and went to stand outside while Mallery, Shirin, and Leah changed.

Leah's outfit was classic bard—poofy shirt under a studded leather jerkin, leggings, and Golden Age Robin mini-boots. A brocaded flat cap with an ostrich feather completed her outfit. A live steel version of the espada ropera hung from her belt in a sheath. She thought back to her first mission and the brace of guns Shirin had handed her. This was much more her speed. But it also meant they were expecting a fight.

Mallery wore scale mail and had a big-ass shield with a sunburst design strapped to her back, a mace slung from her belt. That'd make her the cleric.

Shirin wore a massive robe over a fine silk dress with leather straps wrapped over and around, belt laden with pouches and bottles filled with bright-colored liquid. Wizard.

This wasn't Rom-Com World, where everything was solved with kissing and honest communication, or Science Fiction World, where Roman did the dirty work. On this mission, they'd all have to fight. They'd be a heroic fellowship, adventurers looking to right wrongs and fulfill prophecies. Her hands shook with excitement.

The women switched out to stand guard. The ship had landed smack-dab in the middle of a forest. But everything was cast in a sickly light, thanks to the sun being shrouded in purple clouds, casting the world in weird light.

Leah pointed. "Five bucks says that light is part of the reason we're here."

"No bet," Mallery answered. "The question is, where does it come from, and how do we stop it?"

"How is this going to work? If we're here to patch a breach, do we need to recruit the heroes, levy an army, and lay siege to the castle? I'm totally up for a good siege."

Shirin joined in. "Sieges are much more fun when you're on the outside and sitting in the back, with food, instead of on the inside, eating leather straps." She spoke with the air of someone who had done both.

"Have you been in sieges? Here?" Leah asked, not at all hiding her enthusiasm.

Shirin shrugged. "If *Tough Guide to Fantasy Land* had a bingo card, I'd be a winner twice over."

"I can totally make a bingo card. My bag has parchment, right?"

"I'm sure you can find better things to do with it. Like compose some genre-appropriate poetry or songs to fit your archetype, Ms. Bard."

"Can't I just Olde English up some Lady Gaga and call it good?" she asked, not entirely joking.

Roman spoke from inside the hatch, "'Bad Romance' would make a pretty good Broadside Ballad." He emerged, decked out in polished but dinged breastplate over chain. He had a greatsword slung over his shoulders, and no less than three more weapons slung at his belt. Every inch of Roman's outfit was loaded with weaponry. Human Cuisinart™ in the best tradition of Obsidian RPGs. It was ridiculous and impractical, but because they were in Fantasy world, it worked.

He jumped out of the hatch opening and landed with a substantial thud in the moss-covered clearing.

King stepped into the opening of the hatch, and while he was wearing a shiny metal helmet, it did not have big Kirby-esque wings or other giant swooping parts. It was a standard Norman nasal helm, the rest of his kit a full suit of plate mail. His weapon of choice was a beaten longsword with a far-newer and polished silver hilt, leather grip, and a gryphon-headed pommel.

"How come I get jack-all for armor?" Leah asked.

"Learn to move in the heavier gear and you can wear it on-mission," King said. "Plate is more maneuverable than most people think, but only in the real world. Here, this suit moves like Iron Man by way of Stay Puft thanks to how fantasy stories are told. I've gotten used to it, though. And it'll stop near about anything. Let's get on the road. I want to make town by nightfall in case this breach comes with bonus monsters. See to the camping gear."

For lack of horses, the team had brought a cart. Leah didn't have to pull it, but she did have to load it while Roman backseat-pull-cart-driver-ed her.

King set the ship's Phase Manipulator, and the ship was replaced by a thick stand of trees.

And with that, they were off. Roman trudged along with the gear, while Leah walked behind the cart with Mallery at her side, King and Shirin at the front.

"Any guesses about the plot?" Leah asked, but kept on talking. "I hope we get an invading kingdom or breach in dimensions, like a spirit invasion or something."

"We're in Fallran, which trends really traditional. So, I'm betting on succession war gone messy or a Dark Lord."

"Betting on Dark Lord is like betting that the couple gets together in the end in Category Romance. You're automatically right more than 95% of the time," Leah said.

"Doesn't mean I'm wrong. Three of the last four times we've come to Fallran for a breach, it's been to overthrow a Dark Lord."

"Maybe there will be a good twist this time."

"If we're here, it was probably a bad twist."

Leah nodded, though she couldn't help but be excited. Soon she'd see halflings, dwarves, elves, magic, monsters, and a dozen other impossible things that she'd never expected to see in any greater detail or immediacy than a 3-D IMAX.

They reached the nearest village just as the sun was setting in the distance, purple light fading toward flat black. The sign out front of the small town proclaimed it Ham's Horn.

"Shouldn't there be stars or a moon by now?" Leah asked.

"Yes. There should," Shirin said. "That's new."

"Another question to ask," King said. "Spot me the nearest tavern and we'll get started."

The streets of the town were already nearly empty, giving Leah a quick flash back to the town in her first mission, people running scared from the

Williamson gang. She caught brief glimpses of dirty faces, heads adorned by snoods and flat caps, people turning cloaks against the cooling of evening.

A painted sign of frothing ale welcomed them just inside the town square. Roman hauled the cart toward the stable.

The tavern was a cobbled-together wood-and-thatch Cliché Golem, and Leah loved every inch of it. The roaring fire along one wall, the gnarled wooden tables, the bustier-clad serving wenches, the shadowed booths in three corners, the tired and cloaked parties huddled around the tables, and the timeworn innkeeper behind the bar, barking orders at the girls whose family resemblance was undeniable.

Her hands instinctively moved to arrange her dice or type *LFG* in the chat box that didn't exist.

"Try to look a little less like a fresh mark?" Mallery said, nudging Leah with an armor-copped elbow.

"But...tavern! Bartender. Wenches. Do I need to pose as a wench? I think I could totally wench it up."

The team settled into a corner booth, putting Leah in the corner to minimize the impact of her gawking.

Chapter Three:
So, You Meet in a Tavern

Shirin and Roman went to the bar, leaving Mallery to wrangle Leah.

The Senior Genrenaut pushed her cloak back and took a seat at a stool by the bar. "She's really geeked out about this place."

Roman shrugged. "It's to be expected. We all have our genre kryptonite. Remember the first time Mallery touched down in Rom-Com World?"

Mallery had grinned so hard that she had to take ibuprofen for the jaw pain.

Shirin nodded to the innkeeper, saying, "Hail and well met. My friends and I are looking for supper, drinks, and some rooms for the night." She kept the language strictly by-the-book. They didn't want to stand out, at least not until they'd found the breach.

The big man nodded, wiping his hands on his apron. "Of course, milady. My girls will see to your meal." He moved to a cabinet and found a set of keys. "Have ye need of one or two rooms?"

"Two, please. Adjoining."

"Of course." He picked out two keys and handed one to Shirin, the other to King. "Numbers three and five, on the right. It's three silvers each."

Shirin slid a handful of coins across the ale-stained bar. "Thank you, kind sir. And your name?"

"I'm Jalen, and my girls are Jara, Kara, Lara, and Mara, tallest to shortest," he said with the cadence of a rehearsed bit.

"A pleasure," Shirin said, slipping the key into an interior pouch.

They rejoined the junior team members. Leah was still every bit as excited, talking with her hands and nearly vibrating with excitement.

One of Jalen's daughters came by, Kara from what Shirin could tell, and dropped off five tankards of ale.

"Real fantasy ale!" Leah said. "Prepare for a three-page description of food and drink flavors."

"Please don't," Roman said.

"Please do," Mallery countered.

King huffed. "Focus, children."

Leah took a swig of her ale, then set it down and wiped her mouth with an *aaah*.

"How is it?" Shirin asked.

"Terrible! Notes of leather, lemon, and abject poverty. I love it."

Kara came back around, saying, "Milords and miladies, your rooms are ready."

After securing their gear in the rooms, they returned to the common area, where Shirin returned to the bar, looking for information.

"Jalen, my friends and I are just recently returned to Fallran. What news from the capital?"

The innkeep looked to the window, scanned the room, then looked down. "You've not heard, then."

"Clearly not," Shirin said. "What has happened?"

"The King is dead, and a sorcerer sits the throne. That purple in the air, that's his dark magic, it is; brought the dead back to life. Stick your head outside after nightfall and you'll see 'em, armored skeletons clanking around, purple fire in their eyes like demons."

Shirin put a hand over her mouth, feigning terror. That sounded like a plot thread if there ever was one.

"How can this be? Surely someone has taken up arms against this fiend," she said, following the script and keeping her word choice in-genre.

"That they did, milady. Theyn Lighthall and the heroes of the Battle of Haggen Gap laid siege to the castle with what remained of the royal army. But they…well. They lost. Theyn died; we know that. Haven't heard nothing else from the capital, save for the proclamations from them skeleton heralds the Night-Lord sends out."

"They don't come in here, do they?"

"No, they stay to the streets. But when they speak, it cuts through walls and cloth, right to your very soul. I had a headache for two days when the last one came through, I did. We're due for another one soon, so I've laid in more ale."

"A wise choice, good sir. Thank you for your time." Shirin left another silver on the bar and returned to their table, where Leah gawked at the obligatory legs of lamb.

"Being a vegetarian here is going to be tricky, isn't it?" she asked, looking around at the food on patron's plates.

"Very," Shirin said. "I packed you some protein bars, but they'll only last so long and are hardly appetizing."

"I've got some ideas for recipes that should work even on the road," Mallery said, proud.

Those two weren't exactly subtle. But it wasn't affecting their work, and Shirin found it amusing in a puppy-love kind of way. They certainly weren't as annoying as her teenage son Hassan and his girlfriend. If the relationship started to impact the mission, King would need to know. Maybe he already did, and wasn't saying anything. King consulted her on almost but not quite everything. As team lead, he was expected to have and keep some secrets, for the good of the team and the Genrenauts writ large.

"So, what's our next step?" Mallery asked. She was on her second ale, keeping pace with Roman. Despite her size, Mallery could hold her alcohol like a professional. One of the million skills you picked up as a social operator in the Genrenauts. It took Shirin a concerted effort to get a proper buzz on. Had for more than a decade.

King said, "Next step is, we wait here like a good adventuring party and see what comes our way."

"I know what comes next," Leah said. "Cloaked stranger with an invitation to adventure. Maybe we'll protect a caravan or roust goblins out of a mine. Then we step up and say, "Yes, good sir! We will be your heroes. And then it's off to fame and glory."

"Keep it together, newbie," King said. But he was smiling as he said it. "We're here for the breach, not for glory."

"Sorry, boss, but it's better that I get this all out tonight so I can be functional tomorrow. Also, we're all still slap-happy from three days of standby. Everyone needs to blow off some steam."

King narrowed his eyes but looked like he was accepting her argument. Shirin raised a toast.

"To not having to kill time in the ready room."

"I'll drink to that," Roman said. They polished off their meal and then went back to waiting. Which involved Leah geeking out about fantasy, Shirin reviewing her grimoire, and Roman playing with his knife. Mallery watched the crowd and King kept an eye on the door.

An hour later, their quest-giver arrived.

Chapter Four:
A Cloaked Stranger Approaches Your Group

Leah looked the man up and down. White, unassuming, average height. His cloak was threadbare, somewhere between gray and brown. From the corner of the booth, she didn't have a view of his boots, but she imagined they were just as shabby.

Sliding into their booth in the spot beside Shirin, the stranger leaned into the table and said, "You are here for a reason."

Leah wanted to take that as a straight line but let it stand. The story was starting, and she could hold her snarkiness in order to stay in character.

Probably.

Mostly.

"Who are you?" King asked.

"A friend. I speak on behalf of one who would see the glory of Fallran restored."

Mallery leaned forward, her voice conspiratorial. "And by *glory*, you mean..."

"An heir to the throne found, the Night-Lord deposed, the undead banished," the figure answered.

King gestured to an open seat. "We're listening."

"My patron is secluded in a farm outside of town, away from the patrols. We must join him now; he will explain." The cloaked figure stood and turned toward the door.

"How do we know this isn't a trap?" Shirin asked.

"There are five of you and but two of us. It takes courage to stand up to tyranny. If you haven't the stomach to risk the road at night, then our cause is doomed from the start."

"Nice linguistic ju—" Leah cut herself off before finishing with an out-of-genre word "—justification. It puts all of the responsibility on us."

King stood, hands open and to the side. "But as a show of trust, we will accompany you. If you but give us your name."

The cloaked man gave a slow nod. "Declan. Now we must go before the patrols return."

* * *

The group followed Declan out of the inn, raising some eyebrows as they went.

Their would-be quest-giver Declan retrieved a lantern from the front of the inn and led the group toward the outskirts of the town. The woods closed in once more, casting jagged shadows on the road. The night sky was purple-blue, not yet full night. Leah wasn't sure whether full dark would be black or purple, given the magical which-a-ma-whatsit from the Night-Lord. After all, when you name yourself after the night, you're probably going to want to make your mark on it. Right? Probably.

The road was narrow, only wide enough for one cart. The group carried their weapons with them, though Roman had only one pair of swords, not his entire mobile arsenal. Leah rested a hand on the pommel of her sword. An owl hooted behind her and she nearly jumped.

"Steady," King said.

Declan guided them off the road onto a side path. If they were walking into an ambush, no one from the town would be able to hear them. But knowing her team, it'd take a pretty large group to get the drop on them. Roman and King had besieged an entire base on their own not three months earlier. And this time, they had magic.

Leah leaned over to Mallery. "So, we just wait to get ambushed or not?"

"Not nearly that simple. I cast an aegis over the group as we left the inn. If anything comes toward us with an attempt to harm, we'll know."

The sound of a ringing bell filled Leah's ears, coming from everywhere and nowhere.

"Like that?" Leah asked.

Roman cross-drew his blades. "To arms!"

"What is it?" Declan asked, turning over his shoulder, moving the lamp as if trying to search for the danger.

"I cast a spell of warning," Mallery said. "Something's coming." Mallery shrugged the shield off her shoulder and looped her left arm through the straps. With her other hand, she held her necklace, a golden-winged eagle. "Felur watch over us. Let me be your shield made flesh; guide these heroes on their quest for righteousness."

The figurine glowed bright gold, and the light rippled out, flashing into six spheres, one surrounding each Genrenaut as well as their guide. The spheres faded from view, but Leah felt their presence, like the closeness of a friend. It was a feeling that said, "I've got your back."

Despite the imminent danger, Leah could not help but stare. Magic. No-shit, legit divine magic. "Whoa."

Mallery winked. "Stay with me. I'll protect you."

She could swoon. Instead, she drew her sword and began to sing "Another One Bites the Dust."

"Leah!" King said in a stage whisper.

"It's what came to mind!" she said, then continued with the song. For verisimilitude, used a bad Cockney accent.

King didn't have time to chide her further, since a squad of ten armored skeletons marched into view, coming from the pathway.

"To the farm!" Declan called, setting off at a run.

Roman shouted "Wait!" and followed the man.

Mallery sighed. "And we've already split the party."

Another cluster of skeletons walked onto the path from the other direction, boxing them in.

King lifted his voice and his sword as one. The blade came alive with the same golden light as Mallery's holy symbol. "Form up by the tree there. We fight together!"

Leah moved to Mallery's left, letting the woman's big shield cover her as well. She held her sword at the ready as the skeletons advanced. The first squadron of skeletons split into two ranks: the first wielded swords and shields; the second held halberds high, ready to crash down over the shoulders of their brethren. Deadren? Whatever the collective-buddy noun for skeletons was.

Mallery raised her mace high and called out, "In Felur's name, turn!" A bolt of golden light arced from Leah's mace and forked into five glowing lances. They shot out and disintegrated the first rank, their bones vanishing and armor clattering to the ground. Purple light seeped from the dead, fading into nothingness.

But the second rank took their place and continued to advance.

Behind them, Shirin raised her voice, speaking in what sounded like fakey Latin mixed with fantasyland gibberish. A wave of heat hit her from behind, and Leah sneaked a look over her shoulder, still covered by Mallery's shield. A beach ball–sized ball of flame shot forward from the gem atop Shirin's staff, detonating another three skeletons. That left only two ahead of them, but a full squad still behind.

"Look to the rear!" King said, stepping up to Leah's left. Standing in the center, she was covered on both sides, and felt way less intimidated by the glowing-eyed skeletons bearing down on her.

"Prepare to receive their charge. Watch the halberds!" he added as groups crashed together. Leah swung as hard as she could, her sword clanging off the shield of a skeleton. The halberds scraped and slid off of Mallery's shield, and the fight broke down into chaos.

Leah cut and parried and thrust as best as she could. But slashing/piercing weapons against skeletons? Not so good. Mallery fared far better with her mace, the weapon smashing through bones and metal both. And even cooler, the mace's glow left strobing afterimages as she swung, like dancing with glowsticks in the night.

A pair of skeletons pushed past King's defenses and knocked him to the ground. Leah stepped up, seeing her moment. She cut straight through one of the skeleton's necks, sending its head flying. She turned the follow-through into a parry to block another skeleton's halberd. The heavy blade bit deep into the soft dirt inches from King's knee. Leah grabbed the weapon's haft with her free hand, stomping and hacking the skeleton's arm off to the beat of her song.

This was fun. The dangerous and irresponsible kind of fun, like skydiving, or like what she assumed skydiving would feel like. It was biking without training wheels for the first time, driving without Mom in the passenger's seat. It was letting go, putting years of formal practice into lethal reality. It was terrifying and intoxicating at once.

She sang louder.

* * *

Roman was a blur, greatsword dancing between blade and shield and haft. He parried a skeleton's sword aside and then caved its face in with his heavy pommel.

"Come get some!" he added, jumping ahead to the obligatory *Army of Darkness* reference. It was the least out-of-genre one he could think of.

Declan waved his lantern at a skeleton, doing nothing. He'd be better off using the thing as a club in both hands. Roman fought a retreating battle, giving ground slowly, inevitably, but slow enough to give Shirin time for her spells.

"Igneo Uthia Magnus!" There was a flash of volcanic red light, and the ground in front of him cracked and tore open. Four of the skeletons lost their footing and were crushed flat as the ground rejoined like the closing maw of a blue whale. The sound of crushed bones brought a grin to Roman's face as he continued his dance of death, keeping the three remaining skeletons all busy.

A halberdier smashed through his defense and pushed him back. At the same time, one of the skeletons broke off from the pack and charged for the rest of the team.

"Flanker!" Roman called, lashing out with a kick to drive back the halberdier as his sword danced back and forth with the third skeleton.

"Got him!" King shouted from behind him, taking some of the weight off Roman's shoulders. He shoved the sword-and-shield skeleton back, then spun and beat the halberdier's weapon far off target. He spun the blade over his head and slashed down at the skeleton's collarbone. The magically animated soldier crumpled, dark light going out of its eyes.

"Last one back here!" Roman called, closing on the final skeleton.

"We could use some help!" Mallery called.

"Coming!" Shirin answered, leaving Roman with the last skeleton.

"You could just give up."

The creature's mouth opened wide, revealing a purple-tinged empty maw as it swung its shield at Roman.

"I tried." Roman ducked under the shield, then slashed up under the skeleton's helmet and cut the skull clean off.

He turned and saw the rest of the party facing down another squadron of skeletons. This group was led by a skeletal giant with a club as big as Roman was.

"Well, this is something new."

He grinned and then charged.

Chapter Five:
Giant Bone's Connected to the Fear Bone

Leah considered the pros and cons of the current situation.

On the one hand, giant skeleton. Not great for their team.

On the other hand, that meant giants were a thing! And that was awesome!

Which was about the extent of time Leah had to spare on the giant before the rank of skeletons hit them, turning the loose lines into a straight-up mob.

She tried to stick close to Mallery, but when two skeletons knocked the comedienne back and down to the ground, Leah jumped back and turned, smashing a skeleton's leg into two pieces, sending it tumbling.

"Coming!" Shirin said somewhere behind their group.

Good. Help is on the way, she thought.

First, the other skeleton. "Hey, bucko! Forget about me?"

The construct turned, glowing eyes looking confused, like "What did you say?"

But the confusion was all she needed. She thrust the sword straight through the skeleton's eye socket. Her blade cracked through bone and then went *tink* on the other end, stopped by the helm.

She twisted her grip and wrenched forward, pulling the skeleton to the ground by her feet. She was hoping for a decapitation, but she'd take what she could get.

Leah offered a hand to Mallery. The woman's armor meant she nearly pulled Leah off her feet as she came up to a knee.

"Thanks. Back to back?"

"Got it."

They shuffle-stepped back to the mob, covering one another. King was being overwhelmed; five skeletons surrounded him, hacking at his shining armor.

"With you!" Leah stepped up, hacking and slashing to knock aside one skeleton's weapons and clear a way. Two turned to face her, and she took their tempo to crush one's arm, and then swung at the other's neck with a back-edge cut.

Leah switched to "Hit Me with Your Best Shot" as she tried to pull the attention off King. Mallery joined Leah, pushing the skeletons back.

Off to her right, Roman charged into view, banging his sword on his armor and yelling at the giant.

King got to his feet, and the three of them formed up to face the skeletons.

They set a tree as their anchor on one side to prevent flanking. Mallery's mace swung like a wrecking ball, and King spun his sword in devastating arcs and turns. Leah, in the middle, occupied herself with keeping as many of the skeletons busy as she could, knocking aside weapons, distracting them with the song, as well as some sneaky trips and kicks along the way.

Next time, I'm bringing a hammer, too, Leah thought as her sword *chink*ed and deflected off skeletal armor and bone. It was like trying to break apart a ten-pound chunk of ice with a butter knife—you'll get there eventually, but there were so many better ways to do the job.

"Step back!" Shirin said from behind them. Leah felt the wind pick up, and then a ghostly green foot stomped down from the canopy and crushed half of the remaining skeletons.

"Gadzooks!" Leah shouted as the team advanced on the remaining monsters. Once she got into the swing of things, Fantasy World lingo was just as fun as the rest of it.

Once the grunts were dispatched, the team moved to help Roman, who was playing David-and-Goliath with the giant skeleton, dodging its massive swings and working the skeleton's tibia like a woodcutter with a hand axe.

Together, they surrounded the giant and kept it distracted while Roman climbed the monster's back and unscrewed the thing's head like a lightbulb. A giant, terrifying lightbulb.

The giant's head popped off with a crack, and then the purple light went out of its eyes, and the thing collapsed to the ground in a heap.

Roman crushed the bones beneath him as he landed, then held the skull aloft, grinning. "This one is going in the trophy room."

King nodded, as if to say, "I'll allow it."

"Declan, are you still there?" Mallery asked into the darkness of the woods.

A moment later, a light emerged from the brush, followed by their guide. "Are they gone?"

"Aye," Shirin said. "It is just us and the owls."

"Thank Felur for that. But now I know two very important things. First, you are truly heroes capable of facing this task. And second, the Night-Lord may already be aware of our plan. Quickly, to the cabin!"

* * *

The cabin was homely and homey both, a bit cluttered but entirely plain. The furniture looked carved by the same hand that had shaped the logs of the walls. Mallery imagined the craftsperson that had made the home, the time it must have taken to build an entire house by hand.

But inside, there was only one figure, robed and hunched, prodding at a low fire with a poker.

"I've brought them, Master Ioseph," Declan said as he stepped inside.

The wizard turned, the firelight playing across his craggy skin and hooked nose. He had ruddy skin that on Earth would have indicated Middle-Eastern heritage. "Inside, quickly. The wards are weakened with the door open."

Declan closed the door behind them as they took their seats. "This is Ioseph Bluethorn, Court Magician, Keeper of the Azure Soul, and companion of the late Theyn Lighthall."

The Wizard snorted derisively. "Ioseph will do. Not much of the rest of that means anything anymore. The Company is shattered, our hero fallen. What matters is what we do next."

King stepped forward. "I'm called Kane. My companions and I would see the Night-Lord deposed and peace returned to Fallran. But given that we were just assaulted by twenty skeletons on the open road, it looks like that will be no small task. What do you propose?"

"First, you must know what transpired. The tale of the rise and fall of Theyn Lighthall. For only in knowing his doom can you understand the fate that plagues Fallran."

Leah jammed Mallery with a playful elbow to the ribs. "Time for exposition," she whispered.

Mallery shushed the junior Genrenaut but didn't hold back the smile. She'd been thinking more or less the same thing. Most any wizard you met had several hours of tales and legends they were desperate to share, like when you got a choice role but weren't allowed to announce it until finally, the right people came along and you could spill your guts.

Ioseph reached deep into his robes and drew out a handful of sparkling golden dust. He tossed it into the fire, which crackled and burst, creating a circular field of shimmering gold. It faded to black, then shifted and created a 3-D holographic image as Ioseph began to speak.

Leah looked to Mallery, gesturing to the magical hologram. Mallery smiled, and squeezed Leah's hand.

"Centuries ago, when the Daineg dynasty was founded, my great-grand-predecessor granted the first king the gift of a prophecy."

The field showed a storybook image, like high-quality papercuts but animated. Mallery had spent years studying magic off and on for work, had crafted and called a great deal of it herself. But it never ceased to amaze. When witnessing magic, she couldn't help but become five again, watching fireworks from her parents' van for the first time.

"The prophecy stated that a scion of the dynasty would be its undoing. And so it has been that each generation, the children of the Fallran have distrusted one another, the heir always wary of his siblings. Some Kings exiled their younger children, some sent them on impossible quests, others managed to only have one child, gambling that their heir would live to continue the line."

The field showed short vignettes of each generation, the bold knights battling dragons and rescuing imperiled nobles, the exiled heirs living out their years in waiting in small cottages and mountain hermitages, and more.

The magical holograph transitioned into a great battlefield, pikes and war machines in rows upon rows. Mallery was reminded of the snowflake papercuts where you cut and then unfolded an entire banner of identical shapes.

"Fifteen years ago, during the war against the Akkara Legions, King Uros of Fallran fell in love with a Serani sorceress and broke his wedding vows. He returned home, ashamed. Less than a year later, two children were born to the King of Fallran, younger brothers to Crown Prince Eos."

The hologram showed two figures, back to back, one bright, one dark. "One child, Armand, was born to Queen Valari. The other was the child of the Serani sorceress, Lucenne. As the King's advisor, I reached out to the sorceress and implored her to never bring the boy back to Fallran. He was to be well taken care of, so long as they did not come to our shores."

This much she knew from the surveillance records Preeti and the rest of the teams maintained. But she had a feeling there were more details in store.

A tall figure rushed through the woods, a small bundle under one arm.

"As a precaution, Prince Theyn was spirited away by a trusted member of the royal guard and raised in seclusion."

The magical field showed a boy of maybe ten years old swinging a sword still too big for him at a tree. Beside him, a broad-shouldered man. And beside him, a papercut version of Ioseph himself.

"I visited the boy often, training him in secret so that he could succeed the throne if anything happened to Prince Eos. Or if Lucenne and her child sought vengeance."

"Wasn't the queen even a bit upset that the king cheated on her?" Leah asked.

The Wizard looked up. "The King and Queen keep their own counsel. It is not for us to question."

We'll see about that, Mallery thought. *Best file that away as a plot thread to pick up if needed.*

"Please, continue," King said.

"Barely six months ago," Ioseph said, "the Night-Lord came to the shores of Fallran, leading an army of the undead clad in Serani colors."

The spell conjured up roiling seas and a fleet flying dark flags. Rows of armored skeletons stomped across the beach. The field panned to reveal the shining forces of Fallran, all polished armor and chivalric bluster.

"He met the armies of Fallran on the fields of battle and routed them as if they were children playing with wooden swords.

"I quit the field and returned to Prince Theyn. His time had come. While the undead army made its way to Fallran castle, the prince and his teacher Nolan set out to seek a weapon that could defeat the Night-Lord. The fabled Sun-sword."

The magic showed a young hero lifting a magical sword to the sky. It caught the sun and bathed the vision in golden light.

Chosen One prince raised in secret, magic weapon. So far, this is all going by the script, Mallery thought. But they wouldn't be here if it had ended according to plan.

"But even with the Sun-sword, Prince Theyn could not best the Night-Lord. The prince fell, and our fellowship scattered to the four winds as the Night-Lord consolidated his control over the countryside."

The magical vision showed a map of Fallran, beige parchment turning purple shade by shade as Ioseph finished his story.

Mallery said, "So, if Theyn and the Sun-sword couldn't defeat the Night-Lord, how will we?"

Ioseph's expression darkened. "Theyn was not able to use the Sun-sword to destroy the Deathstone, which turns light into necromantic energy. The Deathstone was once the Hopestone, an ancient artifact of immense power. Now turned, it is the reason the sunlight runs purple now across the kingdom of Fallran."

"The same power that animates the dead," Roman added.

The Wizard nodded.

"Is there another way to destroy the Deathstone?" Leah asked.

"That, my new friends, is what we must find. We will need to search far and wide. Xan'De, one of my former companions, hails from far beyond the sea and knows of many secrets beyond my ken. It is my hope that he will know of something that can best the Deathstone or negate its power long enough to cast down the Night-Lord."

Leah's face scrunched up in frustration. "Are you saying the answer to overthrowing the Night-Lord is 'Let's ask my friend'?"

Ioseph's face tightened into a sour mass of wrinkles. Leah had gone out of genre. *It must be hard to keep to the made-up fantasy dialect when her internal monologue was squeezing at the cheesy perfection of everything around her,* Mallery thought. *I mean, I still have a hard time keeping a straight face here, even after a half-dozen visits.*

She jumped in for the save. "You said Xan'De might know another way we could destroy the Deathstone?"

The wizard picked right back up, like a skipped record finding its place again. "If I knew how to best the Deathstone, I would have done so already. And Theyn would still be among the living. I have given you all the hope and knowledge I have to give. Xan'De and his people, the Matok, may be our best hope, unless one of you happens to know more of artifacts than I."

Shirin piped up. "I may have a way to expedite our search. But I will need to consult my notes. And the spell required may be beyond my capability to cast alone."

The wizard's demeanor brightened. "Truly, you could find an answer?"

"Perhaps. I have traveled across these lands many years and bear writings of rituals from far off." She turned and set her satchel on a desk, producing a stack of ten different tomes. "The enchantment of holding does not also include one of organization. This may take some time."

Declan spoke up. "Please, sit, my friends. There are bedrolls enough for all."

"We have rooms back in the town," Leah said.

King gave Leah the "talk less" look. "And we can return to them in the morning. Shirin, let us try your divination method."

* * *

Shirin reveled in having Ioseph's assistance.

For the most part. Every wizard had their own way of doing things, so for the first hour, they were like cranky odd-couple roommates.

They spent several hours on ritual auguries, using components from his stash and from her mobile apothecary's kit.

The first working was a scrying spell—to learn the purpose and power of the Deathstone. This spell she could have done on her own, but Ioseph's help let them pierce the shroud of protection the Night-Lord's magic provided.

It was as Ioseph had said—the Hopestone had been corrupted. But now she had a working vision and arcane knowledge of how it was corrupted, and to what end.

After the first working, the rest of the team went to bed, with Declan standing first watch.

The next step was to divine the Deathstone's weaknesses. That was far harder. The shroud the Night-Lord had placed over the Hopestone hid it from easy magical analysis. The stone had been made centuries earlier, during the founding of Fallran. If it could not be purified, it would have to be destroyed.

Three hours, five attempts, and a small fortune of magical components later, they had a partial answer, nothing more. Even with Ioseph's help.

The spell's answer was blissfully clear, if not encouraging: *What was once a beacon of hope can never be purified.*

Which meant that they had to destroy the Deathstone. And that'd leave Fallran without its greatest magical protection. They'd close out one broken story and open up the possibility of any number of other dangers. Fallran's storied fate would continue. Another Dark Lord, another immortal threat. And another mission for the Genrenauts.

Ioseph was crestfallen, slumping from exhaustion. And probably disappointment. He was a donor figure that had failed in his role and yet lived to tell the tale.

He was Gandalf if Gondor had already fallen, Dumbledore facing a fascist wizard state under Voldemort.

"Then the stone cannot be saved," he said. "It was pointless to hope, perhaps."

Shirin put her hand over Ioseph's, trying to give comfort. "Hope is never pointless. But sometimes it takes an unexpected shape."

She stood, stretching to work out the kinks in her back from hunching over for hours in candlelight. "This last divination requires that I call on a pact made long ago. I must consult alone, for my source is capricious and does not care for company."

In reality, she was calling in to Preeti for help.

Ioseph nodded. "Of course. Every wizard has their secrets."

"Wish me luck. If the fates are with us, I will have an answer by morning."

She walked out into the night, purple glow dimming the weaker stars. She walked to the edge of the woods, set down a spell of protection, and then activated her comm unit back to Earth Prime.

"Preeti, you still there?"

No answer. Preeti may have gone home for the night, but someone should be there. Maybe it was interference. She called again. Nothing.

She pulled out the comm unit and gave it a once-over. She turned it off and then on again, and tried once more.

This time, she got crackling and the buzz of interference. The damned dimensional storms again. Whatever had been escalating dimensional disturbance over the last year was getting worse, not better. There might come a time, if the storms didn't let up, that the High Council would pull back, restrict deployment even more. There were only so many ships available, and training new Genrenauts took time, even with smart candidates like Leah.

A few minutes later, on her seventeenth try, she got through.

"Hello?" came Preeti's voice through the crackling.

"Mid-Atlantic Actual, this is Mid-Atlantic 3. Do you copy?"

"I copy, Mid-Atlantic 3. What's your status?"

"We've deployed and found the breach. The Chosen One and his fellowship failed; golden boy bought it in the tower with the Night-Lord by all accounts. I need you to run a search through the Artifact database. We need something to destroy an unbreakable gem."

"The Hopestone?" Preeti asked.

"Just so. It's been corrupted."

"That's going to… Give me a few minutes. But stay on the line. I don't know if I'll be able to pick up the signal again if we lose it now."

Shirin stayed on the line, moving around her protective circle to try to maintain the signal. Nothing had pinged her magical sensors, but random encounters were just that.

Minutes later, Preeti had some answers. "Okay, I've got three good candidates. The Wand of Necessity can do whatever you need it to do, but our best records place it on the other side of the world. It'd be hard to get there and back in time. There's also the Shilelagh of Wall Removal, which can knock down any wall or barrier."

"That's close but might not work. What's your number three?"

"The Hammer of K'gon. Made to be able to destroy anything, including the War-Blooms of the Fungal Lords."

"Send me the file; I think we've got a winner. And thank you."

"How's it going?" Preeti's voice had a thread of worry, and something else Shirin couldn't quite place.

"Deploying late will make this harder, but we've got a full team and a fantasy-loving newbie looking to prove herself. We'll do fine."

When in doubt, allay fears and put on a good face. Worked for parenting, worked for the Genrenauts.

Hopefully.

She dropped the field of protection and returned to the cabin, greeted by Ioseph, who replaced the wards on the building. She spent the rest of the night transcribing the file and catching a few winks to ensure she could function reasonably well the next day. Fortunately, she didn't need as much sleep as she once had. Getting older didn't have too many benefits, but that was one of them.

The Genrenauts woke one by one, and as Declan and Roman made breakfast, she gave them the answer they needed to continue the story.

"Four millennia ago, there was a dwarf named K'gon, legendary as a warrior and king," Shirin said.

"The latter tends to require the former," Ioseph added.

"Just so. He built great cities, supported artisans and craftspeople. But most of all, his Hammer is rumored to be able to shatter any object in existence. He used the Hammer to crack the gates of the underworld so that his people could wage war on the demon realms directly. There's more, but the 'shatter any object in existence' is the relevant part for our purposes."

Shirin realized she was rambling. She rubbed her temples and reached for another pot of tea.

"Sounds great! Where do we find it?" Leah asked.

"That's the problem. The Hammer was lost three hundred years ago when the Fungal Lords marched on the dwarven kingdoms. To get to the Hammer, we have to go deeper into the under-roads than even the dwarves will go."

"A perilous task, but the Hammer will be a match for the Deathstone," Ioseph said.

King took charge. "Leah, you head for the Hammer with Roman and Mallery. Shirin and I will collect the other companions. Time is of the essence. We'll meet back here and then find a way into Fallran castle."

Declan stepped forward. "That, I can provide. I moved between the castle and the countryside at Their Majesties' whim. The secret ways are known to me, and I wager that the Night-Lord has not bothered to find them all. Fallran the First was quite thorough."

"Then we have a plan. Ioseph, can you accompany Shirin and me? I'm sure your companions would be more trusting if they saw you among us."

Plus, it wouldn't hurt to have an arch-mage with them, Shirin thought.

The wizard leaned on his staff, looking as tired as Shirin felt. "I have another task, I'm afraid. I must gather the remnants of the royal army." Ioseph took a sapphire-set ring from his finger, then raised it to his lips and whispered. Pale gold light wrapped around the ring and snapped into place, leaving a glowing rune on the sapphire. He passed the ring to Roman. "Wear this, and the companions will know you come with my blessing and protection."

And with that, they were off. They returned to the tavern to reclaim their gear, and then Shirin and King pulled a tag team to haggle a local rancher down on five horses.

Mounted, the team paused at the crossroads that divided the path to the split-level dwarven kingdom of Karn-Du and the roads to the edges of the kingdom. Ioseph assumed that the remaining members of the fellowship would be watching and waiting. They had towns marked on their maps, ready to reassemble the heroes of Fallran.

* * *

King addressed Leah and the rest of the team, light reflecting off his polished armor. He looked every bit the champion.

No longer in the presence of witnesses, King dispensed with Fantasy World language. "We have just over six weeks to do all of this. No side quests unless absolutely necessary. Got it? Use the communicators to stay in touch. I can use messenger spirits if the comms fail, but only as needed."

"This is too cool," Leah said. "Also, about side quests. They're so much fun. Is it okay if we pick up some quirky companions along the way?" Leah asked, trying to let the joke into her voice even as she wanted it to be a real request.

"I'm not going to bother answering those questions. Be safe, and ride fast." King turned and ordered his horse to take off. Shirin followed, leaving Leah, Roman, and Mallery to start off on the path leading into the mountains.

"You're fighting well, but don't forget your role," Mallery said. "If you're the bard, the story expects you to be toward the back of the line of battle, singing songs of prowess or protection."

"I can fight just fine from the front."

This is a job, she reminded herself. *We all play our role.*

"But speaking of songs." She reached for her lute. "I feel like this is the perfect time for some traveling music."

Leah started in on the Peter Jackson film version of "The Road Goes Ever On." She used the song to steady her nerves at not actually being anything resembling confident on a horse. Luckily, King had given her the horse equivalent of Shaggy from *Scooby-Doo*. Totally laid-back and incredibly amenable.

Mallery joined in the song, threading in and out with harmonies. Roman didn't sing, but he did smile.

And so they rode toward the horizon, where purple-tinged clouds met hazy white-tipped peaks. Her heart soared with confidence and excitement. Maybe it was the view, and maybe it was her bard magic already kicking in.

Either way, I'm on an epic fantasy quest. How freaking amazing is this? she thought, marveling.

She sang her heart out, moving from song to song like a Renaissance jukebox stuck on Optimism Shuffle.

Chapter Six:
Heroic Travel Montage, Part One

There's a reason that fantasy novels take the travel sequences in montage or tiny snippets.

Most of cross-country travel is equally boring and exhausting.

Leah, Mallery, and Roman rode for a few hours, took a break to eat some cheese and bread, then rode for another four hours, until they stopped to make camp before the sun set.

Leah's thighs and butt were already sore by the first stop, and practically numb when they stopped to make camp.

"Ow. Ow. Ow. I was not prepared. No amount of pony rides at county fairs could have prepared me for this. Also, this really should have been a part of my training."

Roman said. "Sorry, it was farther down the priority list. We don't keep horses in HQ anymore. Have to visit a ranch down the road."

"Think of it this way," Mallery said. "Chances are, by the time we're done, you won't need that training, and you'll have saved so much time! Plus, this way, you get to talk and see the sights while you learn."

Roman brought them back on-mission. "Ioseph said the skeletons are the most dangerous at twilight, when the sun's light turns dark, closer to the Deathstone's natural shade."

Leah stopped her already-futile attempts to assemble her super-not-modern tent. "But that's just because of the refraction of the light; how does that have anything to do with magic?"

Roman looked at the sun and shrugged. "Hell if I know. It's magic. Never got rated on the stuff. Genre expectations say that the big burly warrior doesn't tend to get to be the mage, so I never really bothered."

The veteran hero stretched, cracking joints as he shook out the day's ride. "Plus, we've already faced them at dusk. If they're easier to take out any other time, then that makes our job much easier."

"So, how far to the dwarven lands?" Leah asked.

Mallery jumped in. "Most of a week. We have the money to pay for one fresh set of horses, assuming we get good value for these at Dougal at the halfway point. And I can help make sure of that. My blessings can detect lies. And I like a good haggling."

"A week to dwarf-land, then what?"

Roman walked over to fix Leah's knot. But then he left her to finish the job on her own. "We get at most two weeks to find the Hammer, then three weeks to get back, assemble the army, and take down the Night-Lord."

"Is six weeks really long enough for an entire epic fantasy trilogy?" Leah asked.

Mallery waved her hand in the semi-universal sign of *maybe*. "With the setup we have, I wonder if it's more like we're coming in at the start of book two. And we've done this before. Time-wise, most of what we do here ends up being riding across the countryside, balancing between haste and not killing the horses." Mallery's horse neighed, as if to punctuate her point. "Until things start ramping up, our most common enemy will be boredom. And with you along, we have nothing to fear from that."

Leah winked at Mallery. "One jester, no waiting." The benefit of being teamed up with Roman is that the action hero DGAF when it came to Mallery and her flirting. Roman was like Mallery's big brother. Or big little brother. Either way, he was chill.

Once they were set up for the night, just out of sight of the road, Roman produced a pot. "Find some water. It's time for stew."

"Stew!" Leah was happy to not have to contain her voice. "I love it. It makes no sense to make stew on the road, but here we are."

She stopped and looked around, turning a three-sixty. "Any idea of where the river is?"

Mallery waved deeper into the forest. "Should be about ten minutes this way. I'll go with you."

Leah walked out the soreness, if slowly. Mallery wasn't too much faster, clanking along with her armor.

"How heavy is that stuff?" she asked.

"Not very. It's elven-made, so it weighs as much as aluminum." She removed a glove and held out her sleeve. Leah slipped a hand into the sleeve and checked the heft of the mail. It was super-light.

"Very nice. So, how much time would it reasonably take to bring firewood?" Leah asked, picking up small branches here and there, then stopping at one larger log section.

"Half an hour. We'll need enough to help Roman start the fire, then more to keep it going throughout the night."

"So, is this where we sneak some actual alone time, or does that come later?"

Mallery's grin was wry. "A little of column A, a lot of column B. Let's work first, then play."

"Speaking of play, you said they made you train bard too, right?"

"Seemed a natural pairing. Not as natural as for you."

"Yeah, but I can't play instruments for crap. And I'm not sure stand-up fits in-genre here."

"Not quite the same, but give it a shot. Bards and Jesters are known for their biting wit here; give it a try and see how the magic of this world enhances it. But you will want to get passable with the lute." Mallery gestured downhill. "Let's head this way."

Leah hurried as best as she could, following the "Clean your plate and you get dessert faster" approach.

* * *

Thanks to the power of story logic, the stew cooked in an hour, somehow. Mallery and Leah went out for more firewood-collecting and more woodlands-necking, returning with two more armfuls of solid logs for an overnight fire.

"You take first watch. Nothing ever happens during first watch. It's always second or last watch." Roman rewrapped his cloak as a pillow. "If anything does come up, just kick the tents. I've got some books in my bag, if you like. Or maybe practice some songs from before the nineteenth century."

Leah waved the lute around like it was made of ick. "I'm not really much of a balladeer."

"You are now." Roman threw a smile, then slipped into his tent and closed the flap. "Good night."

Mallery had decided to take last watch, so she stayed up for only a few minutes before kissing Leah good night.

After their diversion in the woods and a goodnight kiss like that, Leah was a lot less grumpy about being sore from riding all day for the next few weeks.

Left to her own devices, Leah built herself a stack of books, ballads and histories, travelogues and more. A few were the same books she'd read as genre orientation (*A Complete History of Fallran*, an in-world text, and the Earth-Prime-based *The Tough Genrenauts' Guide to Fantasyland*, with apologies to Diana Wynne Jones).

Leah had never been much for reading music, but she had a decent ear. Thankfully, the book of ballads was Earth Prime–based, so each ballad had a header giving the tune. No fewer than fifteen of the ballads were set to the tune she knew as "Greensleeves," another five to "Whiskey in the Jar," and so on. Leah was thankful for the Irish-American community back home and her friends growing up that had been obsessive fans of the Chieftains.

Several times, while practicing a song, her lute started to glow, wisps of light rolling off the strings. While playing a battle song, her fingers grew stronger, able to hold down the strings with ease and far less pain. During a song about an old swordsman and his skill, her fingers moved through the chords almost without her having to think about it, her hands moving with greater speed and confidence.

Magic. She was doing magic. It wasn't as flashy as shooting fireballs or raising the dead, but it was a good start. An amazing start. She'd dreamed about what magic would feel like, what she'd do if she got to go off to Hogwarts or really cast spells from a scroll.

The reality of it was the same and different all at once. She felt the power deep inside, like a groundswell of emotion, the same as when she nailed a skit or won a hard-fought bout in a fencing tournament. It was triumph given form to make change in the world.

Ecstatic, Leah opened a fresh notebook and started writing, slowed by the pen and ink but only just. She copied song titles and effects, checking them against the official bardic text from HQ, fabricated to look like an in-world journal of a famous bard.

She compiled a short list of ten songs that were Council-approved as fitting in this region, and spent the rest of her shift transcribing the lyrics and rehearsing her way through in a soft voice, one eye always scanning the woods around them.

The owls and birds and various sounds of the forest accompanied her. It was Fantasy World forest, which ended up sounding a lot like the meditation/relaxation tapes her aunt Mei listened to whenever they'd go to her house for New Year's.

Eventually, Roman crawled out of the tent and set about arranging his arsenal like Jayne in "House of Gold," weapons laid out in order of size and use next to him around the camp.

"You ready for *So You Think You Can Belt*?" he asked as Leah put away her books.

"I did magic! At least, it better have been magic, or else I'm going to ask what kind of mushrooms you put in that stew. I found three songs so far where the magic kicks in like it's supposed to.

"That's great," he said. "Keep practicing."

"I mean, I'm not going to win any bardic competitions, but it should be good enough for Fallran pop radio. Can Shirin enchant me an auto-tune necklace or something for later on?"

Roman chuckled and shooed Leah off to bed. "Long day tomorrow. If we've got time, maybe some sparring in there to stay fresh?"

Leah rubbed her thighs, still sore from riding. "Only if we do hip openers first."

"Got it. Yoga, then fencing."

And so Leah slipped into her tiny tent, the dark canvas all of twelve inches above her head, and dreamed gloriously silly Fantasy World dreams of heroism and saving the world. They smashed together Jones, Pratchett, Hobb, Tolkien, and more into a magical stew of joy.

Chapter Seven:
Putting the Band Back Together

King and Shirin made good time the first day on the road to the city of Ag'ra, where Ioseph had said they'd be likely to find Xan'De, the Matok warrior-mystic. Ag'ra was a port town and a crossroads. Officially a free city, it was closely allied with Fallran, but ancient magics kept its walls sacrosanct. It was unlikely the Night-Lord would move on Ag'ra without consolidating his hold on Fallran first.

King and Shirin had ridden these roads and roads just like them many times over the years. It was dangerous to split the party, but there was a comfort in being back with his oldest partner on the team. They knew each other well enough they barely had to talk if they didn't feel like it.

As they set off the second morning, Shirin felt like it. "It really is quite fun to see Leah having such a good time on a mission. She hasn't been that excited since Ahura-3."

"As long as she keeps her head on her shoulders and lets her knowledge serve her and not distract her, she'll do fine."

"We all have our loves. Leah tells me that you had some puppy-face going on when the two of you walked into Henriksen's precinct.

"That's nostalgia more than fannishness."

"You say *potato*, I say *pommes frites*."

King's holy symbol glowed in warning, beaming straight into his eyes. "Trouble coming." He held the holy symbol and concentrated on an incantation.

King was pragmatic about gods in genre worlds. Back home, he was a One-God kind of man like his mother raised him, but here, there were many gods, and they were demonstrably real. He'd had several long talks with the Genrenauts interfaith chaplain not long after joining up. These worlds were part of the multiverse, and if God had made one universe, why not others? So, prayers here were the same as prayers there; it's just that there was a different set of lenses, a filtering system. And in Fantasy World, God's Will made itself very clear.

Certainty fell upon him like a summer rainfall, crisp and sudden. *Skeletons.*

"There's a patrol coming. We should get off the road."

Nudging the horses into the woods without a path, they ventured just far enough into the brush and tree cover to be hidden, positioning themselves on the eastern side of the road to minimize the glint of sunlight on their armor, and they waited.

Sure enough, two minutes later, a skeleton troupe clanked by, coming down the road the other direction. King counted twenty spearmen led by a mounted skeleton warrior in full plate.

Shirin petted her horse's hair. Her other hand held tight to her staff. Once they'd passed, Shirin's horse got restless, but they waited still.

The sense of danger dimmed, and they returned to the empty road.

Shirin squinted to make sure the skeletons were out of sight. "Do you think they were coming from Ag'ra?"

"Not likely. There's probably an outpost or garrison in Chandler's Crossing."

They encountered another two patrols over the course of the day, one coming from the Crossing, and one turning northwest toward Weller's Well at the Y-juncture that split off toward Shady Grove.

The second time, they were nearly found out. King's horse, tired from carrying the weight of a large man in full armor, got spooked by one of the skeleton's screams and tried to break for the deep woods. King nearly dropped off the horse, he was hauling back on the reins so hard. His holy symbol warned him of greater danger, so he walked the steed a bit farther into the forest, signaling Shirin with his sword.

Even deep into the brush, King saw the blackened metal, bleached bone, and glowing purple eyes of a skeleton. It had followed them into the woods. But the undead soldier's commander called it back, and the thing returned to the road.

Shirin looked worried when they reunited. "Three patrols in one day? That's some army."

"All the more reason to pass in secret. If the Night-Lord gets word of a gathering force, he'll recall his patrols to repel the siege."

"We will need Ioseph to re-form the army, then. Unless we can pull a Cut-off-the-Head move with the Night-Lord."

"We'll need to thread the needle on this one, to be sure. The companions will help set us on the right path, but I'm thinking we may need to adjust the plan and pull a reversal somewhere. Something to discuss with the others when we check in."

They passed the rest of the day without incident, camping off the road just under a day's ride from Chandler's Crossing. Then another two days to Ag'ra and the first of their errant heroes.

* * *

Leah and company ran into trouble first thing the following morning.

Roman went ahead to scout, while Leah and Mallery rode side by side and talked.

Leah picked up her new favorite-least-favorite topic of conversation: music. "I knew that everyone used 'Greensleeves' as a tune, but this is kind of ridiculous. I hope you and Roman like that song."

"Used to. But it's fine. The story has its expectations. We give the story what it wants, feed into the narrative inertia. Whenever possible, we lean into expectations instead of swimming upstream against them. And here, the story world expects 'Greensleeves' and faux-Irish folk songs and poetry. Stick with that and you've got us covered. The same way the blessings I gain through Felur are Vancian magic that's distinct but only sort of from the arcane spells that Shirin uses. I swear, almost a third of our respective spell selections end up doing the same thing."

Roman came tearing over a hill at a full gallop. He waved them off the road, his other hand on the reins. She could see the worry on his face from half a football field away.

They jumped off their horses and led the steeds into the woods. Roman slowed and joined them, urging them even farther back from the road.

"A skeleton patrol. Ten strong, with shadow wolf steeds and some kind of zombie knight as their leader. They've got captives, coming this way at a forced march."

They tied their horses to an old-growth tree and crept back toward the road, hiding behind shrubbery while Leah kept a lid on the wealth of Monty

Python references that popped into her mind's eye like a set of video game dialogue options.

The skeletons and their dark mounts came into view, hungry slinky things that looked equal parts panther, wolf, and smoke. At their head rode a partially decayed figure in a polished version of the hammered armor the skeletons wore. Its eyes showed intelligence, and Leah caught it barking orders, some kind of threat lobbed at the captives.

Humans, halflings, and some dwarves were mixed in the crowd of the undead squadron. All of the captives were ragged, clothes tattered, some bloodied. They were chained ankle to ankle and pulled carts laden with iron ingots.

"Aren't we going to do something about this?" Leah whispered. "One of them could be a hero in the making or have key information or something. That's how it always goes with these subplots."

"King said no subplots," Roman said. "And ten shadow wolf-mounted skeletons is too many to take, even with surprise."

Leah studied Mallery's face as the comedienne-cleric considered. "I have a spell that might be able to help balance the odds, but it's still too dangerous. And even if we take out the skeletons, then we'd have to escort the prisoners back to safety. And there's a garrison in every town, it looks like. I don't like it. This isn't our moment."

"Are we seriously not going to do anything?" Leah asked. "What kind of crap heroes does that make us?"

Mallery lowered her voice, talking slower. This was her reasoning voice. "We're not the heroes. We're the story doctors. And if we get bogged down here, we'll never get to the Hammer, never set up the story so the heroes can triumph. We're trying to finish an epic conflict, not fight a guerrilla war."

"This is bullshit," Leah said, her voice too loud for the situation.

Roman put a steadying hand on her shoulder. With the touch, she realized that she was shaking with anger. "Keep your eyes on the prize."

Leah bit her lip as the skeletons and their captives passed, the carts rolling along the road. Leah heard a soft, high voice singing, the others echoing in call-and-response form.

Every single fiber of her raised-on-heroic-fantasy being wanted to burst from the brush, draw her sword, and bring swift justice to the skeletons, to be a hero and set the poor citizens free.

But that wasn't her job. Her job was to fix the story, not right every little wrong in the entire world.

But was that really enough? If you force someone to work with shoddy equipment and they get hurt every week, eventually, shouldn't you fix the tool instead of sending them to the doctor? She'd spent the last several months playing the doctor, applying spot fixes along with the team, keeping to the shadows. Help the real hero, delay the problems until the real hero came back.

This world was short on heroes in a big way. The breach had been allowed to fester, and now the problem was bigger than a simple fix.

King kept telling her to take the initiative more, to find her own style. The fantasy genre responded to bold action, to big gestures, and to the power of one person to make a difference.

It was time to step up and answer the call.

"Fuck it." Leah stepped out of the brush, lute in hand.

"Leah!" Mallery called in a stage whisper.

Leah ignored it and played a power chord, or as much of one as a lute could handle.

"Hey, skeleton warriors! Let me sing you the song of my people!"

Mallery brushed the shrubbery aside and took up a spot next to Leah.

"That was incredibly reckless. We're way outmatched here. Stick with me, and we'll do our best."

On her left, Leah saw Roman moving through the brush, doubtless going around to flank. Roman would be their ace in the hole.

Which left her and Mallery facing down ten skeletons on shadow wolves.

"We just need to break some of the prisoners free, and they'll cause a bunch of chaos. Now would be a good time to even the odds."

Mallery grasped her holy symbol, holding it forward and praying in a strong, clear voice.

"Felur of mighty grace, turn your bright light upon us to scatter darkness and crush the foes of life."

She held her mace up high. It turned first into a torch, covered in magical light, then became a tiny sun, light too bright to look at directly. She swung the mace forward, and the light lashed out, going to war with the sickly purple light that animated the skeletons. The zombie knight stepped forward, leaning into its shield to resist the holy lance.

The outline of a muscled woman in armor similar to Mallery's holy symbol formed in the light. It did battle with the silhouette of a purple sorcerer with a gnarled staff. The avatar of the goddess swung at the sorcerer's staff, but the sorcerer parried the blow and pushed back. The goddess swung again, scoring a cut across the sorcerer's arm.

When the light faded, three of the skeletons were gone, their armor clattering to the ground.

But their steeds remained. As did the zombie knight, who raised its voice, shouting, "Charge!"

Mallery raised her shield, and Leah remembered she was a part of the fight, not just the audience. She drew her sword and started singing a version of "Whiskey in the Jar," which was marked in her disguised textbook as a Song of Battle.

The wolves split and started to circle, two bearing right, one left.

"We stay in the middle, they'll pick us apart!" Leah said between stanzas.

"Agreed; follow me!" Mallery feinted one way and then made for the prisoners, slashing at one of the wolves with her shield.

Leah followed suit, forgetting her song as she swung at the wolf. She cut into one of the creature's paw swipes, defending as she attacked. Her maestra would be pleased. The creature's blood came out thick and black and wrong, spraying onto the road and grass and Leah's face.

Ick, she thought, but kept the thought, and her breakfast, down for the moment.

"Keep the song going," Mallery said as they advanced.

She'd gotten them into this mess because she couldn't stand by, and she needed to help get them out of it. If she got them all killed, then that didn't help the prisoners.

The skeletons pressed in, chasing them as they pushed for the prisoners. Leah lost track of everything that wasn't right in front of her. She could hear Mallery calling moves and swinging, but while Leah was good with a blade, she had significantly less experience fighting nonhuman opponents. It was all Leah could do to swing the sword in defensive cuts and maintain the song. And even then, she took a cut along the arm and heard Mallery get hit several times.

This was not my best plan, she thought as the remaining skeletons came closing in…

* * *

There was a fire across the town the night King and Shirin stayed in Chandler's Crossing, but King insisted they stay out of the fight and not make waves.

Not yet.

Two days later, they arrived at Ag'ra, the letter from renowned wizard Ioseph Bluethorn granting them easy access.

And once they were inside, Xan'De was not hard to find. As a port town, Ag'ra was cosmopolitan. Which meant that it had a Matok fighting arena. Xan'De's return had made waves as he rose once again to the top of the brackets.

They found him in his quarters in the neighborhood around the arena. Xan'De's quarters were decorated in the Matok style, all open to receive the sun and the sea breeze, with divans and reclining chairs and outdoor bathing.

Even reclining in the bath, goblet in hand and without a care in the world, Xan'De dominated the room. Easily seven feet tall, wide and muscled, his bare torso tattooed and scarred from years of battle, all four arms adorned with Art Deco–esque geometric tattoos. He bathed with three beautiful women—a dark-skinned human woman, a fair elf, and an olive-skinned curvaceous gnome. King was spared a full view by the magically powered jacuzzi function in the hot tub.

A servant preceded them as they approached.

"Mighty Xan'De, may I present Anthony Kane of the order of Felur's Fist, and his companion, the Wizard Shi'Reen. They say they come with news from Ioseph Bluethorn."

Xan'De set down his goblet and disentangled himself from his fans. "If Bluethorn truly sent you, you'll have a way to prove it."

King drew the enspelled ring and knelt at the front of the tub, not interested in wading in and then having to polish his armor for hours.

Xan'De only took one long step to cross the wide tub and take the ring in one hand. The sapphire glowed as the rune manifested, and Xan'De recoiled as if struck, his eyes flashing the same hue.

Xan'De spoke. "The time has come. We will close the circle that was spoiled. A better challenge than putting the pups here in their place."

He turned. "See to my weapons, and fresh horses for three. My respite is over."

"But, mighty Xan'De, what of the championship?" asked the human woman, wrapping herself in a towel, natural hair untouched by the water.

"I have trophies enough to melt down and forge myself a crown. But a greater fight awaits me in Fallran. This house is yours once more until I return."

The two other women grabbed towels, then slipped on sandals and hurried off in different directions.

"Nolan next, yes? He'll be hiding in Favorton, most like," Xan'De said.

Shirin said, "It's is five days' ride, from my memory."

"For Fallran horses, yes. With my steeds, we'll be there in three."

"Three?" King asked.

"You've never rode a draenkish, have you?" Xan'De's smile was the smile of the daredevil, the man with nothing to fear.

Saving two days would give them that much more time to search. This might just work. Assuming that the rest of the team didn't run afoul of something they couldn't evade. And assuming Leah didn't go off and play the hero.

* * *

Leah's enthusiasm had gotten the best of her. This was dangerous, and an unnecessary delay, but it did provide an excellent excuse for Roman to cut loose.

Roman swung a hammer around him in a reasonable impression of the Mighty Thor, hewing his way through the skeleton's back line.

Mallery's holy smite had brought their numbers down, but the wolves still had the women surrounded.

Roman ran up one of the wolves' snouts, his hammer vaporizing its rider's head. Then he leaped from the wolf's back and dove into a forward flip over the cart towing meager supplies for the captives. He brought the hammer down on the post that served as the central post for the captive's chains.

And with that one blow, he set a dozen humans, dwarves, and gnomes free. He quick-drew and tossed one-handed weapons to several captives in between hammer swings as he kept up the melee with the skeletons. There was a reason he carried an entire armory on his person at all times in this world.

"Stay together! Fight as one! This is your chance for freedom!"

A gnome with a matted beard took his knife to the rope bindings at his companion's legs. Then an older man caught Roman's hand axe and tossed it right into the face of an oncoming shadow wolf.

Roman was the calm center of the storm, moving without doubt, without worry. This fight was not the kind of battle he'd been born for, but it was still Action. And here, he was the hero the scene needed. The hero his team needed.

But for every hero, there was a villain. Or at least an evil lieutenant. The zombie knight caught Roman in its gaze, leveling its sword at the warrior.

All at once, the prisoners were no longer by his side, cowering from the attention of their captor.

"Finish off the skeletons and then help my companions!" Roman shouted as he stalked toward the knight. It had the height advantage, thanks to the steed. But Roman had tricks up his sleeve.

Focusing on his role and that of the knight as his opposite, Roman mentally tossed away his reins, let caution to the wind, and embraced his nature as a Hero. A Warrior.

Roman grinned. Drew his greatsword. And charged.

He cut into the knight's swing, knocking the slash aside. He continued the motion to dodge the shadow-wolf's strike, then cut down into the beast's side, slashing through where its ribs would be. Instead, the blow tore ichor from the creature's form, sizzling on the road.

He pressed his advantage, intercepting the zombie knight's strike. He moved his grip to hold the sword at the hilt and just beyond the halfway point with his other gauntleted hand. He used the leverage to shove the knight's weapon aside and then shoved the blade up and under the undead warrior's breastplate, skewering what remained of its organs.

Roman hauled on the sword and dragged the knight off its dying steed. He let the greatsword drop and replaced it with two long knives. He buried one in the zombie knight's eye socket; the other he used to slit the throat of its steed.

And then he pulled out his hatchet and finished the knight off with several quick hacks to the neck.

Roman wiped coagulated blood off his face and turned his attention to the wolves. To Mallery and Leah. Four of the creatures remained, picking at Mallery and Leah. Mallery's shield had dropped to the ground, the comedienne holding her recently injured arm in close, the mail thick with blood. Leah had gashes along one arm and fought with her off hand.

She's not singing, Roman realized, and saw when she turned that she had been clawed across the mouth as well. Her bardic role had been forgotten. She was still Leah the Comedian, not the Bard. She had skill with a blade, but she wasn't fitting into the story the way she should, even putting aside her brash mistake.

He needed to end this. Now. Before it got worse.

Roman tackled one of the wolves and, with a motion probably too fast to be human, pulled a knife from his sleeve and buried it in the creature's eye.

He rolled off the one wolf and jabbed another with the hammer, forcing it to the ground. Impressively, Leah stepped up and stabbed it in the throat as soon as it was down.

This left just two. They turned, looked at the prisoners, at the three heroes, and then bolted for the woods.

Not so fast, Roman thought.

Roman twisted the handle of his hammer and grabbed the trio of darts hidden in the pommel. He tossed them after one of the fleeing creatures. Two sank into its fur, the poison seeping its way through the beast's blood. It was a demonic beast, but it was enough flesh and blood to collapse thirty feet into the bush.

But one was still fleeing.

"Hey, corpse-breath!" Leah's voice came out hoarse.

The creature stopped and turned.

Now she was fitting her role.

"Yeah, you! You so much of a coward that you won't stand and fight for your Dark Lord?"

The creature cocked its head in the way of dogs trying to figure out what their humans were saying.

But they didn't need to talk with this thing. They just needed it dead. Roman quick-drew the hatchet and hurled it overhand. The wolf was still fixated on Leah's bardic fascination, and the hatchet took it full in the chest. The creature slumped to the ground.

Roman scanned the road, the brush, and the skies.

"It's done," he said, looking mostly at Leah. "But we need to get off the road as soon as possible to avoid the next patrol. Can you still heal?"

"How did you do that?" Leah asked. "That was completely unreal!"

"Later," Roman said. He could explain later. But it was high time she learned about his origins. "Healing?"

Mallery nodded. She dropped her mace and brought a bloodied hand to the holy symbol. As she touched it, she stood a bit taller, shook a bit less.

She prayed under her breath, and a beam of divine light cut through the clouds to shine upon her, Leah, and Roman.

Roman's gashes and bruises faded. Mallery shook out her injured hand, and the wounds on Leah's face closed to soft pink scars.

"That's all I've got left," the comedienne said, tired.

"Thank you, thank you all," the gnome with the knife said, approaching the group. He wasn't actually young—his beard was too full, his eyes not crinkled with age.

Roman bowed. "And thank you for helping. Our horses are in the woods, but we don't have enough for everyone. We'll need to travel off-road. Is there a town nearby we can take you to?"

The gnome turned to his companions. Their conversation spanned across at least three different languages, only two of which Roman understood at all. There was pointing and shouting, but after most of a minute, the gnome turned back and said, "We'll go to Oldtown. There are many places to hide in the hills."

"How far from here?"

"Two days to the south."

Roman looked over to Mallery and Leah. Mallery had collected her gear, while Leah had gone to the brush, presumably to fetch their horses.

They were bearing southwest, so this wouldn't take them too far out of their way. An acceptable detour. King had said no subplots, but they'd just saved a half-dozen lives, and that was always worthwhile.

He didn't relish the dressing-down Leah would get when King found out about it, though. And Mallery looked pissed. It was one thing to lead the team into battle, but to force a fight against orders, with no notice, and get your teammates injured?

That was something else. Mallery had the better rapport with Leah, so he'd let her handle this.

Instead, he helped the former prisoners repack the supplies from the cart and get ready to hit the off-road.

It'd been nice to have Leah look at him like a real person, to not have to go through the weeks or months of odd looks. Her hastiness had forced his hand. But at least now, he didn't have to hide from a teammate. The prisoners, sure. But they were extras. Lives, yes. But they'd be in and out of the story within a week.

And for all that Leah had endangered Mallery and his life, in the end, they had helped people.

They'd gotten to be heroes.

Chapter Eight:
Mea Culpa Maxima

Mallery took point, citing the need to clear her head.

What she really needed was some time to be angry on her own.

They'd nearly gotten killed. Without Roman's Action Hero abilities, Mallery and Leah would be partially digested in the stomachs of infernal wolf-beasts. They'd never get the chance to sip drinks on the beach together, win an Emmy, or grow old together with someone fabulous and brilliant.

Especially since the person responsible for almost getting them killed was the current contender for the role of Mallery's leading lady, the current Plus One in Mallery's dreams of the future.

Leah stayed with Roman and the prisoners, twenty paces back in the woods. Mallery's horse picked through the underbrush, which was much more slow going than riding on the road, but Roman's call to make themselves scarce was smart. It's like he knew what he was doing, and people should listen to him. People who have too much enthusiasm and not enough experience. People who she thought she could trust and then went flying off the handle.

She could understand wanting to help. Wanting to help is a good thing. A great thing. It's why they do what they do. But you go into a fight like that, you need a plan, a real plan. Not to go off half-cocked and hope to banter and sing your way out of it.

Mallery took a branch off a tree with her mace, then put it away and grabbed her holy symbol.

Staying angry wasn't useful. She picked up a prayer. In Hebrew, but gods could speak every language, so it was all good.

She prayed to Felur and Yahweh for guidance, for help with forgiveness, and for strength. There were bound to be more battles ahead, and she had to know that Leah could be counted on.

It was one thing to date someone unreliable, to have fun.

But when you had to count on them to watch your back in life-or-death situations?

That was something different.

"Mallery!" Leah called, catching up.

Mallery pulled back on the reins to slow her steed. Leah pushed aside branches as she approached. The divine healing had closed Leah's wounds, but the scars remained, or would until Mallery could cast another healing aura when her blessings refreshed. Leah looked worried, guilty, and afraid.

"I wanted to give you some space, but then I got too antsy and needed to come up and apologize. I just talked to Roman and apologized to him, and so now I wanted to say that I'm really sorry for going aggro back there when you and Roman told me not to. It was really reckless and selfish, I totally screwed up. We all got hurt and I'm really sorry."

Mallery let Leah's words sit for a few moments as their horses walked through the woods.

"Thank you for that. I was really scared there before Roman came back. You can't just put all of our lives on the line like that. Not when it's against orders and the odds are so bad. King keeps telling us about initiative and everything, but you can't take that as license to pull a Leeroy Jenkins."

"I know. I just saw those prisoners and couldn't stand by on the sidelines. I'm glad you're all right."

"You're lucky that Felur and me are like this," Mallery said, crossing two fingers.

"Lucky for more than that. Roman was…" Leah shook her head in wonder. "I mean, I've never seen someone move like that."

"We can't count on being that lucky again. Not when the breach is this developed. Okay?"

"I get it. Did missions used to be this hard? It seems like just about every job I've been on has been a special circumstance, something out of the ordinary."

"Some missions are harder than others. You're right that it's been worse the whole time you've been on board. HQ still doesn't have a projection for when the storms will let up, and the ops team still isn't certain that the storms are why the stories have been breaking faster and harder. Maybe it has something to do with the Tall Woman you IDed; maybe she's an externality. There's just a whole lot of unknowns, variables out of reach. All the dangers of live theater and more. Which is why we need to be able to count on one another to follow the script and have one another's back, okay?

"Got it. No more subplots. Hammer, heroes, Night-Lord. That's it."

Mallery nodded.

"Okay. That's all I had to say, so I can let you have the scouting to yourself again if you like. Not sure if this is the kind of situation where we hug it out or where we say our piece and give one another space."

Leah had screwed up, and big time. But it had come from a good place, and she was owning up to her failure. Aside from being perfect, what more could you ask for? And dating a perfect person would get tiresome really fast. "I've found that hugging it out on horseback is not particularly easy. I'm willing to try, but I'm about spent on healing spells."

"Totally. I would fully expect to eat dirt trying to pull something like that. Especially in this brush."

"Can you go back to Roman and ask how long he thinks it will be until we can go back onto the road? Then come back and distract me with something silly. I require grade-A peerless silliness to improve my mood."

Leah's expression brightened by forty watts. She saluted in a wonderfully ridiculous fashion, then guided her horse around a tree and back toward the group.

* * *

Leah tried to cheer up the former captives and her teammates with some music, practicing the tunes she'd transcribed the night before. This is what bards did, after all. She picked a song of encouragement, one that was supposed to lighten burdens and calm hearts. She had to focus enough that the magical effect just barely cancelled out the stress of effort, but the rest of the party walked a little lighter, shoulders down, expressions relaxed. But when she stopped, her mind went back on the attack, repeating the sight of Mallery on the brink of collapse, the pain of the wolf's claws at her face.

She picked the song up again, hoping to steady herself as well as the captives.

The freed prisoners had scars on their arms, worn faces and feet. But they also had a spark of hope in their eyes, fanned by Leah's song.

After a few songs, the prisoners started to drift off into the meager tents and lean-tos they'd been granted or assembled. Soon, that left just Leah, Mallery, and Roman.

They chatted for a few minutes, about how the detour would impact their path, and what Shirin and King were doing (hopefully avoiding needless fights, unlike Leah).

When she was sure the captives weren't listening, Leah asked, "Okay, so you said *later*. Now it's later. How did you do all of that? Tapping into the story to awesome when the story needs you to awesome is one thing, but you were practically bullet-timing that fight back there."

Roman took a long breath, the flickering oranges, yellows, and reds of the fire dancing in shadow and light on his face.

"I wasn't born on your Earth. I come from another world. I grew up in the Post-Apocalypse region of Action World, though for me, it was just the Wasteland. I fought, I killed, and I did what was necessary to survive."

Leah looked from Roman to Mallery. She wasn't surprised, wasn't reacting. She already knew. Of course she knew. Why wouldn't she? They were like brother and sister.

"I became a hero of my world. Saved people. As much as I could, and as often. But it took a toll. My life wasn't my own. I wandered from story to story, always a helper figure, never my own man. Until I met King. I was at the end of my rope, running on fumes. And he gave me a way out."

"How long ago was that?" Leah asked.

"Most of ten years. It's a better life. A happier life. But when I'm on-mission, and when the story calls for it, I can call on my original nature, bring the rules of my world with me to another world."

"That is some Campbellian wet-dream *Last Action Hero*–level wonkiness right here."

Mallery chuckled, and Roman looked up at Leah. For a second, she was expecting rebuke. She'd crossed a line of some sort.

But instead, he smiled. It wasn't the smile of a wolf about to pounce, not the easy smile of a predator like he'd get sometime in a fight. This was just Roman the teammate, not Roman the Action Hero.

"I suppose it is. I try not to depend on it, because who knows when it'll give out? I've never gone back, and HQ can't tell me for sure if and when that ability will give out. Every time, I expect it could be my last. But for now, my magic still works."

"So, I've got about a million questions about how that works, but since you're not a lab rat and this isn't the R&D team, I'll leave it be. Anyway, thank you for what you did. I fucked up bad, and you pulled us out of the fire." Leah stood and offered a hand of thanks. Roman took it and squeezed, looking up at her (not too much, though. Dude was tall.)

"I got first watch," Leah said. Roman assembled his bedside arsenal, and Mallery said her nightly prayers. Leah gave her a kiss goodnight before she crawled into her bedroll.

And then it was just Leah, the fire, and the stars.

She'd gotten caught up in the story, and the whole group had nearly paid for it. She'd carry that guilt with her. She'd acted because it was the right thing to do as a person, even if it was a bad call for a Genrenaut. She couldn't shut one off entirely to be the other. Not yet. And maybe not ever.

But she'd do the job. And now? Now she had skin in the game. Duty and responsibility were fine as motivating forces.

But anger? Guilt? A drive for justice? That was Premium, Nitrous-Oxide-Level Motivation.

And she was ready to burn.

Chapter Nine:
Karn-Du

Oldtown had a garrison, but they were mostly occupied in keeping the local population under lockdown. The thing about rural towns was that they were used to being self-sufficient. The King of Fallran knew to leave well enough alone and just accept his taxes. The Night-Lord's hands-on methods were not met well.

Roman, Mallery, and Leah met no resistance as they led the captives around the town into the hills, where they bade farewell. The gnome that had first taken up arms presented Roman with a gift, a small whittled key, a symbol of the freedom they'd provided.

Roman tied the key to a strip of hide and hung it around his neck. Another token to ward away the demons of worry and sorrow.

This key was more proof that he had made a difference, that he'd gotten to help on his own terms. Every time he leaned into his origins, it threw him for a loop. He sometimes regretted leaving, but was haunted by his memories. He still wondered what he was doing pretending to be something he wasn't, questioned his right to use that power away from his home.

He couldn't help but worry about Mallery, about all of them. He'd come through more lethal scrapes than he had any right to. But the rest of them didn't have his gifts.

Roman rubbed the key and kissed it for luck. Another reminder that they'd made a difference. Not just because it was what the story wanted, but because they'd chosen to step in, to save lives.

That pride steadied him. It'd have to be enough. The story was far from over. There would be other tests, and he'd have to be prepared for them.

* * *

Roman held a hand up to block the sun as they rode into Karn-Du. It was the largest aboveground dwarven city in the continent. A whole city built of limestone, carved into the hillside at the edge of a glacial drift.

Stone towers and pyramids rose high, tiered and stacked and arranged by the intricacies of dwarven craft and municipal planning. The dwarves in this region were craftspeople, all of them. No dwarven child grew their first chin hair before they'd reached at least adept status in some craft—sewing, smithing, cobbling, or one of another hundred pursuits. The kings and queens ruled with statecraft; the warlords perfected the art of battle.

Inside the walls, the city unfolded a whole new level, like a fractal. Designs on walls, murals, ornate carts and bags. Every brick, every cobblestone, every garment was made with passion and personality.

The bustling dwarven markets reminded Roman at times of the ramshackle markets back home, where sunburned survivors hawked half-broken technology and shriveled produce. But those comparisons disappeared as soon as anyone opened their mouth and out came the broadest Scottish accent anyone on any earth had ever heard. Genrenauts researchers had traced the Dwarf Equals Scottish meme to Ralph Bakshi's *Lord of the Rings*, and it had been the law of Fantasyland as long as Roman had been on the job.

"Our first job is to figure out where to look for the Hammer. Then we'll need a guide that can take us there. If we're lucky, we can find a guide that knows where the Hammer is. We'll need a guide either way. My Dwarven is rusty."

"And mine isn't much better," Mallery added.

Leah's expression was once again set to Gawk. "So, how do we do that? Troll the bars until we find a dwarf with *Looking for Group* plastered to his head?"

"Basically. The normal fantasy tavern rules apply, but we don't just need any dwarf. We need someone daring enough to plumb the depths, smart enough to lead us where no one has been in centuries, but not so ambitious that they'll demand to keep it for their family or to avenge some ancient slight."

"What could possibly go wrong?" Leah asked, and they set about their task.

His heart rate spiked several times when he saw one or another tall woman with dark hair. But neither was the dimensional traveler they were looking for. She could be in disguise, now that she'd been seen in a second location. They couldn't be sure how much she knew that they knew in this game of cat and mouse.

But neither of the women that surprised him moved the same way the woman in the Western World had. As he approached them, both looked Roman right in the eye without so much as a blink. They were just background characters.

Per Mallery's lead, the pair cooled down their couple-ish instincts in the city. Most civilizations in this world were fairly homophobic, and Karn-Du, largely informed by dwarven social mores, was light on public displays of affection even for heterosexual pairings. Roman knew from experience that people here swung both ways as frequently as anywhere else; they just kept it out of the public eye. More than a handful of taverns with suggestive names served the same coded purpose as gay bars back on Earth Prime had in decades past. Not that he'd been around for those years, but he'd picked it up from Mallery and other queer friends he'd made acclimating to Earth Prime.

After the second tavern, Leah switched from ordering ale for herself first and settled for the task of just buying drinks for the potential guides.

Roman ended up doing a fair amount of the talking, being the one of the three that could parse the dwarven dialects most easily. Leah and Mallery watched his back and shot down drunken dwarf after drunken dwarf's awkward advances, attempts at "accidental" groping, and one marriage proposal from a dwarf Leah caught falling off his chair.

Five taverns into their search, they found what Roman hoped was the real deal. Qargon stood tall for a dwarf, nearly four-feet five inches.

"The Hammer? Aye, I know where it is. At least, where the legends say 'tis. But there are giant ants, fungal blooms, and a hundred other terrors 'tween here and there. Not as if others haven't gone to find it. Most gave up a hundred years ago when the Skull King returned and caved even more tunnels in."

"The cave-ins won't be a problem," Roman said. "Mallery here is a priestess of Felur. And she has blessings that will let us pass through the rubble."

"If she can do it, why haven't they done it before?" Leah asked, butting into the conversation.

"Blessings are not as simple as arcane magic. You ask, and Felur generally grants her favor. But they are not guaranteed, not universally dependable," Mallery said.

"Aye. And my people don't care much for uncertainty when we're planning great works. The expeditions that tried to reclaim K'gon's hall have been trying to take back the whole kingdom at once, or not at all. We're just looking to use the Hammer. Legend says that to claim it, ye must face a test of skill and sway the spirit of K'gon himself. And since K'gon was the greatest craftsman in ten generations, not many have had the stomach to face the spirit's wrath should they fail."

"So, how are we supposed to win when we get there?" Leah asked.

Roman cracked a sly smile. "We have crafts that K'gon has never heard of."

"When does your expedition depart?" Qargon added.

"As soon as possible. Gather what supplies you need; we mean to set out first thing tomorrow." Roman stood to get another round while Leah tested out jokes about Karn-Du and the particularities of dwarven culture.

* * *

Shirin learned quickly that Xan'De's mood was permanently set to "gregarious but cryptic". One of his four hands was permanently holding a wine flask, but he never seemed to get drunk. He didn't make very much sense even before he started drinking for the day.

The trio crested another hill on the southern road bound inland, which would turn toward Hammet, Nolan's likely hiding place.

Just beyond the base of the hill, an old tree lay astride the road, truck cleaved from its roots by a lightning strike or high winds. Several smaller trees were scattered around the larger deadfall.

"A storm the likes of this I've not seen on this fair-weathered land," Xan'De said. "Nothing like the Matok storms, which would tear the roof off of a stone house were it unwarded."

"Not a problem," King said. "We'll lead the horses through the woods and get back on the road."

"By my memory, the woods are thick in this part of the kingdom," Shirin said.

Sure enough, it took no little bit of doing to pick their way through the woods. They had to get down off and lead the horses, Xan'De clearing the brush ahead with his machete-like blades.

King's holy symbol started to glow, reflecting off his polished armor. He took it in hand, squinting.

"I can't tell where it's coming from," clearly frustrated by the lack of clarity.

They hacked and wound their way onto the road, Xan'De wiping the sap off his blades as they prepared to remount.

Shirin cast a spell of protection on the group, which would turn aside several minor blows.

The brush on the far side of the road exploded, revealing a pack of shadow wolves, each standing over five feet tall at the shoulder. Smoky blackness rolled off them as they moved, like a living motion blur.

"To arms! A blood day!" Xan'De said, leaping from the horse, blades in his hands in a flash.

Shirin sighed. She'd been hoping for a quiet day. Relatively quiet. If such a thing was possible with Xan'De around. She raised her staff and started chanting as King took a step forward to cover her.

There were eight wolves and only three of them.

An aura of blessings passed over the heroes.

"Cover me," Shirin said. This fight would take up most of her spells, but if need be, they could camp down early for her to rest. If these wolves were controlled by the Night-Lord, leaving even one of them alive could spell disaster for their plans.

King slashed at a shadow-wolf coming in to flank, pushing it back toward he pack and away from Shirin.

Shirin began casting a Blinding spell. Both King and Xan'De were facing away, the wolves in. The positioning was perfect.

The incantation came first, then the somatic component. Then an act of will to bring it to life.

Shirin closed her eyes, and a burst of light erupted from her staff.

Magic was exhilarating but not intoxicating. Shirin never felt out of control, never swept away in anything. It was work, hard work, but it was still wondrous, even years later.

The wolves whined, and both King and Xan'De struck. Xan'De cut with a one-handed sword and cleaved through the head of one wolf with a massive axe held in his upper two hands, stabbing another with a sword held in a lower hand. At the same time, King impaled one through the neck with his longsword.

The Wolves pulled back and spread out, trying to surround them.

"I have the flankers!" Xan'De said as he dashed to the side. "We must fell one more immediately!"

Shirin prepared a spell to create a wall of force to cut off one angle of attack.

To her left, King hacked at the other wolf, sword glowing with righteousness and humming a resonant major cord.

"Speed, friends!" Xan'De said behind them.

Xan'De impaled one of the flanking wolves.

The wolves regrouped, just four of them left.

Shirin threw up a wall to cut off their escape, and from there, the fight ended quickly.

"That," King said as they stood in a trio, back-to-back-to-back, making sure there wasn't a second wave, "was a trap. The wolves couldn't have felled the trees that way."

"Agreed."

"Many things are possible, but not all are likely."

"What do you think it was?" Shirin asked the foreigner.

"The Night-Lord's servants were dangerous enough to lay this trap. We felled not a few of these things on our journey back with the Sun-sword. But now we must retrieve our horses and lay many leagues between us and this trap, lest the wolves' keepers return to this trap and catch us up."

Shirin called out to the horses. They'd tried to scatter but hadn't made it far through the heavy brush. Her horse had some cuts where it had crashed through underbrush, but a simple blessing from King closed those quickly.

Xan'De's injuries took a full five-minute prayer, depleting King's limited healing capabilities from his granted paladin powers. But then they were off, making good time for Hammett.

* * *

After several days together, Mallery, Leah, and Roman found that Qargon was a skilled guide and far more attentive on the road. He limited himself to one or two small drinks in the evenings. Once they got away from the prying ears in the city, he also went on at length about the skill and handsomeness of his husband, a famous (according to Qargon) tailor who had made garments for the nobility from Ag'ra to Serana and beyond. She was honestly glad that their hyper-macho warrior guide was queer. In past trips to this story region, she'd learned that this world was as homophobic as you could expect from an imagined pseudo–Middle Ages. She and Leah didn't have to tiptoe around him for anything other than the general politeness of avoiding blatant PDA.

Once you saw past the Drunken Dwarven Adventurer exterior, there was far more to Qargon than expected.

The three of them politely grilled Qargon about his history and views on the world, from the best way to sharpen an edge to dwarven views on homosexuality (not pretty, unless you kept it very secret; propagation of the clan was very important, which meant children).

"There's more than a few times when dwarven nobles married at near the same time and were very, very close, you see. Bit of fertility magic and some discretion, and ye can live something close to a happy life. For commoners like me and Derjin, it's not near as complicated. We've made peace with our clans. His wealth'll pass to his niece, mine to my brother, and we're left to our own devices as long as we don't make pretensions of upward mobility. With his skills, Derjin could aspire to the high merchant class, buy his way to a family legacy. But we've made our choice."

"I wish loving as your heart guided you was as easy with my people," Roman volunteered. "We suffered long and hard, and with survival a daily struggle. Most anyone would kill for water or food. They didn't need any other excuses. One man loving another was taken as weakness in the eyes of the strongest and most aggressive. So I kept my head down, carried on my affairs in the shadows, until I was strong enough not to face all challenges with force."

Mallery put a hand on Roman's shoulder. He didn't often share stories of his home, his old life in the Post-Apocalyptic story world. Even in this way, framed to avoid breaking concealment protocols. It was a display of trust.

Qargon nodded, compassion written across his face.

It was a good move, executed well. Qargon had shown vulnerability, and Roman matched it. Roman pretended to be a novice at the social maneuvering, but for anyone compatible with his background as a warrior of the broken roads, Roman was a social force just by being himself. More than Mallery could fake even on her best days.

Sometimes truth was better. Even it was fiction.

Leah took notes the whole time, sometimes with pen and ink, sometimes just filing things away. Mallery was learning to read when something was being tossed around in the Stand-Up Material tumbler of Leah's mind.

As the quartet made their way into the mountains, they traded roads and forest for tunnels and torches.

"I was expecting that Roman here would have to hunch," Mallery said as they walked through the outer tunnels.

Qargon harrumphed good-naturedly. "The builders of these tunnels weren't of a mind to make the passage easy for humans or elves. But this section was carved not long after the second Gergian war, and what they were keen on was leaving room for siege weapons, to help keep the war on the side of the surfacers. Meant that the warlords commissioned more ballistas and siege towers, fewer drills and cave collapsers."

Roman hunched anyway. "I'm not interested in opening a gash on the top of my head if I put a hair too much spring in my step. If I'm getting a scar from this quest, I'd like it to mean something other than clumsiness."

"We'll come to a bottleneck with high ground ahead, natural resting point. You'll be able to relax your neck, giraffe-man."

They reached the divide some minutes later and took a break. Roman's neck cracked and crunched as he stretched it out, kneading the bunched muscles as he sat and gnawed on some tack.

Qargon gestured with his axe. "We head left here, then the path spirals down a ways and levels out for a few miles. There's an abandoned outpost where we can bunk for the night, then two days' travel to the cave-in at Ru'kal, where things start to get tricky."

"And that's where I'll come in," Mallery said. "I can get us through the rock, as long as you can scout us pockets of air for when the spells wear out."

"Not a problem," Qargon said. "Dwarven construction can handle minor problems like hundreds of tons of rockfall collapse."

Leah practiced her ballads as they marched down from the Y-split, cycling back and forth from songs using the Greensleeves theme until Roman suggested she take a break to "rest her voice." Better he ask than she. Mallery got that Leah had to practice to get confident with the bardic spells, and wanted nothing less than to nag her significant other. She'd been that girlfriend in the past, and it had gone poorly for everyone.

She started up again an hour later, but Qargon called, "Quiet. I see something ahead."

Something glowed light green in the tunnel below.

"What is that?" Leah asked.

Mallery answered. "Luminescent fungus. Grows in the under-roads. It's really quite pretty in those big caverns. Lights up the geodes like a permanent fireworks display." She'd never seen a colony quite this big. Their last quest underground had shown her plenty of glowing fungus, but in smaller chunks, mostly for lighting tunnels and small caverns.

"Who uses it for light, aside from dwarves?"

Qargon lowered the torch, stopping for a moment. "Oh, any number of a myriad monsters that wander these under-roads, now that the dwarven kingdoms don't patrol anymore. Most are opportunists, not likely to attack an armed group, especially with a dwarf in the lead. Best have someone watch our backs, regardless."

Roman drifted back to rear position, leaving Leah and Mallery in the middle.

Leah stayed quiet, her practice forgotten.

They reached the first fungal blooms, misshapen mushroom stalks and caps glowing with a sickly green light, color somewhere between mucus and moss.

Qargon halted. "Something is wrong. This fungus is not the ones from the songs. They're hive blooms. Very dangerous."

Mallery wrinkled her nose. "Up close, they're not nearly so nice to look at. More of a stench-ridden mound of decay."

"Aye, that they are. And where there are hive blooms, the dregs of the old Fungal Lords' armies cannot be far away. Best stay on your guard, all. Ready your blades, blessings, and ballads."

"I need to write that down," Leah said. "That would be an amazing title for something."

Branching pathways opened up to the tunnels, large enough to crawl through, like an ant colony.

Qargon led on even as their choice of paths multiplied exponentially.

"This is the main tunnel—you can tell from the finished ceiling." The dwarf lifted the torch to illustrate his point. The main tunnel was not only larger than the side pathways, but the roof and side walls were mostly jagged edges rounded off, leaving an uneven-but-cultivated look.

Lights emerged from the tunnels, drowning out Qargon's torchlight.

"Get ready," Qargon said, pulling a hand axe from its loop at his belt. "Stick together; don't let them isolate you. And avoid their bites."

"They what?"

"The ants," Qargon said. "They're controlled by the hive blooms. Made to be slaves to the fungus and ensure its spread. They were one of the simpler but more dangerous creations of the Fungal Lords. Hit them wrong and they'll explode; spores will get into your lungs. Then you become one of them."

"That's not the least bit terrifying." Leah drew her sword. "I'll keep them busy and you smite them?"

Mallery brandished her mace. "A fine plan."

The ants' rustling grew louder.

"Here they come," Roman said, his voice brightening with the coming battle.

* * *

Roman drew his shorter sword and a hammer. The narrow tunnels made his larger weapons impractical. He could use the greatsword as a spear, but that'd only keep them at bay for so long. "No chance we can outrun them?"

Qargon laughed. "As much chance as a cask of mead staying sealed after a battle."

"Understood." Roman pulled the kerchief around his neck up, refolding it as a crude mouth guard. He took a wide stance, lowering his center of gravity to receive a charge and to free up some overhead space.

Staccato sounds of legs on stone echoed through the tunnels, growing louder by the moment.

Mallery said, "I'm going to try to shut some of them off." Chanting rose from behind Roman as he watched glowing figures approach.

Each of the ants was three meters long, standing a meter and a half at the shoulder. Fungal blooms dotted the grey-furred ants' bodies in an irregular pattern, but most had blooms emerging from their heads.

Leah had burst into song, a tune of strength and valor. Roman felt his already-powerful moves enhanced by the bardic magic. It felt not unlike being back in his home world, where the very nature of reality in the story region helped guide his aim and bolster his stamina. But it was not the same, didn't come with the same sense of obligation and being boxed in.

It was just power, and he'd use every bit of it to protect people and do his job.

Roman chucked a hand axe at an oncoming ant. The blade cleaved into the mushroom-dominated head, and the creature slowed but then kept coming, its movements more jerky.

"Do we need to watch out for spores?" Leah asked.

"Worry about tha…" The sounds of steel on chitin rose from Qargon's direction, swallowing the dwarf's words.

Roman focused on the battle before him. The ants were more than big enough to bowl him over if given the chance. So, he'd have to make sure they didn't get the chance.

He swung the hammer at the ant's probing leg, batting it aside. He grabbed the axe out of its head when the thing turned its maw. He kicked and swung and pushed the thing back, standing his ground, then dove to the side when another fungus-taken ant barreled out of a tunnel, leaping at him.

Roman pushed off the side of the tunnel, turning to face the new attacker. The ant lashed out with its front legs, catching Roman across the back and forcing him to the side. The fungus-ridden ant opened its maw, and Roman led with his blade, head down as the sword pierced the creature's maw and then cracked through its head, scattering spores.

He slid out from under the beast as it collapsed, but the sword didn't come with him. He drew a knife and continued, slicing the air to hold off another.

"Two down, two coming," Roman said, passing the information back.

"Three back here," Qargon answered.

Light blazed from Mallery's shield. "Keep them back just a minute longer and I will have a solution for a half-dozen."

A minute was a long time in a fight. Roman filled the tunnel as best he could while still being able to move. The ants were big enough that they could only come two at a time, barring new attackers from overwhelming the heroes all at once.

But they just. Kept. Coming.

Roman wove a defensive pattern, but since he was forced to use his shorter weapons, the ants could counterattack more easily. He left the knife in a spore-free shoulder and stepped back to slide the longsword off his back. He'd be restricted to short cuts and thrusts, but it was three times the reach. And now that he knew how they moved…

Longsword in hand, he cut into the ants' movements and jabbed the tip at them to punish any advances.

He speared one through the head, shearing the fungal bloom with it. The creature dropped to the floor beside its companion, filling the tunnel. Roman lunged forward, blade first.

And missed.

The ant dipped under his blow and bowled him over.

And then kept going. Roman took a hand off the sword and grabbed a leg.

The creature dragged him along the ground, twitching its leg as it went. The result was total disorientation. He lost all sense of up and down.

But he did know one direction: where the ant's leg was. He dropped the longsword and drew another dagger, then brought his dagger-holding wrist to the one holding on for dear life and, using one hand as a brace, started cutting the ant's leg off.

Leah shouted the chorus of her song, sword whipping through the air as she held the creature at bay.

Roman sheared through the leg, and the creature bellowed, spores spreading from its blooms.

"Watch the spores!" He rolled back and got to his feet. He plucked the longsword off the ground and spun it in a short half-cut that took off another leg. That was enough to get the ant's attention. He scuttled crab-wise, putting his back to the pile of dead insects.

The ant followed the threat that had just harmed it, putting its back to Leah. She slashed straight through the thing's abdomen, a perfect cut that caused the thing to shriek, a cloud of spores shaking free from each of the creature's blooms.

Roman stabbed the ant's maw, then a short slice to chop off the main plume.

Another one down.

Within a heartbeat, another creature crawled past the pile of ants and pounced for Leah.

Chapter Ten:
Heroic Travel Montage, Part Two

Nolan the swordsman was easy to find. To start, the town of Hammett was barely worth the name—literally one crossroads with a building at each corner: one tavern, one church, one general store, and one smith to support the dozens of farms in the area.

They stabled the horses at the tavern and walked inside. The tavern was tiny room for maybe thirty, but most of the tables were empty. They'd dodged three more patrols between Ag'ra and there, each between ten and twenty strong.

The tavern being empty made it all that much easier to find their missing swordsman bent over the bar, drunk as a kid on their twenty-first birthday.

Nolan wore an unassuming longsword in a worn scabbard leaning against the bar beside him. From the nicks and dings on the hilt, King guessed that sword had seen regular use for most of a decade, if not more.

King stood back and let Xan'De approach his companion.

The big foreigner filled the room with his booming voice. "How many drinks is that? I will gladly catch up, but I need to know where to start."

Nolan turned, eyes red, unfocused.

"What?"

King and Shirin settled up with the tavern owner, a man named Rangel, room and board for all four of them.

He left Xan'De to speak with his friend. No need to complicate the situation. With the party reassembling, he and Shirin could step back, let the story take its course, nudging it here and there. Stories wanted to resolve, wanted to fix themselves. He just hoped that the rest of the team was having as easy a time of it with the Hammer.

* * *

When the St. Bernard–sized ant jumped for Leah's face, she didn't have the time to panic, or think, or do anything other than what her training told her to do. So, without thinking, in between verses of her song of battle, Leah took a step the side and cut into the creature's mandibles and shoulder, cleaving into a leg at the end of her cut.

The fungal ant dropped to the ground, blackened half-congealed blood dripping to the tunnel floor.

Her fencing background made her a very combat-ready bard, and thanks to weeks of practice, now she could sing and fight with nearly no problems.

Leah spun the blade over her head and cut again. Her instinctive move had left Mallery without further cover. The cleric was deep in battle-prayer, invoking lances of faith and divine shields and all that good stuff that was helping them stay ahead of the as-of-yet unending stream of ants.

And they just kept coming. A small armory lay scattered on the tunnel floor around Roman, all of the blades he'd thrown, dropped, or lost in the thick chitin of the fungal insects. Brain-jacked ants probably would not respond to her biting wit, even with the bardic magic behind it.

But if she lost her handy-dandy side sword, all she had was her lute and a knife in her boot. Sword it was.

Mallery finished a spell, and before Leah's eyes, four of the ants up the tunnel sank into the rock, vanishing as if beneath choppy waves.

At that, the other fungi seemed to decide to cut their losses. The brain-jacked ants broke and ran, disappearing into the tunnels, leaving behind the corpses of the fallen and sprinkles of spores spotting the floor.

"That was a right cracking fight, wasn't it?" Qargon wiped his axe off on a spore-less portion of an ant's abdomen. "Good to know you lot are worth your salt in a battle. Good moves, there. Don't take much to magic myself, even gods' magic, but right handy to have around in a pinch."

"Everyone okay?" Roman asked, pulling down the do-rag he'd used as a filtering mask.

"All limbs present and accounted for," Leah said. "Well done, Sister Mallery."

"Felur's earth blessings are versatile. But I won't be able to use that one again today."

Qargon lit his torch once more and pointed down-tunnel. "Well, for now we're safe. Best get moving, case anything else rattling around the tunnels thinks this is a good time to pile on. Scavengers and the like. Follow me."

* * *

Nolan and Xan'De agreed that the best place to look for Alaria was in the darkest, nastiest back alleys of Yordin, the port city to the southwest of the capital. Which meant a swift ride across the bulk of Fallran.

They dodged patrols, getting very handy at predicting their schedules. And when the skeletons were off book, Shirin's incantations and the blessings of Felur protected them.

Which meant that a week into their ride across the peninsula, they were getting pretty bored. Xan'De and Nolan rode together. The two men, though from vastly different backgrounds, got on in the way that King associated with old compatriots. Shorthand, abundant in-jokes, and a great deal of nonverbal communication. He gave them their space, let them take the lead.

The latest report from Leah, Mallery, and Roman indicated that they'd gone underground, guide in place, bound for the Hammer of K'gon.

No further word from Ioseph about the state of the army.

Now more properly seen as the resistance. The skies of Fallran still ran purple, nights longer each day even as they headed into summer. Each day, the Night-Lord's hold on the land grew stronger. But that was the way the story went. It was always darkest before the dawn; the cycle had to run its course before the heroes could rise up and cast down the evil overlord. All running textbook so far.

Which was why he worried. Since the spring and just before Mallery's mishap on Western World, none of their cases had run this smooth. If the forecasters were to be believed, the weight of popularity helped the story here progress as it should. The beats of a heroic quest were as popular and widely known as ever. Fantasy had become so popular, it now had its own reality TV shows, on top of the millions watching the latest fantasy epic on premium cable.

There'd be a reckoning when they touched back down in HQ, but that was a problem for later. The team didn't need to know that he'd fabricated the flight plan and deployment order. The mission came first, and King would handle the repercussions.

Chapter Eleven:
The Buried Kingdom

After another long day of walking, some walking, and more walking, Qargon led the team into a vast cavern.

The view took Mallery's breath away, and it made no signs of coming back.

The claustrophobic tunnels opened up to a massive cavern, carved with precision and beauty into the living stone.

And before them, though marred by many hundred tons of rock-fall, was the Fortress of K'gon.

Mallery tried to imagine the subterranean city as it had been, lit by bioluminescent stone fixed in the firmament of rock above the city, glittering lights in an infinite rainbow approximating white light filling the cavern like daylight. The expert craftsmanship of the city, every stone a masterwork, made with care and precision and love, a calling card and story to be recounted for generations to come.

Even a half-mile away from the main building, she could discern the detail, gargoyles and embellishments and entrancing fractal designs, older versions of what she'd seen on the surface, like the difference between early and late Byzantine imperial architecture. Her mind chewed on the differences between the styles, then she put it aside and focused again. This wasn't the time to stop and gawk. Especially because Leah was.

She stepped back and got Leah's attention, breaking her from her awestruck state.

"Beautiful, right? But we need to keep going."

Leah shook it off and looked ahead. "Right. Sure."

Back on track, Mallery's mind tried to turn back the clock, removing piles of boulders and shattered buildings, and imagining the pristine city it had once been. K'gon's masterpiece would never recover, even if the dwarves did manage to reclaim the city.

"How did this city fall?" Mallery asked, neck still craned up to take in the city, ruined though it was.

"Our folly. Hubris, like most of the ending of dwarven epics. We expanded throughout the foundation of the world, continued to explore and expand, ever-new canvases of stone and steel we could use to reflect our brilliance, refine our craft. But we weren't the only beings to make our homes here below. The kings of dwarven lands came to be rivals, turning their backs on one another in pursuit of glory and immortality through craft and deeds. So, when one kingdom came under attack and called for help, the besieged king's cousins did not answer. And one by one, the under-kingdoms fell, until it was too late. The descendants of K'gon and Varek fled to the surface, abandoning the great subterranean cities."

"And how long ago was that? Didn't the dwarves figure it out after the first kindgoms fell?" Leah asked.

"Dwarves aren't known for our quick changes in judgement. We bear grudges like another art form, and our royalty live a long, long time. Some tales say the early kingdoms to fall succumbed nearly as much due to betrayal and long knives as they did to the creatures of the deep darkness."

"Shit," Leah said. "I'm sorry. To lose places like this, to lose your home…"

Mallery thought of her relatives that had fled the USSR, others that had barely escaped the Holocaust. It seemed like her people were always being chased out of home after home. It wasn't a fate she wished on anyone, even in her darkest hours, fleeing from the anti-Semitism that flared up on the Internet and daily life. She'd tried bitterness on from time to time, but it always left her hollowed out.

Unfortunately, Fantasy World was no stranger to bitterness and vengeance. It followed the same zero-sum approach so many people on Earth had: grudges between peoples, back and forth, until everyone goes down at once.

Qargon led the party down the pathway to a long bridge over a chasm, one of three such bridges, each leading to a fortified corner of the fortress. One bridge had crumbled under the weight of the cave-in, and another had a thirty-foot gap in the middle.

The bridge before them was intact but covered in rubble, dozens of pieces that earned the label of "boulder".

"This is my cue," Mallery said. "Everybody get close. And hold hands. Thinking positive thoughts would not hurt, either. The spell will let us pass through rock, but since we're standing on rock, it requires concentration, and active attention to which rock you want the spell to let you pass. Hold my hand, and even if you falter, I'll catch you." She added in a wink for Leah. Even in a crowd, she tried to make Leah feel special, to not forget their nascent relationship even as they focused on work. They couldn't just switch it on and off. If this was going to work, they'd have to find a way to be partners in both ways at the same time without compromising the mission.

Qargon offered Roman a meaty hand. "It's a damn sight better than trying to bring an excavating team. Bring a group of fifty, we'd have lost ten to the ants, another ten to their spores, and the size of the party would have attracted a deep burrower. This is better, as long as your magic holds up."

Leah grabbed Mallery's hand on one side and Roman's on the other.

Mallery chanted in Fantasy World's version of Not-Latin, her hands twisting and dancing in ritual motion.

"Mighty Felur, hear your humble agent in this world as she requests your blessing and grant of passage through these trials."

Pure white light beamed from her holy symbol. Her tabard stirred like she was standing in a wind tunnel. Mallery's body filled with the certainty and power of Felur, as great a high as a standing ovation from a sold-out house.

She focused that power into the blessing they would need to make their way through the stone.

"Focus on standing still."

Mallery's ears popped, and she felt her footing begin to slip into the rock. It felt less like quicksand and more like sticking her feet in hot water after a long day of dancing. She focused, and her feet stopped and stabilized. She lifted her feet and visualized herself stepping on the stone, and so she did.

"Watch your footing," Mallery said. "You'll have to consciously pass through each stone. We'll be here for a while, but we should get at least an hour of movement per casting. And I can perform three of these in one day, four if I push myself. Let's not have it come to that.

"And another thing," she said as they set out. "Don't break the contact, especially not when you're in the middle of stone."

"Or what?" Leah asked.

Mallery's response was flat. "You can guess *or what.*"

"Got it."

They moved slowly but steadily. Most physically able adults hadn't needed to consciously think about walking in many years. For Mallery, it was back to being in physical therapy from the last time she'd gotten injured on the job. She'd had to work her foot back into fighting form over the course of several weeks before the medical team cleared her for fieldwork again.

It was also the weirdest bath she'd ever taken standing up. And clothed. And armored. And holding hands with several people.

Mallery had lived a full and interesting life, but magic? Magic was a whole other conversation. A different level of experience and oddity.

She kept up the chant to Felur, maintaining her concentration amidst her wandering thoughts and the strain of keeping a physical bead on everyone in the group through the chain of touch. "Felur of holy might and blessed transport, deliver us through this trial that we might raise a great victory in your name…"

The next hurdle was to accommodate for the fact that all four of them had noticeably different-length legs. Roman could outpace them all, so he stayed in the back, taking small, measured steps. Qargon lengthened his stride to set their pace fast enough to move well. The four of them crossed the bridge, and by the time they got to the fortress itself, they were moving at probably three-quarters normal walking speed—a leisurely stroll instead of the near-marching pace they'd used through the tunnels.

"Praise be to you, Felur, just and wise…"

Mallery's eye was constantly drawn up and about to the beautiful details of the stone working. There were rotten ruins of wooden boards and scraps of decomposed cloth as well, but the stone endured, even where it was marred and worn down or shattered beneath the collapsed rock. Shining plates of the cavern's overhead mantle caught the luminescence and scattered light among the shadows in the crushed fortress, light bouncing up and around at odd angles, disorienting her. She held tight to her companions and kept walking, pushing forward as Qargon led them through the ruined Fortress of K'gon.

They passed the battlements and the courtyard, their light growing dim, down to Qargon's torch, which bounced off the rubble, casting odd shadows on the surface of the rocks. As they moved through solid rock, the light disappeared entirely, leaving them to trust Qargon's sense of direction and keen dwarven darkvision.

Sometime later, they reached an open area with little rockfall, an untouched kitchen long since picked bare. Qargon set his nearly spent torch in a sconce and lit another, placing it on the opposite wall.

"Here's a good place for a respite."

Mallery exhaled, dropping to one knee. She steadied herself on her shield.

"Are you well?" Leah leapt to Mallery's side in a sweet display.

"I will be fine. Holding your concentration for most of an hour…"

"Not easy?"

She managed a weak smile.

"I'll take care of the provisioning, then." Leah fished out the cheese and bread and dried meat they'd packed, handing bundles around to the group. Qargon passed on the bread and water, instead opening his wine flask, wetting the food his own way.

Roman took the food with thanks, leaning against the wall next to a rusted-out stove, the exhaust feeding up. Mallery imagined the smokestack piping all the way to the top of the fortress, then dispersing as soot up the mantle of the cavern, some industrious dwarves on cranes or giant bats scrubbing off the roof of the cavern to keep the luminescent and reflective plates active and their city lit.

"How much further to the chamber with the Hammer?" Leah asked.

"I'd reckon another hour, maybe two. We have to get to the heart of the fortress, then down into the burial maze. That'll slow us down, not because of the stone, more because of the traps and puzzles."

Mallery had taken a seat, shield sitting by her side. She looked wiped. "You didn't say anything about traps and puzzles earlier."

"K'gon's a dwarf lord. They're all buried with traps and puzzles. Artisans from around the world came to compete to contribute protections to his tomb. But don't worry. I've a nose for traps. And the three of you have shown yourselves to be quite resourceful, so we'll muddle through."

"Muddling isn't my preferred way of doing anything," Roman said. "What else can you tell us that we'd need to know before we get there?"

"Aye. There's three things you need to know about dwarven burial traps…"

* * *

King woke to a guttural scream of alarm. A shadowy figure, hooded and cloaked, stood above him, the canvas of his tiny tent pulled back. But the screaming was coming from somewhere else.

Xan'De crashed into the assailant as King reached for his sword. The foreign-born warrior tackled the assailant out of King's sight, giving him the time to grab his sword and slide out of the tent.

The fire had died down, but the moon was bright, defying the Night-Lord's shadowy influence.

Unarmored, he was vulnerable, but the sword was all the armor he'd have that night.

Another nine figures stood around the fire, already fighting with the remainder of his party. Nolan's blade clashed with that of an assassin, sparks igniting in the darkness. Shirin held several assailants at bay with electrified fingers reaching out like white-hot tentacles.

"Form up!" King said, shuffling toward Shirin as two more cloaked figures with long knives started to circle him. He lashed out with a reverse cut at the shoulder. The figure ducked under the strike and lunged forward. King parried the blow with a back-edge cut and riposted with a slash across the chest, sending the killer to the ground.

The other assassin tossed a dagger, which embedded in King's knee, his sword out of place to parry, the range too short to dodge.

King cried out in pain, which alerted Shirin. She raised her staff at the killers with an incantation.

He touched a hand to his holy symbol, and healing warmth raced to his wound. The damage was still done, but he'd be able to fight until he could cast a proper healing prayer.

Faced by a kite shield and a longsword, the killers kept their distance, switching to thrown daggers and darts. They flanked as they went, trying to box the team in. Xan'De rampaged through out the camp, a whirlwind of mayhem. Nolan dispatched assassins with practiced ease, but their numbers kept up the pressure.

They fought for most of a minute, two more assassins falling to the heroes' blows.

A whistle cut through the sound of combat, and the remaining assassins backed off, disappearing into the brush. Nolan went charging off after them, until Xan'De caught up and pulled the man back.

"Patience, old friend! Where one trap is sprung, another two lie in waiting."

Nolan puffed, face red from exertion and rage, but he let himself be contained by the Matok.

"How did they breach our defenses?" Nolan asked.

King's mind went straight to the Tall Woman, though he had no evidence. If he were in her shoes, infiltrating a story being worked by a rival team, a three AM assassination attempt would be very high on his list of maneuvers.

Shirin closed her eyes, hand clutching her staff. "The enchantment has been dispelled. This would have taken someone with impressive magical capabilities."

King nodded. "That would be a tall order," he said. She nodded, taking his meaning.

"But what matters is that we're unharmed." King shifted weight and winced. "Mostly."

King put his weapon aside and sat. Shirin helped him dress the wound. When that was done, he intoned a longer prayer to Felur, which closed the wound.

"So, who do we think they were?" King asked.

Nolan snorted in derision. "Assassins from the Night-Lord, I'd wager. We've seen killers like this before."

Xan'De nodded. "They plagued us all the way to the castle. Each time, we were able to rout them as we did tonight, but they are formidable."

King said, "Well, I'm not going to get any more sleep tonight, so I've got watch." *Got to work the story. Figure out what her next move will be*, he thought.

"Nor I," Xan'De said. "Perhaps we can speak of philosophy, as you suggested."

"I'd be honored. Nolan, Shirin, get some sleep if you can."

Shirin nodded. "One of the advantages of getting older. Any bunk will do. I'll get to sleep now and wake for last watch to prepare my spells."

Nolan sat with his blades, cleaning and re-polishing, then crawled back into his tent.

King set another log on the fire. He leaned over and blew on the embers, coaxing them back up until they caught on the log. "I'd like to go back to the beginning. How is the Ay-eh different from the Yui?"

"The Ay-eh is all living things known and unknown," Xan'De said, taking a seat beside King. "Yui is the unity of all known things, past and future. They are like two axes, intersecting in the observable now."

"So, gods are of the Yui, but not the Ay-eh."

"Indeed. And ancestors are of the Ay-eh but not the Yui."

"So, each Matok's life circumscribes an area comprising the second derivative of a function of Yui over Ay-eh, as more things become known and living things move from alive to dead and from un-being to alive."

"Just so. And you spoke of a man and his cave. Did the man truly believe that shadows cast on the walls were the whole of reality?"

"Ah, no. The man and the cave is a story meant to teach the lesson that observable reality, what can be seen and perceived, is merely an interaction of senses with physical existence."

"So, Plato's shadows did not include Yui."

"Only a small slice of Yui, if I take your meaning. No men were willing to leave the cave, so they saw only manifestations; their worlds were small."

"They did not expand their Ay-eh."

King smiled. "I believe we're beginning to understand one another."

And so they talked on, in hushed voices, until the sun came up. King changed details and names but still managed to learn a great deal about Matok philosophy through story and complement it with mythology and philosophy from Earth Prime. The risk of cultural drift was incredibly low, as Xan'De's people were the Eternal Other—the Matok had not made a major impact on any kingdom or region in the Fantasy World in the two hundred years that it had been observed by the High Council.

But more importantly, he gained an understanding of the Matok and built trust. Even as he gave Xan'De and Nolan room to drive the story themselves, it was necessary to retain a strong relationship so he could "advise" and count on his words being heeded. It was a delicate balance to strike, a game of push and pull, like guiding a student through a rhetorical maze without ever letting them in on the joke that they were being led.

The morning came, and with it a fresh wave of fatigue. He brewed the coffee doubly strong that morning, promising himself he'd take last watch the next night to get himself a chance to catch up on sleep.

And soon, they'd be back in the capital, with real beds. And all-more-present danger.

* * *

Leah was on an honest-to-goodness dungeon crawl. Single-file party walking, trap-disarming, monster-fighting dungeon crawl. They battled bronze-and-gold automata animated by dwarven artifice, and dire rats that would make a Baltimore wharf rat jump on a boat and sail back to England.

If it weren't for Qargon being around and not in on the dice-chucking, ten-foot-pole-using jokes, she'd be cracking up. As it was, she quipped bard-style, drawing on her stand-up skills to find the right overlap between insight and joke about their surroundings and the care required to move through the tunnels the way they were.

"Something you don't hear about much is trap-finding speed. That gait where you balance expedience with care. Just fast enough to make good time, just slow enough to avoid blundering into poison darts or endless pits."

Working stand-up into her bardic paradigm also helped her stay focused, to look for hidden traps and other dangers. Qargon and Roman had enough dungeoneering skills to steer them right, but it never hurt to have backups.

Qargon led them into a new room with a similarly low roof. Leah had to stoop a hair, and Roman had taken to walking on his knees, strips of leather tied around his leggings as low-rent kneepads.

"Ach, this one here is a classic," Qargon said to the group as they stood in the doorway. "See the tiles here?"

Each tile was marked with a set of dwarven runes. "These rooms are built to test a visitor's knowledge of the life of the honored dead. K'gon in this case. We have to walk only on the right tiles and in the right order to recount one of the legends of K'gon."

"And you know these legends?"

"Aye, of course. The trick is figuring out which legend to use. There's snippets here from at least three."

Leah said, "I have a song for translation, but I imagine it'll go easier if you just do that for us."

"Aye," Qargon said. "You'll be wanting to save your strength."

Leah pulled out her journal, turning to a fresh page. She'd already filled dozens of pages taking notes on Bardic magic and songs, but plotting out a grid for a puzzle was 100% a valid use of parchment.

Once again, it turned out that a lot of dungeoneering came down to being prepared and taking your time. Leah took notes while Qargon sorted through the tiles and their associated tale snippets. Roman stood guard while Mallery rested, exhausted from all of those earth-shaping spells.

After the first few steps were decided, Leah piped in, drawing on her Genrenauts-honed sense of story progression. Dwarven legends, she'd read, used a four-act structure, where tension built and built, the action circling the climax until all the threads connected at once, the climax like a lodestone to complete an arch.

The three of them agreed on everything up to the last three pieces. They stood a mere twenty feet from the far side of the room.

Mallery pointed forward. "There's got to be at least three tiles left. That completes a perfect square of four stanzas of four."

"But there's only two lines left in the tale." Mallery pointed at the tile diagonally to her left. "K'gon's friends forged their fears into axes and faced the four lava fiends." Then she pointed to another tile in the final row. "And so, the fiends defeated, K'gon split the heart of the Lava Lord and brought peace to the under-realms."

Qargon tugged at his beard. "Aye, but that's only fifteen lines. There should be a sixteenth."

"Maybe the ending is in the far doorway?" Leah suggested.

Qargon held his lantern out toward the doorway. "There's no runes on the stone in the far landing."

Leah pointed. "But look, there are runes on the door frame. I count two on each side, and I think one on the underside of the lodestone."

"Aye, that'll be it. Well done, bard." Qargon hopped the last two tiles and reached out with a hand-axe to tap a rune in the doorway, which glowed.

The room shook, and the runes faded back into the tiles. The far door clicked and swung open, revealing the next hall.

Qargon clapped Leah on the shoulder with a meaty hand. "We'll make a proper tale-singer of you yet, young lady."

Leah staggered back, falling toward an incorrect tile. Mallery grabbed her hand and pulled her back. Leah squeezed her thanks and caught the comedienne blushing.

Leah pulled herself up and steadied. "For now, I'll settle for getting the Hammer and returning to the surface in one piece. I'm starting to miss the sun. And as someone who almost never sees the sunrise, let me tell you that is not my natural state of being."

"There was once a year where I never saw the sunrise," Mallery said. "The theater life."

"I didn't know Felur had theater."

Mallery recovered with practiced ease. "I wasn't always a priestess."

"Aye, I suppose. And I can understand yer impulse. Too long aboveground and I get twitchy, like I'm liable to step outside and fall into the sky. It won't be much further before the Hammer. Keep on."

* * *

Sure enough, after two more long hallways and a "fill the bucket" puzzle straight out of a computer RPG, they reached the burial chamber of K'gon the Mighty.

The room was tall, three dwarven stories or so, and every inch of it was carved and painted, perfectly preserved. A dozen arts and crafts filled the room—earthenware, weapons, textiles, scrolls of poetry, and more. A great king of craftsmen, honored in every dwarven discipline.

In the center of the room, resting in the hands of a life-size golden statue of K'gon carved into the sarcophagus, was the Hammer of K'gon. It looked like the love child of the Weta workshop and something out of Jack Kirby's *Thor*. It was ornately carved steel, runes and fractal designs on every inch. The Hammer had a flat, square head bigger than Leah's face, sloping back into a curved point on the other end. The head was mounted on a leather-wrapped handle, two feet long, with a spiked metal cap on the bottom.

"Cool."

"This is the final rest of K'gon the Mighty. It is venerable, it is sacred, it is far more than a place of mild temperature. Next we decipher how to call forth the spirit of K'gon to seek his blessing and receive the Hammer."

Mallery spoke a few quick words, then scanned the room. "This entire room is glowing with magic. And the Hammer is noon-day-sun levels of powerful." She shook her head and looked again, not strained this time. "All I can tell is that this is the Hammer. Or a decoy so good that no one could tell the difference until the artifact was used."

Qargon approached the sarcophagus with reverence. "Aye, this is the Hammer. I can feel it in my fingers, down to my gut. On my beard, this is the Hammer." Qargon continued to speak, his voice low, even. He spoke in dwarven, but it sounded different from what she'd heard before. Maybe Old Dwarven, or a high speech dialect.

"What's he saying?" Leah asked.

"It's what you'd expect," Roman said. "He introduced himself, his craft, and his lineage. Then some stuff I can't follow."

"So, what do we do?"

Mallery set her shield down. "For now, we wait."

Qargon continued, then waved the group forward. They came up and stood beside him.

"What now?" asked Leah.

"Patience, tale-weaver. Dwarves are not hasty people."

So, they waited. Leah focused on the sarcophagus, the craftsman's hammer, which looked for all the world like Mjolnir did in Marvel comics.

What felt like an hour later but was probably only a couple of minutes, a gong rang out from everywhere and nowhere, and white wispy smoke began to seep out from the sarcophagus. The smoke gathered atop the sarcophagus, taking the form of a dwarf. Of K'gon. The ghostly K'gon stood atop its mortal remains, a spiritual hammer held in its hands. He wore beautifully-crafted scale armor, and a geometrically-pattered helm over intricately-braided hair and beard.

"You come for the Hammer. For the power to destroy and remake. But to earn my masterpiece, you must present me with a work of equal magnificence. What works have you to earn the Hammer of K'gon?"

And here we go.

Chapter Twelve:
The Hammer of K'gon

The spirit of K'gon looked down at them from atop the sarcophagus.

The group huddled up.

Qargon said, "As suspected. We'll each get one chance to present our greatest display of skill. If none of our displays are deemed worthy...well, it'll be bad. I'll go first. And if none of our offerings satisfy the old man, then be ready to run."

That's not ominous or anything, Leah thought, looking up at the spirit, its face neutral with a hint of disapproval. But that was basically resting face for dwarves.

Something clicked in her brain. Leah smiled and dropped to the floor, sitting cross-legged. She assembled her writing materials, parchment, pen, and ink.

"I'm going last," she said, writing shorthand (or as best as she could with quill and ink). She produced the notebook she'd been using to record her observations and notes about Qargon and dwarven culture, the bits and pieces of material she'd been assembling since they hired the dwarf.

Qargon stepped forward, presenting his axe. It was a work of beauty, functional and elegant. Leather straps in different colors held emblems and badges, which he'd described and identified over their days of travel together. Each represented an accomplishment, an alliance, or a memory of a failure become a lesson. His whole life was in that axe, its construction and the tale it told since it was forged.

"Mighty K'gon, I present you my greatest accomplishment, my axe, Fear-crusher, forged by my own two hands and adorned with a living memory of my deeds."

The spirit took the axe from Qargon's hands and appraised it. K'gon tested the balance of the haft, spinning it slowly through several cuts and spins. It thumbed the edge of the blade, then raised the axe and looked down the haft.

Leah stopped paying attention after that, focusing on her display. She liked working on her feet, but with improv, you had people to work off of. But going into an untested stand-up routine only a week in the making? That was a whole other level of trouble.

* * *

Mallery pondered her approach while K'gon evaluated Qargon's axe. They had four chances, total. *What would impress the spirit of a dwarven hero? A soliloquy? Some divine blessing?* Leah was scribbling away, clearly already on some track. Roman had years of heroic adventures to draw from, or a sales catalog's worth of weapon demonstrations with his overloaded kit.

What could she do that was different enough, distinct enough? From what she knew about dwarves, it would need to come from the heart but also display skill.

K'gon took a deep breath, and then handed the axe back to Qargon.

"This is a marvelous work, cousin. I applaud you for the skill and care it took to forge, and congratulate you for the accolades you have earned with it by your side."

Qargon perked up, eyes gleaming.

"But it is not worthy of the Hammer."

Their companion folded in on himself, heartbroken. He accepted the axe and slumped backward. The dwarf needed consolation, but they didn't have time to waste.

Roman stepped forward and offered up a tale of his heroics, the dune buggies and motorcycles of his home replaced by chariots and horses. But still, it was a classic tale—a noble hero, people in need, a journey across harsh conditions with would-be slavers nipping at their heels the entire way. It was a Max tale, from not long before he left his home and came to Earth Prime. He'd said many times that it was the story from his past he was most proud of, that had almost made him want to stay despite the endless repetition and desperate conditions.

And he told it fabulously.

When he finished and stepped back, Qargon said "A fine tale. Your accolades should be remembered and celebrated. But I am a legend of my people. I drove away the Fungal Lords, led a host of thousands. You were a hero to dozens, and their lives have meaning. But your story is not worthy of the Hammer."

Roman tensed for a moment, and Mallery raised a hand to calm him again. It was a hard move, trying to compare heroism to a legendary figure in Epic Fantasy World. Post-Apocalyptic just operated at a different scale. In a world where ninety percent of humanity was gone, saving a few dozen was like saving thousands. But Roman couldn't exactly make that clear. Not without revealing the reality of where he'd come from. "I'm from another plane" would take even more explaining. Draw attention and scrutiny that they didn't need.

Roman squeezed Mallery's hand and stepped back, accepting the dwarven spirit's judgment.

I'm up, Mallery thought, and stepped forward.

She spread her arms and spoke a spell that she'd only used once before, channeling Felur's power to speak to the spirit world.

Wind stirred from nowhere and everywhere to rustle her tabard. Her holy symbol glowed white, then became as a prism, every color in the rainbow shining out and illuminating the tomb.

But that was just the special effects.

Mallery reached out to the spirits of the dwarves buried with K'gon. She felt them with a sixth sense—not quite touch, not quite hearing, but somewhere between the two. It was the same sense she got when she was really nailing a bit or fully in character. Call it flow, call it the zone, or call it the touch of God's love, it was all one and the same.

She reached out to them one by one, tugging on the threads to draw forth the spirits.

She reached out to K'gon's shield-bearer, his lifelong servant and friend. One.

She reached out to his sister, his loyal critic, master craftswoman, builder of his great machines of war.

Two.

And she reached out to his wife, a legendary smith, who had crafted him armor so fine that it could not be penetrated by spell or blade.

Mallery reached up with her holy symbol, and the light filled the room, going full whiteout. She felt the air crack. The spirits strode forth from behind her.

She turned and saw the dwarven ghosts, each a different shade—the shield-bearer blue, his sister grey, his wife red.

"My liege," said the shield-bearer.

"Brother," said his sister.

"My love," said his wife.

K'gon's eyes went wide, but only for a moment.

"Mere parlor tricks. Spirits are mere echoes. Were you to truly bring my loved ones back to me in the flesh, hale and whole, then the Hammer would be yours."

"They're every bit as real as you, great craftsman," Mallery said. "Talk with them yourself if you still doubt."

The three stepped forward, rising onto the sarcophagus. The four began to speak, and Mallery could tell just from their body language that their conversation was a private one, words left unsaid.

She stepped back, bringing the others with her. "Let them have their moment. Divided three ways, the spell will not last long."

"Good," Leah said. "Give me a few more minutes, and I think I've got something that will knock him dead." She cocked her head, looking back at the ghost. "It'll kill. Nope, not that, either. The comedy sayings, they do nothing! Good thing I didn't try to use them against the skellies. But yeah, close to done. Stall for me."

The ghostly companions did the stalling for them for ten minutes solid. Mallery tried not to pry, only glancing back on occasion. She saw hugging, arguments, tears, and finally, reconciliation.

"Priestess, you have my thanks," K'gon said, his ghostly companions standing at his side. Mallery released the spell, and one by one, the spirits dissipated, flowing back to their earthly remains.

"That was a great gift you have given me. Too many words left unsaid, grudges I was too stubborn to set aside."

Mallery beamed, neglecting to hold in her pride. She'd hoped this would work. They were a team, but there was little wrong with wanting to succeed, to be the one to pull it out in a clutch situation. You put in the work in the chorus, but it wasn't wrong to want applause for your solo.

"But this art is known to me. It is mighty, but it is the blessing of a god, not the prowess of a mortal. It is not worthy of the Hammer."

What? Mallery bit the word back before she spoke, shouting only in her mind. She had to keep her cool. An angry dwarf spirit was way worse than an unimpressed dwarf spirit.

"I am very sorry to hear that, mighty K'gon. But I am glad to have done you a service."

"A boon you will have. Should your final companion's display fail to prove worthy of the Hammer, I will repay your kindness in giving me ten minutes of my life again by summing those spirits by giving you a ten-minute head start before releasing the tomb's wrath upon you."

That's dwarven mercy for you, Mallery thought.

"Child," K'gon said, regarding Leah. "Your turn has come."

Leah said, in classic fashion, "Gulp."

* * *

Leah stood, her notes in hand. At least this time, she didn't have to wear heels.

She walked forward, finding her light at the middle of the room, standing between the two torches at her sides.

"Good evening! Or is it morning? I can never tell down here. Silly me, I forgot to bring a clock."

K'gon did not respond. *Okay, so, not the best opening.* Leah stopped and cocked her head. "Which makes me wonder—before clocks, how did dwarves tell time? Was it just dead reckoning, or do the bioluminescent plants and rocks have their own time cycle? All these years living on the surface and I never learned how things worked for dwarves. Read countless epics about parties of heroes, always including a dwarf, but all the scribes were human. So, of course, I never got more than a stereotypical view of your people."

Leah started pacing, working the room, turning so Qargon, Mallery, and Roman were in view. She was more comfortable with an audience. Or, more specifically, with more of an audience than the Ghost of Judgy Dwarves Past staring her down from his eminently lootable but probably-trapped-as-hell sarcophagus.

"But now I've traveled the under-roads, seen the beauty of dwarven cities. Proper dwarven cities, mind you. I mean, Ag'ra is nice and all, but that's like saying that Hammett is a human city when Fallran City is right there, just fifty leagues away."

"Anyway. Something I wondered about dwarves is whether the incredible patience is an inborn thing, or whether it's cultural. And I've always been afraid to ask—it's kind of insensitive, and it's always hard to ask awkward questions. I remember kids asking me about my eyes, and gods bless them, they weren't being mean, they'd just never seen anyone like me before, and they had more curiosity than courtesy. And it seems like dwarves have it even worse. You hang out in your amazing castles and kingdoms, keep the surface lands safe from the terrifying monsters from the underneath, and most surfacers never even bother to find out what dwarven people have really contributed."

The spirit started nodding along with her. *Building rapport, good. Keep it up,* she told herself.

"And speaking of monsters—those fungal ants? Terrifying. I wish there were more dwarves around, because I bet if they were, I'd have never seen those things. Zombies are one thing, but fungal zombie giant ants? I may never sleep again. Not without a stack of charms and walls taller than an elf standing on a giant's shoulder."

Leah snuck a peek at K'gon, as she'd mostly been avoiding direct eye contact. One, because he was dead and kind of creepy, and two, because now that she had started, she was going to get through her material, failure or not. And then she was going to be ready to run. Not too different from her comedy career back on Earth Prime, actually. Just replace drunken "fans" making sloppy passes with dwarven death traps, and they were practically the same.

Okay. Not that similar, she admitted to herself. But still dangerous.

"So, anyway, the thing about dwarven cities I like best is that they're beautiful at every distance, from every angle. On the horizon, the skyline is magnificent; it tells the story of the city like a beautiful silhouette painted against the backdrop of darkness.

"You get closer and see the larger designs, the thoughtfulness that went into the municipal design—everything has its place; it's planned, not like human cities that sprout up which-what-ever way like an untended field."

Leah paused and risked looking K'gon right in the eyes.

"And then you walk into the city and you find yourself surrounded by brilliance. Countless lives' work in every single inch of the city. Fractal designs carved into walls, murals on every surface, weapons with histories and names, clothes so brilliantly constructed and tailored that no two are alike. Every block is a fashion show and an art gallery, and a gladiatorial arena. Dwarves pursue excellence like it was water and breathable air. They yearn for it, always striving, never settling.

"I've only just recently seen dwarves and dwarven construction with my own two eyes, but damned if I haven't been waiting my whole life for it. And for that, all I can say is thank you.

"And while you're at it, can you tell me how those awesome braids work? I'm thinking of growing a beard."

K'gon looked down at Leah, his face impassive.

Her racing heartbeat switched from "performer's high" to "ready to run".

The dwarven spirit took a breath, *Which is weird because it's not like he was breathing, right?* and laughed.

He laughed. From dour to delighted, the laughter changed all of the lines of his face, making him look like a kindly uncle.

"That was not any art or skill known to me. It fits no established aesthetic traditions, no recognizable crafts."

K'gon the Mighty, master builder, warrior, leader, smiled. "Brilliant. Singular. Real experience, shared with honesty and humility, and yet confidence."

"Wait, you liked it?" Leah asked before she could stop herself.

Did I do it? Did I really pull this off? she thought.

"I was perplexed at first, but then both flattered and honored. What do you call this art?"

Emotional whiplash brought her back from panic and confusion to pride. "It's an obscure form of bardic performance. Standing speech." It was barely comedy, more like the autobiographical portions of a comic's larger set. But it worked. *Holy crap, it worked.* The thought echoed in her mind.

"Entirely distinct, yes. Unlike tall tales, limerick, or shaggy Jek stories. Quite impressive."

K'Gon continued. "What is your name, child?"

"Leah. Of the Tang clan."

"Leah of the Tang, you have shown your prowess, shared with me an art style unknown to my people, and opened my eyes to a new way of understanding my world. Your gift was yours alone to give, not granted, and not a mere display of prowess."

He continued. "Your gift is worthy of the Hammer."

Hell, yeah! Leah thought, pumping her fist.

The spirit stepped forward and held the Hammer out toward her, balanced in both hands.

"The Hammer will shatter any surface, break any shield or armor. But it can only be wielded by the worthy."

Whoever wields this Hammer, if she be worthy... Leah heard in her mind.

She set down her notes and stepped forward to accept the artifact. It dropped into her hands like a ton of bricks, but within a millisecond, it was lighter, no heavier than a baseball bat. She tested the weight, taking a couple of two-handed swings. The weight distribution was different from a longsword, but not too different. And it handled like a dream. It wanted to swing, wanted to cut through the air, but twisted and moved, the haft responding to the smallest torque.

Leah stepped back and saluted K'gon with the Hammer, then rested it on her shoulders. She turned to the others and said, "Well, how about that."

Mallery's expression was mixed between pride and disappointment. Her blessing had been nothing short of astonishing—thoughtful, poignant, and unforgettable. It should have been her. But in the end, Leah had been the one to take away the prize. This would be a thing.

Any time only one of them got to win in some solo quest or get the singular spotlight, the other would feel left out. Especially since so much of their background and training put them in the running for the same archetypes and roles in stories.

She tried to nip that disappointment in the bud. "Your spell was amazing, Mallery. You might not have seen, but I was totally crying when K'gon was talking with his wife. It should have been yours that he chose. I just poured my heart out."

Qargon's smile was somehow wider than his face. "That was no mere outpouring. That was a tapestry. I'd heard it in small bits and pieces, but the way you wove it together was as masterful as any dwarven tale-spinner!"

I saved the day because it turns out dwarves are an easy mark for stand-up. Who knew? Maybe King did. He was crafty like that.

Leah would have liked more time just with Mallery. Would have to get around to that later, make sure she felt as good about her offering as she really should. "Thank you! I honestly had no idea that he'd be as moved as he was. I just knew that it was my best opportunity to show him something he'd never seen or heard before."

Roman asked, "So, does this mean we don't have to escape the tomb as it crumbles around us?"

Qargon gestured toward the exit with his torch. "Let's not wait around to find out."

Even if they'd had to flee the tomb, Leah would still have the Cheshire-cat grin slapped on her face.

As it was, when they ran into another pack of giant fungus-ridden ants, Leah was ready, McGuffin in tow.

Chapter Thirteen:
For Want of a Thief

Nolan and Xan'De led King and Shirin all around the capital, through pubs and brothels and black markets and bolt-holes.

But Alaria, the fellowship's designated rogue, was nowhere to be seen. Her trail had gone dead weeks earlier, not long after Theyn's death during the failed siege.

Which meant that when Mallery/Leah/Roman's group signaled they'd successfully recovered the Hammer of K'gon and were on their way back to the capital, King knew he'd need to make a choice sooner rather than later.

They had less than three weeks left on their timer, or risk the world getting its hooks in them. Going over by a day or two wasn't out of the question, but they still had to get back to the town where they'd landed, even after they'd toppled the Night-Lord.

He'd considered just giving the Hammer to Theyn's friends and letting them have at it. But from the team's report, the weapon was bonded to Leah. And he had little reason to believe the remaining companions could defeat the Night-Lord on their own, even if the Hammer could be transferred.

Every day, the skies got a bit more purple, even at the sun's zenith. King gave it another month before it was purple midnight-dark twenty-four hours a day. Not that the Night-Lord seemed to have a plan of how to manage agriculture that way, but Evil Overlords weren't well known for their agricultural acumen.

The breach was nearly two months old now and was well on its way to becoming permanent. He could only guess at the level of ripples back on Earth. There'd be a huge resetting of the status quo, assuming they could patch the breach and get home in one piece. It'd been years since a breach lasted this long. This region and a few others operated in longer time spans—days on Earth Prime equating to weeks or years in-world. That would mitigate some of the impact. But they'd started three days behind, and when you combined that with the increased ferocity of the breaches in the past year...

There'd likely be several more missions to this region and the others in Fantasy World over the next few months, as the ripples played out across a dozen other stories. In the meantime, hundreds, maybe thousands of people would burn out on their jobs, their art, their relationships, unable to imagine brighter alternatives, happier possibilities. The liberating and conciliatory power of Fantasy would be weakened. And given where current events were, the results could be disastrous.

But for the moment, there was only one mission, one breach, one team. His.

Spending all this time in taverns and boardinghouses was also eating deep into King's purse. Stay much longer and he would need to start sharking locals at cards to cover their room and board.

King decided to head the problem off at the pass and start generating some income. But it was really all a cover for working counterintelligence. Looking for spies or informants for the Night-Lord.

And for the Tall Woman. He still wasn't sure Leah's theory was right, but it hurt little to stay on the look-out.

After the assassination attempt, he'd kept his eyes peeled every waking moment. And his worry went to overdrive any time they entered a settlement.

Every day, one or another woman caught his attention. A flash of hair, the confidence of movement. But they were never her. But he still kept his guard up.

The Tall Woman had moved through criminal circles on the Crime World, and if Leah was right about her being a rouge Genrenaut, maybe she'd do the same again.

King scratched the polish off his shoes, ruffled up his clothes, and walked several blocks over to find a tavern that had been on Shirin and Xan'De's list, where no one had seen him in at least a couple of years, the last time the team had come to the capital on a mission.

Affecting a slight limp, King walked into the Split Purse, the kind of thieves' bar found in every city and many larger towns.

King slipped to the side and waited a moment as his vision adjusted to the lower light. Though it was midafternoon, this place forfeited natural light in order to keep the windows closed.

The tavern was only half-full, down a half-dozen ruffians from its usual crowd.

The criminal ecology of Fantasy World regions was fascinating. A city like this would have a proper thieves' guild, maybe even two or three competing factions. They'd have their own cutpurse bureaucracy and pecking order, which meant he had to be careful which lowlifes to swindle and when.

Thanks to that criminal ecology, there was always a game of cards happening at the Split Purse, any hour of the day or night. And there they were—several regulars, including, a dismayed merchant being fleeced of his jewels, an unshaven roguish type, and an off-duty city guard with a bawdy serving maid on his lap.

King affected the British-esque accent of Elara, making him present like an out-of-towner totally out of his element.

"Hello, friends. Can I join your game? It looks very interesting."

The unshaven rogue grinned, showing a silver tooth, and pulled over a chair. "Of course, friend. Take a seat. We're real friendly-like."

And so King went to work.

* * *

Two hours later and fifty coins richer, King bought his new friends a round to thank them for the game, then stood and made for the exit.

And when the roughs caught up to him two blocks later, chasing him into an alley, he did them the favor of not hurting them too much. They didn't even have the courtesy to fight together.

One lunged at him with a rusted knife, overhand. True murderers knew to stab for the gut, quickly and repeatedly, like a jackhammer. Going overhand gave him time to step to the side, grab the would-be killer by the wrist, and respond with a jab to the solar plexus. King wrapped the grab into a quick hold and tossed the thief into a pile of refuse in the alley, turning just as the other sore loser came at him with a knife.

But this one could fight. King dodged back, and the knife-swipe cut into his leather jerkin. Sensing a more dangerous opponent, King danced away again and pulled a knife out of his boot.

"This will go better if you just walk," King said, dropping his accent.

The tough's answer took the form of a lunge. King rolled to the side, pushing the striking arm away with a backhand block. He countered with his own thrust, low and fast. The tough dodged forward out of the way.

The men turned and squared off again.

They circled, changing guards and grips, left hand to right, overhand grip to underhand. King read his opponent, watched the shifting of his weight, the rhythm of his breath.

The tough got tired of waiting and stepped forward with a slash at King's wrist. King raised his hand and turned to slash into the man's blow, scoring a cut along his assailant's forearm.

The mugger winced but had the skill to catch the knife in his other hand without missing more than a single beat.

But one beat was all King needed. He closed on the sore loser and wrapped his free hand around the tough's other arm and pulled them both down. King turned and laid the tough out on the ground, his unwounded arm pinned beneath him, knife out of play.

King knelt on the man's back, knife tip to his assailant's neck.

"You could have walked. You're lucky I'm not the killing type when I don't have to be."

King clocked the man over the head with the pommel of his knife, and the tough dropped unconscious. That move only worked in story worlds, but it was damned effective.

Taking a spare cloth from his pouches, King tied down his cuts to stem the flow of blood.

Then the Genrenaut rolled both men, checking their coats and pockets for loose change (to teach them a lesson) and for any spare intel or jobs they might be working (to teach King more about what was going on in the city). His first search turned up a half-dozen spare Vekk, but neither men had any useful intel on hand.

They'd been too long idle in waiting for the rest of the team. There would be other waylays, complications designed to keep the story interesting, until the team was reunited. It wouldn't be long. But in the meantime, he shouldn't go out on his own anymore. It had been reckless to do so already. But the closer to the end of the mission they got, the closer he got to facing the music, to owning up to what he'd done to pursue the mission. He'd used the judgment he'd gained in decades of service and acted according to the spirit of the Genrenauts' mission, rather than the letter of the Council's dictate. He'd been telling Leah to follow her instincts for months, to trust in her judgment. It would be hypocritical if he didn't do the same.

King walked the remaining block to their tavern, unsurprised that there'd been no city watch response to his altercation. Half the watch had quit town when the Night-Lord had taken over, and what remained were all in the pockets of the rich—they didn't come downhill anymore except for graft and indulgence. But no guard meant he got to keep his coin and the robbers' purses to boot.

Shirin spotted him from the team's habitual booth in their tavern and nodded. King gestured to the private room, preferring to manage his wounds quietly instead of advertising the fact he'd been in a fight. The Night-Lord was bound to have spies throughout the city, people ruled by fear, pressed into service because of a kidnapped loved one.

"What have you gotten yourself into in my absence, fearless leader?" Shirin closed the door as King lowered himself down onto one of the beds, wounded arm clutched to his chest. Each room slept two. Xan'De and Nolan's room was next door, though he hadn't seen either in the common room coming back in.

"Went looking for a friendly game," King said. "When I won too many games, they got a lot less friendly."

"It seems like you've been looking for a lot of friendly games this week."

"Seems like. That ends now. The world's trying to keep things interesting for us while the others make their way back. That means we need to lay low so we can expedite and force the finale."

King unwound the strip of cloth and rolled back his sleeve, biting his lip as the dirty cloth pulled out of the wound. He used a simple healing prayer, then dressed the wound.

"You and I can stay put, but Xan'De and Nolan are ready to start a tavern brawl at the drop of a hat."

"That's what worries me."

"Back to the common room? We can at least try to keep an eye on them."

King played along, but worry continued to creep up on him, cutting away at his confidence in their chances of success. And if he brought them there and they stayed for nearly seven weeks only to fail? Well that would look even worse to the Council.

Hurry up, kids. We need to move into Act Three, and soon.

* * *

A magical hammer was an infinitely better weapon for fighting skeletons than an espada ropera, as Leah learned time and time again on the road back from the dwarven lands.

In the two weeks it took them to get back out of the under-roads and head back toward the capital to meet up with the remaining companions and other Genrenauts, Leah had put the Hammer through its paces, and was already thinking of ways she could take it with her when they went back to Earth Prime. Just hang it up in the ready room or stow it away in her personal gear section for their next trip back to fantasyland.

She fought with artifact and jest alike, bolstering her allies and crushing all opposition.

And by night, she continued to practice her songs, keep up her sword (and hammer) play, teach Qargon about human comedy, and carve out precious moments alone with Mallery. They'd been there, in Mission-Dating mode, for over a month. It was amazing getting to see her every day away from the prying eyes of HQ. Roman didn't care, and Qargon had clued in at some point along the way, and helped give them their privacy.

Leah had never had this much time with an SO this quickly. She'd always been in school or working, or traveling for comedy competitions or trying to work the open-mic circuit. It was simultaneously almost too much while never being quite enough. It was always still Mission-Dating, not alone time on their own terms.

"We're so taking a long weekend after we get back. We can do a spa day, then hit the museums, go to the Eastern Shore…" Mallery had a different plan of what they could do when they got back nearly every day. She painted this whole story of their immediate future, and every version was fabulous. They just had to make it through the end of the mission first.

And so it was, five and a half weeks after they'd arrived in Fantasy-land, Leah, Roman, Mallery, and Qargon arrived at the capital city, ready to bring the Night-Lord's dark reign to an end.

Or die trying.

Chapter Fourteen:
The Council of Heroes

Two teams reunited in an unassuming cottage at the edge of the royal woods, far from the center of the city. Declan answered the door, and the party filed inside. The cottage had once been a hunting lodge, from the look of it. Roaring fire, empty spots on the wall where game would be displayed.

But now, the place was one hundred percent wizard-y. Crystals, beakers, bags of components, a great silvered mirror, pillars of marble, and a cauldron large enough to classify as a jacuzzi. The whole place was lit by crystals and oddly colored candle flames.

They filed into the cottage in several groups, spacing their arrival out to not attract notice. Mallery, Leah, and Qargon were the last group.

In total, they numbered five Genrenauts, a dwarf, three of the failed fellowship of Theyn Lighthall, and a chatelaine. It made for a very full room. There were hugs and introductions and heroic stories of battles traded back and forth.

Leah immediately apologized for her mistake on the road, even though they'd called it in weeks ago.

"That was incredibly reckless. I expect you made your apologies to the others already?" King asked.

"Of course. I begged forgiveness, and forgiveness was granted."

King looked to Mallery, who nodded. As did Roman.

"In that case, I trust you've learned from that mistake and proven wiser in the meantime?"

"That I have. To the best of my ability."

"Wisdom indeed! She earned the right to bear the Hammer of K'Gon!"

Qargon said, busting into Genrenauts business. He raised Leah's hand holding the Hammer. The artifact shone like it had been professionally lit. Mallery, Leah, and Roman introduced Qargon to the remaining companions, and Nolan asked where Alaria was.

"She's not with you, and she never appeared when we were searching. That's suspicious, isn't it?"

Ioseph called the group to a long table. "She's always kept some things to herself. Perhaps she fled, her spirit broken. Perhaps she betrayed us to the Night-Lord for coin. Or perhaps her real place in this tale is yet to be told."

"Well-said, Ioseph," King said.

Being the wizard that he was, Ioseph had exactly the right number of chairs around his table. Mallery wasn't sure if that was a magical talent or a genre-derived one, and she supposed from their perspective, it might as well be the same thing. Just like how Tolkien wizards were never early or late. Except when they were.

Wizards were as close to Genrenauts as this world came. The long view of history and destiny, a bit of manipulation of the cosmology. But only wizards got the pointed hats and the huge gem-laden staves. That staff-plus-gem combination was traced to the Peter Jackson *Lord of the Rings* films, though there were instances from long before.

"Please, be seated," the wizard said, pipe in hand. Another classic affectation. A little bit of her pined for tobacco, a throwback to her most nervous Broadway days.

"How fared your quest to reunite the army?" King asked.

Ioseph's face turned dark. "The army is scattered, its leaders taken and turned. We must take the castle directly and confront the Night-Lord ourselves. There are many such matters to discuss, but first, dinner. I don't believe in planning on an empty stomach."

Nolan and Xan'De sat, unfazed, as if they'd gone through this routine many times before. Mallery had as well, just not this specific routine. If King were leading the show, there would be more legal pads and seminar-style discussion.

Ioseph raised his staff, then rattled off a paragraph's worth of not-Latin. Blue light settled over the bare table, and in the blink of an eye, a feast appeared— roast duck, stuffed pheasant, several stews, salads, candied fruits, complicated vegetable arrangements in the shapes of monsters and fantastical creatures, and a half-dozen carafes of wine, with just as many pitchers of ale beside.

That was a new one. She shared a look with Leah and started pouring the wine.

Ioseph chuckled, seeming to bask in the Genrenauts' delight. "Sit. Eat. Drink. Tonight, we plot a revolution."

And a happy ending, Mallery thought.

* * *

Leah avoided the urge to overeat. It was easier, given Fantasy World's predisposition toward just about all food being one or another type of meat. So, as the Genrenauts and companions crept through the tunnel, which ran from the safe-house pantry all the way through to the castle's grain stores, the only heavy weight in her stomach was from nerves.

They'd been there, working on this story, for longer than she'd spent in the field for any five other missions. The sense of momentum, of building to something, pressed in on her closer than the narrow halls and low ceilings of the tunnel. The regulations and mission logs said that Fantasy World missions could last longer, as did those of some Science Fiction and Romance regions. Any region where the most popular stories played out over the course of months, even years.

Every one of Leah's missions so far had been short-term, more like a movie or TV episode than an entire novel or hundred-plus-hour computer role-playing game. But she'd put in hundreds of hours in the field there, had time to grow into her role, to level up. She'd become a competent rider, a solid lute player, and, given K'gon's blessing, an impressive bard.

Maybe this is what it's like to be a Real Genrenaut, she thought.

Her mind back on her work and the task at hand, she focused again on the world in front of her. Mold and mustiness filled the stuffy air, but they walked the two miles under the city without incident.

"As I suspected," Declan said. "The Night-Lord doesn't know about the secret ways. Though of royal blood, he is not of Fallran."

Ioseph stroked his beard. "Regardless, we must expect heavy resistance as soon as we come upon anyone not of the household staff."

Nolan added, "I know the quick routes through the castle; between me and Declan, we should be able to lead you right."

Xan'De nodded. "Upon the edge of a knife, the dancing leaf relies on the wind to avoid becoming its own neighbor."

"And what's that supposed to mean, sorry?" Roman asked.

"He means that we're in a difficult situation, and we need all circumstances to go our way so we don't die."

The Matok smiled.

Declan raised a finger to his lips as they approached the far end of the tunnel. They sneaked the last hundred feet, Leah keeping the Hammer of K'gon resting on her shoulder. After two weeks of practice, she felt more than comfortable with the artifact, in no small part thanks to feeling like it weighed about half of what it should while still hitting as hard.

She'd been voted down on trying the Hammer on ruins or trees, but everything else she'd tried shattered in the face of the Hammer.

Let's just hope the Deathstone isn't an exception.

They came to an old wooden door, clasps rusty but functional. Declan opened the door and disappeared into the cellar, then returned a minute later, waving them in.

Once inside, they split into two squads: Leah with the companions, Declan with the rest of the Genrenauts. Which meant that Leah was the stand-in for Theyn Lighthall.

She was basically the Chosen One. It was all coming full circle. The stand-up bit about the Chosen One had gotten her the job, and now it was her turn to be the Special instead of the orphan from Iowa. She'd just had to wait about fifteen years for her chance. Now she was storming the castle to defeat a Dark Lord and save the kingdom.

Eat your heart out, Orphan Joe from Iowa.

The cellar gave way to a hallway, then a stairwell, then another hallway.

Where are the skeletons? she wondered. The party continued, Declan leading the companions, Genrenauts behind. Leah stood between Xan'De and Ioseph, Nolan at the back.

They stepped into a wide hall. Declan pointed. "From here, we can bear right, and then it's straight up the tower."

"I sense great sorcery afoot," Ioseph said. "It's permeated the very walls. Fates only know what abominations the Night-Lord has wrought in our absence."

"Take the left way," Nolan added. "It's less visible from the balcony."

Declan followed Nolan's suggestion, creeping along the left-hand side of the wide hall, adorned with tapestries of the former Kings of Fallran, their epic deeds. Every twenty feet sported a lit brazier, yellow-orange flame a welcome change from the purple tainting the sky both day and night.

Halfway down the hall, the lights went out, replaced by a sickly purple glow at the center of the room. And as light filled the great hall, everything changed.

And at the center of the room, standing beside the source of the light, stood a cloaked man, tall but slim. His arms were raised, hands crackling with magical power.

The Night-Lord laughed, his cackle echoing throughout the hall. And as it resonated, skeletal troops poured out from every exit, cutting the heroes off entirely.

"Welcome back, old friends. I see you've brought new offerings."

Three figures stepped out from behind the glowing stone, the Deathstone.

One was a leather-clad Latina, decked out in assassin gear with knives galore. Her face was covered by a veil, short black hair drawn up like an anime heroine, right down to the blue streak of hair at her temple.

Beside her was a slim man, fair-skinned with black hair. His whole look exuded Dark Prince, embodying the antihero or lovable villain mold. He picked his nails with a gold-hilted knife, face locked into a haughty sneer.

And at their center was the Tall Woman. Leah was right. It was the same woman who had been in her first mission, run poor Theo Long over, and interrupted his reconciliation. The same woman who had taken shots at King and her just weeks before, who had killed the inadvertent killer Ricardo Hernandez. She was back again, traveling across dimensions to interfere with the story worlds. For what reason? Was she following them, or were the ripples her fault and they were following her? What was her relationship to the Night-Lord? What did she want? Who were these people with her? Minions? Or were they a whole team of dimensional travelers?

Questions bounced around so fast that her mind became an overworked racquetball court. She pointed an accusatory finger and said, "I was right!"

King gave her a short nod that said, *Yes, but be quiet right now.* His nods said a lot. Perks of being the boss.

"What are you doing here?" Nolan asked, his eyes locked on the Tall Woman.

She raised a finger and *tsk-tsk*ed him. "You're in the presence of royalty. Be silent."

The group shifted into fighting positions as the skeletons closed in.

Leah grabbed the Hammer in both hands, plotting a path through the melee to get a clean shot at the Deathstone. Nolan took a step over to stand by her side. She nodded at the older swordsman as he drew his blade. Nolan raised his blade as the skeletons charged.

In the heat of battle, time slowed. The old warrior turned.

First, she wondered why he was turning to her. He raised his pommel and Leah realized too late what was happening. She couldn't raise her weapon in time. The last thing she saw was Nolan's pommel coming down on her head. She felt a sense of completion, of book-ending. She'd claimed the Hammer, proven her theory right. All to die right before the finale?

Was this really the end?

The last thing she remembered was thinking *What the eff?*

END EPISODE FIVE

Episode Six:
The Failed Fellowship (Part Two)
The Heroes of Fallran

Chapter One:
Tower Defense Game

Leah awoke to the sound of howling winds. Her head throbbed, and her vision was foggy like someone had wrapped her up as a cheesecloth mummy. The world was lit in purple, and as her eyes tried to focus, her ears gave her far clearer input.

"Good, you're awake. How do you feel?" It was Shirin, her voice strained but steady.

Leah sat up and focused on the dark blur that she thought was Shirin. Colors sorted themselves out from one another, especially after Leah remembered that everything would be in a purple filter thanks to the Night-Lord's world-dominating, skeleton-animating toy.

Mallery sat beside Shirin. They were both safe. What about the others? What had happened?

"Where are we? Dungeon?"

Mallery nodded. "Tower cells. And the rooms are enchanted, no magic allowed. We've tried everything. Cantrips, blessings, rituals, prayers. Nada."

"That's a good trick. Always hate when the bad guy locks up the heroes but doesn't remember who he's dealing with. It's just lazy. Seems like this one has read the Evil Overlord Manual."

Mallery grinned at the reference. At least she was safe. Safe-ish. No more in danger than any of them. If something had happened to her while Leah was out...

Not useful, she told herself.

Shirin waved toward the door, which had a tiny grated glass window. "King and the boys are locked up across the hall, but the skeletons took all of our equipment, including the comms. And the rooms are soundproofed."

Leah pushed herself up onto the hanging cots of the room. The walls were gray stone, tinged by the same purple light to look almost metallic, like their world had been inexplicably crossed over with cyberpunk.

That'd be cool. Thaumopunk needs to be more of a thing, she thought aimlessly.

"So, what's our move? With no magic, it's down to like faking illness or taking out the guards when we're en route somewhere."

Shirin walked over to the window, looking out into the purple dawn. "Narrative logic would suggest that the Night-Lord will want to gloat at us at least once before he kills us. That'll be our opportunity, unless something else comes up."

"So, why do you think the Tall Woman is here?" Leah asked, picking up on the gnarliest of the loose threads in the story. "Were those people with her other dimensional travelers? What are we going to do about her?"

"I got knocked out before I could get that much of a read on them," Mallery said.

"Our first priority is to patch the breach. If we can bring the Tall Woman and the others in, then that's a bonus. But for now, we need to focus on escaping."

Leah gestured to the room. "Right now it looks like all we have is time. And judging by when she showed up, I'd bet dollars to donuts that she's playing some role in the story, which makes her part of the breach."

Leah sat up on the cot with Mallery, resting her head on the taller woman's shoulder. She was talking a good talk, but this was the worst situation she'd been in yet. No weapons, no comms, nowhere near enough information about the new characters added to the story.

Mallery wrapped Leah in her arms. No matter what, they'd face it together. "I'm glad you're okay."

"Me too. And it's nice to be able to talk normally again without breaking concealment protocols."

"The danger of ensemble stories," Shirin said. "King, Roman, and I once spent nearly six weeks traveling with a Chosen One Princess on a mission most of a decade back. It was a standard deliver-the-McGuffin-to-the-Axis-Mundi kind of quest, but her protectors had all died before they could reach the palace.

"Roman had just joined the team a month before the mission, and trying to pass his Post-Apocalypse cant off as generically foreign was a trip and a half."

They passed the hours trading more stories of Fantasy World. Gritty war stories of holding a castle against legions of orcs and goblins, heroic tales of lost heirs, and comedic tales of puns gone berserk and magical academies that bore a hilarious resemblance to mid-twentieth-century American universities, complete with academic infighting and bitter rivalries over comparatively small stakes. Some of the stories Leah had heard during their three-day hold before the mission, but these tellings were different. What else would you expect from professional storytellers?

And sure enough, after their morning meal (moldy bread with un-moldy and therefore un-tasty cheese), an armed force of skeletons came into the room to bind them with manacles, hand and feet.

Another force met them on the stairs with King and the Genrenauts. Leah risked looking over her shoulder and saw the Tall Woman's fantasy companions in the back.

But no Nolan.

Leah prayed to nothing and everything. *Let me get my hands on my sword and I will wreak righteous vengeance upon you. This I swear.*

Also, they needed to get out, soon, because that thought was entirely too Fantasy-World-y.

But first, the lair of the Night-Lord.

* * *

King wracked his brain, looking for escape scenarios, as the skeletal forces led them into the solarium, where the Night-Lord awaited them, the Tall Woman and her crew in tow. Including Nolan. The four interlopers stood off to the side, Nolan's friendly expression gone, replaced by a haughty smile.

We got played. Hard. Had the Tall Woman pegged that they were on to her in Crime World? Then she what, set this all up as a trap?

Was Nolan another rogue dimensional traveler, or a local plant? Another variable. Maybe the Tall Woman was the only dimension-hopper; maybe she had a whole team of her own, from Earth Prime or recruited across story worlds. Too many variables, King thought. He needed more information for his report to be sure.

I can deal with that after facing the council, he decided.

He needed to get face time with them to start to pick out some truth to lay a better foundation for all of his speculation, or it'd just be flights of fancy, even with his experience. And moreover, they needed photographic or video evidence. Something solid to take to the council.

There were any number of ways that the Tall Woman could have made the crossing. There'd been rumors of others that could travel between worlds—that maybe one of the Science Fiction regions could have developed the same technology as the High Council. But from the way the Tall Woman's squad held themselves, he'd bet good money they were a unit. She'd recruited them or they'd all been in this from the beginning.

The Night-Lord stood, throwing open his cloak in that trademarked supervillain fashion. The cowl was still drawn forward, making him guess the Night-Lord was either totally babyfaced and therefore really unassuming, or scarred by the forces he controlled.

"I trust you have all been enjoying your accommodations? I wanted to make sure you had a view of my sky," he said, one cloaked arm gesturing to the oversized windows out on the barely red dawn, the artifact's necromantic pall nearly complete.

Ioseph Bluethorn struggled against his captors, skeletons hands-on even though the wizard's hands were bound in rune-laden manacles. "We have no desire to be your audience, Armand of Serani." The Night-Lord's stance stiffened at the mention of his real name. "The Light will find a way, even if we fall. The dwarves will rise, the Matok will assemble the clans, and your reign will be but a footnote."

The Night-Lord walked right up to Ioseph, coming up next to the long-limbed wizard.

The Night-Lord held up his hand.

"No, it is you who will be the footnote. In the section marked THE DOOM OF FALLRAN.

"Ioseph Bluethorn, last court wizard of Fallran, who spectacularly failed both in protecting the crown and avenging it. He died at the hands of Our Glorious Leader on the eve of his ultimate victory."

The Night-Lord's hand glowed, and in a blur, it surged forward into the wizard's chest. The overlord pulled and ripped out a fist-sized sapphire. Ioseph's clothes dropped to the floor, empty.

"Holy Obi-Wan Kenobi!" Leah said.

Circumstances were bad enough that dressing the newbie down over breaking the masquerade protocols was pointless. She was a bard who looked as foreign as he did; she'd be expected to speak of things unknown to Fallran or Serani.

Rather than chastising Leah, he watched the Tall Woman and her crew.

Sure enough, their body language and expressions told him they *did* get the reference. Which meant they'd been to Earth Prime, or other Earths that shared the narrative — Near Future SF, Romance, or Action, perhaps one or two others from outside his territory.

King decided to press his luck for more intel.

"So, who are your friends? I've seen their leader before, and I can guarantee that she's out for her own agenda, and she's as likely to stab you in the back the way that he did to us and Theyn."

"A convenience, a way of expediting the process. They're mercenaries, well paid. They're just wise enough to know how to pick the right employer."

"The people most likely to be betrayed are the ones who are certain that they won't be."

"Well said, traveler, but irrelevant. My victory is at hand. Tonight, a lunar eclipse will give me all the time I need to cast an eternal darkness across the land, the solar power of the gods of light held at bay by the Moon Goddess and her shadowy children.

"And you will all be here to witness. But not yet, not now. There are too many preparations. And without your precious wizard, no chance to escape."

The Night-Lord gave a dismissive wave. "Take them away. I must finish my work."

King locked eyes on the Tall Woman for as long as possible, until a skeleton grabbed his head and turned him toward the stairs.

Options narrowed before his eyes, and King could not see a way forward. He was running short on options for a happy reversal.

But he had to trust in the story. They all had weak points, edges, opportunities built into the ebb and flow of every tale type.

It required patience, insight, and the bravery to put everything on the line when the opportunity presented itself.

No matter the cost.

Chapter Two:
Cribbing from Edmond Dantès

Leah was done being patient. Which meant that her best approach for figuring out an escape plan was to pace.

Angrily. She'd pace so hard, her Robin Hood-y booties would wear down and then the skeletons would have to come in to give her new shoes and she could crack their skulls together in true heroic fashion and bust everyone out of the tower.

It was her best plan so far, but it'd take a while. The skeletons hadn't reacted when Shirin faked illness, nor apparently when Xan'De bloodied his hands against the door.

Mallery meditated up a storm, still trying to reach out for some kind of divine intercession. But Felur wasn't listening, or couldn't hear. Which was alarming in and of itself. What could trump a god's omniscience?

Not to mention that Leah was still getting used to the idea of being in a world with demonstrably real gods. She venerated her ancestors like she'd been raised, but in a "respect your elders" kind of way more than a "their spirits will literally guide your hand" way.

So, if the gods were really real, shouldn't they be able to do something? Or was it that the cell and the manacles just stopped the god from being able to intervene? Because then it would mean the magic was trumping divine power, which was a whole different barrel of scary. Like antimatter scary.

Were gods so puny here that evil overlords could just head them off at the pass with some cold iron and a rune pattern? She'd seen Mallery's magic do some pretty awesome things, but it seemed like divine source or no, it was still magic, and one kind of magic could cancel out the other. She searched her memory for what the Genrenauts' texts said on the matter. Before this mission, it'd all been theory to her, and only now that she'd been here and done magic herself did she have visceral context for all of the theorizing.

Cosmological uncertainty kept Leah awake when Shirin and Mallery had both gone to sleep, napping during the daytime to be awake for the big finale when the Night-Lord sent for them once more.

Which meant that Leah was the only one awake when the sound of metal on metal started up in the late afternoon.

Leah kicked Shirin's cot, then Mallery's. The women snapped awake, another trick of the veteran Genrenaut that Leah had yet to master. Leah pointed at the door as the sound continued.

Mallery's hair was mussed and slick with sweat. The captors hadn't exactly been forthcoming with the hygiene supplies.

The skeleton guards didn't take this long when opening the door with keys. *I mean, they have skeleton keys, after all.*

She held in her joke but mentally logged it in the file labeled TERRIBLE PUNS.

Which meant…

The figure in the hallway when the door swung open was no skeleton. It was a woman, russet-brown skin and short wiry hair. She was broad at the shoulder and wore loose gray clothes and a worn leather vest. She held a blackened knife and a metal pin, her lock-picking tools.

By the description they'd given, Leah suspected that this was Alaria, the missing member of Theyn's party.

Finally, the break they'd needed.

Alaria held the knife up to her mouth, not needing to say "Shh."

The three women composed themselves and stealthed out into the hall, where Xan'De watched the stairs as the woman padded soundlessly over to the last cell.

Leah stepped over lifeless skeleton heaps to stand by Xan'De at the stairs. "Alaria?" Leah mouthed, pointing to their rescuer.

"Indeed. Wisdom kept her from the fold; now we have our chance to away." He gestured to a grappling hook and its tailing rope hanging out a window five steps down the spiral staircase.

"What happened to 'the walls are unclimbable'?"

"Alaria has made a history of finding ways in and through impossible boundaries before."

"Nice."

The door to the final cell swung open, and Alaria waved the group out.

"Down the rope. Do not let go. While you hold it, you will be able to walk down the tower walls. Let go, and the enchantment will not give you footing."

Shirin climbed out the window and started descending like it was no big thing to jump out of a two-hundred-foot-tall tower and start descending.

Leah asked, "What about the Night-Lord? He's doing the big evil ritual thing tonight!"

Alaria grinned. "We're getting out of the tower, not the castle. I stole your gear before I came up to the tower. It's at the base of the rope. Then we find another entrance into the castle and make our way to the Night-Lord's quarters."

"You're next, bard," King said, waving her out the window.

"If you say so…" Leah stepped up into the window, holding on with both hands. She squatted down, grabbed the rope, then spent several seconds switching between positions, trying to both psyche herself up and figure out how one climbs out of a window when howling winds were basically begging for you to self-defenestrate into their loving embrace.

"Hurry up," Roman said. "Left leg out, brace yourself, and turn to your right and grab the rope with both hands."

Leah followed the directions and got herself outside the tower, feet in place, holding onto the rope for dear life. But with the rope, she felt nearly weightless. She reached down and practically floated down. Hand under hand, she started descending like it was a breeze.

"I want one."

Roman climbed out after her. "Ask very nice and perhaps Alaria will give it to you as a parting gift once you shatter the Deathstone."

Leah held to her number-one goal during the descent, which was to not look down. She watched Roman's descent, calm, smooth. The action hero looked down as he closed the distance between them, and Leah turned her gaze to the wall.

The roof of the castle slanted down at about a twenty-degree grade, so Leah hopped off the rope and immediately sat down, holding the crest of the roof. Shirin had moved away from the tower, putting gear in order. She handed Leah her leather jerkin, then the belt, sword in place.

"Hammer?"

"It's not here," she said. "Not surprising. Night-Lord wouldn't want to let that thing out of his sight."

"K'gon said that only I could wield it."

"Carrying something and locking it away are different from wielding it."

"So, first we get the Hammer, then we take out the Night-Lord?"

"Sounds good to me," Roman said, dropping from the rope to a squat, crab-walking across the roof to join them. Shirin slid his pack over to him, and the man began arming, strapping on weapon after weapon.

One by one, the Genrenauts and companions took to the roof. Alaria came down last. Still holding the rope, she gave a flick of the wrist and the grapple unhooked from the tower and came tumbling down, landing conveniently in the rogue's free hand.

So cool, Leah thought. *Gotta get me one of those.*

"You're welcome. Now get yourselves sorted so we can finish this. I'm getting real sick of the color purple."

"Where were you this whole time?" King asked.

Alaria scanned the roof, still on the lookout. "When Theyn fell, I vanished into the crowds, laid low while the Night-Lord solidified his control. took over. Then I tracked down Nolan and began to follow his movements. He met regularly with this other group, foreigners with strange manners and their own coded cant. Nolan was a traitor the whole time, allied with the Night-Lord."

Xan'De fumed, nose flaring. "He was a brother to us. We bled together for months. A traitor, the whole time?"

"I'm afraid so," Alaria said. "This group of his, they've been allied with the Night-Lord even before his ships struck land. They must have sent Nolan to oversee Theyn's training, then turned on him when he confronted the Night-Lord. I followed Theyn up the tower, hoping to help him in those final moments if he needed me.

"I saw Nolan come up behind him, but the storms and wind drowned out my voice, and my dagger missed. Nolan felled Theyn and then saluted the Night-Lord. I knew I couldn't defeat them both, so I ran. I ran as fast as I could and stayed hidden. Then I went after Nolan. I never caught him on his own; the others were always nearby.

"But I knew if I stopped Nolan before he betrayed the group, his allies might escape. So, I waited."

"Except now the wizard is dead and the world is mere hours from a magical apocalypse," Leah said.

Alaria's grin returned. "Bluethorn's not dead."

"What?"

"Wizards bind their souls to a gemstone. If you seize the gemstone, you capture the wizard as well. That's why if we break the Deathstone, we'll be victorious. The Night-Lord has made that his soul gem."

"First, we get the Hammer," King said, bringing the team back to order the way that he always did. "Then, my team will contain Nolan and his friends while you, Xan'De, and Leah foil the Night-Lord's plans." He looked over at the sinking sun.

"We don't have long. Let's get moving."

* * *

Alaria led Mallery and the rest through the halls, dodging patrols to avoid tipping their hand.

"Patrols will find out you're gone soon enough, but let them rush the tower first. Gives us more of an opening."

"Do we have a minute before the next patrol?" Shirin asked.

"You should be good."

Mallery wasn't so certain. The Fear had crept up on her again. That fear of pain, of death, of missed opportunities and interdimensional disaster. *Great feeling. Big fan.*

Shirin raised her staff and cast another spell. When her eyes opened again, they were flat black, but she moved with purpose. "The Hammer is this way."

Divine magic was generally happy-making. The god's love wrapped you up, guided you. The arcane magic Mallery had done as a bard felt different. It felt more like dipping a ladle into a pool of Power and taking a drink.

Once again, she was happy to be the cleric. Also, better armor.

They turned the corner into a hallway with a single door and a right turn at the end.

But there was a skeleton patrol in the middle.

"Raise the alarm," said the skeleton leader.

Mallery stepped forward. "No." She raised her mace and gripped the holy symbol in her other hand. A chorus erupted in her mind, nearly Gregorian, but all in higher voices, altos and sopranos.

A flash of holy light filled the room, drowning out the purple glow animating the skeletons.

When the light cleared, the skeletons were no more than piles of bleached bone and forge-beaten arms and armor.

"Daaaamn, girl," Leah said.

Mallery winked.

Again, glad to be the cleric. Once the mission was sorted, she and Leah could spend some time outside of work again. Stolen kisses and walks to collect firewood were all well and good, but it'd be nice to have a date without the imminent threat of arcane ambush.

Alaria grimaced. "No time for gloating. Get the Hammer, and then we need to double back before another patrol finds these."

Shirin held her staff out and started chanting again.

Mallery's heart began to race as their plan came together. Excitement and hope pushed the Fear to the sidelines. For now.

Mallery, Alaria, and Leah raced up the stairs once more.

"If he's got it anywhere, it's in the treasure room."

They fought past several more skeleton patrols, each just the right size to threaten them without barring their way entirely.

The story is on our side, Mallery thought. The Hammer was what they needed to patch the breach, and its weight had kept the Night-Lord from securing it too well. The story wanted to be fixed, needed to be fixed. The world itself was bleeding, aching to be whole once more.

Alaria picked the lock on treasure room, and when it opened, Leah raced inside.

The room was huge. Far larger on the inside than the tower would allow.

"How? Also what?"

"The kingdom of Fallran is the richest in the known world. How are we to find one artifact in this?"

Mallery spoke a prayer to Felur. "Great Felur, grant us your wisdom. Grant us true sight so that we might recover the Hammer of K'gon and put things to right." Felur would be the story world's agent, helping them once again.

Mallery's eyesight shifted, gold-white ghostly images of everything layered on top of her normal vision.

"Follow me," she said. Mallery scanned the shelves, which numbered in the dozens. They walked past countless treasure chests, stacks of carpets, scroll cases by the dozens. There was enough treasure for a dozen heroes to retire on. And even so, it was depleted. The section marked FORBIDDEN MAGIC was picked nearly clean. The blessing led her past scrolls and suits of armor and artifacts of many sorts to a simple, unadorned chest.

"It is protected by a magical lock."

Alaria grinned. "There hasn't been a lock created by wizard or man that can keep me out." She produced a set of lockpicks that glowed with their own magical aura, and set to work.

Alaria knelt by the chest for several minutes, working deftly but carefully. Twice the chest lashed out with purple energy, trying to strangle the thief. And twice the three of them beat the tentacles back until Alaria could try again.

At last, the lock clicked and the chest opened, revealing the Hammer of K'gon.

Leah grabbed the McGuffin and hugged it to her chest.

"Thank Felur," Mallery said. The story had come through.

Now they had to do their part.

Leah swung the Hammer around like a set of keys on a lanyard, grinning ear to ear. "Now to the finale. This ends tonight."

That's my girl.

Chapter Three:
The Deathstone

Shirin, the Genrenauts, and the companions moved as fast as they could go without drawing the attention of the guards. Even Qargon was silent as they prowled the halls.

Alaria and Xan'De led them through the winding passages of the castle, which were already beginning to look shabby and unkempt.

The rogue spoke to them in a low voice. "There will be several patrols ahead. I'd expect a fight the whole way to the Night-Lord, and he'll likely have time to prepare."

Xan-De added, "Several of us are likely to die. Those that survive will sing tales of this day."

"I would rather we try to all stay alive and sing tales about one another anyway," Leah said. "After all, you have a bard in the party."

Xan'De and Qargon took the fore, Leah followed with Alaria at her back, then the rest of the Genrenauts, starting with King and Roman in the back, their two parties set.

Sure enough, the next floor up, with tapestries and sconces galore, was also filled with skeletons, all heavily armed.

And the battle was joined.

They fought through three groups of skeletons, each larger than the last. The third group was led by another zombie knight. Roman dueled the undead lieutenant while the rest of the heroes felled the minions as quickly and quietly as possible.

The *quietly* part was all thanks to Shirin and several judicious Silence spells. They made no sound, left no opportunity for the undead to raise an alarm.

Soon, they came to the stairs below the royal wing.

Another skeleton force met them there, dozens strong.

Either they'd heard something echo through the hallways, or the Night-Lord had magical surveillance.

All pretense of stealth was gone. Now there was only blood and steel.

* * *

Xan'De and Qargon tore into the skeletons' ranks, and in Leah's hands, the Hammer of K'gon shattered any armor or blade that stood in its way.

Swinging the Hammer, she burst into a Song of Battle, singing about shield lines and heroic soldiers, belting as loud as she could to be heard over the din.

The time for stealth was over. She wanted the Night-Lord to hear her coming.

This was her chance to be the Chosen One. And she wouldn't fail. Not again. Not with Mallery and the team depending on her. With a whole nation, world, and multiverse depending on it.

This is what she'd joined the Genrenauts to do.

A half-dozen skeletons went down in an instant under the heroes' combined first strike. The Night-Lord's forces fell back and set the shield wall, spear-wielders behind.

They advanced, a wall of beaten metal and stabby death.

Shirin's staff sucked in air. A green light leapt up and split the sky, calling down lightning bolts from a fresh-made storm cloud in the hall's vaulted ceiling.

The lightning disintegrated several skeletons. The wooden haft of several spears caught fire. But where humans would have flipped out at being lit on fire, the burning skeletons merely hurled the spears at the assembled heroes.

The group scattered. Xan'De, Qargon, and Roman charged, with Leah making for the corner. Leah shattered the shield of the skeleton nearest the wall. Seeing her opportunity, she started to fold the skeleton's line in on itself, destroying everything in her way. In her mind, the song switched to "Another One Bites The Dust," though she stuck to her genre-appropriate tune.

Roman slid in to cover her, batting aside spears and keeping the other shield-skeletons from pressing in on her all at once.

With the shield wall shaken and the heroes' spells crashing down in green and white light, arcane and divine both, the assembled heroes broke the skeletons' line.

And then the Tall Woman and her squad arrived. The skinny man with the fair skin had lightning dancing between his fingertips, and Nolan strode forward with a greatsword, moving with perfect form as he advanced in a high guard, ready to split someone in two. The Tall Woman carried a nicked and beaten longsword. Beside her was the leather-clad Latina with two long knives, her eyes locked on Alaria.

There they were. Now Leah and the team could get answers.

* * *

King shouted as he tackled one of the remaining skeletons. "We'll hold the others; break through and get to the Night-Lord!" The undead soldier braced its shield, so King threw his mass just below its center of gravity and sent it reeling. The advantage of fighting skeletons: they were at most one quarter the mass of a flesh-and-blood human.

King pointed his sword at the Tall Woman and said, "You've meddled with your last story. This ends now. Your team against mine."

"If you're looking for a fair fight, you've already lost, Kane," she said. "But if you lay down arms, maybe we'll let you join the winning team."

King took a middle guard, waiting for his opponent to step into range. She entered with a horizontal cut, which he countered with a pacing step and a high cut.

"Why are you doing this?" King asked. "You've traveled across great distances to vex my team in our missions. Give me answers and we'll take you all alive."

She ducked under his blade. Spun into a cut for his leg. He pivoted on his other foot and cleared her blade, then stepped back to reset.

"Your offer of compassion is commendable," she said. "But you're offering refuge to the woman about to grind you beneath her boot. That's not so much compassion as it is delusion."

"If you're going to grind me beneath your boot, at least tell me your name."

She scoffed as she parried his blade away and stepped back to re-set. "Careful, there. You're veering into the territory of Romance. You can call me Raven."

King took a snapshot of the battlefield in the moment granted by her momentary retreat. Story-world logic would let the two of them carry on a normal conversation while fighting, but then he'd get fully drawn into the duel and lose his commander's view of the battlefield.

His side had cleared out most of the skeletons and were now trying to break through Raven's line. The hidden camera on King's belt was recording the whole thing, taking a record to share with the High Council.

If they pulled this off, maybe he'd have enough to validate Leah's theory about this Raven being a rogue dimensional traveler and justify his going AWOL.

But the Hammer of K'gon could not be stopped so easily. Xan'De and the companions kept the dimensional interlopers off Leah as she mowed through the skeletons. They'd break through. Especially if he kept their leader busy.

King delivered a diagonal cut with a pacing step forward. It was one of the Meisterhau from German swordsmanship. In a kung fu movie, they'd be called "Ultimate Techniques". In reality, Meisterhau were just refined versatile moves that formed the cornerstone of a style, serving simultaneously as attack and defense.

Raven met the blow with one of the only viable counters—the same move. But she parried hard, making up for King's greater mass. He let her press through, flipping the blade around his head to cut at her jaw, just below her helm. She spun her blade into a parry, barely offsetting his blade, but striking at the same time.

They both took cuts—hers a glancing gash to the jaw, his a cut across his waist.

King dropped to a knee, years of training keeping him in form enough to slash at the woman as he fell. She stumbled back, retreating into her line.

Pure stubbornness hammering his cry of pain into words, King shouted, "Push through!"

Looking through the cracks in the line, King saw Leah jogging down the hall, Xan'De at her heels.

King pushed himself to his feet, using the longsword scabbard as a cane. This gave him a vantage on the fight.

With him a step back, they were outnumbered, four to five. But Raven had stepped back as well. The two commanders barked orders, though Raven's voice was weakened, one hand glued to her jaw to stem the tide of blood.

The dark cleric raised his mace for a spell, probably healing, but Mallery batted his weapon down, white light clashing with black shadow.

"Hold them!"

Roman moved with the grace of experience, attacking and defending with every strike. He covered Shirin against the blades of Raven's Genrenauts while pressing the team's black-clad rogue, but it was costing him. His armor had gashes and rents, blood seeping out. But the fighter wasn't slowing. He was born for combat, born from action, and he would hold.

Let's just hope the rest of us last as long, King thought.

* * *

Leah huffed and puffed as she followed Xan'De and Alaria up the stairs. Even lightened by magic, the Hammer still weighed something, and she'd been in go-go-go mode for some time, on top of crummy tower-dungeon sleep.

But she'd been training for this, endurance, cardio, weights. This was her biggest mission yet, in the genre she'd loved since she was a kid.

So, she pressed on.

Leah heard a voice in her mind, saying, *Keep it together. You can do it.*

Surprisingly, it wasn't Mallery's voice, nor King's or Shirin's or Roman's. It was hers.

She could do this.

A chorus of moans echoed down the stairs, punctuated by a familiar scream.

"Ioseph!" Xan'De said, racing ahead, leaving the other two behind.

"Dammit!" Alaria answered, pounding up the stairs to follow.

"Wait for me!" Leah called up the hall, huffing as she scaled two stairs at a time, wishing for the thousandth time she'd been born tall. Even like two inches taller. Assuming it was all legs.

No big deal, just wielding the super-weapon here. No reason to hang out and protect me from evil death—blasts.

The battle was joined before she crested the top of the stairs. The clang of steel on steel, spiritual moans detonating like grenades, and the *thwipp* of thrown blades.

At the top of the stairs, she saw Alaria and Xan'De pressing the Night-Lord, while the Deathstone spewed death bolts. Alaria dodged and jumped, weaving under and leaping over the magical bursts, trying to take the fight to the sorcerer. The fist-sized sapphire that housed Ioseph's spirit floated beside the Deathstone, waves of purple energy battering the floating stone. Twinges of purple light invaded the edges of the sapphire, surging toward the center but being pushed back like waves upon a reinforced shore.

"Bring me my harem pants…it's Hammer Time," she said to no one in particular. But she'd been saving that line up for weeks, and dammit, she was going to use it before the battle was done.

Leah hit the landing and leaned forward into a sprint, the Hammer held in both hands before her.

She zeroed in on her target.

Just get to the heart. Get to the heart, break it, and that's game.

Zaps of necrotic energy raced toward her, but she kept going. They screamed past her ears, most deflecting off the Hammer. One caught her in the left shoulder. Her armor aged and crumbled, as well as the clothes below. Her shoulder ached worse than the time she'd sprained her back, like someone had dumped thirty years of arthritis on it all at once.

She kept going. *Just get to the stone,* she told herself on repeat.

More blasts arced by as Xan'De and Alaria pounded away at the Night-Lord's defenses, purple shield fading with each hit, the impact rippling across the otherwise-transparent dome.

Thirty feet away. Leah lifted the Hammer over her shoulder, left arm going from dull ache to a sharp, thousand-needles stabbing pain.

But she held.

Just keep going.

The Night-Lord wound up a bigger blast. Like, turn-you-into-dust bigger. And he knew exactly where she was going. He'd barely have to aim. She leaned left, trying to circle around, maybe get the giganto-gem between her and the blast.

But he was too fast. The Night-Lord tossed a ball of necrotic energy overhand like an all-star pitcher, and time slowed. But she couldn't move faster, couldn't dodge like in the movies. She just saw doom coming for her with a screaming skull image at its head, jaws wide, like it was going to swallow her entire life in one gulp.

She ducked, diving, trying everything she could to get out of the way, but it was all too slow. Her brain was on super-speed, but her body wasn't with the program, and in the end, it'd all be for nothing.

So, that's what it'd come to. A heroic death in the pursuit of saving a fantasy kingdom she'd only ever visited once, where stew was a real travel food, dwarves were masters of every craft except stand-up, where Jewish comediennes were holy paladins, and mouthy Chinese-American girls were bards.

Less than six months onto the job and her ticket was already getting punched. She'd figured it might end this way, hero's death and all. But she was expecting she'd make it to fifty, maybe beat King's record. The old guy would come and speak at her funeral after his second hip replacement, gravely old-man voice telling jokes about her bad improvisational comedy and tendency for leaving her notebooks strewn about the ready room like dirty laundry.

Except.

Xan'De moved like quicksilver, like everyone else had gotten the slow-mo memo and he had responded by thinking, *I laugh at these rules! They are not for me.* The foreigner hero, warrior-poet and weirdo, threw himself in the way of the oncoming death bolt.

It consumed him, layer by layer. It tore apart his clothes, then shredded his skin, muscles, and bones, the necrotic spell spending itself to consume the hero.

The world snapped back to full speed, and Leah scrambled upright, only ten feet from the Heart.

"Do it now!" Alaria cried, heartbreak cracking her voice. She saw the assassin lady drop smoke bombs like they were going out of style. A moment later, the floating stone was in reach.

"Hammer, don't fail me now." She bound forward, throwing her entire weight, heart and soul, into the blow. She smashed straight through the gem, which shattered into gravity-defying pyramid-shaped shards around her as she plowed through now-empty space.

Leah tumbled into a heap on the other side. Her landing was as ungraceful and embarrassing as her previous moment had been inspiring and heroic. *You win some, you lose some.* At least Mallery and the others hadn't seen that.

She found her feet and stared down the Night-Lord. His super-weapon was a pile of brittle purple glass on the floor.

And outside, the sky was clear, rose-red sunset untainted by magic.

She pointed the Hammer at the Big Bad, savoring the moment. "This is where you give up." The appended *comma, asshole!* was implied but unsaid.

The Night-Lord gathered another burst of energy, a blast as big as the one that had killed Xan'De.

But before he could strike, two serrated blades popped out of his chest as Alaria appeared out of the smoke.

The bereaved thief raised the Night-Lord off the ground, then pulled them him apart in different directions, leaving the Would-Be Evil Overlord in several cloaked pieces on the ground.

Whoa.

Alaria's face was covered in blood spray, her chest heaving in deep, angry breaths.

And like that, it was done.

The room went silent. So silent, she could hear the barest strains of combat from down below.

The sapphire clattered to the floor, still glowing. It shook, rattled, and then burst into a plume of blue light.

And as the light faded, Ioseph Bluethorn stood in its place, his clothes fresh, his face clean-shaven. It made him look fifteen years younger. He leaned on his staff, then looked up, blue eyes as bright as ever.

"Well done, my friends." He stood slowly, like he was shaking out a leg gone to sleep. "But the battle is not yet won. Secure the castle. I will return."

He slammed the butt of his staff on the tiled floor and transformed into a ball of blue light. The light arced out the window, vanishing beyond the castle.

"What in all that is weird and wonderful was that?" Leah asked.

Alaria lowered her blades, looking between the window and the place where Xan'De had been. "I…I don't know. He's never done that before."

Leah looked to where Xan'De had died. His axe lay on the ground, it alone untouched. Leah squeezed Alaria's shoulder. "I'm sorry about Xan'De. He… I didn't…"

"He knew his role, and he will be remembered. You promised a song, and I expect you to deliver."

"His deeds will be sung in taverns and courts across the continent for a thousand years," Leah said, mustering as much Bardic Dignity and Gravitas as she could manage.

Alaria managed a sliver of a smile, and they regrouped.

The adrenaline of nearly dying, shattering an artifact of world-ending power, and seeing the Night-Lord skewered all within a minute was as energizing as the time she'd pounded energy drinks to pull an all-nighter and finish her capstone project in college. Remembering that, she knew the only way to not collapse was to keep going.

"Reinforcements on the way!" she shouted as they charged down the stairs. Leah watched her footing to avoid taking another epic spill right after her big triumph.

Please let them be safe. The sight of Mallery falling in battle flashed across Leah's mind, and for a second, she couldn't breathe.

Focus on what's real. Until you see her, you don't know if she's safe. If any of them are safe. Xan'De said that people would die before the day was done, and he was right. Dramatic Irony has been satisfied. Right? Worry and excitement made a vicious cocktail in her mind as they rejoined the battle.

They hit the lower floor running. At the far end of the hall, the Tall Woman and her team raced to a dead end adorned with nothing more than two torches and a portrait of some old noble.

Nolan pulled one of the torches and the portrait swung forward, revealing a secret passageway.

Sneaky bastard, Leah thought. If they escaped, then there would be no physical evidence of the Tall Woman's appearance. Just more testimony. They needed to bring her in for questioning, find out how she traveled across dimensions, what she was doing to the stories and why.

There was no way Leah could catch them.

But the Genrenauts were in pursuit, bloodied and beaten but still whole.

Leah's heart soared at seeing Mallery still up and running, as well as the others. Xan'De would be the only one to fall today. All five of the Genrenauts would be going home.

King shouted something at the retreating villains, but the words were lost in the distance.

The dark prince pulled a horn from his robes and blew, the crackling of magic enhancing the horn's blast. It rattled her very bones and raised every hair on the back of her neck.

"What is that?" she asked as Alaria raced ahead to join the battle.

Leah heard a deafening screech from outside the castle.

But not far outside.

The side wall of the hallway collapsed inward as an immense red shadow crashed into view.

Great sweeping motion cleared the smoke, and revealed a thirty-foot-long mother-effing red dragon.

The secret passageway was closed, the Tall Woman and her team gone, the dragon in their way.

"Dragon!" Leah cried. All of a sudden, she was eight again. Not only was she the Chosen One to lift the curse on the land, she'd get to fight a for-reals dragon.

Chapter Four:
Sword-ed Affairs

Dragon dragon dragon!

I'm fighting a mother-loving dragon!

Leah's inner monologue continued to flip out even as her reflexes got with the program and her voice projected a Song of Courage, helping to negate the dragon-fear she'd read about in the Fantasy World gazetteer.

Leah and Mallery fought hip to hip, the cleric covering her with the massive shield as they maneuvered Leah around for a clean shot with the Hammer.

How many couples get to fight dragons together? Not so many. Probably almost none. Almost no lesbian couples, that's for sure.

The dragon's claws were the size of Leah's torso, and the thing's tail was longer than any New Year's Day parade dragon she'd seen.

This was an occidental dragon, of course. Proper dragons didn't just randomly attack people, not unless those people had been incredibly wicked. No, this was a straight-up red-scaled, flame-breathing, randomly murdering European dragon. Summoned by the dark prince guy's horn or some spell or the Night-Lord's final counterstrike, deployed too late to save his life, but not too late to threaten the team and prevent them from capturing their dimension-hopping quarry.

The dragon let loose another gout of flame, sending the heroes scattering. Shirin's arcane shield deflected the flame but imploded under the pressure, singeing the woman's robes.

This was supposed to be cleanup, but it sure felt like the main event.

Epic fantasies and their nested stories.

Kill the Dark Lord, then capture the evil Genrenauts, but defeat the dragon first, then bring peace to the realm. They had to wrap up every subplot as well, even as they'd tried (mostly) to keep the subplots limited.

Less worrying, more fighting, she told herself. She swung the Hammer at the dragon's tail. It smashed scales like they were made of Legos. *Chalk up another one for K'gon,* she thought.

The dragon roared in pain but fought on.

It laid Roman out with a swipe of one clawed hand, then gouged Alaria's arm with a barely dodged bite.

They were wearing it down but paying the price along the way.

The dragon breathed fire at King. With Fantasy-World armor, there was no way he could dodge. Mallery leapt forward and took the gout on her shield, bracing against the flames.

She didn't need to think, didn't even worry. She just jumped right in.

My girlfriend is a hero, she thought.

Pride gave way to worry as the dragon lunged forward to swallow Mallery whole.

"Hell, no!" Leah shouted. She bounded forward and choked up on the Hammer. She let swing a horizontal slash, putting all of her weight behind the blow. The blow shattered several of the dragon's teeth just as it was about to snap its mouth shut over Mallery.

Gotcha, she thought.

The great wyrm writhed in pain, coiling up to protect itself.

"Re-form!" King called, and the heroes stepped into formation.

Mallery and King stood side by side, joined by a dazed but still-moving Roman. Leah joined them, playing the Song of Battle, her whole body buzzing with magic and adrenaline. Shirin stood a pace back, staff raised. And Alaria moved to flank.

When the dragon uncurled, they were ready.

To open their barrage, Mallery tossed a lance of light at the creature's rump and Shirin let loose with a cascade of ice bolts that fired at machine-gun speed.

Alaria chucked a long dagger at the thing's eye, Roman dodged its claw-strikes to bury a sword to its hilt in the creature's breast, and King cut three toes off at once.

And then they kept going. They had the beast on the ropes but kept striking, kept casting, and kept swinging.

Leah threw in the chorus from "We Will Rock You" as they pushed for the fight's endgame.

"Stay on it!" King shouted. "We will be triumphant!"

Leah swung once more, the Hammer shattering a patch of scales, exposing bloodied muscle. Then they pulled a Combined Arms Bard the Bowman, concentrating their fire on a single armorless spot, and struck.

And like with the Black Arrow and Smaug, their blows struck true. The dragon swayed, then drooped and crashed to the floor, raising a cloud of dust. The heroes were knocked to the ground by the force of the creature's collapse.

But only the good guys got back up.

"Everyone alive?" King asked.

"Slightly singed, still bleeding," Shirin said.

Roman growled, "Left side's numb."

Leah said, "Slightly necrotized arm, but I'll live."

Mallery said, "A few cuts and a body's worth of bruises."

King ran to the secret passage and pulled the torch handle.

Nothing happened. He pulled again, then moved and pulled the other one. "Come on. Why won't you work!"

Roman stepped up and pulled the painting from its fixture but revealed only a flat, seamless stone wall.

"What sorcery is this!" Roman shouted, getting into it.

King pressed his hands to the wall. "Everyone on me."

They poked and prodded and searched. Shirin tried a spell of Opening, Leah sang a Song of Cleverness, but nothing they did could make the passage reappear.

Shirin produced a scroll from her bag and read it, the words burning up as she went. The entire scroll vanished in a burst of magical flame, and Shirin turned a complete three-sixty, her eyes lit with green fire.

"I cannot see them, sense them, or feel their presence on this plane. They're gone. All that remains is a lingering magic at the door. This must have been a spelled portal, designed to let them escape and then close forever."

Roman pounded a fist on the wall. King looked defeated, deflated. They'd come home empty-handed again.

"Everyone is still wounded," Mallery said, setting down her shield. She took her holy symbol in one hand and raised it to the unclouded sun. "Join hands. Let us receive the blessing of Felur."

They formed a circle, hand in hand. Leah squeezed Mallery's hand, and was rewarded with a wink. The look on her face told Leah that there was more to say. Later.

"Great Felur, we dedicate this victory over a beast of darkness to you. You who have borne us up with your righteousness. Please grant your grace to us, your soldiers on the field of glory, such that we may fight on."

She was good at the inspirational-praying thing.

White light descended from the heavens and filled every hollowed-out or pained part of Leah's being, leaving her whole and uplifted and not at all jittery, the worry and wonder from the tower evening out into a pool of calm and hope.

"Praise Felur," Leah said with a happy sigh.

Looking around, Leah saw the same sense of calm from the others. Wounds were closed, burns healed, and spirits lifted.

Mallery had an absolutely beatific look on her face. "That was was…not what I expected. It was several times the greatest blessing I've ever been granted. Felur is truly pleased."

Alaria grinned. "She's not the only one. Night-Lord vanquished, evil artifact destroyed? All that's left is cleanup."

King looked to the stairs. "But Raven and her party escaped, and we still don't know what their real mission was. We'll scour the castle, make sure they're not still here and somehow hiding from scrying. And along the way, we can clear out any remaining skeletons."

"Then we go down to throw open the gate and proclaim the kingdom's liberation."

They spent several hours searching the castle before King relented and called for them to make for the front gates. King was fuming, frustrated in a way that was all too reminiscent of when he'd nearly lost himself in Crime World. This Raven, as he'd called her, was getting under his skin, too.

"We'll find her," Leah said, a hand on the team lead's shoulder. King squeezed Leah's hand.

"I'm supposed to be the one offering encouragement."

"We all do our part. But right now, we have a story to finish, right?"

King nodded. It wasn't an indulgent nod of a parent to a child, or a teacher to a student. This was a nod of peers.

"To the gates," he said. And so they went.

* * *

King and the Genrenauts found a crowd assembled at the gates, clubs and knives in hand. Shattered bones littered the far side of the moat at their feet.

They lowered the drawbridge and met the charging citizens with open arms. King pushed Alaria to the front, the recognizable hero.

As the crowd shifted, Ioseph Bluethorn appeared, stepping forward to greet the one surviving member of his party—barring Nolan, the traitor.

After months, they'd confirmed the Tall Woman was a dimensional traveler. They'd all seen her, could add their voices to Leah's once-tenuous theory. But without a suspect in custody, the Council might still be disappointed in their results. In his results.

The next few days moved quickly. The surviving companions held a ceremony to honor Xan'De and Theyn's lives. The surviving nobles of Fallran appointed Alaria and Ioseph Protectors of the Realm, until a new heir could be determined.

As soon as the ceremony ended, Ioseph grabbed King and the other Genrenauts, running through the possibilities and candidates. But the wizard's voice was rote, more frustrated at the prospect of tedium than worried about a succession war.

King said, "We will need to disembark soon. Our own lords call us home so that we may prepare for our next holy mission."

"I understand. But first, let me express Fallran's eternal gratitude."

Ioseph threw open his arms and proclaimed, "Let there be a feast!"

Chapter Five:
Fallran's Gratitude

Alaria, Ioseph, and Leah were the honored guests of the celebration, a receiving line as long as the soccer-field-sized Great Hall. Nobles and courtiers emerged from the rocks of privilege they'd been hiding under while the Night-Lord had the run of the castle.

King watched as the nobles threw together a feast in less than a day's notice, bringing in prize pheasants, calves, and more. Fortunately for Leah, Fallran was also known for its desserts, so while the roasted pork and steaks were off the menu, Leah was also presented with tarts and small cakes to her heart's content. She and Mallery were inseparable that evening, even disappearing from the party at the same time.

Something to deal with later. He'd suspected something was going on, but it hadn't interfered with their performance as of yet. In fact, King would bet good money that Leah's feelings for Mallery were no small part of what had given her the narrative juice to make that home-run swing that had turned the tide in the battle against the dragon. Every story world recognized and respected love, not just the Romance regions.

As the official section of the feast died down, King led the team in their customary denouement toast, though this one was tinged with more fatigue and worry than most. Especially for him. They'd patched the story, set Fallran back on course, but they'd seen companions die and spent six weeks of their lives on a mission they'd soon learn was never approved in the first place.

He kept a brave face, laughing and celebrating with the team, raising somber toasts to the victorious dead. Only two remained from Theyn Lighthall's original party, three if you counted the wolf in hero's clothing.

471

King did everything he could to hold the scene in his mind, spent a moment focusing on each member of the team, this team he'd assembled by hand, storytellers and heroes all searching for their story, for a place to fit and do good. And what good they'd done.

Don't get too drunk on the nostalgia, he told himself. The wine was doing a fine job of that on its own.

"Are you all right?" Shirin asked at a whisper.

"Just tired. And not relishing the six weeks of mission to summarize in the debrief."

Shirin chuckled, then poured him some more wine. "Live in the moment a bit longer. We won't be back here for a while, I imagine."

That's what I'm afraid of. But King drank the wine and focused on the moment, on his team, on the family he'd built and now put in danger in pursuit of a quest he still had not completed.

Chapter Six:
Homecoming

The next day, the team bade Alaria, Ioseph, and Qargon farewell and rode out of the capital, their bags laden with treasure and gifts from nobles currying favor and jockeying for position in the inheritance struggle.

Leah sang the whole way back to their ship, in a contagiously excited mood, especially since she could go back to singing Earth-Prime songs instead of rehearsing a broadside ballad for the thousandth time.

But thanks to six weeks of solid practice, her singing voice was in rare form, her fencing skills had never been better, and she had a one-of-a-kind World-Saving Artifact of her very own.

"Are you sure we shouldn't leave it here, like a sword-in-the-stone kind of thing?" she asked. "Not that I don't want to have my own magic hammer at home."

"We've tried that before," Shirin said. "The artifacts go bad when their Chosen Bearer leaves the dimension. We didn't notice it at first, then when our team arrived to address a breach created by a poisoned wood taking over the countryside, they traced it back to the sword left behind by one of Mendoza's artifacts left jammed into a tree stump, Zelda-style. The sword was sentient, and it did not react well to being abandoned."

Leah cocked her head, looking down at the Hammer in its saddle harness.

"Wait, so is this thing intelligent? I feel like I would have found out by now. And maybe that sword was just really co-dependent."

"Let's not take any risks, alright? You can store the Hammer in the supply wing with the other artifacts."

"Also, does anyone else ever consider how ridiculously amazing it is that every HQ has its own mini-Warehouse 13?"

Ahead, Roman shrugged. "Just makes me more confident that we could fight off the National Guard and FBI if we needed to."

"Because it's also totally normal to daydream about fighting off the National Guard and FBI."

"Don't sass. Preparedness is next to godliness."

"I'm not sassing. If I were sassing you, you'd know it because you would be properly cowed by my brilliance."

And so they rode on, reaching the forest outside the village where they'd first arrived.

They let the horses loose, sending them off in the direction of the town. Someone could use them. There was always a need for road-worthy horses. Maybe some enterprising team of adventurers would come along and ride those horses to even greater glory.

Or maybe an ogre would find them and have a midnight snack. Who knew?

King dropped the camouflage on the ship, and Leah restrained the urge to hug the big metal tube when it revealed itself.

"Home! Hot showers, TV, indoor plumbing, and proper vegetarian food."

Leah continued to chatter as she did the walk-around with Roman, Shirin squaring away the gear as King headed inside for the pre-flight sequence.

Within minutes, they were airborne. Or dimension-borne. They were off. Not in fantasyland anymore.

The return passage was bumpy, but the storm had mostly passed on. And after a hero's feast and an epic win, some stomach-churning turbulence wasn't too much of a bother.

She'd completed a full circuit of the team's major regions in their beat—Western, Science Fiction, Romance, Mystery, and now Fantasy. With this report filed, her position would come up for review, and she'd be able to apply for a permanent position. Because it wasn't like she was going to do anything else with her life now that she'd gotten hooked on the delights and the danger of professional dimensional-interventionist story doctoring.

Comms came back up halfway through the journey.

"This is Mid-Atlantic Actual, come back."

"Mid-Atlantic Actual, this is Mid-Atlantic 3 inbound after a successful mission," King said.

"Glad to be coming back. We missed your voice out there," Shirin added.

Preeti answered, "Your flight plan hasn't been logged. Please stand by so we can clear up a berth for you."

King threw some switches, the ship's crossover slowing. "Standing by, Actual. Disturbance kept our cross-world comms down, couldn't be helped."

No answer.

The ship sat in not-quite-anywhere, waves of dimensional energy hitting the ship, tossing it back and forth like a toy in a bathtub.

"Do you think something's gone wrong?" Shirin asked.

"Maybe one of the other ships was damaged in a dimensional crossing?" Leah volunteered.

"Could be," King said. "Hold tight; we'll be home soon enough."

Something was wrong. Story senses or just a general gut feeling, whatever it was, was going off.

Preeti crackled back onto the comms. "You are clear to approach, Mid-Atlantic 3."

"Roger that. Mid-Atlantic 3 coming in."

Her calm tentatively harshed, Leah grabbed the Hammer out of her bag again and carried it over her shoulder as she lined up to climb down out of the ship.

The main hatch opened, and as the light equalized, a booming voice filled the ship. "Angstrom King, get your traitorous ass out here right now."

Say what?

* * *

King climbed down the ladder to see Ricardo Mendoza standing on the hangar floor, the man's eyes as filled with cold fury as he'd ever seen.

"The Council is on the line. I suggest you don't make them wait."

And here came the judgment. No time to prepare, to debrief his team. Just straight to the principal's office.

"Good job, team. I'm proud of all of you. I'll be back," he said, then set off at a jog, making for the comms room. On the way, he saw that team members were posted at every exit. They were expecting him to rabbit.

Deanna, Mendoza's right-hand-woman, was standing by in the comms room, her arms crossed. *Great, a babysitter,* he thought.

"Deanna," King said with a nod, taking the position. As he stepped into place, the screens snapped on all at once, revealing the five shadowed figures of the Genrenauts High Council.

The center figure, D'Arienzo, spoke first. "Angstrom King. You have served with this organization for nearly thirty years. Your clearance rate is exceptional, and while we have been lenient in the past in acknowledgment of the efficacy of your unorthodox approaches, this latest stunt of yours is beyond the pale."

King stood strong, keeping any expression or response off his face. *Let them yell, then move on.*

D'Arienzo continued. "In the next few minutes, you will explain to us why you contravened a direct order, inappropriately requisitioned Genrenauts assets, coerced personnel into breaking regulations, and made an unapproved deployment where you implemented narrative interventions without guidance, irrevocably changing the course of that world's history."

"It was the right thing to do. I do not pretend to understand the Council's methods, as I know you have a greater plan, a wider view. But that world was on my beat, I saw a breach getting worse day by day, and I saw my window. So, I broke the letter of the regulations in order to serve the spirit of the organization. My team was not informed of my disobedience; they believed this was an approved and sanctioned mission.

"Which it should have been in the first place," King added. "The disturbance cleared, and there was clearly a breach, as your readings will have told you by now given the fact that we have a stable patch."

"During the mission, we found and confronted the same dimensional traveler which I alerted you to several weeks ago. Previously identified as the Tall Woman, we have now learned that she goes by the name or call sign Raven."

King sent the data packet with his video footage of the final battle.

"You can see her here with several companions. I suspect that they are part of her cohort, traveling across dimensions as well. With the possible exception of Nolan, a swordsman who had been part of Theyn Lighthall's fellowship and is the likely traitor leading to the original story breach."

Several councilors' silhouettes shifted. That had ruffled their feathers.

Insubordination or not, this recording was incontrovertible.

He waited several minutes while they watched, standing tall.

Gisler broke the silence. "King. It's one thing to take your mantle of team leader too seriously and ignore the chain of command. But wasting our time is not something I'd ever expect from you."

One of the screens blinked and switched to display static and white noise.

"We scanned the entire video, ran it through scene-selection algorithms. But we didn't have to. It's hundreds of hours of static."

"What?" King asked. "That's impossible. I got them on the record. It's all there."

"Look at it yourself, King." D'Arienzo gestured to a display panel.

King stepped forward and scanned through the footage, running the same analytics and algorithms that made his video reports take an hour or two instead of dozens. Back before they had the algorithms, it had taken most of a week just to compose a thorough report.

Static. It was all static. Dozens of recordings, the proper length and timing, but all static. No vocal or environmental audio.

Nothing.

"I don't understand. She must have tampered with it somehow. Some kind of Faraday cage or EMP. Maybe the dragon."

For the first time in years, he found himself sweating under the lights of the presentation room. Everything was spinning out of control, and it all came back to Raven.

King tried to appeal to logic. "Can you explain why all of the metadata is there but the recordings show nothing but static? You and I both know that's never happened."

D'Arienzo said, "It would have been very easy for you to doctor all of the video. That way, we have only your word to trust. Your word that we cannot trust.

The unnamed Councilor said, "The fact remains that despite being of sound mind and a veteran of this organization, well aware of the delicate interconnectedness of Genrenauts activity around the world, you still conducted an unapproved mission and made massive changes to the world. And you came back with no real evidence to justify your insubordination. We would have deployed your team when the time was right."

"The time was right," King said. "And they were the right changes. We patched the breach mere hours before the world would have been thrown disastrously off course. You've seen the ripple reports. It would have been a disaster. Epidemic-level morale degradation, at the very least. And this country can't handle that right now."

Gisler cut in with characteristic snark. "Perhaps Mr. King is actually making a bid for our jobs, asserting that he knows how to protect interstellar balance better than we do."

"That must be it," said another Councilor, another of the mysterious ones that had yet to show their face.

"Regardless of your motivations, and despite the efficacy of your solution to the breach, your actions have put this organization at critical risk, endangering other missions and depriving your base of one of its ships. Another breach is now twelve hours farther along than it would have been if you'd followed orders."

This was preposterous. "A twelve-hour handicap against a massive ripple. I'll take that trade-off."

"Again, it was not your decision to make."

"Perhaps we have given the outlying bases too much autonomy," one Councilor said, more for her colleagues' benefit than King's.

"I agree," said D'Arienzo.

"A discussion for another time. First, we must deal with the matter at hand."

"Angstrom King, your status as team leader is hereby revoked, and you are to be placed on indefinite unpaid administrative leave, effective the minute you stepped back inside Mid-Atlantic HQ to lead your joyride."

And there it was.

"What will happen to my team?"

"Ricardo Mendoza will oversee your team, with Ms. Tehrani as his second. Mr. Mendoza is a loyal team leader with decades of experience and a cooler head."

Cool head, my shiny ass. Mendoza's beat included the most commercial, most mainstream sub-genres. He drove his team hard, flew off the handle at insubordination, and refused to think outside the box. He created cookie-cutter patches, one-size-fits-all solutions to nuanced narrative conundrums. He was a blunt instrument; King's team was a twenty-tool Swiss army knife.

"Councilors, with all due respect..." King started.

"You've proven you have no respect for the authority of this Council, King. You are dismissed. Stand down until we call for you again to determine whether your role in this organization can be salvaged."

And with that, the screens blinked out, going dark.

"Pardon my saying, sir," Deanna said from behind him, "but you didn't need to goad them. I've never seen that go well for anyone."

"That's never happened to video of yours, right?" he asked, rubbing his head, six weeks of growth making a mess of his hair.

They'd taken his team from him. They were his world. The team, the work. All because of Raven and her machinations. He thought he'd won the battle even if Raven escaped to fight again. Now he saw that she'd played him with the dragon and the portal.

"From the ground, everything you did is right. But the Council sees everything from ten thousand feet up. We believe in the mission, believe in the Council's judgment."

"I got tired of waiting for permission to do my job. And this whole thing stinks. If there's more going on at the top level, they need to read us in, or our experience and judgment count for nothing."

Deanna joined King as they walked out into the hall. "I get that, sir. But right now, you need to debrief your team before the Council tells me to escort you from the premises. I wager you have about ten minutes."

King swallowed his anger and started jogging again, this time to his team, the one thing left in the organization that made sense.

* * *

Shirin broke out the emergency wine.

Leah shouldn't have been surprised that there was emergency wine, but she was glad that it existed.

Looking through the ceiling light through the three-quarters opaque red liquid, Leah tried to reconcile her emotional high with the instant shock and dissonance that had come with their so-called welcome back to HQ.

"Did you all know we'd gone rogue?" Leah asked, finally.

"No," Roman said. "But you saw the breach. We all did. We needed to be there."

"Then why forbid us?"

Shirin paced. Her comfy nook lay barren, pile of biographies and histories piled around the bowl chair like the arms of a throne. "Let's wait for what King has to say."

Mallery returned to the ready room, dressed in a fresh set of clothes, towel-drying her hair from the shower.

They were back, but not Home. Home was a place where the problems were familiar. Maybe all wasn't at peace, but you knew the score. Uncertainty tore away the protection of home like a grumpy bear ripping the top off your tent as it looks for your picnic basket.

HQ had become more like home over these last months, but only because of the people. But this room wasn't home, not now, even with Mallery, Roman, and Shirin around.

Without King, this was just a room, they weren't quite a team.

They'd saved the world and lost their true north in exchange.

This isn't how the story was supposed to go.

But she was a Genrenaut.

A Genrenaut could change a story when it went off track.

"How do we fix this? Talk to the Council? Write the most amazing mission report ever? Fly to London and browbeat them directly? We just overthrew a world-threatening sorcerer. We can fix some red tape. Did anyone get footage of the Tall Woman's team? Audio? Anything?"

Shirin didn't miss a step. "We can check, but King's camera broke, and with all the energy I was throwing around, nothing of mine could record. For now, we wait for King."

Mallery got a blow-dryer out of a drawer that Leah swore had been filled with office supplies. "The Council is as high as it goes. They have their reasons for doing what they do. A year or so ago, we held off on a mission to Science Fiction's world for two weeks. Just like this time, we were climbing the walls, desperate to deploy. We realized that a meteor had hit the region, that that was the breach. All of our sensors were down, no intel. We had to wait while the Council sent drones through and collected data, figured out where we could deploy.

"They lost three drones to stray fragments, smaller meteors the big one had gathered in its wake; they kept hammering the world for ten days. But eventually, they found survivors and we had our answer. We deployed, gathered up the survivors—all scientists, not a leader among them, overwhelmed by fear and grief. We got them onto their Ark and sent them on their way."

Mallery continued. "If we'd ignored orders and deployed right away, no chance we'd have been able to find the survivors. Probably would have peppered by meteorites."

Roman piped in from the treadmill, even at a sprint, feet pounding. "King made the call, and we did the job. But he didn't trust the system. And the system works. It's worked for thirty years. We all do this because we believe in the system. What he did was brash and dangerous. He put us all into a vulnerable position. But he didn't abandon us, and we won't abandon him."

As if on cue, King slid through the door, slowing from a jog.

"I don't have long. Security is coming for me. But I'm not going that way."

King looked both ways, up and down the hall. "I'm sorry for misleading you. I had to track down the Tall Woman. I don't have any doubt. Not anymore. You cracked this, Leah, and now we're on to something big. If you don't want to stake your careers on it, I understand. But you know they're out there. Next time, you'll be prepared."

Leah walked up to King. "How can we help?"

"Do your jobs. Follow Mendoza or whoever they give you. But don't forget what we saw there, what we've seen building for months. Those people are making changes to the multiverse, and we need to know why. That's what I'm going to try to figure out."

King extended a hand. "Ms. Tang, I'm sorry that your apprenticeship has been so troubled. As far as I'm concerned, you've earned your wings. It has been an honor to have you on the team."

Roman killed the treadmill and slid off, landing both feet at once on the carpet. Shirin met their leader first. She leaned into him and they hugged. They spoke at a whisper, and Leah refrained from eavesdropping, stepping back to let her teammates have their moment with the boss before he went off to do whatever it was.

Roman went next. The men exchanged a hearty handshake, then into a hug. The former soldier teared up.

"Thank you for giving me a new purpose and a new family. If I can't be there to watch your back, you've got to do it yourself."

"I will. Look after the team for me."

"Always."

Mallery stood on her toes to kiss King on the cheek, then buried her head in his chest. "Come back to us, boss. I can't go back to Broadway. I've gotten too used to playing the big parts."

"If I can, I will."

"Do or do not; there is no try," Mallery said, eyes puffy.

King glanced to the side, then sighed. "Time to go. Thank you all. It's been an honor."

And then he was off at a run. Headed for the quartermaster's wing.

Leah pointed in King's direction. "What is he doing? Should we follow? I feel like we should be following."

"We don't follow. We stay right here and do our jobs," Shirin said. She crossed the room, sat down in her chair, and picked up a book in the most dejected fashion possible, curling into herself and disappearing into her reading.

Roman returned to his treadmill, and Mallery retrieved a pair of beers from the fridge, opening them on the way and slipping the opener back into her pocket.

"This sucks," she said, taking a seat. "I say we drink in protest."

Leah raised a bottle and toasted.

The beer was cold. So cold, almost unbearably cold after six weeks of lukewarm ale and barely cooled wine. It was too bitter, too sharp, too full-bodied, and it was perfect.

"Do you always get reverse culture shock coming back from Fantasy-land?" Leah asked Mallery.

"Not always. Sometimes, we get the job done in just a couple of weeks, and it feels more like coming back to work after vacation. Though to be honest, nothing's been normal for a while. My hospital stay aside. You figured out the trend of breaches early, and now we've got real evidence. And if there's one thing I know about King, it's that when he's got a lead, nothing will stop him. Not even the High Council."

Klaxons filled the room and hallways.

But they weren't a breach alarm.

This was the security breach alarm.

"Roman, on me," Shirin said on the way out of the room. "Mallery, Leah, stay here."

"What the hell is going on? Did we come back to the Bizarro-verse or something?" Leah said, totally adrift.

"Stand down, both of you." A confident, barely familiar voice cut through the alarm from the hallway. "Charlie Team, attention."

Ricardo Mendoza filled the entrance to their ready room, arms crossed behind his back. He was younger than King, mid-forties, hair full of product and locked into a perfect early Mad Men–era style. Leah'd never seen him look particularly happy, but right then, he looked like someone had just handed him a bag full of crap and told him to paint with it.

The team stood, beer and books and treadmills forgotten.

"Angstrom King has been relieved of his position as Team Leader. So now, your team falls to me. I know that King kept you all close. I am not Angstrom King. You are specialists, and I will value your skills and your judgment. But I am the final arbiter for all mission-critical decisions, and you now report to me. Are there any questions?"

Silence.

"Good. I want your mission reports in the next hour. Then take two days off. Thirty-two hours of comp time will be added to your records as recognition for the long hours. King swears that none of you knew he was deploying without leave, and he's a man of his word. The breach is sealed and the world stable. Let's just hope that King didn't set off an unforeseen ripple and put us all in more trouble later on.

"Those reports are due in an hour. Good night."

And with that, he left.

Leah waited until his bootsteps faded into the distance, then picked up her beer and took a long, cold swig, already assembling her thoughts for the report. "Well, this is going to be a barrel of laughs."

Paperwork. After all the adventure, suspense, and danger, it all came down to paperwork.

Leah finished her beer and retrieved her tablet from her locker.

She opened a mission report template and started typing.

Once upon a time, we were forced to wait for two days while a breach got worse and worse, then our boss decided to throw out the rulebook and do the right thing, even though we didn't know we were breaking the rules at the time...

She sighed, deleted the paragraph, and started again.

Mallery came over to join her.

"As soon as we're done with these, I say we blow this popsicle stand."

Leah looked to the door, where King had left. "Do you mean...quit?"

A shadow crossed Mallery's face. She was considering it. "I mean leaving work at work and reminding ourselves that we have lives beyond being Genrenauts. Lives together."

Her heart was racing. This was all wrong. They'd fixed one story and come to find their own had careened off course.

Leah nodded, squeezing the comedienne's offered hand, using the touch as an anchor.

Her mind was everywhere but in the present. The past, her time on the team, the lessons she'd learned from her teammates. Mallery's smile, Shirin's quick wit. Roman's silent strength and wicked moves. And King, the friendly rulemonger gone rogue, and the wonderful turn her life had taken since that open mic at Comedy Corner.

And now King was gone, off to put things right. He'd brought her in, trained her, and she'd made a place for herself on the team. He'd led them to victory even when they weren't supposed to be fighting, and they'd done the work. But now he was gone, and they were on a short leash, tethered to a drill sergeant-slash-nanny.

Screw this, Leah thought. They'd take the time, and then figure out what the next chapter would bring.

As she powered through the report, her mind drifted back to King.

Knock 'em dead, boss.

Epilogue:
Boldly Going Somewhere

King dropped from fifteen feet in the air, instinct taking over as he landed into a roll.

Head snapping up, he scanned around him in all directions. Sand and dirt, as far as the eye can see. Rolling dunes, nearly faded tracks, and wreckage, rusted and burnt-out skeletons that had been cars, once upon a time.

The sun beat down like a jackhammer, punishing waves of heat sapping his energy. He took the sunglasses, jacket, and wide-brimmed hat out from his bag. Then he checked his waterskins, uncurled the belt. He slid the machete into one side, sawed-off shotgun into the other.

His Road Warrior ensemble in place, King checked the compass on his pocket watch. His bolt-hole was a mile northwest. Assuming it was still there and unmolested, he'd have gear needed to track Raven and her team.

He started singing a spiritual, mind drifting back to church as a kid, the choir singing up front, a hundred voices joined as one.

And he started walking. Every three steps counted as two, sand robbing him of inches every bit of the way.

But it wasn't far to the cache, even in this heat.

And he had plenty of thinking to do along the way.

Find Raven and her people.

Beat them, trap them, and drag them back to HQ.

Drop them in the Council's lap.

And get his team back.

END SEASON ONE

If you enjoyed this book, please consider writing a short review on your favorite book retail sites. Retailer reviews boost visibility and can help new readers find series that may go on to become their favorites.

Acknowledgments

Genrenauts began with a single tiny seed of an idea:

A woman from our world, transported to a fantasy-land, where she ends up in front of the King & Queen of a land plagued by a traitor in their midst. The young woman, being a fantasy fan, instantly points to the goatee-wearing advisor standing by the throne and says, "It's him! It's the vizier!"

Because it's *always* the vizier.

That small vignette, with the genre-aware woman solving problems using her knowledge of story structure and familiar tropes, would eventually grow into the six-novella season of adventure science fiction you hold in your hands now.

It's all Lee Harris' fault, really. Lee and I were colleagues at Angry Robot, and working together, I came to appreciate his keen eye for SF that combines action, adventure, and interesting speculation. Tor.com very smartly snapped him up to be the Senior Editor of their novella project, now called Tor.com Publishing. I'd already been looking at maybe pitching something for the novella project, as I'd seen authors like Matt Wallace writing series of novellas independently to great effect.

So I gave myself a challenge — come up with a series to be written in novella form, for a digital-first publication approach, that would let me re-connect with the readers of my Ree Reyes Geekomancy series, while branching out to a broader readership, and do so in a way that Lee would like.

Enter the genre-aware woman and the vizier.

As I often do, I took the seed of an idea and I started bouncing it around in my mind. It accreted influence and touchstones, from **Leverage** and **Redshirts** to **Quantum Leap** and **The A-Team**. I thought about each novella as a mission, for a procedural adventure serial. I thought about

Babylon 5 and its long-arc storytelling, where episodes built into season arcs, which built into series arcs.

I got so excited about the idea and the long arc that I sketched out a five season arc for the series. Lee got on board with the idea and we signed a deal for the first two episodes of season one, enabled by the fabulous Sara Megibow, my agent. And so I went to work.

It was the first time I'd written connected shorter works, and I quickly found that the 25-30k word size fits me really well. Long enough to tell a story with some substance to it, but not so long that I get bogged down in the Mushy Middle. It was like writing a weekly adventure TV show all on my own, with no one telling me what I could or couldn't do.

I've had a lot of help in this journey, from many different parts of my life. I've thanked these folks in the individual episodes along the way, but they deserve the thanks again.

So here's a quick tour of thank yous to people who helped make **Genrenauts** possible:

First, my wife, Meg White Underwood – my best friend and #1 brainstorming buddy. Meg is as fine a reader for characterization as I have ever met, and I am very grateful to have her feedback on this and all of my work.

My parents, David and Becky, who helped nurture my insatiable interest in storytelling.

Bryan Roberts, Andrew Reyes, and all of the Game Preserve family – flunkies, cashwrap monkeys, and more.

Hundreds of fellow gamers across the years, from my elementary school D&D group to card gamers, tabletop RPGers, the Embracing the Muse LARP (players, STs, and staff), and my college gaming crew - Jack Norris, Jason Inglert, Jim Wong, Jonathan Crum, Joe Bowman, and Miranda Wagoner.

Megan Christopher and Ron Mitchell, for the gut check right as the idea for Genrenauts first took shape.

Dave Robison, Master Brainstormer, for helping me unpack the core concept and explore the many possibilities.

My marvelous beta readers - Beth Cato, Effie Seiberg, K8 Walton, Daniel Bensen, A. Jarrell Hayes, Michelle Jones, Jason Kimble, and Jay Swanson. You all helped me find my way through the forests of revision, to know which jokes were working, which were not, how to push myself to explore the character's voices and personalities most effectively and honestly, and helped me make sure that the series was doing its job.

Patrick S. Tomlinson, for feedback on stand-up comedy.

Marie Brennan, Delilah S. Dawson, Matt Wallace, Howard Tayler, and all of my other colleagues and friends that have helped spread the word and get the series in front of readers. Every blurb, review, and signal-boost has meant the world to me.

The brilliant Mary Robinette Kowal, for lending her talents to bringing the **Genrenauts** stories to life in the audiobook editions. Props also to her top-notch audio engineer, Andrew.

I am incredibly grateful for the support Tor.com has given me, in launching the series, promoting it, and generally being fabulous to work with. Thanks to Lee Harris, Irene Gallo, Mordicai Knode, Katharine Duckett, Carl Engle-Laird, Christine Foltzer, and to Peter Lutjen for creating the first two covers and setting the series style.

Sean Glenn picked up seamlessly where Peter left off, building out the covers for the individual episodes.

Thomas Walker rose to the task of bringing my vision for the omnibus cover to life, and went far beyond what I could have imagined, creating a piece of art I will treasure for many years to come. Working in publishing, I've come to appreciate the power of a good cover, and I have been very blessed in this field with this series.

Bryon Quertermous answered my call with excitement and insight, serving as the developmental editor for episodes three through six. Bryon challenged me to dig deeper, to be sharper, to not be lazy with my comedy or sloppy with my explanations. He pushed me to write the stories to the absolute best of my ability, and for that I am incredibly grateful.

And then Richard Shealy came along with a fine-toothed comb, delivering copyedits that cleaned up my mistakes, pointed at places where I could be even that much clearer and crisper with my prose. Copyeditors are always worth their fee, folks. They keep you from face-planting all over the page. And if you do it even after they've given their input, that's on you (or for this series, me).

When I decided to take the reins of **Genrenauts** to publish independently, Margot Atwell was there to help me bring Leah & the crew to the Kickstarter community, where it has grown and become stronger than ever.

Sara Megibow, aka The Agent of Awesomeness, helped seal the initial deal to give Genrenauts life, and has been a partner and advocate for the series every step of the way.

And saving the best for last, my eternal gratitude goes out to the three hundred and twenty-one backers of the **Genrenauts: The Complete Season One Collection** Kickstarter, who made this edition possible. You rock!

OBSERVER

Beverly Bambury, Levi Ryan, Louise Lowenspets, Mary Mascari, Tieg Zaharia

RECRUIT

Aaron Clites, Aaron Jamieson, Adam Danger Taco Rakunas, Adam Woods, Aidan Elliott-McCrea, Aitor, Alasdair Stuart, Alison Fleming, Aly Ross, Amanda Nixon, Anders M. Ytterdahl, Andrew Kinzler, Andrew Turnwall, Andrew Wilson, Angela Carlson, Anthony C. Senatore, Ashley Nunn. Aulne, BeePeeGee, Beth Cato, Bitter Old Joe O'Toole, Brendan Hong, Brian M, Bryan Young, Caitlin Jane Hughes, Carla G. Chiodi, Carol J. Guess, Caroline Mills, Cat Vincent, Chloe Ng, Chris Vincent, Chris 'Warcabbit' Hare - City of Titans, Christopher C. Cockrell, Christopher Nickolas Carlson, Colin Newell, Coral Moore, Corey McKinnon, Courtney Schafer, Daniel Chadborn, Daniel Rhodes, David Annandale, David Holden, Denise Lhamon, Di, Dominic Quach, Dustin Gerald Fickle, Eduard Lukhmanov, Elizabeth Poole, Elsa Sjunneson-Henry, Enrica "Cool Whip" Jang, Eric Buscemi, Evelyn Sawtelle, Ferrett Steinmetz, Gavran, Gerald Gaiser, Gillis Björk, Glen Sawyer, Greg Noe, Haley McDonald, Hisham El-Far, Hugh J O'Donnell, J.R. Murdock, James Classen, Jason M. Hough, Jen Baluk, Jen Woods, Jens Heinrich, Jibreel Ford, Joanne BB, Joel Cunningham, Joel Fischer, Jon Lundy, Jonathan Killstring, Jordan Thomas, Joris Meijer, Josh S., Josh Storey, Joshua B. Marin, Julia Rios, Julie Winningham, K.J. Larsen, Kat Feete, Kate Heartfield, Kerri Regan, Kevin Henderson, Kristy Griffin Green, Kristy Mika, Lennhoff Family, Lily Carnahan, Lord Admiral Matt Gould, Mari Kurisato, Matt (Twpsyn) Hill, Matt Dovey, Matt Hurlburt, Matt Leitzen, Mattia Forza, Max Kaehn, Mayer Brenner, Megan Christopher, Megan E. O'Keefe, Meghan Ball, Meredith Gene Levine, Michael Bentley, Michael Bernardi, Michael Hicks, Michael J. Martinez, Misha Dainiak, Mitch Eatough, Mitchell Shanklin, Monica Valentinelli, Monica W., Mur Lafferty, Natalie Luhrs, Nehemias Bailon, Nicholas Dao, Nikki Tysoe, Noel Rappin, Nor Azman, Oko, Paul Jackson, Paul Swanson @AssortedNoise, Paul Weimer, Peter Hansen, Peter

Tieryas, Philip Harris, Poppa Connelly, R Devine, Rachel Neumeier, Rebecca Smith, Renata Vander Broock, Rhodri Morgan-Smith, Robin Hill, Ron Jarrell, Ross Williams, Royal Hinshaw, Sarah Williams, Sean, Shawn Ta, Sheryl R. Hayes, Sidsel N. Pedersen, Sir Lee of the Yorkshire Harrises, Smashingsuns, Solomon Foster, Sophie Lagacé, SorchaRei, Stephanie Cranford, Sven of the Dead, SW Sondheimer, Tessa Brunton, Tevin Deante' Hill, Thomas Butler, Timothy Reid, Tom Nugent, Trish E. Matson, Wright S. Johnson, Yannick Allard, Zac Derenne, Zvi Gilbert

GENRENAUT
@johnpatrickmcp, A. F. Grappin. A. Jarrell Hayes, A.C. Wise, Aaron R Corff, Adam Leader-Smith & Megan Browndorf, Alan Weir, Andrea Phillips, Andrea Tatjana, Andy W. Taylor, Angie Pettenato, Ann Chatham, Anna Campbell, anne m. gibson, Barb Moermond, Barry Welling, Becca Horn, Beth Bernobich, Brian O'Conor, Byron J. Hartsfield, Charlotte C. Royal, Claudette Dorsey, Dan Layman-Kennedy, Daniel P. Haeusser, Deborah Stanish, DecodedParadox, Devan Barlow, E.M. Markoff, Ed Potter, Elizabeth A. Janes, Elyse M Grasso, Emily Gilman, Ethan Doubleday-Everett, Gregory A. Wilson, H. C. Newton, Jack Vickeridge, James Dawsey, James 'Jimbeaux' Silverstein, Jason Youngberg, Jayson "Luftwaffle" Utz, Jeremy C. Zerby, Jo Robson, Joel Pearson, John Appel, John J Houlihan, Jonathan Boynton, Julio Capa, Kelman Edwards, Kevin Brock, Kristianne, Legion of Leaches, Liam Frazier, Liam Glans, Lothair Biedermann, Marcia Franklin, Marianne, Martin Cahill, Martin Jackson, Megan E. Daggett, Melanie R. Meadors, Melissa Harkness, Melissa Shumake, Michael Kindness, Michael Lee, Miriam Krause, M'liss Garber, Mo Foley, Mon Capitain, Nitin Dahyabhai, Patti Short, Paul E. Olson, Paul Morell, Paul Townsend, Pete Milan, Ragnarok Publications, Raida, Ryan Trottier, Sarah Celiann, Sarah Schweitzer, Scott F Couchman, Shawn Belton, Soli-chan, The Shean-Joneses, "Nexus_General", Tom Sias, Twigs, Tyler Smith, Vaughn Barker, Victoria Irwin, Whitney E. Novak

OPERATIONS
Andrew Folk, Andrew R. Mizener, Darren Radford, Dave Robison, Joyce Ann Garcia from McAllen Texas, Khurrum, Laser Eyes, Mary B. Rodgers, Missy Katano, Nathan Beittenmiller, Russell Duhon, S. Brown, Sam Dailey, The Pinckneys, Tommy G. Junior Agent

GENRENAUTS FIELD OFFICE
Game Empire, McLean & Eakin Booksellers

SPECIALIST
Alex von der Linden, Amber Simpson, Kent Rice, Laura A. Burns, Rob Durand, Steven Larson, Victor J Kinzer

VETERAN GENRENAUT
Adam Zabell, Andy Barker, Joe Bowman, Phil Jourdan, Sally Novak Janin

NARRATIVE TRAINING
Dave Heyman, Sturm "Gabriel Kabik" Brightblade, Kyle Anderson, Michael Melilli

35595926R00277

Made in the USA
Middletown, DE
10 October 2016